Played

by Lisa Lennox

This is a work of fiction. The authors have invented the characters. Any resemblance to actual persons, living or dead, is purely coincidental.

If you have purchased this book with a 'dull' or missing cover—you have possibly purchased an unauthorized or stolen book. Please immediately contact the publisher advising where, when and how you purchased this book.

Compilation and Introduction copyright © 2010 by
Triple Crown Publications
PO Box 247378
Columbus, OH 43224
www.TripleCrownPublications.com

Library of Congress Control Number: 2010941674
ISBN: 978-0-9825888-1-9

Author: Lisa Lennox
Graphics Design: Valerie Thompson, Leap Graphics
Photography: Treagen Kier
Editor-in-Chief: Vickie Stringer
Editors: Cynthia Parker and Caitlin McLellan

First Trade Paperback Edition Printing 2011

10 9 8 7 6 5 4 3 2 1

Printed in the United States of America

Acknowledgments

As always, I want to thank Vickie Stringer, publishing goddess, and all the wonderful staff at Triple Crown Publications. There is no other company I'd rather be with. Thanks as well to my talented editors, Cynthia Parker, Alisha Yvonne and Caitlin McLellan. Played received the magic touch and I couldn't be happer with the end result. Thank you Christopher Means for your good eye.

Lastly, I want to thank my wonderful, priceless fans. You encourage and inspire to endless bounds.

Dedication

This book is dedicated to those writers who remain true to their craft. Stay strong, and remember why you write. Words restore and show us the way.

1

She was naked before I poured my first drink. Draping a fresh towel loosely around her petite five-foot-three, one hundred ten-pound frame, she danced slowly in the mirror by the headboard, which hung over the bed laced with sticky sheets. Kneeling there, she touched her body seductively. The thick, cool air from the window unit blasted at her body, causing her hair to blow in its heavy current. I pretended not to watch her reflection from the mirror above the dresser.

"You think they'll find the place this time?" I asked, face buried in a glass of vodka with no chaser.

"I hope so. The Madison Inn is a good location. Two of 'em already called my phone lookin' for the spot, so they should be on the way." She looked out of the window, hips moving to the rhythm of some stripper anthem playing on the CD player.

Everyone called her Tiki. No one cared to know her real name, not even me. She was a mixed breed; the sexy results of a black and Asian unprotected sexual encounter. I met her through a friend, and all I needed to know was that she was only about her business and didn't keep up with any drama. I needed her on my team.

The raggedy room smelled like damp, soured carpet and stale cigarettes. It was hard to breathe, but it was an upgrade from the roach-infested hotel we occupied the night before. Tiki walked into the bathroom, and I pulled the top comforter from the bed and threw it onto the floor. I heard somewhere that hotel staff less frequently wash comforters than sheets. My imagination got the best of me and I imagined the bodily fluids of whomever the previous occupants were. The thought almost made me sick.

"What are you doing, Taj?" She turned around and looked at me, pulling her thick, black hair up from her shoulders into a ponytail.

"I'm getting ready."

"By taking off the covers?" She lifted the comforter from the floor.

"They don't wash these all the time. Do you know who was in here before us?"

Turning her nose up at what I said, she walked into the bathroom. I picked up my duffle bag and followed her in.

"So, what are you wearing tonight?" she asked.

"Something I snatched from Victoria's Secret. I just hope it fits."

"It don't matter if it does or doesn't. You'll be coming out of it soon." Her lips formed the most attractive smirk I had ever seen as she put on her outfit for the night.

There was a knock and we both looked at each other; suggesting to the other to check it out.

"Why don't you go, Tiki, and I'll jump in a quick shower. Please."

"All right, chick. Make it quick. Showtime in fifteen."

"Gotcha."

It seemed like I couldn't get clean enough. In spite of liquor-induced sweat and the heat from the shower, I still felt dirty having to shower in such a filthy place. The miniature bar of soap broke into pieces in my washcloth, which forced me to make do with what I had. Rinsing, I was careful not to wet my hair. Then I heard heavy footsteps walk into the bathroom. My heart sank into my stomach.

"Tiki?" I called.

"Nah, shawty, you straight. I just gotta piss real quick." I peeped from behind the shower curtain at the man. He unzipped his jeans stitched with the True Religion emblem on the back pocket, a good indication that he had money to spend.

"And your name is?" I asked with an attitude as he relieved himself. I was offended that he would enter without knocking.

"It's Terrance."

"Ok. I'm Taj." He reached out in an attempt to move the curtain to the side to see the goods, but I stopped him, playing nicely. "Make yourself comfortable and I'll be out in a minute."

"All right. All right." He walked out and closed the door behind himself. Although he didn't wash his hands, I was glad he wasn't one that had to be forced out.

I tiptoed around the dirty, wet towel Tiki laid on the floor from her shower which now held several of Terrance's filthy footprints, and I applied lotion and body oil from shoulders to toes. Tearing off the tags from the bra and panty set, I put them on and let my hair down. Every silky, black strand lay properly in place. I puckered up for a glossy finish then slid on my black four-inch pumps. I was ready to begin.

Walking out into the room through fogged clouds of weed smoke made my shower a waste of time. Music was still playing as I counted seven men seated around the bed passing a blunt. As I looked on, I noticed three more stood by the dresser, each refilling their half-empty glasses of liquor. All eyes were on me but Tiki was nowhere in sight.

"Fellas, ya'll seen Tiki?"

"She stepped out for a minute. She said she'll be right back," Terrance offered.

Just then, Tiki walked into the room with her fresh towel

still wrapped around her, two men following her. They were extremely tall, and handsomer than any of the other men already in the room. This brought the total to twelve.

"Where you find them?" I asked.

"Wandering—looking for a good party," Tiki responded, her eyes scanning the room. "A hundred dollars a head, right fellas?"

"We got you, sexy. Damn! It looks worth it to me," the tall dark-skinned one said. He licked his lips and pressed them together, then turned toward the other man. "What you think, Mike?"

"You ain't even gotta ask, man. You know I'm down," he replied, adjusting the rim of his cap.

"Mike, huh?" I leaned over to touch him, shoulder to shoulder. "You ready?"

"Let's do this." His cap cast a shadow over his eyes and I could see his perfect smile, straight white teeth and extremely plump lips.

"Umph!" I smiled.

He blushed a bit, smiled, then lowered his head, fidgeting with his cap.

I reached behind me and turned off the main light in the room. Tiki pressed pause on the CD player for our announcements. All eyes were on us as we walked over to the bed and kneeled in its center, with our legs gaped open, forming a V-shape, giving a sneak peak.

"Ok, guys," Tiki said, closing her legs. I did the same as she turned around and faced the crowd. "I need some form of ID. If you don't have it, I'm sorry, but you gotta go." Eagerly, some men reached into their pockets while Tiki continued. "If you've been here before, you know the rules."

A few gasped, others sighed while someone chimed in, "no weapons, no touching, grabbing, fighting or jacking off ..."

"Well, that is, no touching *us*," Tiki interjected.

"If you feel like you cannot abide by these terms," I continued, "leave now. But ..." I placed my index finger in my mouth and seductively removed it, "the price of admission is still one

Triple Crown Publications *presents...*

hundred dollars." After all the ones who couldn't pass the cut shuffled out cussing and spitting, the remaining men reached into their pockets without taking their eyes from me.

Tiki collected the money and put it behind the bed in an envelope. "One last thing," she added. She held her cell phone in the air and light illuminated the darkest areas of the room, flashing across everyone's eyes. "This is what I call *your* life-line."

"At midnight, I will make a phone call," I said, finishing her statement. "If for some reason that phone call is not received, the police will be here before you can think to run." The men spoke amongst each other. "I only have to press one button to reach the authorities so don't try anything slick."

Up to that point, there hadn't been a need to phone the authorities. We never rehearsed an escape route in the event that something went wrong, and we hoped that no one would give us a reason to do so.

"With that said, let's begin." Tiki walked back over to the CD player and pressed play. Walking slowly to the bed, she climbed in with me.

We began with some kissing, then she unfastened my 34D bra with her mouth as she cupped and massaged my breasts with both of her hands. Easing out of our panties, we both took turns touching, rubbing and licking each other until an hour had passed. No one left the room, but we were so busy entertaining that we wouldn't have noticed if all of them were gone.

Performing sexual acts with one another, in front of others, served as our occupation. It was quick and easy money. I was doing shows for almost a year when I met Tiki. Before her, I would perform with various friends who just needed some quick cash to get by for a while. But I needed someone more dependable—someone who needed this life, this profession, as much as I did. I found it when I met Tiki. She was not only good at entertaining; she was professional and down for whatever at any time. The bottom line for Tiki was the almighty dollar.

P l a y e d

What may have been a lot of dough to many quickly became pocket change to us. After three thousand dollars slid through our fingers for a weekend's work, anything less may as well have been pennies, and we spent it as such. We quickly became addicted to it, like some of the drugs we used on a regular basis to escape the reality of our profession.

Tiki and I hustled for different reasons. Money was her main priority, and it kept her from enjoying life. Me, on the other hand, I enjoyed life. I loved educating myself, even through others. I thought I was as smart as they came with a sexiness to match.

There was a time when I considered working as an exotic dancer. It seemed to be a far more acceptable way of making money than engaging in sexual acts with women in hotel rooms. But I never pursued that path, because the bottom dollar told me differently. I just knew that the mediocre pay that I would take home every night after being molested by men, *and* having to tip the DJ and bouncers for their services from my hard-earned cash, made stripping a waste of time and entrepreneurship very attractive. After trying to expand the business, I realized that other partners weren't reliable, so I stuck to what I knew worked—and that was the Tiki and Taj duo.

Tiki was loyal, but I never let my guard down. If she was anything like me, she'd look out for herself first. She was human, so she could not be trusted.

Triple Crown Publications *presents...*

2

Waking up at 2 o'clock in the afternoon, feeling the after-effects of the alcohol and drugs, I slid my head underneath my pillow and willed myself to go back to sleep. Unable to, I looked around my apartment.

To the naked eye, it appeared that I had everything. A little further examination would reveal that it was the total opposite. I was a wreck. My one-bedroom apartment was barely furnished; it only contained a couch and a twenty-seven inch television which sat on top of a TV stand. The main living area was clean but my bedroom was a complete mess, scattered with costumes I didn't feel like hanging or folding and accessories thrown everywhere. I kept my place dark, like how I felt on the inside.

Finally peeking my head up from underneath the pillow, I looked at my cell phone and it flashed red, indicating that I had an unchecked voicemail message. It was Shai, a close associate who I hung out with on occasion, especially if she was paying. Shai was the only child of a doctor–teacher couple, and being sheltered and spoiled made her want to do what she wanted more than the average street kid. Unbeknownst to her parents, their white-collar occupations afforded her much more expensive drugs than the typical marijuana plant.

Listening to my message, I learned the place to be that evening was at her house on the west side of town. Since I had no prior plans, I decided to head over. There would be all the recreation I needed.

Hours later, I arrived at Shai's, prepared for whatever was to jump off.

"What's up?" A tall guy opened the door after I rang the bell. He sported a faded Chicago Bulls jersey and some outdated Jordans. "Who you ma?" he asked, eyes barely open, pressing all his body weight against the door.

"I'm Taj," I responded, annoyed.

"And? What's that supposed to mean?" His marijuana-induced high caused his eyes to drop that he could barely see me.

"Nigga, let me in! I'm Shai's friend." I stormed past him and clutched my Dooney & Bourke bag closer to my side. He closed the door and disappeared to another room.

Shai's place was like walking into a whorehouse. There were four bedrooms, all void of adequate furnishings. Only Shai's room held a bed and dresser and she was the only one allowed to fuck in it. The rest of the house was fair game for anything and anyone else.

Looking for Shai, I walked into the clouded room. The artificial light that flashed from the fifty-two inch television illuminated three figures that were sitting across from it. One of the figures looked like a girl. Carefully walking closer, I called out hesitantly, "Shai?"

"Naw, shorty," a male voice boomed. "She in the last room on the left."

Turning to walk out of the room, I made my way to the

back of the house. I heard music that became louder as I approached the last bedroom. I knocked but no one answered. I knocked again.

"Shai?" I called out, opening the door slowly.

"Come in," someone moaned.

I opened the door. As I entered through a light haze of smoke, I saw a girl sitting on a chair near a dresser and night-stand. She wore a long, loose-fitting spaghetti-strap dress with her hair curled and pinned loosely into a bun. Her legs were crossed, sexy and seductive. She was focused on some-thing else in the room and paid me no attention. I wondered for a moment if she was the one who invited me in.

Sexual sounds began to softly fill the room, and my eyes scanned the surroundings. I noticed that Shai was on the bed, in plain view, engaging in sexual activity with some guy I'd never seen before. The girl in the chair didn't move; she was merely a voyeur captivated by the sight. I walked past her, par-tially in hopes that I could snatch her interests from what was going on but also to get a look at the plethora of dope that was laid across the nightstand. There were pills for the pill pop-pers, coke for whoever snorted and weed for those who played it safe. I grabbed a little blue Ecstasy pill and crushed it between my back teeth for a quicker effect, swallowing with as much saliva as I could create.

I moved closer to the dresser, turned around and lifted my body to sit on it. My feet dangled two feet from the floor. Not before long, I felt tingling in my temples—an indication that the Ecstasy was beginning to take effect. I pressed the back of my head against the mirror hinged to the dresser, then slowly adjusted myself for a better view. My focus wasn't on Shai and her taking a good pounding from the back: I've seen that numerous times before. Instead, I stared at the girl in the chair, unable to take my eyes off of her.

The music stopped and Shai's wails filled the air.

The girl's lips turned up in a smile at the corners, and then she reached for the water bottle near her ankle on the floor. She glanced my way, stood up and walked over toward me.

P l a y e d

"What are you lookin' at?" she whispered directly into my ear. I noticed Shai was nearly passed out on the bed.

"You," I flirted.

The woman leaned in and placed her left hand next to my thigh, slightly touching it.

"Like what you see? Or, can you see? How many?" She held up three fingers. Her gold tennis bracelet slid down her tiny wrist.

"One," I replied, eyes half closed.

"Oh, my. You'll have to do better than that."

"There is only *one* of you. I can't focus my attention anywhere else."

The woman smiled, then lowered her head.

"Don't blush," I teased. "I'm sure that's nothing new to you."

"And what makes you say that?" she asked, still grinning.

"If you don't know, then I don't either. What's your name?" I began to stroke her arm uncontrollably. The effects of the drugs were overpowering. She didn't move, but instead leaned in closer, lifting her hand and interlocking it with mine.

"It's Santina, but everyone calls me San."

"San," I repeated.

"You wanna go somewhere and talk?"

"This *is* somewhere, but if you mean privately, sure, yeah, I'll go."

She grabbed my hand as if to help me down from the dresser, and I began to stroke my hair compulsively. The Ecstasy made it seem as though I could feel each individual strand flow through my fingers. My other hand held on to San's arm for balance, and we walked out of the room.

We sat opposite each other on the carpeted hallway floor, beneath the heavy clouds of smoke. It was quiet. There was no one else there.

"You never told me your name," she said.

"Did you ever ask for it?" We spoke as if in battle.

"Why are you so difficult? What's your name?"

"My name is Taj."

"And how you spell that?"

"T-A-J."

"Sounds like a boy's name. Not a name for someone as pretty as you."

I smiled at her attempted flirt, but I barely had enough focus or strength to keep my posture against the wall.

"So, who do you know here?" she asked.

"Shai. She's my homegirl. We went to school together."

"Really?" she looked at me. "I didn't take you for the private school type."

"It wasn't private. Where do you think she got her ruggedness from? Not some nun singing hymnals."

San laughed. "I doubt that would be the case, but OK." She continued to giggle.

"Do you know the guy who was with Shai?"

"A little. Met him last time I was here." She hung her head. "Shai and her damn boy toys."

"Jealous?"

"Nah, not at all. I don't have a problem getting who I want." She looked directly at me. "*If* I want them bad enough."

"If you want them bad enough?" I repeated with a knowing smile.

"Don't be too flattered." She straightened her dress, then crossed one leg over the other. "I have someone at home. What about you?"

"A girl?" I asked.

"I'm talking to *you*, aren't I?" She smiled. "Her name is Kendra."

My heart dropped. "No one," I responded faintly. With the help of the wall, I lifted myself up from the floor and threw my bag over my shoulder.

"Shhh ... wait a sec ... what's that sound?" San looked puzzled.

"What sound?" I looked around and tried to hear what she heard.

"It sounds like water. Is it raining?"

"Oh ... no." I raised my eyebrows in acknowledgment, then

P l a y e d

11

pointed toward the back door. "It's the lake behind the house."

"There's a lake out back? I've never seen it."

"Yeah. It's not too well-lit back there. You can barely see it at night, but if you're quiet enough you can hear it." I pulled my keys from my purse.

"Where you going? You leaving?"

"Yeah, I gotta work."

"Time does fly when you're getting high." She smirked. "I wanted to spend some more time with you."

"I really gotta go."

"Can you drive yourself? You're really messed up."

"I'm a big girl. I can drive. Tell Shai I said to call Taj."

"I know your name. You don't have to remind me," she said with an attitude.

I didn't say goodbye to her. I didn't care to look back as I walked closer to the front door. For all I knew her head was still pressed against the wall as her high escalated in the darkness behind her eyelids.

I felt hurt and rejected, even purposeless. Rejection on any level always forced me to examine myself, and whether or not I was worthy to have what others had. It wasn't that San was involved with someone. It was simply that I was not. And that was something that performing shows couldn't help me purchase. Almost as much as I resented relationships, I hated the idea of lacking something even more.

With each step toward the door, I felt my chest become heavy, resting in the pit of my stomach until the weight and disappointment forced tears down my cheek. I didn't stop for a moment to question my behavior until I was outside approaching my car. Then, I realized and thought to myself, *I'm high as hell.*

Triple Crown Publications *presents...*

3

It was Wednesday, two weeks later, when I received a phone call from Shai. I felt my phone vibrating beneath my thighs as I was sitting in the chair at Happy Nails, a Korean nail salon, having eyelash extensions applied.

"Hello?" I answered, eyes closed tightly.

"Girl, whatchu doin'?"

"Getting my eyelashes put on."

"Oh, you want me to let you go?"

"No, girl, you ok. Damn, it's been a minute. It took you this long to call me?"

"Girl, I've been busy. Anyway, let me tell you. Someone been blowin' me up to get your number," she said, then paused. "You wanna know who?"

"If you wanna tell me."

"My friend, San."

I remained silent.

"I told her I wouldn't give her your number, so I'm finally calling you to give you hers." She paused. "You want it?"

"Text it to me. I can't see right now, remember?"

"Alright then. Bye." She hung up.

It took Shai three days to text the phone number to me, and I still waited a week to call. As far as I was concerned, San and I had little to nothing in common, and to top it off, she was in a relationship.

It was almost 3:00 a.m. when I placed the first phone call to San. I'd had a long night working with Tiki, and I needed to hear a voice other than rappers on the stereo. I settled into my car, double-checked that I had all my earnings for that night, and then stuffed them into the glove box. I fastened my seat-belt, then dialed her number.

"Hello?" she said, wide awake.

"Why aren't you asleep?"

"I just got in. I went out tonight."

"Where'd you go? Wait, first, do you know who this is?"

"Of course I do. I went to a nightclub near the beach."

"Sounds fun." There was silence. "Well, I don't want to keep you up, just talk to you briefly and—"

"What are you doing tomorrow?" she cut me off.

"Nothing. Why?"

"Make sure you call me. I want to see you."

"OK. Make sure you answer."

We said our goodbyes and both ended the call.

After waking up around noon the following day, I noticed I had three text messages from San. I called her without reading a single one and made arrangements to meet up at my favorite bookstore near the mall. I didn't want to overdo it, so with a bare face and a pair of large-framed sunglasses, I threw on a tight pair of Lucky Brand jeans, a J'adore Dior top and sprayed a bit of perfume.

We pulled up to the bookstore at the same time. She noticed me first and signaled by honking the horn of her newer-modeled midnight blue Toyota Camry. We exited our cars quickly and made our way to the entrance. San wore a tight pair of light blue jeans with rips and tears throughout, along with a waist-length black halter. She applied her make-up lightly for daytime wear, which only minimally enhanced her natural beauty.

We greeted each other with a hug and went straight to the row of books that we found most appealing.

"Why is it that African-American fiction books all have pictures of half-naked women on them?" she asked as she picked up a book from the shelf.

"I think it has something to do with what appeals to the urban community. Think about it." She looked at me. "What's in most hip-hop videos?"

"Oh, I see. Well, we'll never see a Danielle Steele book with a half-naked white woman on it." We both giggled.

"You ever wonder why bookstores designate a section for African-American fiction? Or, what makes a book African-American fiction—the writer being black or the book's content?"

She looked baffled. "So, you read a lot?" she asked.

"Yeah, in my spare time," I said, browsing the Omar Tyree section.

"What do you read?"

"Anything that can keep my interest long enough to get through it, but I really like books that can teach me something."

"I've been writing for a while now," San said suddenly.

"What have you been writing?"

"Nothing major, but I've actually never been big on reading. I'll put a book down after a few chapters and never pick it up again."

"Perhaps you weren't reading the right books—good books."

She walked to the opposite side of the shelf and began to finger through a couple of novels. From time to time, we would both glance up from the never-ending rows of books and catch each other's eyes. I couldn't see her lips, but her eyes smiled back at mine. I picked up the latest E. Lynn Harris

P l a y e d

novel and walked around the corner to join her.

"Ready?"

"If you are," she answered. "Is that what you came here for?"

"Maybe. I won't know what I like until I've read it."

San shrugged her shoulders and led the way to the cash register. We made plans to go to the mall after leaving the bookstore. She wanted to look for a gift for her mother's birthday, and I didn't mind picking up a few things. Leaving her car in the parking lot, she hopped into the BMW I rented for that week and we headed to the mall.

She was quiet for most of the ride, only turning down the music once to compliment me on having such a nice car. I smiled and said "thank you," but it was too soon for her to know about what I had and how I had come to have it.

I noticed that she looked from the passenger side window as if she was hoping that someone would save her. From the way she would focus most of her attention on drivers of other cars, crossing pedestrians, and buildings we'd passed, I felt like I was kidnapping her and she wanted to finger "HELP" in a heavily fogged window.

"Are you OK?" I turned down some old-school Keith Sweat I had been playing all week.

"Yeah. Why you ask?" She continued to look out of the window.

"Well—because of that." I raised my hand to indicate her demeanor, and she was forced to look at me. "It's like you're looking for someone to save you. If you're uncomfortable or something, I can take you back to your car."

"No, I'm fine." She looked at me, then turned back toward the window. "I guess there are a few things on my mind."

I didn't bother to ask her about those things. I figured if she wanted me to know she would offer that information.

We rode the rest of the way in silence, but once we arrived at the mall, she wouldn't stop talking. Every outfit she saw put her in the mind of one of her friends—the whore, the conservative, the church girl, and even herself. From time to time, I would drift away from her just to hear her voice dying in the distance. I could tell she may have been a little nervous and had to constantly find something to say to avoid the common awkwardness of hanging out with someone for the first time. It wasn't upsetting, just irritating.

"Ahh, that's cute." She came from behind.

"Yeah, isn't it?" I held up a pair of khaki shorts made for toddlers.

"So, you got a kid, huh?" She picked up a different pair of shorts from the rack. "I have a daughter, too. Her name is—"

"I never said I had a kid." I turned and walked away.

"Well, my daughter's name is Sarai." She followed behind me.

"Isn't that a Biblical name?" I asked.

"Yeah. She was Abraham's wife in the book of Genesis, who was so beautiful that Abraham had to tell the Egyptians that she was his sister in order to avoid being killed. And—"

"I know the story." I cut her off. "And where is your daughter?" I asked, stopping to look at clothes on a different rack.

"My mom's. I just need to get myself together then I'm going to get her. I can't wait to bring her home to me. It's been a year. You have no idea how much I miss her."

Oh, but I do, I thought. *You have no idea.*

Sarai became the topic of the afternoon. San went on to tell me how her ex-boyfriend would abuse both her and her then four-year-old daughter. Once she was able to support and protect her daughter, she would take her from her parents' home.

I learned that San worked in the public library for a year and barely made enough money to pay her bills. On the night I met her, I had wondered what solace drugs and alcohol offered her—what void needed to be filled there—and I had finally discovered it. San confiding in me was beyond anything that I could fathom; she talked to me as though we were old friends. I learned more about her in those few hours than I'd learned about close acquaintances I knew for years. She was honest and didn't hold back the details of her life no matter

P l a y e d

how disturbing the truth may have been. I, on the other hand, kept myself in enough darkness to hide what I feared would allow someone access into my world.

We made several plans to see each other and kept each one of them: dinner on Tuesday, lunch on Thursday, a movie on Friday. After a month, my time became divided between work and San. I never questioned the relationship she informed me she had when we first met. Besides, we didn't consider furthering whatever our relationship was. It wasn't sexual, but it was just as fulfilling: we both vitally filled a void in each other's life. I saw true beauty throughout San, beauty deeper than her attractive physical attributes. It was not that she had eyes as lovely as Saharan sands, but the way she looked at me with them—not that her calves and thighs were tight and toned, but how her walk defined her confidence; it was the way she smiled, touched and talked as though we were old friends.

I found no faults with her, but even so, I tried to keep my guard up.

Triple Crown Publications *presents*...

4

San invited me to a poetry spot downtown one Saturday evening. She wanted me to hear a new piece that she'd written, so I agreed to go along.

After about fifteen minutes of being there and listening to other poets, it was San's turn.

"Next, we're going to hear from a little lady who has been performing here with us for the past year. She's going to bless us tonight with a new piece." The emcee looked at her. "San, you're up. Give it up for her, ladies and gentlemen."

San gave me a nervous smile and rose from the table. I gave her a smirk in response and watched as she walked away, touching the backs of people she knew.

For a moment, I felt like a character in Alex Hairston's *Love Don't Come Easy*. She nervously turned the pages in her notebook before she began.

"This piece is not yet titled." She looked up from her notebook toward the audience. "Even my—thoughts become unclear as I—strain to express myself with word—stuttering unto paper—never thinking imaginable that I would be here—enraptured in this sea of confusion and self-misguidance—"

I had never heard her perform before. Her demeanor was so different; completely transformed. Her voice demanded the attention of everyone in the room. Her body language made her seriousness clear and evident. I was lost in her words. Finally, she ended the piece with a flirty smile and a "thank you," and then made her way back to the table, smiling with relief.

"You were great, San."

"Thank you," she beamed.

"Were you nervous?"

"Well, I always get butterflies before I go up. Then, I'm OK once I get started." She grabbed my hand. "But did you really like it?"

"Yeah, it was one of the best ones tonight."

"Well, it was about us."

"Us?" I was appalled. Although I was enraptured by San's performance, I had paid more attention to her movement than her words.

"Yeah." She nodded and smiled.

The emcee spoke again, and for a moment, I was saved.

"Let's listen to the next one," I said quickly. "We'll talk about yours later on, OK?"

She nodded her head again.

Two more poets performed, and San and I didn't say anything to each other. I checked my phone and realized that the time had passed quickly. I was supposed to meet Tiki at 11:30 for work that night, so I had to say goodbye to San.

I gently tugged at her shirt to get her attention. She turned to me, eyes wide.

"I have to go," I mouthed, and pointed to the door.

"Now?" she asked.

She reached for my hand, but I pulled back. "I have to work."

She looked disappointed and motioned to walk out of the room where we could hear each other and not distract others. Once outside, she stood in front of me and folded her arms. "Where are you going, Taj?"

"I'm curious to know what puts you in a position to question me?" Her jaw dropped a little. Hesitantly, I added, "But if you must know, I'm going to work."

"You don't have to be so damn cold toward me, Taj." She turned as if she would walk away, and then stopped in her tracks. "Ah, man, come on. What is this, Taj? What's going on?" It appeared as though she was about to cry.

"What? What do you mean?" I pretended to not understand her sudden outburst of emotion.

"I try my hardest to not question anything but you're so secretive in everything you do. We've spent almost every day in the last month together but I don't even know where you live or where you work. Why—why am I an outsider?"

Her emotions transferred to me. I realized how much I kept her out of any and every part of me. I didn't feel that I was obligated to let her in, but I felt remorse knowing that she didn't deserve the treatment I dished out to her. No one was ever so eager to know more things about me; they only accepted what I offered them. San was different.

"I'm not ready to tell you yet, San," I said, placing my hand on her right shoulder.

"Are you a prostitute or something?"

"No, I'm not!" I felt the heat of anger on my face.

"And? What are you?" She waited for me to respond, but I offered nothing. "I thought we were friends, Taj."

At that moment, I thought about waking up the following day and not hearing her voice, or sharing another meal with her, or even exchanging one good book with her for another one. More importantly, I thought about the void—that inescapable emptiness that existed before I met her. I couldn't endure having such a gaping hole in my life again. As much as I was afraid of losing San, I was afraid of experiencing *loss* even more.

P l a y e d

"Let's go." I grabbed her hand and rushed toward the exit, fearing I would be late.

She didn't say anything on the ride to the hotel. She just sat there with her arms folded, staring out the window. Ten minutes later, we arrived at the Hyatt downtown on the river. San evaluated her surroundings, and by the look on her face, I figured she believed her assumptions were right, and that I was indeed a prostitute. I parked in the garage adjacent to the hotel and told San to get out. I went to the trunk and pulled out my duffle bag.

"No, I'm not an assassin if that's what you're thinking," I said, trying to lighten the mood.

She didn't say anything.

We took the elevator to the sixth floor and walked down the corridor to Room 623. San followed me in. Tiki sprung from the bathroom in powder blue lingerie and black patent leather pumps, putting on an earring.

"Girl, where you been? You were supposed to be here a half hour ago. Hurry up and get dressed." She walked back into the bathroom without noticing that someone else was in the room.

"Sit over there," I said firmly and pointed to a chair in the corner, "and please don't wander around. Don't talk to anyone."

"But there's no one else here," she said, confused.

"Listen to me." I walked up to her, our noses only inches apart. "Please … please don't judge me." She broke eye contact with me and sat down. What shocked me most was my own behavior. I actually cared what she thought of me. *Am I deeply ashamed of myself?*

I showered and dressed quickly, nervous that San would be exposed to some drunken crowd that assumed every woman in the room was a part of the show. Before I exited the bathroom, Tiki already begun to play music. I assumed that the night's crowd was already arriving. I was about to open my world up to San and it made me sick to my stomach. There was no need for a drink; I couldn't have felt higher, or more nauseated for that matter.

A crowd gathered around the bed where Tiki sat. All attention was on her half-naked body. The bathroom door creaked as I closed it behind me, and a few turned to look. San sat up in her chair, examining my body—the black fishnet stockings connected to the hot pink garter belt with matching bra and thong. My body glistened in pure jojoba oil. My hair was pinned so that only a few strands fell in my face. After a few seconds, all eyes were now on me. San sat back in her chair and watched as Tiki began to lay down the rules: no weapons, no touching, grabbing, fighting or jacking off.

This night, the price was one hundred and fifty dollars because of the niceness of the hotel. The men dug into their pockets and threw the money on the bed. Tiki collected it, and it was time to begin.

We both kneeled on the bed, facing each other. Her lace, one-piece costume covered only her nipples. I was excited, so I went for them, grabbing and sucking, flicking her nipples with the tip of my tongue. She moaned. I slid a hand between her thighs and stroked her, applying a bit of pressure where I assumed her clit would be. She pressed harder against my hand. It excited me more. I grabbed her waist and kissed her, then flung her body down on the bed, showing some aggression. I gently put my hand on her right knee and slowly pulled her right leg toward me, opening her legs enough to give the crowd a look. We continued kissing as I slid my finger inside her. She gripped my forearm tightly and pushed it in deeper.

I was so lost in what was going on in the show that I forgot about my guest that night. Tiki and I were maneuvering each other on the bed, a sexy transition, and I looked out into the crowd for San. The chair in the back of the room was empty. I scanned our audience; she was nowhere in sight. San was gone. But I couldn't seem distracted at that point. It was a situation I would have to deal with at a later time.

After the show, Tiki and I packed up and said our goodbyes to our guests. I had every intention of calling San as soon as it was all over, but I realized that I'd left my cell phone in the

P l a y e d

car. I just wanted to make sure that she was OK and that we were still cool with each other.

It was almost 2:00 a.m., and the hotel lobby was empty. No one was coming or going; even the reception desk was deserted. The door slid open automatically, and I walked out. San was sitting on the curb, shoulders slouched forward, arms resting on her thighs.

"Hey, you." I stood next to her.

She looked up at me and pulled at her fingertips.

"Wow! Is it that bad?" I laughed faintly.

"You know, the only reason I'm still here is because my purse is in your car, and I couldn't get a taxi to get away from here without it. So, please," she stood up and dusted the back of her jeans, "if you would give me my purse I could—"

"Wait a minute. You wanted to see this. I didn't bring you here to upset you."

"Just give me my purse."

"No, you're not going anywhere like this." My concern surprised me as much as it might've surprised her. "And you can be damn sure I'm not letting you take a taxi this late."

"Oh, like you give a damn about someone else besides yourself now?"

"What? Where is this coming from?"

"Just get my damn purse."

"I'm lost." I pressed my hand against my forehead, confused. "I'm not giving you anything! I thought we were cool, San. I thought you would understand. You've seen this all before. You saw it the night I met you. With Shai." I paused for a moment. "You know, this is my fault." I reached inside my handbag and withdrew my car keys. "I knew it. This is why I don't let people in."

"Is that what you think you did, Taj? Let me in?"

"Come on. Get your purse." I started to walk away.

"Is that it?" She placed her hands on her hips.

"It's what you wanted, isn't it?" I stopped and turned to her.

"No, no it's—"

"What then?" I yelled.

"It's you. It's you that I want, Taj. Can you not see past all the walls you've built up around yourself? I've never met anyone so beautiful, but too damn *stupid* to realize when someone genuinely cares about them." There was silence as I stared out into the street. "Just get my purse!"

I had no response for her. I walked to the car and unlocked the doors by keyless entry.

"It's open," I told her.

She reached in through the passenger side, pulled out her purse, and threw it over her shoulder. By the time I placed my bag in the trunk, she was gone. I looked around the lot, into the darkness. There wasn't a single shadow. "San?" I called. There was nothing.

There was no movement in the parking lot. I shined the headlights, on high beam, in the vicinity around the hotel. She was gone.

There wasn't a single part of me that believed San wasn't being sincere. We were close friends after all, but even that was new to me. Of course...there was some attraction to her on my end, but I had made up in my mind to keep my distance from her. *What could I offer her?* I thought.

It had only been 24 hours since I last heard from San, but I already felt that something was missing. The void quickly came back into plain sight. Considering we were together almost every day for weeks, I knew that it would be difficult without her—at least for a while. I decided to count that day as Day One toward the recovery process without her. *Pretty soon,* I thought, *she'll just be considered another person in my past.*

Played

5

I sat in the farthest, quietest corner of the bookstore reading. It was late, 9:00 p.m. perhaps. I was so consumed with the book that I lost track of time. To preview a book that I was intending to purchase, to me, meant that I would have to read at least the first three chapters. By then, I read five. It was indeed a must-have. I walked to the counter, reaching in my purse for some cash to make the purchase.

"How are you this evening?" the cashier asked.

"Good," I replied, still digging through my purse. I found a twenty-dollar bill and finally took notice of the person behind the register. She was gorgeous. She had the cutest dimples, and her smile was close to perfect. Her skin was a flawless shade of brown, and her hair was jet-black and hung to her shoulders. I handed her the book.

"Oh, this is a good one. I've read it before."

"Really?" I asked.

 Triple Crown Publications *presents...*

She nodded.

"Then that means we have the same taste in books."

"Maybe so."

"I wonder what else we have in common." I smiled, trying to make her feel comfortable about a woman making passes at her.

"Who knows," she shrugged her shoulders.

"What's your name?" I asked.

"Brandi."

"Oh, I see. It says it right there on your—" My eyes were fixed on her chest as we completed the transaction.

"Don't mind her. She's a big flirt," a familiar voice behind me said. I turned quickly.

"San?" She was standing behind me holding some children's books, wearing an extremely large smile.

"What? Thought you would never run into me?"

"Yes—no. I mean—" Noticing I was done, she moved past me to the register.

"I would like these please," she told the cashier.

"I mean, it's been weeks. How have you been?"

"If you wanted to know the answer to that, you could have called me weeks ago."

"Are you still mad?" I thought about what she said for a moment then told her, "You didn't call me either." The cashier seemed to try hard to pretend she wasn't listening.

"I was never mad at you." She picked up her bag and took her receipt. "Thank you."

"Then, what was it?" I followed close behind her.

"If you don't know the answer to that, then—"

"Why are you so hard with me now?" It seemed as if the tables had turned.

"Listen." She turned to look at me. "It's not a big deal to me anymore. What you do." She smirked. "We're still cool. As a matter of fact, I was going to have a drink across the street. Do you wanna go?" She paused for a moment. "Oh, or do you have to work?" she added sarcastically.

"No, I don't."

Played

"Come on then."

We walked out together. Our cars were parked next to each other, but she wouldn't have known. That week's rental for me was a midnight blue Jaguar, one of my favorite rides. We took her car to the bar directly across the street from the bookstore and ordered one drink after another: a top shelf margarita, a blue Long Island, a few shots of Patron and even a couple of Jell-O shots. It seemed like forever since I had last spoken to San. I didn't realize how much I actually missed her until she was in my presence again. We didn't discuss the events of that night; it was like it never happened, and we picked up exactly where we left off. San talked about how she was closer to getting her daughter to come home with her and how she was working at the poetry spot as a server for some extra cash. There was nothing new going on with me. Everything was always the same with me.

"I don't think you should be driving now," I told her. "Let me take you home."

"I'm fine." She could barely keep her eyes open. "You don't have your car anyway."

"I can drive you home."

"No. I'm fine. Thank you though."

"Are you sure? I really don't think—"

"Yeah—actually, you can drive me—to your place."

I looked serious. "My place?"

"Exactly. We're friends, right?"

"I mean—yeah. That's no problem."

"Really?" She seemed stunned that I agreed. "Let's go then," she said, possibly fearing that I would change my mind.

San could barely walk in the parking lot. I drove her car back to the bookstore and changed cars. I figured it would be more of a liability if I left the rental there overnight. I helped her into the passenger seat, and she immediately put her head back, hardly noticing that she was in a different car. I never invited anyone into my apartment, but it was the price I was willing to pay for her companionship—anything to prevent her from disappearing again. I hoped that she would appreciate seeing it. But as I thought about it, I realized it was possible that revealing more of my lifestyle would have an adverse effect and drive San farther from me. Either way, it was risky.

When I pulled up to my apartment, I noticed San was on the verge of passing out. Getting out of my car, I walked to the passenger side, opened the door, put her arm across my shoulder and held her waist to help her out of the car and into the apartment. I sat her down on the couch, then went to my bedroom and grabbed a fresh blanket from my laundry basket and the blanket from my bed. When I returned, I saw her dipped to the side, giving a drunken moan here and there. Putting a small pillow behind her head, I stretched her out and put the blanket on her body. The room was quiet, except for the clock on the wall that made a tick tock sound. It wouldn't have seemed so loud had my senses not been marred by the alcohol. I could feel the hairs standing in my ears with each stroke. The sound was like a drum. I put the blanket on the floor and lay down until I eventually fell asleep.

"Wake up, sleepy." The sun was up and so was San. She leaned over the edge of the sofa and touched my face with the back of her hand.

"What time is it?"

"Morning."

"Ha ha. Very funny."

"You asked. Are we at your place?"

"Yeah. This is where you wanted to go, right?"

"Um, yeah. It's comfortable." She looked around at the few pieces of furniture sporadically placed around the living room. "I like your couch, but why aren't we in bed?" I was surprised by her forwardness.

"It's a mess back there. And I wouldn't want you to wake up and—"

"Can I see?" She was like an Energizer bunny. She moved

Played

29

the covers from her body.

"Did you have a cup of coffee or something already this morning?" I asked, watching her jump up from the couch and begin walking down the hallway. "Don't say I didn't warn you!" I yelled as she opened the door.

"Wow, you're right! You sure have a lot of clothes and shoes, but the room is very spacious." Her voice gradually faded, an indication that she was getting deeper into the room. "What's this?"

I got up from the floor and rushed into the bedroom.

She was holding a blue blanket and standing over a small brown box tucked off in the corner.

"That? That's nothing," I said, trying to take it from her.

"No, wait a minute," she snatched back. "Micah Anthony Kingston," she said, reading what was stitched into the blanket.

"Give it to me."

She seemed to notice I was getting upset. "Give it to me!" I said more forcefully, taking a step forward. She quickly reached for my hair and lifted it from the back of my neck and read, "M-A-K," aloud. "I was wondering what that meant."

"San, please don't—" I reached for the blanket again with tears clouding my eyes.

"I won't judge you, if that's what you're thinking. I just know that you have a lot of secrets, and day after day, I'm discovering them." She dropped the blanket back into the box and looked at me. "So, how old is he?"

A tear dropped from my eye. "Who are you? FBI or something? Why you asking me all these damn questions?"

"Taj, you're so full of it. I don't feel bad for asking a question that a *normal* person wouldn't have a hard time answering."

"He's five now," I answered, aggravated, wiping my face, angry that I showed some type of vulnerability.

"Is he with his father? Your parents?" She folded her arms and waited for an answer.

"Look, I don't have time to be questioned by you," I

huffed. "This whole thing was a bad idea." As I turned to walk away, she grabbed my arm.

"No. Stop walking away from me," she demanded. "Just talk to me, Taj. I only want to understand what's going on with you. Why you do the things you do . . . what makes you—drives you?"

"Don't give me poetry, San. My life is real. You wouldn't understand that."

"And so is mine," she replied softly looking into my eyes. "What do you want me to do?"

"Just be what I want you to be," I uttered from some-where.

"What? And what's that?" She laughed faintly.

"Just be there—*here*. That's it."

"No." She folded her arms. "You can't dictate how people act, what they say and what they do. We put up with who and what people are, or we don't. It's that simple."

"I was raped, San. My mom died when I was a kid, and who the hell knows who my dad is. My foster parents could-n't have given a damn about me. I lived in that house for three years—three years! I didn't have anywhere else to go, so a crackhouse became my home for months. I had noth-ing!" Another tear escaped my eye and I tried my hardest not to let more fall.

"Who raped you?" she asked hesitantly, staring at me.

"My foster brother." I forced it out but sucked up the need to cry. "He was older than me, bigger than me, stronger than me. My foster parents didn't listen. They said it was my clothes, the way I wore my hair, the way I walked, how I tip-toed from the shower to my bedroom. It wasn't *their son*. It was me." I turned away and started to fold some of the clothes from the bed in hopes that I would distract her and end her questioning.

"But where is he—the baby?"

"The state has 'em." I found it hard to swallow. I gave up folding clothes and looked at San. "He was born with dope in his system."

Played

31

She looked shocked.

"I tried, but I couldn't cope with everything that I was going through, and they took him from me."

She leaned in to hug me. I rested my head on her shoulder and held her tight.

"Shh now. You'll get him back."

For a moment, I felt that he was better off exactly where he was.

Triple Crown Publications *presents...*

6

I had never spent so much time learning to care for someone before. It was the least that I could do for San, after all she'd done for me. Four months passed without either of us realizing it. I spent numerous days hiding behind bookshelves with her, chatting with her at her work, and rushing through performances at night to try to make it back to her. Even though our relationship wasn't sexual, her girlfriend Kendra had become a distant memory. All of our time was now spent on talking to each other, indulging in novels that San actually found she enjoyed, or watching old flicks. We frequently took trips to Atlanta, staying at the Hilton Downtown and blowing money in stripclubs just for the fun of it. Escaping our day-to-day routine became a day-to-day goal for us, but it primarily came at my expense. After learning I owned a passport, San began to dream up other ideas for escape, and money got strange.

P l a y e d

Prior to meeting San, I was very keen on my spending habits. But now money had become an issue. There were no longer moments that I would decline to do a show. I was desperate for money and had not heard from Tiki in almost a week. Her phone was disconnected, but one evening when San and I were on the way to dinner at one of our favorite seafood spots near the beach, she called.

"Hello?" I answered, putting our conversation on hold.

No one spoke.

"Um ... hello?" I asked again, only louder.

"Girl, it's me."

"Tiki? Where you been?"

"I'm in Alabama right now. My grandma died, and I'm here with my people."

"I'm sorry to hear that," I told her, not feeling the least bit remorseful. "So, why are you calling?"

"I just wanted to let you know so you won't—"

"Naw, it's cool. Just call when you get back." I closed the phone then threw it on the dashboard. San grabbed it and asked what was wrong. I offered nothing.

I knew I should have been more understanding, sympathetic even, but she was my only way to make money, and she was hours away, which created a huge problem. Part of me even wondered if her grandmother really died at all. Knowing Tiki, it wouldn't surprise me if she were in the Caribbean with some overweight, buck-toothed, retired athlete who offered her money. That's just how the game was played.

At dinner I was extremely quiet, plotting my next money-making move. Robbing a bank was always at the top of my list, but how would I actually pull it off? Then, I considered a check-writing scheme that would tie me over until Tiki returned. That idea quickly went out the window when I considered possibly having to pay the money back when or if I was ever caught. One thought led to another. San wasn't the type to talk without someone else contributing to the conversation, so there were moments when neither of us spoke.

"So, we're gonna sit here and not say anything to each

other?" she asked, stirring her Patrón margarita with a straw.

"There's nothing to talk about," I answered curtly.

"Why? I know something's wrong. Maybe I can offer some advice or something."

"Tiki is out of town." I lowered my eyes, knowing I was on the verge of vulnerability. "I need money, but I can't make any without her."

"Don't you know anyone else? Shai, maybe?"

"Hell no! Who would want to see her tacky ass doing a show? We'll have to pay folks to watch it." We both chuckled.

"Well," she hesitated, "maybe I can help you out."

I looked at her. "San, I don't want your money. I—"

"No, I didn't mean money. I meant I can help you with the show." She stared at me. I was surprised to say the least. How could I have expected her to make such an offer?

I shook my head. "We're friends. I can't mix the two. I want to keep things the way they are."

"Well," she shrugged, taking a sip of her margarita, "don't say I didn't offer." She looked off, continuing to sip her drink.

I didn't need a new business partner or a sex partner for that matter, but I did need money. I trusted her, and after fifteen minutes of pondering her offer, I accepted it. In that moment, I had no idea how the situation would play out. I should have been happy to have an opportunity to make money, but for the first time, I was nervous. I had seen San naked on a few occasions—fitting rooms in clothing stores primarily, but not during intimate settings. During those times I saw her body I searched almost every inch of it for the slightest flaw and I uncovered none. I imagined kissing the purple butterfly on her left shoulder and found myself staring at it quite frequently, but a part of me was afraid to touch her. I didn't find her body to be sexy, just beautiful.

After dinner, the rest of the evening was spent contacting some guys I knew in order to arrange a show for Saturday night. I managed to scrounge ten who were willing to pay at least one hundred dollars, making our earnings for that evening a thousand dollars.

Played

"Can they touch us? What if they touched us ... what if the police officers come ... what if we're robbed ... what will we wear?" were only a few of the questions San asked. I could tell she was nervous about it. I answered all of her questions positively, breaking down the particulars of how the shows operate, even if I never stopped to think of it myself. I wanted her to feel safe, comfortable. Moreover, I wanted to protect her.

Saturday arrived quickly. San and I spent most of the day shopping and getting manicures and pedicures. I had my lashes refreshed by the Koreans while San waited. She despised anything artificial. Her hair and nails were always natural. She wore very little makeup, if she ever wore any at all. On the other hand, I openly accepted any enhancements that would make me stand out from the ordinary woman. Not that I couldn't stand out enough without them, but I liked to come across as, or at least feel, untouchable.

We carried our things to a room on the fourth floor of the Hyatt in downtown Jacksonville. San barely said anything when she sat her overnight bag down in the corner of the room. Every once in a while she would release a heavy sigh, and then sip more of the rum and Coke she'd mixed in one of the glasses from the wet bar. I decided not to drink or use drugs that night at all; I wanted to be aware of everything that was going on around me.

"Should I get dressed now, Taj?" San asked, sitting at the edge of the bed.

"Well, what time is it?" I replied, looking around.

She looked at her watch. "Almost eight."

"Yeah, you can jump in the shower then. I'll get in after you."

She stood from the bed, walked over to her overnight bag and removed some of her belongings. "Where are the razors? I really need to shave."

"Look in the bag by the door. I think I packed them there."

She did, then went into the bathroom only to emerge after half an hour, wearing only a towel. Her hair was pinned into a loose ponytail and her makeup was applied lightly. Her features resembled those of a doll, exaggerated yet beautiful. I couldn't determine whether or not I wanted to fantasize about her or feel jealous. I was truly torn. I walked past her without speaking and went into the bathroom to prepare myself.

After twenty minutes, I was applying makeup behind the locked bathroom door.

"Taj?" San called out, attempting to turn the knob.

"Yeah?" I responded.

"Are you almost finished? It's almost nine and—" her voice trembled.

"Don't worry. I'm almost done."

"Well, OK. I'm not opening the door if someone knocks. Just know that."

"That's fine. I'll get it."

She was sitting in the chair next to the bed when I walked from the bathroom. I went over to the corner near her to stuff clothes into the overnight bag. She smelled sweet. Her legs were crossed, and I could see every inch of her right thigh. They were extremely toned. Her costume was a simple two-piece bra and panty set that we picked up at Frederick's of Hollywood in the mall. The set was peach and was lined in brown lace. Her shoes were gold in color, which matched her accessories: a gold bangle, hoop earrings and gold necklace dangling two interlocking C's.

"You look very nice."

"So do you," she replied.

"Are you ready?"

"Um-hmm," she nodded.

Our first set of guests arrived five minutes after nine. I never saw this crew at a show before, but it was obvious that the four of them had been at a bar before coming to the hotel. Each of them reeked of alcohol and slurred a little when they spoke. But for the most part, they seemed pleasant, like they weren't going to give us a hard time. Two of them walked over to San while she sat in the chair. She leaned forward to shake their hands. I felt it would be the beginning of a very long night.

Played

Others began to pour in not long afterward. There were a few familiar faces in the crowd whom I had to introduce to San. By 9:30 p.m. all ten of our guests had arrived and I locked the door in order to begin the show. Since San had never done a show before, I talked the entire time, laying out all the rules for the night: no weapons, no touching, grabbing, fighting or jacking off. San assisted in collecting our base pay of one thousand dollars. Tips would follow.

I signaled for her to go over to the bed, and then I turned off the lights in the back of the room in hopes that it would make her more comfortable if she wasn't able to see some of the guys. With the light of cell phones, I was still able to look out for those breaking the rules, but in any case I figured that I was more alert that night given my sobriety, and that I would catch any awkward activity.

The men were extremely quiet, staring at San on the bed. I pressed play on the stereo and kneeled on the floor between her legs, resting my head on her lap. She caressed my face for a moment, then leaned in and ran her fingers down my back, stopping at my bra strap. I looked up at her, and she grabbed my face and slowly moved toward me for a kiss. I braced myself. Our lips pressed softly at first; her lips were so smooth and plump. I couldn't break away, instead pressing harder, longer. I cupped her chin with my right hand, keeping her mouth engaged with mine. Our tongues danced subtly in the space between our lips' meeting place. I lifted myself from the floor—lips still entangled with hers—and helped maneuver her body farther on the bed.

She crossed her legs while lying flat on her back. My hand began at her tight abdomen and inched down past her panties to her thigh. I whispered, "Let me in." She slowly opened her legs. I made circles on her chest, abdomen, and thighs with my tongue, then hesitantly tugged at her panties. She seemed to have finally blocked out the idea that ten other people were in the room watching us. She helped me take off her panties, using the tip of her index finger to pull them down her thighs, then maneuvered each leg to remove them completely. She moved so seductively, never losing eye contact. She moaned subtly, sexily, but any more would have been too much.

She positioned one hand on each of her breasts, massaging them. I reached for her right hand and placed it between her thighs. She began to massage there as well. The men began to stir a little, wanting a closer look. I brought my knees up to a doggy-style position and started to stroke myself. San had flipped a switch within me. I was only inches away, but I refused to sink my head between her thighs. I wanted to start over at her mouth again, kiss her slowly, softly. I did. She wrapped her arms around me, tight. After a few minutes, I made my way down again. I didn't come up for a while.

We switched positions numerous times. We incorporated a toy or two, but we spent most of the time interlocked in a kiss, and before we knew it, an hour and a half had passed. The show was only intended to be an hour long. I finally pried my hands away from her body and reached for my cell phone. "It's over," I whispered to her. She looked disappointed.

By the end of the show, we had made almost four hundred dollars in tips, bringing our total for that evening to fourteen hundred. When the room was clear, San sat straight up in bed, removing the covers and revealing her breasts. She was obviously comfortable around me in the nude. A part of me didn't want to look at her. I wanted the images of her and I being intimate to be completely erased from my mind so we could return to just being comfortable enough to talk about anything. What could I have said to her at the point without coming across as awkward?

"So, that was it, huh?" she asked, maneuvering the cover to look at the mess we made.

"Yeah, wasn't much to it," I responded, putting on a T-shirt, without a bra.

"I actually liked it. I got paid to have great sex."

"Easy, right? Here . . . here's your money." I attempted to hand over seven hundred dollars in cash.

"What's that for?" she asked me, looking at the money and then back at me. "I said I was helping out. I'm not Tiki."

Played

"Are you sure?" I wasn't going to argue about it because I needed the cash.

"Yeah. Why don't you treat me to dinner or something? We'll call it even."

I smiled. "That won't be a problem."

A week later, I treated San to dinner. We dined over Bang Bang shrimp, fresh salmon and several glasses of wine at Bonefish Grill near the beach. But my encounter with her on the night of the show forced me back a few steps. At one point, we were inseparable, but now I found myself ignoring several of her phone calls throughout the day. I thought of her more but wanted to speak with her less.

My actions seemed unexplainable, but what was clear was the presence of emotions I now felt that I had never experienced for anyone else in my entire life. I didn't know how to handle them. San challenged everything I believed in: that people are naturally selfish beings who will stop at nothing to get ahead and are willing to hurt or leave others behind in the process. She had become too close for comfort, and I didn't know how to handle it. Of course, it was frustrating to her. Several voicemails contained deep sighs of aggravation which never received a response. But I no longer wanted her in a position as my friend. I had to determine how she would fit into my life, if at all.

Having only spoken to San twice in a two-week period, I finally became worried when I hadn't heard from her in three days. At first, I figured that she was over my little game of not answering whenever she called, but when *my* calls went unanswered, I knew that something was wrong. I called her three times; each one was quickly directed to voicemail. By 8:00 p.m., she hadn't returned any of my calls or messages, so I decided to drive over to her place.

San lived only twenty minutes from my house, but the neighborhoods were extremely different. She lived alone on the north side of town, where thugs and hoodlums with dreads lined the streets wearing long white tees. I rarely visited her—not because of the neighborhood, but because she preferred to come to me. My guess was that my place was like a vacation spot compared to hers. She didn't make a lot of money and wasn't the type to live beyond her means. Her new Camry was her most extravagant possession, but she had plenty without having it all.

Children ran barefoot in the streets and in her apartment complex. Women sat on their porches doing hair, smoking cigarettes, and talking on cordless house phones. San's car was parked outside, but there were no lights on that were visible from the street. I parked near her car and ran up the stairs. The neighbors were attentive, admiring the red Mercedes I rented that week. By the second knock, the door opened.

"What are you doing here?" She wore red boy shorts, a black halter that tied behind her neck, and tube socks that almost reached her knees. Her hair was pinned up off her shoulders. Her eyes were puffy and her nose was red.

"I came to check on you. Are you sick or something?"

She examined herself. "No, I'm fine."

"It doesn't look that way to me, San. If you want me to leave I will, but don't lie to me."

"Come in." She stepped back to open the door just enough to let me in.

There were dishes stacked in the kitchen sink and paper scattered all over the living room floor. The air was damp, like cool air hadn't circulated through the space. She flung her body onto the sofa and tapped a box of cigarettes, relieving it of one. "Want one?" she motioned toward me. I declined and sat next to her, wondering when she started smoking.

"Well, I'm still confused about what's going on here."

"I've been doing all I can to bring Sarai home. Everything."

"I know. You've been working hard."

"That's just it. The county has had a significant budget cut, and my job is out the window." She started to sort through some papers on the floor.

"You can get another job, San. What about something temporary?"

Played

"No! I can't do temporary. I just want to be able to take care of my daughter and not keep scrounging around for employment."

"You will, San. I'll help you."

She looked at me through bloodshot eyes. "So, is that it? You'll help *me* now?" She sat up and continued. "Everything is so damn easy for you. You need money; you do a show. You don't want to be bothered with someone, you don't answer your phone. I can't do that. I have to deal with my issues. Unlike you, my issues are real and there are no easy resolutions."

Taken aback by her comment, I stood up. I refused to apologize for who I was and I was not going to engage in an argument with her. "I'll go."

"Go ahead." She looked up at me from the couch, holding the cigarette between her fingers that were pressed to her lips.

"Call me if you need me," I tried.

"For what? You never answer your phone."

I never felt sorry for her until that moment. Discovering that she had a weakness was momentous. I searched all over to find something that made us relatable. She finally became human in my sight, even attainable. It wasn't my intentions to prey on San's weakness, but only at that point did part of me want to give her everything she needed—her daughter and security. And that wanting made me feel helpless. For the first time, I didn't have an instant fix. But I wanted to do anything to help her. I left her apartment, walked down the concrete stairs quickly and rushed to my car. I opened the sunroof to let in some cool air then drove away.

Ten minutes into the drive from San's house, my cell phone rang.

"Hello," I answered.

"It's me," San spoke.

"What's wrong?"

"Nothing. You said to call if I needed you."

"Yeah?"

"I need you."

There was nothing that I could say. A sense of excitement rushed through me. She finally said what I regrettably feared to feel for her, and I realized that I needed her just as much. It wasn't simply for sexual pleasure as it had been with others in the past, nor was it based on the fact that we shared a friendship, but because over time, I learned to trust, respect, and love her.

Played

7

Soon after the episode at San's apartment, she became my partner in crime, and a great one, might I add. I hadn't heard from Tiki in weeks, and a friend was in need of some fast cash. Of course I wouldn't refuse an opportunity to make some money, so I was all in.

San was dependable. She never stood me up or made excuses about why she couldn't work, even though she may not have been feeling well that day. She always wore a smile. It took her a while to get the idea that what we did wasn't just a sexual encounter between two women, but a performance for others. She and I practiced role-playing on nights that we were not performing. We practiced moaning and several movements that were more enticing, inviting. She mastered seductive lip biting and bedroom talk. Most times I was turned on by listening to her.

Three months of working passed, and we'd made enough

money to last for at least six months. She moved out of her crummy residence and we relocated—together. Our apartment was located on the south side of Jacksonville, near the beach. It was more expensive than either of us could afford without the other, so we split the bills down the middle. There were three bedrooms, two-and-a-half baths, granite countertops, glossy hardwood floors and a fireplace in both the living room and the master suite. It was a piece of art, which only increased in beauty when San added pieces she collected from a trip to Atlanta.

For the most part, San and I shared the master suite. We hadn't declared to be in a committed relationship, but no title could have brought us any closer. We were truly partners in every aspect of our lives. There was a spare bedroom, fully furnished and decorated, in case one of us decided to move out of the master suite. The third bedroom held two twin-sized beds for the day that our children would be able to come and stay with us. And that day came for San not long after moving into the new place.

"Guess what?" She came into the kitchen while I was chopping onions to add to a skillet of browning ground beef.

"What?" I stirred the mixture then poured it into an awaiting pot filled with spaghetti sauce.

"I'm going to Tampa tomorrow."

"OK. It's not like you haven't been twenty times since I've known you."

"But wait! Not only am I going to Tampa, I'm bringing something back with me."

I turned and looked at her. "Oh, come on. No more knick-knacks from your mom's garage. If she didn't want it, I don't want it either. It's only going to collect dust just like—"

"No," she said, cutting me off. "Maybe I should have said that I'm bringing *someone* back with me."

I gripped the spoon with which I was stirring the bubbling spaghetti sauce even tighter. Something prevented me from breathing properly and my vision slightly blurred. I immediately knew who she was referring to: Sarai. A part of me want-

P l a y e d

45

ed to be happy for her, but I couldn't be. Micah, my own son, still seemed so far out of reach. Even after several inquiries, I hadn't received any phone calls or correspondence regarding his whereabouts. His foster parents had moved away, and there was no urgency to find him since the state believed he would be better off without me.

For a moment, I reflected on the last time I saw him. That day, three different narcotics were running through my system. I was barely able to open my eyes, but he didn't know any better. He laughed and giggled on my knee until he was taken away for a final time.

"Well, aren't you going to say anything?" San giggled, grabbing me from behind.

"That's nice. I'm happy for you." I turned back to the stove.

"Ahhh, is that all?" She positioned herself to be able to look me in the face. "What's wrong? Are you crying?"

"No, it's the onions. I think they got into my eyes or something." I grabbed a towel from the counter and wiped my face. "I really am happy that she is coming home, San. It's what you've been wanting for some time now."

"I know. I can't wait!" She hugged me closely.

Four days later, Sarai was there. She wasn't as I pictured her. I thought she would be the spitting image of San: light-skinned, pointy nose and big, beautiful eyes. She was the total opposite; dark and subtle, with secretive looks, but gorgeous nonetheless. Sarai was extremely soft-spoken and playful and would laugh at even the idea of something funny. At 4 years old, she had her mother's intelligence and absorbed everything she learned.

Every other day San took Sarai on some type of educational adventure, be it to the park, the zoo, museums or the beach. It was pleasing to watch the two of them together, but it only reminded me more of what was missing in my own life. It took weeks for me to connect with Sarai. I kept my distance, but as time went by, she began to cling to me. Our favorite place was on the sofa in front of the television in the evenings.

Triple Crown Publications *presents...*

She would snuggle up close to me and watch old episodes of the "Fresh Prince of Bel-Air," or I would allow her to watch some cartoons on the big screen. We didn't become close enough for me to feel as though I was a motherly figure to her, but close enough for me to truly care about her.

Between San's time in front of the computer writing her life away, her frequent Tampa visits and spending time with Sarai, we started to perform less and less. We weren't in dire need of money or anything, but I liked to keep stacking as much as I could just in case. We were down to performing once a week, which was a major reduction compared to the four to five times a week that I was accustomed to. One night after leaving a performance, I decided to discuss our infrequent show situation with San as we loaded the trunk of my Lincoln Navigator with our belongings, preparing to go home for the night.

"So, how do you feel about me doing shows again with Tiki?"

She ignored me, pretending not to hear anything I said.

"Did you hear me?"

"Umm. You said something about Tiki. What was it?"

"The shows. Would it be cool if I did them with her again?"

She dropped her overnight bag into the trunk. "What do you think?"

"Well, I wanted to ask because I know you're busy with writing and with Sarai and all. I need to make money but I just didn't want to put any more pressure on you."

"Yeah, thanks for being so considerate," she said sarcastically.

"What do you want me to do, San?" I asked, placing another bag in the trunk.

"You can do anything but do a show with Tiki." She faced me with a hand on her hip. "That was the old you. Don't go back to that."

"No, that's where you're wrong," I barked angrily, upset by her remark. Staring hard at her, I said, "That's still me."

"So, what? I'm not in this with you anymore?"

P l a y e d

"Yes, but I just want to be on the grind like we used to be. You have other things going on, but there's nothing stopping me."

"Talk to me about it then. What's wrong with talking to me first?" She reached down and placed the final bag into the trunk. After she closed it she placed her hands on her hips again.

"I *am* talking to you about it."

"No, you're not. You came to me with your own solution. A ridiculous solution, might I add." She stared at me, awaiting an answer.

"Well, I apologize for that, but the fact still remains—"

"And what about Sarai?" she interrupted. "I don't want to do anything to lose her again."

"What? Are you serious?" I threw my hands up in the air. "Doing this is what got her back to you in the first place."

"Yeah, well, now that I have her back, I don't plan on losing her again."

"Then I need a new partner," I told her seriously, and walked to the driver's side of the truck.

She climbed into the passenger side, fastened her seatbelt, and placed her right hand on her forehead. She was silent for some time. I stared at her for a few seconds, thinking that it would trigger some sort of reaction, then buckled my own seatbelt and started the engine.

"I'll pick it up. We'll perform more," she said, compromising, not looking at me.

"Do you mean that, San?" I asked, seriously.

She looked out of the window. "Yeah, I mean it."

She didn't.

We continued to perform one show a week, on nights that were most convenient for her. I complained and argued until my voice became raspy and my throat began to throb, but she always got her way. It became a constant argument, week after week. I even threatened to not come home some nights but I never acted on it. My life had done a complete one-eighty. I was in love with a woman, living with her faithfully, caring for her daughter, and hustling less because of her. I lost control of my life, even though a part of me found some solitude and happiness where I was. But the question that plagued my mind constantly was how long I would remain there.

Played

8

San spent a lot of time at the computer, writing. I believed she finally found her niche, but we couldn't pay the bills with it. That is, until her great aunt, Margie, had become a well-known activist in her South Florida community and wanted to put out a book about her childhood struggles and adult challenges. She called on San for help, and San was more than willing to do everything she could. When she was finally presented with this opportunity to profit from writing, her excitement changed the entire mood at home. She did everything with a smile—the dishes, taking out the trash, and even bathing Sarai.

The following weekend San made plans to drive to Tampa for a face-to-face interview with her aunt. She packed very little the night before; just some jeans and cute tops, no make-up or heels.

"Are you gonna miss me?" She leaned in to kiss me.

Triple Crown Publications *presents...*

"Maybe. Your side of the bed will be quite empty."

"Mm-hmm. Well, it should be." We both laughed. "Make sure you pick Sarai up from school today."

"How could I forget that?" I straightened the collar on her shirt.

"All right, then I guess I better get going. I'll be back tomorrow night." She grabbed her bag, walked to the front door then turned for a final goodbye before she exited. "I love you."

"Yeah, me, too. Drive carefully."

She left. I spent the remainder of the afternoon getting rid of clothes I hadn't worn in a while so that I could hang up some of my new things. San's closet was nicely organized. She shopped less than I did, opting for higher quality, not quantity. I, on the other hand, liked a bit of both. The hours passed quickly, and I figured I might as well pick Sarai up from school for her to spend the rest of the afternoon at home with me.

It had been four hours since San left, and I hadn't heard from her. I attempted to call her twice enroute to Sarai's school, but she didn't answer. The drive shouldn't have taken her very long, and her not answering my phone calls was extremely out of the ordinary.

Time passed slowly as I waited to hear from San. Still, I managed to watch "Finding Nemo" and two episodes of "SpongeBob SquarePants" With Sarai.

"Can we play dolls?" Sarai asked.

I looked at her and was touched by her innocence. "Sure, go get them."

She hopped up off the couch to retrieve her dolls. Just as she returned, I looked at the clock. It was 7:00 p.m. and I still hadn't received a phone call.

"Where's my mom?" Sarai asked as she combed the hair of her black Barbie. She sat next to me on the sofa with another doll so I could play.

"She'll be back—as soon as you wake up tomorrow." I stared blankly at the television.

"But I want—I want to see her," she whined.

P l a y e d

"Not tonight, Sarai. Are you hungry?" I asked, hoping to distract her.

"Yeah. I want corn dogs."

"Ok." I got up from the couch and went to the kitchen to prepare them.

I was placing the corn dogs in the oven when I faintly heard San's ringtone on my phone. Rushing over to the coffee table to grab it, I tried not to alarm Sarai with my urgency.

"Hello? Hello?" I spoke quickly, walking into the bedroom and closing the door.

"Hey, you," she said softly.

I felt a sense of relief hearing her voice. "Oh, God. Tell me you're OK."

"Yeah. I'm sorry I haven't called, but I realized that I left my cell phone charger at home. Look next to the bed. Is it there?"

I looked. It was plugged in the outlet next to the night-stand. "Yeah, it's there. You scared me."

"Well, I didn't want to waste my battery but I wanted to tell you good night." I heard her yawn. "I'm really tired."

"Oh, OK, but Sarai wants to talk to you before—"

"No, I'll see her tomorrow. Give her a kiss for me OK. I'm about to—"

"Wait, she's right here and she really —" The phone went silent. "Hello, San? San?"

I'd never heard of her being too tired to even speak to Sarai. I thought back to the conversation and realized how she failed to say she loved me. Then my mind became clouded with the thought of her being with someone else.

My mind ran through all sorts of scenarios until I remembered she'd left her jewelry, favorite perfumes, cosmetics and her sexiest lingerie at home. But on the other hand, nothing could hinder her from buying new things if she wanted to. Shaking the thoughts from my head, I refused to spend my entire evening wondering what was going on with her. I fed and bathed Sarai, then put her in bed, leaving the door to her room open slightly to reveal the light from the kitchen. Before I left, she spoke.

"Can I sleep with you?" She sat up in bed.

I turned around and looked at her. "No. You're a big girl."

"But I'm scared." She rubbed her eyes.

"Want me to keep your light on?" I flipped the switch then stood in the doorway with my arms folded.

"No, I—I want to sleep with you." She looked at me sleepily, barely able to keep her eyes open.

"Come on." I turned off the light and followed her into our bedroom. She climbed into bed on San's side and got under the covers. I walked over to her and kissed her on the cheek as her mother instructed me and told her good night. She fell asleep instantly.

I didn't manage to fall asleep until 2:00 a.m. Sarai made her way to my side of the bed. I paid attention to her sleeping form. Her features were so angelic, almost glowing. She looked peaceful, innocent, just as her mother had been when we first met. I thought of Micah Anthony, my son. I wondered what he was doing, if he was sleeping as safely as Sarai, if he missed me as much as she missed her mother. I envisioned him lying there next to me. For an instant, I could feel his breath on my shoulder, his foot pressed against my thigh, sense his warmth. Then the thought was gone.

The next morning, I made breakfast for the both of us—scrambled eggs and cheese, biscuits, sausage and grits. It was more food than the two of us could finish, but we tried our hardest to stuff ourselves. Sarai lay down for a nap around noon while I cleaned the breakfast dishes from the morning. I stood over the sink, passing one dish at a time, thinking of San and how she hadn't called all morning. When I finished the dishes, I decided to call her. Grabbing my phone off the kitchen counter, it startled me as it rang in my hand, displaying an unfamiliar number.

"Hello?"

"Taj, girl, what's up?" she spoke quickly.

"Tiki?"

"Yeah, man, listen. I need a favor."

"What kind of favor?"

Played

53

"I'm serious man. We can get paid." Her words ran together.

"For what, Tiki? What are you on? Why you talking so damn fast? I don't have time—"

"It's just for two hours, Taj, please. You know the rapper, Lil' T? Girl, anyway, him and his crew wanna see a show. And he really payin'. You know what I'm saying. Come on, girl."

"Girl, I can't."

There was silence.

"You know what—OK." The conversation became serious. "I never left your ass out to dry, did I? You know, I didn't even trip when you stopped our hustle. No one got money like us, Taj; now when I really need you, you won't even take a moment to consider. I didn't know you were that damn cold!"

She rambled on for some time before I interceded. "All right. Where at?"

"What? You gon' do it?" She sounded surprised.

"Yeah. Where, how much and how long?"

"Three Gs each. At a hotel on the beach and two hours."

"All right. Two hours only," I emphasized. "We have to do it around nine though. I can't be out too late."

"OK, I hear you."

She gave me the hotel name and room number. Disconnecting the call, I thought about San. I knew I promised her I wouldn't do any more shows with Tiki, but three thousand dollars in two hours was an offer I couldn't refuse. I already thought of ways to make it up to her.

My thoughts were broken when I heard Sarai laughing at something on TV. I had no idea what was so funny, but I couldn't refrain from laughing. She danced around the apartment, sang, played with toys, and we even went for a walk to the playground in the complex. I pushed her as high as I could on the swing, only for her to request to go higher.

"I want to fly," she told me.

"People can't fly, Sarai."

"Yeah they can. Keep pushing!" I pushed her a little higher and she giggled each time she went up. "My mom said I can do whatever I want to do." She let go of the chains and opened her arms as if she were flying. "I'm gonna fly. Make me fly, Taj."

"Oh, no!" I grabbed the chains to the swing to slow it down. "Don't do that! You'll fall and hurt yourself!"

"No, God will pick me up. Right?" She looked up at me. "He won't let me hurt, will He?"

I couldn't think of anything else to say. I'd never had a religious talk with a 4-year-old. "No, he won't," I confirmed.

The day turned to night, and we hadn't heard from San all day. I packed my things for the show, but I became nervous that there might be no one to watch Sarai, so I placed a few calls. After my sixth call, I had no luck. I looked at the clock. It was already half after eight, and I was desperate. The only other person I knew to call was Shai, and she agreed to watch Sarai.

With little help from me, Sarai put on her shoes. I brushed her hair and added a few barrettes. She went to her bedroom to get her favorite doll—the black Barbie.

"No, leave that here," I told her.

"Please," she pleaded. "Can I take her? I won't leave her."

"No. Your mom hates when you take toys from the house." I took the toy from her and put it on the kitchen counter. "Come on, let's go."

She pouted.

Shai's house was only a ten-minute drive from the apartment, and when I pulled up to the driveway there were no other cars besides hers parked outside. Shai answered the door by the second time I rang the doorbell, wearing a forest green robe and smoking a cigarette.

"Girl, put that out before you kill yourself," I said, grabbing Sarai's hand to walk inside.

"When it's my time, it's my time." She took one last puff and threw the cigarette into the grass. "Well aren't you a pretty little lady," she said, noticing Sarai standing beside me. "Come on in here."

Shai's house was dark as usual, but there wasn't an enormous cloud of smoke or loud music in any of the rooms. Sarai was calm. She sat on the sofa and laid her head on a throw pillow propped in its corner.

"Are you sleepy?" I caressed her face with the back of my hand.

"No," she sighed. "When is my mom coming?"

"You'll see her later."

"I wanna go with you," she whined.

"No, I'll be right back." I looked at Shai, then back at Sarai. "Auntie Shai is going to give you some cookies but you have to be a big girl if you want some now."

"I know, but—"

"Be good. I'll be right back."

"You going to get my mom—to bring her home?"

"Yeah, I'm going to get her, but you have to be good though."

She started to cry, obviously struggling with the idea that I'd have to leave her there in order to bring her mom home to her, a Catch-22. "OK." She dried her face on the pillow.

"I'll be right back." I looked at Shai. "Keep an eye on her. She just likes to watch cartoons. She'll sit still."

"Girl, I got her. Go on." She waved me away.

Sarai sat up and watched me walk away. I felt terrible for leaving her, but I knew I would come back to her in two hours.

It took another fifteen minutes to get from Shai's house to the beach where I was performing that night. Getting out of my car, I could hear the waves crashing on the shore and could smell the salt of the ocean water. I couldn't think of anything more than making as much money as I could in that couple of hours.

Seeing the hotel, I began to get closer and became focused on the task at hand. Taking the elevator to the third floor, I could already hear music playing from behind the thin walls. When I arrived at the room, I knocked on the door, and when it opened, a cloud of smoke rushed out into the hallway. The room was full of men, perhaps fifteen. There was barely space to walk around. I spotted Tiki talking to one of the guys, but it wouldn't have served any justice calling her name since she wouldn't have heard me over the music anyway. Once my eyes became adjusted to the haze, I noticed the guy she was talking to looked very familiar. This could be Lil' T. He wore a plain white T-shirt and a gray wash pair of Rock & Republic jeans. He had on minimal jewelry, only one ear was pierced, and he wore a large-faced watch that glistened in the light.

Tiki looked different. It had been three months since I last saw her. She was thinner, but not a healthy thin. The lingerie she wore fit loosely on her and it wasn't like her to wear the same outfit twice. I finally understood why she needed the money so badly.

"Hey you." I walked up to her from behind.

"Heeeeyyyy!" She gave me a big drunken hug and looked at me. "It's been a minute. You look good."

"So do you," I lied.

"Are you ready to get started?"

"Yeah, let me change first."

She pulled me into a corner by the arm. "No, we don't have time for that. These niggas ready to pay us. They don't give a damn about what you have on. You're already late so let's get this money."

"What am I supposed to do?" I noticed she was still gripping my arm so I snatched it back. "And let me go!"

"Play it off. We'll role play."

I looked puzzled.

"Just pretend like you just got home from work, and I've been waiting. Then undress. You *are* wearing matching underwear, right?"

"Yeah, but—"

"Come on. Let's start."

She went over to the dresser and turned the music down. Tiki collected the money from Lil' T first. I assumed she would lay down the rules as well since this was primarily her gig. Instead, she jumped into the bed and looked toward me to begin.

P l a y e d   57

The hair on my arms began to stand. "Tiki, what about the rules?"

"Oh, yeah, right." She propped up on her elbows, then said, "Anything goes!"

"What!" I was horrified.

"You heard me right. Girl, let's get this money," she whispered.

All eyes were on me. I couldn't just walk away. Breathing deeply, I dropped my bag and pulled my hair up from my shoulders and pinned it. I slowly unbuttoned my black and white polka dot blouse and removed it. The men were quiet. Tiki got on her hands and knees and slowly crawled over to me. She unbuttoned my pants and slid them down my thighs. My plum-colored, lace underwear was exposed for everyone to look at. I stood at the edge of the bed as she gripped my ass tightly and licked my panties like they were ice cream on a stick. I pulled them to the side, and the men leaned in for a better look. She made circles on my skin with her tongue. I climbed into bed on top of her, and we kissed passionately.

I inched backward onto the bed, ass raised in the air, exposing my goods as I went down on Tiki. About a minute into the ordeal, I felt someone's hand on my thigh, making its way to my treasure.

I turned and looked at who touched me. He had more gold in his mouth than Mr. T had chains and there was a huge bulge in his pants. "What the hell are you doing?"

"Chill, baby."

"Oh, hell no." I protested, crawling to the top of the bed.

"It's OK. Just let me do you," Tiki said with a smile. "Let me do you." She made her way down south.

For a moment what she was doing felt great. I never thought that I would miss having sex with her, but I did. Although it was business, it was still very pleasurable. It was only sex with Tiki, but it was intimacy with San.

Tiki's body began to move back and forth rhythmically and she started to moan while she continued to eat me. I was in my zone when I opened my eyes and looked toward the end of the bed. Tiki was being screwed from the back by the man who touched me. I saw him take his dick out and ram it into Tiki again. That's when I noticed he wasn't wearing a rubber. When he saw me watching, he stared at me and began to go harder and Tiki totally lost all control and focus. Inching toward the edge of the bed, I kept my eyes on him as I reached toward the floor for my shirt. I put it on, stood up, threw on my pants and grabbed my bag.

Lil' T grabbed my arm. "Where you going lil' mama? The party just gettin' good."

"This is not how I party. I have to go."

"No, you won't. Not until I get my money's worth."

"You can get plenty ass elsewhere. You don't have to pay me for it. Let me go." I snatched away from him and left the room.

I didn't care about Tiki's safety in that room full of men. As far as I was concerned, she put herself in that predicament so she had to deal with it. I was so angry with her and with myself for that matter. During my drive to Shai's, I only wanted to get San on the phone and tell her all about it, but I knew it wasn't the right time to make a confession.

It was at that moment that my phone rang. I figured it would be Tiki, but it was San. I couldn't think of anything to say to her. *Was she home? Had she been calling for a while?* So many thoughts raced through my head before I had the courage to finally answer the phone before she went to voice-mail.

"Hello?"

"Hey you. Are you sleeping?" I could hear the wind blowing through the window of her car.

"No. Where are you?"

"I'm getting on the road now. I should be there in about three hours."

"It's after 10, San. Why are you leaving so late?"

"Because I wanted to," she told me.

I was shocked.

"What? Where'd that come from?"

P l a y e d

59

"Nowhere."

"I haven't heard from you. What have you been doing? Who have you been with?" My blood was pounding.

"Let's not go there, Taj. I came to do what I said I would do. I just got caught up. That's all."

"Caught up with what? With who?"

"See, here we go. Every time—" San's voice was drowned out by sirens from a passing emergency vehicle.

"I didn't hear you. Repeat that," I yelled as I heard a multitude of sirens echo loudly, then became faint in her distance. "No, don't worry about it. Even Sarai wanted to speak to you last night, and you couldn't make time for her. What's up with that?"

"What are you trying to say, Taj? I'm not a good mother to my child?" She paused. "Sarai. Where is she?"

"She's—" Lights were flashing against Shai's house as I pulled onto her street. Three police cars and an ambulance were parked out front.

"What? I didn't hear you."

"Let me call you back."

"But wait! I was—"

"Let me call you back, San."

I don't remember disconnecting the call or actually putting the phone down. Entranced, I stared at each light as it lit up the scene. I slowly got out of the car and closed the car door, barely noticing the people to my left or my right. My vision was focused clearly on the front door of Shai's house. At first thought I assumed that some fool had overdosed on some bad cocaine or Ecstasy, and it was my fault if Sarai was exposed to it. I wanted to grab her, bring her out OK. I wanted to tuck her in that night like I did the night before, sit on the sofa and watch cartoons and play patty cake. The thought hit me hard and fast.

The front door was wide open, so I walked in. Shai was sitting on the couch where I last saw Sarai, with a cigarette in her hand. For some reason she was alone at the moment; no police, no Sarai.

"Shai, what's going on?" She stared at the television, unresponsive. "Where is Sarai?" I yelled, frantic now.

She moved slowly. I assumed she was high. When her eyes finally met mine, I noticed one tear had made a path down her cheek. She spoke slowly. "Don't be—don't be mad at me."

"What?" I felt as though someone were stomping on my chest.

"She wanted to walk the puppy, and I told her 'yeah.' I said, 'stay away from that water out there. Don't go by that water.' She went by the water and—"

"She's 4, Shai! She can't walk a dog by herself! Where is she?" I left Shai sitting on the sofa and ran to the back of the house. "Sarai? Sarai, baby, come here." My limbs numbed, and I became weak. The back door was open, so I walked through it. There was a gurney out by the lake with a small body on it with people attending to it. "Oh, God, no."

"No, no, no, no. Wait. No." A police officer grabbed my arms and held me from behind.

"Ma'am, we can't let you go over there. You understand?"

"No, no, wha . . . what . . . what's happened? Where is the girl? The girl? Please, God, no."

"Ma'am, let's go inside, so I can ask you some questions."

"Dammit! Let me go!"

"Ma'am, I'm not here to fight with you. I need you to calm down and come with me. We're taking her to the hospital."

"Will she be OK?"

"Come with me."

He led me back into the house. I could barely walk or see through my clouded vision. My eyes were beginning to swell, and I was getting hoarse. I sat on the sofa next to Shai.

"Ma'am, are you related to the little girl?"

"No, I'm a friend of the family. I was watching her. Well, I was, but not tonight..." Thoughts rushing, I became attached to the officer's features. His eyes were piercing. One of his bushy eyebrows was raised. His pale complexion contrasted with his dark facial hair.

"What's her name?"

P l a y e d

"Sarai. Look, where are they taking her? I need to go." I stood up.

"Ma'am, have a seat." He motioned for me to sit back down but I didn't. "Where is her mother?"

"She's out of town. I mean, she's on the road—on the way back here."

"We'll need to contact the girl's mother."

"Will she be OK? Tell me, dammit! What can I do?"

"She was in the water a long time miss," he told me, playing on my worst fears. "We're doing everything we can. Now, we need to contact her mother so that she's aware of what's going on here."

I couldn't move. I plopped back down on the sofa. My hand landed on the damp pillow propped in its corner; the same pillow where Sarai laid her head and begged me not to leave her. My chest pounded faster with each second. My next move would be to lash out at Shai, strangle her, kick her, punch her, anything. She sat there, head titled back on the sofa, eyes barely open, unresponsive. I wondered when they would detain her; if they would prosecute her.

The lights outside began to dim as the rescue vehicles drove away. They had taken Sarai with them.

I grabbed my keys from the sofa and jetted for the door.

Unable to sort through all the thoughts in my mind, I didn't know what to do. I didn't want to call San, but she had the right to know. I was scared, hurt and frustrated. Driving twenty miles over the speed limit didn't compare to how my mind ran. I went back and forth about calling San the entire drive to the hospital. I thought about her being on the road, her safety. A part of me decided against it, even though I figured that if it were my child I would want to know immediately.

My hands trembled as I picked up the phone to call her, and having to do so invoked an even greater sadness. Although it was a clear night, my visibility was almost zero, so I pulled off the road. I sat there for five minutes, closing my eyes tightly, hoping that it was only a dream and I would soon wake up. It was a still night. My eyes were still swollen, my throat still felt as though it were closing...there was no waking up from it. Finally I pressed the call button on my phone. My heart pounded and my breathing became painful; each exhale triggered a high pitched sound effect from somewhere within me. I pressed the phone to my ear but my call went straight to voicemail. I was relieved for a moment, but it didn't take away from the pain I felt in my heart.

They set Sarai up in a room, in the dark. There was no one else there. I gave the nurses as much information on her as I could, then they closed the door and gave me a moment alone with her. The room was bare, only a bed and a stool and no equipment. That was an indication that no further attempts would be made to save her. Sarai was dead.

There was a bright white light shining from above her bed. She seemed more angelic than the night before, even more peaceful.

"Sarai." I walked over to the bed and softly touched her neck, one of her most ticklish spots. "Wake up, baby. Laugh for me, please," I whispered. There was silence.

She was cold, her lips a shade of blue. I wanted to pick her up, take her home and take care of her—play with her again. "Can you fly now? Did He catch you?"

P l a y e d

9

*L*eaving the hospital, I drove home in complete silence. The apartment was cold, and extremely dark. I dropped my keys on the coffee table and turned on the kitchen light. On the counter, Sarai's Barbie laid naked. I felt lower than I ever had before. I took the doll into the living room where I last played with her, and, feeling the quiet, thought of going into the bedroom and packing my things. I figured that San wouldn't be able to live with me after she found out. Then, I thought to go into the room and grab my bottle of Vicodin. I wondered how I could live with myself after what I had done. In the end, I just sat there.

Keys rattled outside the door. I couldn't look. San walked in with her bag and dropped it at the door. She didn't notice that I was there. Her keys clanked against the coffee table. She finally looked up and grabbed her chest.

"Dammit! You scared the hell out of me," she screamed.

I didn't say a word.

"Why are you sitting out here?" She stood in front of me with her hands in the back pockets of her jeans. "Baby?"

I raised my head. "Yeah?"

"My phone died on the way home. I hope you aren't mad. We didn't actually see eye to eye last time we talked." I didn't say anything.

"Wow! That was a long drive," she continued, walking toward the kitchen. "I don't think I want to do that again anytime soon. There's some crazy folks on the road, too." She opened the refrigerator and looked inside. "What did you eat?"

She walked back to the living room and stood in front of me again, her arms folded. "Taj, what's wrong with you? Why are you—" She paused and looked around. "Where is Sarai?"

I lowered my head and pressed both of my hands against my face.

"Taj?" she said, getting louder. "Sarai? Baby, mommy's home!" She began to frantically search the apartment, then stood in front of me. "Where is she, Taj?"

"Sit down, please," I mustered up enough courage to say.

"No!" she screamed, on the verge of tears. "Tell me what's going on. Where's my baby?"

"She's gone," I yelled. My nose was red, runny and throbbing.

"Where is she?"

"She's gone, San. She's ... dead."

San cocked her head to the side and looked at me. Then, she laughed in disbelief. "No, no she isn't . . . She—" Seeing the state I was in and my seriousness, she grabbed her throat and began to gasp. "What—"

"She drowned—in the lake—behind Shai's house."

"*Shai's* house? What in the hell was she doing at *Shai's* house, Taj?!"

"I can explain, but I don't think it's a good time to—"

"Oh, God. You're serious." Her legs buckled, and she fell to the floor. Her eyes were void of emotion. "And where is she now, Taj?" she whispered.

P l a y e d

"The hospital—Shands. She's—" San picked up her keys from the table and walked toward the door. I stood up and walked toward her. "I'm coming with you."

"NO! NO!" She sobbed and shoved me out of the way. "Get away from me! I don't want you to do or say anything to me right now! I'm going to get my baby."

I let her walk out, feeling everything and nothing.

"I'm sorry," I whispered to myself. "I'm sorry." I plopped down on the sofa, laid my head on its arm, and drifted off to sleep.

Light was shining through the window when I finally awakened. My hair was disheveled and clothes wrinkled. I looked around the room but there was no one there. I went to the front door and looked outside. San's car was still gone. Walking to my cell phone, I picked it up and looked at the Caller ID. I had no missed calls. Walking into the bedroom, I sat on the edge of the bed and called the hospital.

"Shands Jacksonville. This is Pat. How can I help you?"

"How can I check on a patient, ma'am?"

"Well, is the patient admitted or in the ER?"

"Neither. Sarai Campbell. She died last night and was brought there."

"Ok. Hold on a moment please." She placed me on hold and music played in the headset.

"Ma'am, there is no one here by that name. I'm sorry."

"She was there last night. I saw her. When did they remove her and where did they take her?"

"I'm sorry, I'm not permitted to share that information with you."

My face tightened.

"What do you mean not permitted to share that information with me? My name is Taj Jenson and I was there when she arrived."

"I'm sorry ma'am. Hospital policy. Is there anything else that I can help you with?"

"Yes, you can tell me where she is!"

"I'm sorry, ma'am. I can't help you." She hung up.

I sat there looking at the phone, confused. Perhaps it was all a dream after all. I jumped up from the bed, went into the living room and looked around. Everything was in place, like any other day that San would drop Sarai off at school then head to the local coffee shop to write. My eyes scanned the room and I noticed something on the floor beneath the coffee table. I walked over and picked it up. It was Sarai's Barbie that I fell asleep with the night before—the night Sarai died.

The hot water from the shower was soothing as I tried my hardest to recount the events of the previous evening. I felt like I was trapped in a horror movie, or that someone was playing some kind of sick prank on me. Walking back out into the bedroom, semi-wet and wrapped in my towel, the bed looked more inviting than ever. I climbed in, threw the sheets over my head, and wept. With each cry, spasms moved through every internal organ, forcing my abdominals to contract and my biceps to tighten. I wondered what would happen with San and me. Would she leave me now? Could I go back to life without her? I never answered why Sarai was at Shai's house in the first place, and I wasn't prepared to tell her. It would only make the situation worse.

10

For the next two months, Tiki called at least twice a day, seven days a week leaving messages threatening to kill me when she saw me again for leaving her alone at the show. I disregarded each of her threats and refused to answer calls from unfamiliar numbers.

I didn't hear from San, but kept track of her by monthly bank statements that were mailed to the apartment, which indicated that she was spending minimally in Tampa. I thought she would never return, but at the end of two months she did. She refused to talk about anything that went on that night, or anything much else, for that matter. I was curious, but I didn't want to force her to address anything she didn't want to. San was extremely quiet most times and expressionless.

Taking up the space in the guest room, San and I barely spoke; only to ask if the other was hungry or not. The routine

 Triple Crown Publications *presents...*

went on for three weeks. No longer were we friends or even partners. We were strangers forced to live under one roof. There was no love there. I felt so undeserving of her presence that I quickly forced myself to adjust to our awkward behavior. From time to time, I would send flowers to our apartment with messages handwritten on tiny cards, only for the flowers to be left on the counter with the unopened envelope.

I woke up one night, about a quarter after one, after having fallen asleep on the sofa while watching TV. There was no sign of San. I glanced to the bouquet of flowers on the counter and noticed there was only one surviving rose. I also saw that the note card was no longer attached.

"San?" I called out as I rose from the sofa. There was no answer. I figured that she might've left or was asleep, so I went to the bedroom to get undressed.

There was light flickering beneath my bedroom door. I opened it slowly, and there was San, lying on her old side of the bed with a candle on the nightstand next to her. She was sleeping. *What is she doing in here?* I thought. She appeared peaceful, angelic, nestled comfortably under the feather-stuffed down comforter. I didn't wake her. I stepped out of my clothes and lay in the bed beside her. She rolled over, turned toward me, put one arm over my shoulder, and held me tightly. I fell asleep.

"Hey, you," she whispered. Light was shining through the bedroom window. She was lying on my chest, propped on her forearm.

"Yeah?" I said sleepily.

"Want breakfast?"

"Um, yeah, sure."

She jumped out of bed and went to the kitchen. I could hear pots and pans colliding and didn't know what to make of the situation. I figured that this was better than silence, so I went along with it. I showered and slipped on a robe. Stepping out of the bedroom, I could distinctively smell the bacon, bis-

P l a y e d

cuits and the cheese eggs being scrambled on the stove. San turned her place in the kitchen and smirked. I returned her gesture with a friendly "hello" and sat down on a bar stool where she placed champagne flutes filled with orange juice.

"How was your evening?" she asked.

"Fine." I looked at her.

"I guess that's good."

"Is there something you want to talk about, San?" I hoped that she was ready to talk about Sarai, but I feared that she would question me about that night.

"Yes, there is." She scraped the eggs onto a plate next to the stove.

"Ok, what's that?"

She moved the plates to the counter in front of me then rested her hands on the sink. "I want to move."

"To where?"

"Away from here. Atlanta maybe, even Houston."

"Why so far away? Why not Tampa, where your entire family is?"

"They're not my family."

I looked at her concerned by this admission.

"And I can't stand being here anymore. I'm constantly reminded of—of the past. I think it would do us both good if we just packed up and left next week."

I almost choked on the biscuit I stuffed into my mouth. "Next week?"

"Yeah. We have money in savings, and we could always make more if we needed it." She made her way around the bar to sit next to me. "What do you think?"

"Um, I don't know San. I'll have to think about it."

There was no part in my mind that would even consider leaving Jacksonville. The entire situation was extremely odd. We hadn't spoken for almost three months, and all of a sudden she's ready to pack up and leave with me.

"I have a way for us to make five grand," she told me.

"What?" I was really curious. "In one night?"

"Yeah, there are some guys that want a private show. They

got a lot of—"

I thought about the last show I did with Tiki and refused to go through it again. "No, I can't."

"But why? Let's just make the money, get out of town, and start over."

"Maybe I don't want to start over, San." I looked at her seriously and tried to understand where she was coming from. But I couldn't figure it out.

"Don't be so selfish."

"I don't have time for this," I mumbled under my breath and left the room.

She never brought it up again. We both understood that eventually our funds would be depleted, and we needed to make more money, so we began doing shows again. We started off light, with only five to six men in attendance, then increased to our typical twelve to fourteen attendees. There was no longer any passion or excitement in our performances. We were acting, completely. The only improvement that occurred within the home was that we were finally communicating about some things, even though we seemed as distant as ever.

It was December, a week before Christmas, and San and I planned one last show before the holidays. Afterward we would spend Christmas in New York, a place she had never been. The show was to be held at a hotel on the south side of town. San informed me that she'd arranged for twelve guests to show up that night. It was the first time she had taken full control of a show and I was shocked. I prepared as I usually had, but she did not. San showered at home and wore her lingerie beneath jeans and a T-shirt. When I asked why she was preparing at home, she said it was more comfortable, convenient, and that she was tired of lugging all of the bags to the car at the end of the night.

This particular time, San drove her car and we arrived at the hotel two hours before the show was set to begin. After I was dressed we lay across the bed and expressed how excit-

P l a y e d

ed we both were about our trip to New York. We talked about visiting Times Square, watching a Broadway play and shopping in Harlem and on Fifth Avenue. She made me smile again for the first time in a long time. For a moment, there was that old energy between us that was there in the beginning. I played with her hair while she lay on her back. She caressed my shoulder with her fingertips and we laughed together.

There was a knock on the door, and we jumped up from our relaxed positions in bed. I sat up, back pressed against the headboard, legs crossed, while San went to the door. She turned to look at me before she opened the door, making sure I was ready.

"Heeyyyy!" San reached up to hug the two men walking through the door.

"Hey, girl. You looking good." The man had to be about six-foot-four, two hundred forty-five pounds, all muscle. He was dark-skinned, very clean-cut, and was wearing a pair of Rock & Republic jeans and a blue collared shirt he probably picked up at Express.

The other guy looked more serious. He hugged San without saying anything. He wasn't as big: six-foot maybe, one-ninety. He had on a pair of basketball shorts, a T-shirt, and could have used a good shave.

"Hey, you must be Taj." The clean-cut guy reached over the bed to hug me.

"Yeah. What's your name?"

"Leon." He smelled sweet.

"Well, it's nice to meet you, Leon," I flirted. "Who is your friend?"

He turned his head, looked at the man then back to me. "Um, that's my boy, Tony."

"Does he talk?" I asked loud enough for him to hear me. He was sitting in a chair on the opposite side of the room.

"Yeah, I talk," he responded. His deep voice caused me to tremble a bit.

Leon talked with me for a while, and San entertained Tony. I was expecting at least ten others, and it was almost a half

hour after the show was set to begin. I excused myself from our conversation about Jacksonville's new developing communities and pulled San away from Tony.

"Where is everyone?"

"I don't know," she shrugged. "I had confirmation."

"Are you sure?"

She nodded her head.

"We can't do it with just these two."

Tony overheard me and looked directly at me. "Why not?"

"I'm not talking to you," I told him, then looked back at San.

"Probably not, but you're going to give me what I came here for. This already paid for."

"We haven't collected any money from you yet," I reminded him.

"Like hell you didn't. I gave ol' girl over two stacks."

I looked at San who was staring off in another direction, but could clearly hear the conversation. "What did you buy for two stacks?" I felt butterflies, and not the good ones.

"A good time." He smirked.

I grabbed San's arm and started toward the bathroom. Tony jumped up to block our way, arms extended.

"What are you doing?" I squeezed San's arm tighter but she didn't say anything.

"Come on. I get one hour, right?"

San nodded her head but remained silent. I finally understood what was going on. This was San's plan to get us out of town. I let her go and backed away from them. I noticed that Leon was standing near the bed, observing, arms folded.

"Taj, I can't give their money back. I can't," she said, remorsefully.

I looked toward the front door, at the three of them, then back at the front door again. The dresser was behind me, holding bottles of liquor we'd bought for that evening. The balcony was on the opposite side, closed and locked.

Quickly, I grabbed a half-empty bottle of Grey Goose then charged at Tony. I hit him as hard as I could and ran toward

P l a y e d

73

the door. The bottle didn't break. It only made a loud thud as he fell to the floor. I couldn't remove the latch at the top of the door fast enough to open it before Leon grabbed me from behind and threw me near the bed. San disappeared. Tony stood up slowly, holding his ear. "DAMN! You stupid bitch!"

"I'll give your money back. Just let me get it," I pleaded, getting up off the floor.

He walked over and slapped me with the back of his hand. My body lay stretched over the bed. I attempted to crawl to the phone but he pulled me back by the ankle.

"Please, don't hit me any—"

His fist collided with my jawbone. I felt a snap, a burning sensation then warm fluid oozing from my flesh. My mouth had become too impaired to speak or yell but he didn't stop there. Each blow he gave me delivered pain on contact; a severe tingling in one eye, then the other. Blood gushing through my nose made it impossible to breathe. There was that drowning sensation in my nose and throat. I was suffocating. He cussed and yelled with every blow he delivered to my body, but his sounds were soon overpowered by the ringing in my ears. I lay there, silently praying for him to stop—for him to become so tired he'd quit, but when he did, he no longer hit me with his hands. I couldn't make out what the object was, but it was as solid and hit as hard as a baseball bat, delivering instant agony to my head, abdomen, and chest, until after a while I was no longer able to see, hear, speak, or move. I could barely breathe, let alone put forth the energy to cry through the beating. And after a while longer, I felt no more pain as I slipped into a state of unconsciousness.

There was a moment that I recall waking up in the middle of the ordeal. I was lying face down across the bed, the lower half of my body unsupported by the mattress. I was being penetrated, deep inside. Each movement was like sandpaper entering and exiting my walls. In the darkness behind my swollen lids, I wailed as loud as I could. I couldn't feel the moistness of tears on my cheeks, but they had to have been there. I tried to block it out of mind, but the pain was unbear-

able. My knee-jerk reaction was to stop him. With my left arm I reached behind in attempt to push him away. He grabbed and twisted my arm, pinning it against my body. I attempted to scream out, but gagged on my own blood instead. And then, I caught a glimpse of her, San, standing in the corner of the room, arms folded, watching as though she were a guest viewing the show. Then, I went unconscious again.

P l a y e d

11

There was a series of beeps echoing for what felt like an hour before I completely opened my eyes. It became obvious that I was in a hospital room. The sheets were white and crisp. There was an IV machine next to the bed along with other equipment that created the beeps that resonated in my mind. I couldn't feel anything beyond the aching throughout my torso. My neck was incredibly stiff and I felt heavy and swollen. Wiggling my fingers was painful. My left arm was in a cast resting on my chest, so I explored my body with my right hand. Some parts were more swollen than others.

I could recall the events that led me to the hospital, but I had no memory of how I got there. It remained difficult to see through my swollen eyes but, needless to say, they were better than they had been.

"Somebody," I whispered with a voice low and raspy. "Somebody, please."

Triple Crown Publications presents...

No one came. No one heard me. I drifted back to sleep.

"And what's her story?" a female voice asked.

"We don't know yet, but she's better than she was when she got here."

"Well, of course, she has the best doctor in the city," she said, flirting.

I couldn't open my eyes fast enough, heavily under the influence of whatever was in my IV.

"If you say so." I heard the door open and close.

"Who could have done this to such a pretty girl?" a male voice spoke. I could hear his pen pressing hard against whatever he was writing on. He hummed Luther Vandross' "If This World Were Mine" and remained in the room for only a moment, then was gone.

After he left, I mustered enough strength to open my eyes and sit up in bed as best I could. There was a cup of grape juice and a cup of yogurt next to the bed. I drank two gulps of juice, then examined the room. I was alone, somewhere. I looked at the telephone. The receiver read: *St. Vincent's Medical Center.*

The door opened.

"Someone's awake." It was a white female with dark brown, shoulder-length hair, wearing blue scrubs. She came over to the bed and checked my IV. "How are you feeling?"

I looked at her through the small openings I had for eyes. "I'm OK. I guess."

"I'm going to send Dr. Carter in to have a look at you since you're awake."

"Ok. Can I ask you a question?" I asked in a whisper. "How did I get here?"

"You can ask the doctor about that." She turned to leave.

"Thank you."

The clock on the wall indicated it was after 8:30. I could only assume that it was night because no sun reflected through the windows at the rear of the room. I had to have been there for at least sixteen hours. I thought about leaving. I recounted the previous night's events, wondering where the hell San was,

P l a y e d

and how I was going to mess her up when I saw her again. My pain turned to anger, especially while thinking that they could have permanently scarred my face, my most valuable asset.

A man wearing jeans and a collared shirt walked into the room. He was fairly handsome, tall, and in great shape. I noticed his biceps before his face, which topped it off. He looked serious.

"How are you feeling?" He closed the door.

"Are you the doctor?"

"Yes, I am. I'm sorry about my attire. I was heading out to meet some friends and heard that you were awake."

"That's ok. I just wanted to be sure you weren't a stranger coming in to ask my personal business."

"I understand that." He looked over the machines.

"I'm feeling fine though. Can I sign out now?"

"Nooo, no, you can't. We need to talk about a few things first." He pulled up a small, rolling stool and sat near the bed.

"I don't want to talk about anything. I really think I'll feel better if I just went home. I hate hospitals."

"You can start by telling me your name," he said, ignoring everything I told him.

"Taj Jenson," I replied, annoyed.

"Do you have any close relatives that we may contact? With your permission, of course."

"No." There was an awkward silence. "Are you going to just tell me what's wrong with me, or am I going to be here for another hour while you rack up on a huge medical bill? Hasn't it been over twelve hours already? This is ridiculous."

"Calm down please. You've been in here for two days, not hours."

My eyes widened.

"You suffered a concussion, a lot of bruising and swelling. Your left arm is broken in two places, and you—" he paused for a moment. "When was the last time you had intercourse?"

"A while ago. Why?"

"I'm sorry to tell you this, but there is a lot of bruising and swelling in your vaginal area."

I looked toward the ceiling.

"Ok, whatever. When can I leave?" I knew there would be a series of questions following, and I wasn't going to answer them.

"Ms. Jenson, you were raped, and I can't imagine how you may be feeling right now, but you need to speak with the officers who can help you with this."

"No. I don't need to do anything. Can you just sign the paper so I can get out of here? Forget it. You don't need to sign anything. This is a free country and I'm—"

"Not going anywhere," he told me, cutting me off. "Listen, I don't want you to make a decision that may jeopardize your health, so I'll hold off for a moment on contacting the authorities to let them know that you're awake, only if you promise me you won't disappear in the middle of the night."

"No cops?"

"I'll have them on speed-dial if you want to talk, but I won't contact them without your permission."

I folded my arms.

"No, no cops," he reminded. "Get some sleep and we'll talk about this more in the morning."

"Thank you," I said to him before he left the room.

He nodded his head and was on his way.

I hadn't considered the fact that I was involved in a crime, the fact that my blood was smeared over hotel room sheets and that my body was found beaten and unconscious in a public place. That hadn't clicked until the moment Dr. Carter came into my room. There was no way I was going to speak with authorities about the incident. How could I explain that this was just a good-deal-gone-bad and that my supposed girlfriend set me up? I was expecting for the finger to be pointed back at me. The situation would be reminiscent of my childhood, where I was to blame for everything in spite of being the victim. How would I know for sure that I wouldn't be arrested for my part that evening, arranging for men to pay me to perform a public sex act? That was the problem. I had my life, so everything else had to be buried in the past.

Played

My first objective was to get out of bed, a task that would take me almost an hour to achieve alone. My body seemed detached from my central system that held everything together. The swelling had decreased significantly, but parts of my body still remained sore and bruised. The first time I confronted a mirror, I hardly noticed the person behind the black-and-blue blotches that covered my face. Everything was intact, at least, just temporarily damaged; nothing I couldn't recover from with the help of pure cocoa and shea butters. My lip was healing well, and so was the inside of my jaw. I was weaned off of heavy medication but doctors were still monitoring my progress.

Two more days passed in the hospital when Dr. Carter realized no one was coming to visit me, so he checked on me more often than he should have. Once, he brought me an arrangement of fresh flowers and a teddy bear that read "Get Well Soon". He was friendly—sometimes too friendly, asking me about my personal relationships and family. But when his questions were ignored, he changed the subject. I saw him as this ordinary, borderline goofy guy who made a slick attempt to get close to me. Even though I admired his physique in many ways, his personality was barely up to par. All in all I sensed power behind that doctor's coat, which was his most attractive quality.

"They're letting you go home today." He stared at the chart he held, facing away from me.

"Well, don't be too happy about it," I barked sarcastically. I sat at the edge of the bed, fully dressed in a shirt with a colorful map of Florida printed on the front and some blue gym shorts I'd purchased in the hospital's gift shop.

"I'm happy that you're well enough to go home, but I still have some concerns about your wellbeing. You know, what landed you here in the first place. I don't want to see you here again, not in that way."

"In some other way, perhaps?" I giggled.

"Maybe. I just want you to be careful, and if there is anything you may need in the future, you know where to find me.

Triple Crown Publications *presents...*

OK?"

"OK."

Dr. Carter prescribed some pain medications and antibiotics, then handed me a few other sheets of paper as well as a plastic bag that contained a set of keys, some lip gloss, and a pair of earrings that were gathered from the room before the ambulance transported me. He slipped me his card and advised me, if I had no general practitioner, to follow up with him at his office within a few weeks. In all, I spent five days in the hospital recovering from the rape and beating. I was still not operating at 100 percent, but I was able to care for myself without the help of others and with hope that the remainder of my scars, wounds, and pains would vanish as quickly as others had.

"Who's coming to get you, Taj?"

I was silent, realizing the thought hadn't crossed my mind up to that point. I contemplated calling a taxi, which led to the thought that I needed money, then to the idea that I had no wallet, no cash, and no cards.

"I'll call someone," I said.

"OK, just keep in mind what I told you." He reached out to shake my hand. I sensed that he would rather have a hug by how deeply he stared into my eyes and how firmly he gripped my hand, slightly pulling me toward him.

"Thank you for all your help. I will."

He walked out of my room for the last time.

Where was I going to find money to pay for a ride home? Where was home? Was San still there? So many thoughts clouded my mind when I was released. A part of me felt safe and comfortable in a hospital bed with people catering to my needs. But it was time to go. I had no choice but to face whatever else was ahead of me.

I used the phone next to the bed to dial the credit union where San and I kept our savings from performances, only to learn the account had been emptied. Only three dollars and eighteen cents out of over twelve thousand dollars we had saved remained. Catching my heart in my throat, I told myself that I couldn't panic and let everyone else know that something

P l a y e d

was wrong. Instead, I simply inquired about public transportation, and a lady at the nurses' station arranged for me to briefly meet with their Social Services department. Because of my situation, they arranged a one way cab ride home for me. I was thankful.

I arrived at my apartment an hour later.

My Navigator was gone but a strange car sat in its parking space. The sun was completely hidden, but I didn't notice any lights on inside the apartment. I pictured San being there, wanting to harm me even more, but then I figured that nothing could hurt as bad as that initial beating, or as bad as the betrayal I felt.

I reached into my bag for the set of keys but noticed that the door was cracked open. Cautiously, I peered through the tiny slit in the door and was met with darkness. There wasn't any movement or sound. I pushed the door open with my cast. "Hello?" I called out, hoping no one would answer. I flicked the light on and I stood there. There was absolutely nothing. Everything we worked hard for was gone. No furniture or television. Even the Laurie Cooper painting I bought was gone. I shook my head when I saw a broken vase and the last bouquet of flowers I bought for San scattered over the carpet.

Walking into my bedroom, I found that there were no clothes left hanging in my closet; there were only underwear and folded T-shirts—which I called house clothes. My bed was still there, stripped of the Jacquard comforter set I purchased from Macy's a week before. Sarai's old bedroom was intact; nothing was taken. I returned to my bedroom after evaluating the apartment, sat on the edge of the bed, and observed my surroundings while scratching at the cast on my left arm, which made a zipping sound. I regretted every moment I'd spent with San, from the day I met her and how much I'd let her in until now. I realized it was two minutes before Christmas. Merry Christmas to me.

12

All I wanted to do was rest and sleep—something I never wanted so much of before. I had no desire to talk to anyone either. That was OK though because I had no clue where my cell phone was. It was either left back at the hotel room or San had taken it. Either way, I no longer cared. Each day, I recounted the events of that evening, the feeling of being pounded numb, the blank look on San's face, her refusal to help me and the idea that I could have died.

Strolling into the kitchen after two days, I remembered I had a little something stashed away in the freezer that could help me out in times of trouble. Looking inside, the cold air hit my face as I dug deep into the back. Behind the mixed vegetables, I found an ice cream sandwich box that I always kept in there. San didn't like vanilla ice cream, so she had no need to go into it. I opened it and the little money I had hidden away—two hundred to be exact, was still there. I never told San about my hiding place for some reason. I guessed this was the reason why. Then I thought of what I would do next—if I was going to move away, or ever work again. For the time being, there was nowhere else for me to go so I called apartment maintenance, reported a break-in and had the locks changed. I didn't need any more trouble.

My appointment with Dr. Carter was six weeks after I was discharged from the hospital. It was the third Wednesday in February and by then I realized that most of my scarring was minimal. A good liquid foundation covered what remained on the outside, but on the inside, no one could help me. Still, I was grateful for how well Dr. Carter treated me while in his care. He was so compassionate, and I was sure to thank him when I saw him again.

As best as I could, with my arm still in a cast, I curled my hair in loose spirals and fingered the curls apart for a softer look. Sifting through my dirty clothes earlier in the week, I found something suitable to wear for the appointment—a blue blouse by Chanel that revealed most of my back with the deep V-cut and a pair of Dior jeans. By then the bruising back there was barely visible. I smiled when I checked several of my jeans pockets: I found three twenties that I forgot about stuffed into them. Finally, I stood in the mirror for almost an hour, making sure that each imperfection on my face was covered flawlessly, yet subtly. It was the first time I dressed up since that night.

Because I had no transportation, I called a taxi from my neighbor's. The old woman was kind enough to extend her help if I needed it and I thanked her.

The address I gave the driver provided me with a sixty-dollar-round-trip ride across town, but it wasn't to the hospital like I thought it would be. It was an office building. Going to the floor and suite that was listed on Dr. Carter's business card, I approached a receptionist who was completing a sudoku puzzle.

I placed my left arm with the cast on the counter and asked, "Is Dr. Carter here? I have an appointment."

"And your name?" she said with an attitude, as though I

were interrupting her.

"Taj Jenson." She looked at the computer screen. "Ok. Sign there and have a seat." She went back to the puzzle.

I sat across from a little girl holding a black, anorexic-looking doll, whose mother was paying more attention to her telephone conversation than to her. The little girl wouldn't look away. She stared directly at me. I picked up a copy of the Cosmopolitan from the coffee table — *How To Make Him Crave You* stretched across the cover. Fifteen minutes later, a young, Hispanic woman wearing scrubs appeared in the doorway and called my name.

"Yes," I responded.

"Come with me. I'll take you back." I followed her down a long, empty hallway past several closed doors. "You can wait in here and the doctor will be with you."

"Thank you." I walked into the room, placed my Burberry bag on the leather swivel stool next to the counter, then sat on the exam table. Before I was able to get comfortable, in walked Dr. Carter wearing a white lab coat and khaki-colored pants.

"Ms. Jenson, how are you?" He reached out to shake my hand.

"I've been well. Just taking some time to heal and take care of myself, you know."

"And as far as I can see, you're doing a wonderful job. You look . . . umm . . . great."

"What was the *'umm'* all about?"

Dr. Carter's eyes shined as he looked down at his chart and then back up to me. "It's difficult not to compliment such a gorgeous lady while I'm working. I should have arranged for you to see another doctor in my practice to make this less awkward, but I figured I'd take the risk." He laughed.

"Your practice?" I looked at him in amazement.

"Yes ... I'm an internist and this is my practice."

My eyes widened in shock. Not only was he fairly young, but he had his stuff together, legitimately. "Well, after the way you treated me at the hospital, I would have insisted on seeing *you*, Dr. Carter." I giggled. There was no denying some sort of

P l a y e d

attraction.

"After today, you won't have to see me anymore, so I'd prefer that you call me James."

"James Carter," I said, liking the sound of it.

The remainder of the appointment went as planned. He checked my heart, lungs and abdomen to make sure the swelling was gone or at least subsiding. Dr. Carter and I also managed to find time to talk about politics and the failing education system. He was certainly opinionated on both. Before I left, he sent me to an orthopedic office just down the hallway to get my cast removed. We chatted again while we awaited the results of my X-ray. Two hours passed before I knew it and, regretfully, it was time to say goodbye. I promised him it wouldn't be the last time he'd see me.

That evening, once I arrived home, I called him at the phone number listed on his business card from a prepaid phone I picked up at the local Walmart. It went to voicemail.

"Hey, James. It's me, Taj," I said seductively. "It was really nice seeing you today. Maybe we can have dinner soon." I left him my number and hung up.

Within the hour, he returned the phone call and we made plans to meet for a late Thursday night dinner. I saw it as an opportunity to finally impress him outside of the office.

For some odd reason, I expected dinner at the local TGI Fridays, Chili's or Ruby Tuesday, and at most a visit to the local Japanese hibachi grill. He surprised me by taking me downtown to Morton's. The blue neon light over the bridge shimmered over the St. John's River as we crossed. James told me that the steakhouse was a spot that he frequented when he wanted the freshest seafood or an impressive steak. I was stunned that he would show me so much attention with nothing in return. I was so used to doing for myself; now a man, who I hardly knew, wanted to do for me. What did he want from me?

We pulled up to the valet and James left the keys in the ignition and climbed out to open the door of his black, late modeled Range Rover for me. The cool breeze lifted the scent of Amor Amor from my sweet spots and filled the surrounding air. I stepped out of the car, one blue suede BCBG stiletto slingback at a time, and grabbed his hand to enter the restaurant.

We dined on colossal shrimp, lobster, and sea bass, along with two glasses of the restaurant's best Riesling, which was then followed by a deep conversation, in which he revealed a previous failed marriage and his struggle to move on from it. He never revealed specifics, only mentioning that his ex-wife was "selfish in every way imaginable" and that he's "happier now than he's ever been." I imagined ways to make him happier. James was someone that I became curious about and was not simply an object to be conquered and devoured, as other men had been in my past.

"How was your dinner?" he asked, placing his wine glass back on the table after a sip.

"It was really good. The mango salsa on the sea bass totally made the dish. How was yours?" I looked over to his plate. He had barely eaten anything.

"It's great. I don't have too much of an appetite this evening. I guess my mind is a little preoccupied."

"Would you like to share?" I offered.

"I already am." He lifted his glass again. I blushed and lowered my head, then removed my napkin from my lap and placed it on the table. "Are you ready to leave?"

"Whenever you are." I folded my hands in front of me where I rested my chin.

"You're beautiful." He paused. "I mean, I know you hear it quite often, but you're gorgeous beyond your physical beauty. As cliché as it sounds, there is just something about you."

I smiled. "Well, wait 'til you've known me for a month. You'll be dying to get rid of me." We both laughed. He paid the tab, and we left the dining room area, but not before I stopped by the ladies' room to check my makeup and add a dab of perfume to freshen up.

James put on his leather jacket, but the way he did it was like something I'd never seen before. He exuded power and dominance, yet there was a gracefulness to his movements, and a sensitive side I could see through his conversations and interactions with me. *How could this man be single*? I thought.

The valet brought his car to him. James allowed me to get in first, then tipped the valet and joined me.

"Where to ma'am?" He smirked, fastening his seatbelt.

"Perhaps you won't mind takin' me 'round to the Piggly Wiggly."

We both laughed.

"I wouldn't consider myself the average Ms. Daisy, so why don't we try that again."

He chuckled more. "Is there anywhere that you would like to go?"

"No. It's pretty cool out here, and I've had a long night. I think it's time that I turned in."

"Do you have to get up early?" he asked with a raised eyebrow.

"No. I just—"

"Wait, what is it that you do again?"

I was completely caught off guard. "A little bit of this, a little of that," I answered, attempting to be cool.

He gave me a look and I knew what it meant. He wanted to know.

"I work in the entertainment industry—you know, promoting, booking, and modeling—a bit of everything." I stared through the windshield, not wanting to read an expression on his face again. I could tell he knew I wasn't being truthful.

"Well, I'll get you home so you can get some rest. Tomorrow is my only day off this week. The office is closed and I'm not on call at the hospital. Hopefully I won't get an emergency. I'd love to spend more time with you this evening, though."

I looked at him. "Thanks, but it's really not a good time, James. I had a great time with you tonight though." I knew that if I gave in and became too available, my relationship with him would have been shortened. A few sips of wine and flirting would most definitely lead to sex, causing my value to depreciate at least 60 percent.

"It's cool. Maybe we can meet up next week some time. *If* you're not too busy."

I knew he was being sarcastic, reacting to my horrible lie that lacked creativity. How could anything that I have to do compare to his position as a physician?

"What do you want from me, James?"

"Huh?" He looked at me seriously.

"Me. What do you want from me? The way we met ... you know there's more that meets the eye, but why me? What are you getting out of this?"

He looked at me, then sighed. "When I saw you, Taj, there was something about you that intrigued me. Although I'm a doctor, I'm a man too, and I'm *intrigued* by you. I don't want anything more than to get to know you."

We drove in silence, not sure of what to say to the other. When we arrived at my apartment complex, he dropped me off, then checked the backseat to make sure I wasn't leaving anything behind.

Even though he didn't bother to get out, he leaned across the seat and slowly pressed his succulent lips against mine. "I had a good time, Taj."

"Me too ... and thanks again for everything."

"I'll call you tomorrow. You have a good night."

I got out of the car, walked to the door and let myself in. Once I got inside, I attempted to turn on a light, but nothing came on. Feeling my way around, I found another switch, and flipped it. Again, nothing. I listened closely and there were no audible sounds. *Damn,* I said to myself. My electricity was off. I stumbled to my bedroom and located the box that was filled with house clothes, and retrieved what felt like sweat pants and a shirt. I dug deeper and found a pair of socks. A lot was on my mind as I pulled out an old and tattered blanket. Settling into my bed, I recounted the events of that evening. I silently prayed that things would change for me. They had to.

13

James and I spent the next four evenings together. Sushi one night and Italian the next. The following two nights, we opted for our favorite seafood restaurants. By our sixth date, James wanted to create a more personal atmosphere for the two of us, so he invited me to dinner at his place. A man never cooked for me before, let alone a man of his caliber. The idea made me anxious and thrilled.

When I wasn't dining with him, I was raiding whatever was left in my pantry, feasting on old canned goods and crackers that kept well. I ate them sparingly, not knowing when I would be able to eat a full meal again. The little money that I had stashed away was almost gone, which meant that I needed more. Resources and an occupation were not unobtainable to me, but they were difficult to find. I received no responses from the applications I put in online at the library. Still, I wasn't hurting enough to beg for a minimum wage gig either.

The market that James frequented was near my apartment, which was great since I didn't have a vehicle and not even enough money to take the bus. After shopping he headed over to pick me up. I dressed comfortably in an old, fitted pair of Seven Jeans and a cheap baby doll tee that read **Don't Be Jealous** on the front. He grinned as I walked to his Range Rover.

"What's funny?" I asked, climbing inside.

"Nothing. You're gorgeous—even when you're not trying." He continued to smile and I noticed his dimples in the faint evening light.

"What? Am I too dressed down? Is this OK?"

I was fishing for a compliment.

"No, no. You're fine. I've just never seen you dressed this casually. Which is a very nice look, might I add."

And there it was, the compliment I so desperately needed. The groceries were already laid across the backseat, so our next destination was his home.

The drive took almost twenty-five minutes across the river and through some wooded areas. The community he lived in was hidden behind towering spruce trees that lined the main road. James signaled left then turned onto a gravel lot. For a moment, I could see nothing. The road meandered a bit and seemed to have a downward slope. But as we descended, I could see a giant structure in the distance. I didn't want to appear mesmerized by the size of his house, so I sat in cool silence.

"OK." He put the gear in park. "Would you mind grabbing that bag from the floor? It has a bottle of wine in it, so be careful."

"No problem." I was trying not to admire the surroundings, as if I were accustomed to such a lavish lifestyle.

A beautiful red brick design created the driveway, which encircled the white fountain in front of his house. We took eight steps up to the front door, which was four times larger than the average entryway. He placed a few bags on the

P l a y e d

ground to free his hand in order to unlock it.

It smelled sweet inside, like scented candles had been burned for hours. The marble floor of the foyer led to a case of stairs. I followed him to the right, toward the kitchen, passing the untouched living room and a dining room area with seating for at least sixteen.

"You must have a large family," I said.

"Yeah, I do. Sometimes it's a good thing. Sometimes not so good." We chuckled a bit.

"Do you do a lot of entertaining?" I staged questions to distract him from my amazement, but I could tell he knew what I was thinking.

"Well, when I'm not working, I typically have a few close friends and some family over. But, for the most part, I go into the city to see them. My place is really far out and not too easy to find." He placed the groceries on the counter then took the bag from me. "You're welcome to look around, if you like." He set the bottle of wine down and retrieved a glass from the cabinet.

"No. I'm fine. Maybe you can show me around later."

He smirked and poured me a glass of wine. "I need to change. Make yourself at home." He unbuttoned his shirt as he walked away into the distance.

The kitchen was spotless—not a dirty dish in sight or a single spatter on the counter or floors. There was a sink built into the center granite island—something I had never seen before. There was no décor, only stainless steel appliances and top of the line pots and pans hanging above.

I sat in silence, taking it all in, until I heard him coming up behind me. He flipped a switch on the wall, and the color blue splashed on everything white within the kitchen. I turned toward the ceiling-to-floor windows behind me and noticed a swimming pool illuminated with blue lights and surrounded by various poolside furnishings.

"That's beautiful!" I had to say it. His home deserved a compliment.

"Thanks. It's one of the things I like most about this house," he confirmed.

Never mind the huge rooms, expensive furnishings, or the idea that maybe only 10 percent of Americans could afford to live the way he did. It was the blue light shimmering from the depths of his pool that was most amusing to him. I was certain to believe that.

He removed a few pots and pans, made some hot, sudsy dish water, then cleaned them in the sink.

"I rarely cook, so these things probably sat up there collecting dust," he commented, with his back turned toward me.

"Did your ex-wife live here with you?" I asked.

He was quiet for a moment. "Yeah, she did. But let's not ruin our evening talking about her. It's going pretty good so far." He placed a pot and a pan on the stove and turned it on.

I didn't want to say all the wrong things, so I changed the subject by asking him about work. Afterward, we discussed the failing, improperly funded education system yet again and the rising cost of healthcare. We discussed Obama's healthcare reform bill and how it's affecting his practice as well as the hospital. Sitting there talking with him, the pool and the lavish surroundings gradually faded away in the heat of our spirited debate.

The air began to fill with the aroma of fresh sautéed seafood and garlic. Occasionally, he would stop and take a sip of wine while the food sizzled in the background. He made cooking seem so tireless and simple. I didn't believe he rarely cooked.

"We've known each other for a little while now." He stood in front of me on the other side of the bar. "Can I ask you something?" He took another sip of his wine.

"You can ask me anything. It's 'will I answer' that should be the question," I said playfully to not upset him, but I was serious. When people begin a question with a question it is never a good thing.

"I've been wanting to ask you this for a while, and no real opportunity came up until now."

P l a y e d

"What's up?"

"That night you came into the hospital—how did you get there?"

"An ambulance. You know that."

"You know what I mean," he said seriously.

I took a moment to think by taking a few small sips of wine. I knew that if I didn't respond it would affect the rest of the evening and perhaps the relationship we were trying to establish. I was just upset that I hadn't come up with something ahead of time. In all honesty, I tried my hardest to forget that the entire thing ever happened. My only reminders were my healing scars and the dark and empty apartment that I went home to every night.

"I was at a party with a friend—a really close friend, and things got out of hand. There was an altercation between me and some guy, and the next thing I remember, I woke up in the hospital—and saw you." The story I told him was partially true and I hoped he wouldn't question it. I stared directly into his eyes, addressing him as he tried to read me.

"Do you remember what the altercation was about?" he asked, turning away to check on the food.

"Money and someone touching me," I told him, again, somewhat truthfully.

"Well, where was your friend?"

"She left me there."

"I guess I can assume that you two are no longer friends." He turned to me again.

"No. I haven't seen her since that night."

"Do you know if she's OK? Something could have happened to her, too." Lines began to form on his forehead.

For a moment, I thought of San—her safety. What if they had taken her and had done the same thing to her, or even worse, what if she was dead somewhere? What if they turned on her after she turned on me, then robbed us of all of our things in the apartment? I hadn't thought about that until then.

"Taj?" He walked over and placed his hand on mine.

I snapped out of it. "Yeah, I'm sorry."

"You OK?"

"I'm fine. Just thinking."

"I'm not going to get into your business," he leaned in closer, "but if that's what really happened that night, you could've told me then, and police involvement wouldn't have been such an issue."

"There is *nothing* more to it." I stuck to my story, feeling the heat rise on my cheeks.

He looked at me and took a deep breath. "You ready to eat?"

After what he asked, I lost my appetite, but I wouldn't disappoint him by saying so.

As we ate, James insisted that we play ten questions in ten seconds. It was something that he'd made up in order to get to know someone as fast as possible. We were to answer each other's questions truthfully regardless of how embarrassing or personal it was then move on to the next—no further questions asked. Through my participation, I learned that he was the only son of five siblings, his father died of cancer when he was eleven, and that he was the only person in his family to attend college. We also discussed what it meant to keep our distinctive intimate circles of friends (not that I had one), and the matter of trust, among other things. His past relationship with his ex-wife was a touchy subject, so I didn't mention it.

After dinner, we went to the family room where we became intimate. The comfortable L-shaped leather couch was the focus of the room, while the fifty-two-inch plasma flat-screen television provided a bit of entertainment when we came up for air. He was a great kisser, not giving too much tongue or too little. He knew when to break the lip-locking action and simply press his lips against mine. But, I began questioning if he wanted to be with me, because not once did he lean in and grab my waist, caress my breast or put his hand on my thigh. He did nothing, as if the kiss was all he needed. That made me want him even more.

Positioned on the right side of him, I reached for his left hand, which rested on his thigh. Interlocking my small fingers with his, I tightened my grip while pressing my lips harder against his. I pulled him toward me and he gave in for a moment.

"Hold on." He stopped what we were doing and leaned back for a moment. I was seriously waiting for him to tell me that he was gay, and that he just wanted to be friends.

"Yeah? What's wrong?" I asked, wiping away lip gloss smeared on my chin and above my lip.

"Is this something that you want?" he asked me. "I mean, I didn't bring you here to do this." He looked at me closely.

"I just want to be with you. Is it something that *you* want?"

"Never mind me. I wouldn't ever make you do something *you* don't want to do."

Then, it all clicked. James saw me as the victim that had gone into the hospital three months prior to that moment. He didn't know how to approach me with the idea of having sex, considering the circumstances. I decided to play along.

"I know...and I trust you." It sounded good. I slightly touched his chin and leaned in for a kiss.

He put his arm around me and pressed his palm against the small of my back, forcing me to lean back on the couch. I allowed him to take control, and within seconds, he was completely on top of me, and we were interlocked in a kiss. He paused for a second and grabbed the remote. I assumed he would turn the television off, but he changed the channel to a twenty-four-hour R&B Soul station. An oldie, Carl Thomas' "Summer Rain," was playing. After he placed the remote on the coffee table, he quickly lifted his shirt over his head. It was quite obvious that he worked out. By the impeccable cuts and bulges, I found myself wondering when he found time to create such perfection.

He became the aggressor: everything I wanted him to be. I could feel him growing through the basketball shorts he had changed into earlier. I was pleased, so I decided to help him a bit by removing my jeans. It was quite a rushed move, but I didn't see a point in taking our time.

I could feel my wetness as he grinded against me, but we

stayed locked in a kiss no matter what our lower halves were doing. I felt him maneuver his body, moving his hands to our lower regions. He began to pull off his shorts with his hand, then inched them down to his ankles until they were completely off. There was warmth between us—breathtaking warmth that created a rush of hormones straight to my brain and nearly caused an anxiety attack.

He reached for my panties, but instead of taking them off, he merely pulled them aside, then quickly attempted to insert himself.

"Wait." I pressed against his chest in protest.

"What babe? What's wrong?" He was out of breath and as anxious as I was.

"Got a condom?"

"No, I don't," he said remorsefully, closing his eyes, then reopening them to focus on me. "Do you want to stop? I know this is awkward. I just want you so bad right now." Before I could answer, he kissed me again, and I became lost in it. Time went by and I pretended not to notice that he was making a second attempt to penetrate me. I slowly felt him inch himself inside of me. I moaned to signal my approval. I realized how much I actually trusted James, and at that moment, I trusted him with my life.

Played

14

*N*o matter how many evenings I spent with James at his home, I never slept there. Three weeks passed since our first sexual encounter, and between his schedule and the busy schedule I pretended to have, we managed to have sex on eight different occasions. But overstaying my welcome was not an option. I wanted to give him time to miss me, time to have the desire to come for me at the end of a long workday. I must admit, however, that having him pick me up and drop me off at all hours of the night made me feel remorseful, because while he worked, I slept and had nothing else to do.

After another dinner out we made our way back to the car, holding hands the entire ride back to my place. I needed to stop there to grab a hat on the way to James' house. In the car we shared genuine laughter about a Kat Williams video we rented from Netflix.

When we arrived at my complex, I crossed my fingers

and hoped that the management hadn't placed a bright orange eviction notice on my door. At that point, rent was almost forty-five days past due and counting. As we pulled into the lot, I didn't notice any signage near the door. *Coast is clear*, I thought.

"Babe, would you mind if I use your restroom?"

I never invited him into my apartment and for good reason. It was my space and I wanted it to stay like that. He already knew me intimately. I just wasn't ready to give him even more: the truth. On the times he tried to come in, I always came up with some excuse as to why he couldn't. I probably came across as being a slob, having lied to him several times about it being too messy for me to have company over. But I didn't want to recommend that he drive up to the local Gate Food Post, six minutes away, in order to use a public restroom when one was only twenty feet away and available.

"Umm, sure. If you have to go." I was hoping he would say there was no urgency.

"OK. Thanks."

Getting out of the car, he locked the doors and we proceeded toward my apartment, trying to make small talk along the way. All the while I was quickly trying to cook up an excuse as to why I had no power. No genius idea would come to me other than to pretend to not have a clue why the lights were off, so I went with that.

"Here we go," I said, pushing the door open.

"Damn, it's colder in here than it is outside," he remarked after he went inside.

"Yeah, it is," I said, trying to sound surprised. I took a few more steps inside before I attempted to flip on a light. Nothing happened.

"Hmm, the bulb must have blown." James stood with his arms folded in the moonlight that shined through the window. "Let me try another one." At a loss of what to do, I simply stood there while James tried two other lights with the same results. Perplexed, he took a long look around the

Played

room, and even in the dark I could see his brows furrowing. "Where is your furniture?" he asked, concerned. "Your place is empty."

"Umm, I sold it to make room for something I ordered at that new store. You know, the one in the town center." I flipped another switch, and I knew it was time to step up my acting. "Oh, wow."

"What?" I heard coming from a shadow.

"Something really *is* wrong with the power!" I walked to several light switches and flicked them on and off.

"Well, your neighbors have power. I could see their lights when we walked up."

"That's strange," I admitted. "I'll look into it tomorrow and get it all straightened out. The bathroom is this way." I grabbed his hand and rushed him to the bathroom inside the master bedroom where I knew the most moonlight would shine if I left the door open. Even in the dark I could tell that he was being extra-observant by his slow pace and lack of conversation.

"Just leave the door open, and you can use the light shining through this window. I'm stepping out."

I sat on the edge of the bed in the corner of the room and waited to hear the last drip of urine splash against the toilet water. I heard him zip, flush, then run his hands under the cold faucet water.

"Tell me this," he said to me, his eyes adjusting to the dark as he moved to stand in front of me. "Why have you been living in the dark? Is there something going on? Because I don't understand this." He folded his arms.

"What do you mean? I had power this afternoon. It was probably disconnected by mistake or something."

"You might want to keep your day job, because lying is not your forte." He turned and walked back to the bathroom. "Really, Taj. You mean to tell me that a woman *with* power typically has three candles on her bathroom sink, two very visible flashlights, several D batteries strewn across the floor, and a load of blankets on her bed? I think the question is: How long have you been *without* power?"

I didn't want to speak. I was embarrassed and ashamed. Crawling under a rock wouldn't have been enough. I would have rather been bludgeoned with one.

"Actually, for now, it doesn't matter," he continued. "Get your things, and let's go." James walked to the empty living room and waited. I did as I was told, moving slowly in the bedroom, gathering some toiletries, underwear, and my favorite sweatshirt. Everything was in the laundry, which I had no money to wash.

We didn't speak the entire ride back to his house. I felt like a teenager who had just been chastised by her father for breaking curfew, sneaking out of the house or having sex while her parents were at work. But for some reason, I liked it. To know that he wanted what was best for me—to the point that he was upset when I didn't have it—made me realize how much he cared.

"We both need to get some rest. I have to be at the hospital by six." He opened the front door, and I entered in silence.

We made our way to the bedroom, and I undressed down to my panties and bra and climbed into bed next to him. He turned over and put his arm around my waist, kissed me on my neck, then told me good night. A sense of relief had come over me, and it wasn't long before I shut my eyes completely and went off to sleep.

The next morning he was gone. The place was quiet and there was a note on the nightstand, written on a paper towel from the bathroom: plain, unlike the floral printed paper towels in the kitchen. It read: **Don't leave**.

Hungry, I threw on one of his T-shirts and went downstairs to raid the pantry. I started at the fridge, which had been stocked with fresh fruits, some condiments, sandwich meat, bottled water and two percent milk. There was some toasted oats cereal in the pantry, so I poured a bowl, chopped up a banana and added milk.

P l a y e d

The idea that I should go snooping around crossed my mind after breakfast, but the urge wasn't strong enough for me to actually do it. I just wanted rest, to lie down through the morning and possibly do nothing all day. Life in this house was good and my body craved the comfort.

When James returned home that evening, I was sitting out by the pool. I had prepared a turkey club sandwich for him with items I found in the fridge and then laid it on the counter. I left the kitchen light on, so I was able to see his smile from the pool before he looked in my direction and saw me sitting there. He picked up the plate, grabbed a bottle of water from the fridge and came out to join me.

"What a kind gesture." He sat down next to me, near the edge of the pool.

"It was all that I could do, considering you don't have too much to work with."

"I try not to keep food that I don't eat regularly. It goes bad too quickly," he told me biting into the sandwich. "So, do you cook?"

"I'm pretty good in the kitchen. I like learning to make new dishes more than anything."

"Well, when I'm finished with this, we'll go to the store to get a few things."

"No problem."

James didn't bother to talk about the night before. He didn't ask how long I was going to be staying around, or ask about the occupation I proclaimed to have. Possibly he wanted to keep me there. Between bites of his sandwich, he talked about work—how a little girl had broken her arm by supposedly falling from a swing. He said he suspected child abuse because the parents wouldn't allow the girl to speak when he questioned her about the incident. I found the story interesting, and for some reason thought of Sarai.

We went shopping that evening, and I purchased some fresh vegetables, some poultry, a few steaks, and a few slices of tiramisu. That evening was similar to all the others spent there, except in reverse. Instead of sex and then a shower, we showered first, then had sex and fell asleep—together.

The following morning when I awoke, James wasn't there again, but there was another note hidden slightly under a set of keys that read: ***Don't go far. I want to see you when I get home. Enjoy your day***.

I walked through the kitchen to the garage, passing a piece of platinum-colored plastic on the counter. It was the card he used to purchase groceries. There was no note regarding the credit card, but I picked it up from the counter anyway. I opened the garage door and felt around for a light switch. Once I found it, I saw a beautiful, black Mercedes SL600. For several moments I simply stood in the doorway and admired the expensive piece of steel. I thought of all the places I could go, but wouldn't.

The wood grain dash was clean, clear of even a speck of dust. The leather seats were warm and comfortable. It had been months since I sat behind the wheel of European-engineered steel. It had been too long. There were only twenty-five hundred miles on the car. "Damn! A nice ass car that he never drives. He's crazy as hell," I said aloud and laughed to myself. I left the house in it, but wasn't gone long. I didn't want to take advantage of James's generosity.

By 4:30 p.m., it was time to prepare dinner. The oven was set on broil, and I placed a skillet on the stove to sauté some potatoes. The aroma of fresh herbs and broiled steak began to fill the air. Singing and humming songs that resonated in my mind from watching music videos, I floated around the kitchen. Last, I put a few ears of corn in boiling water, preparing to wrap them in foil with some butter and fresh herbs.

Ten minutes before James was due to arrive, I ran to the shower to freshen up and have the clean scent of Caress on my skin. Afterward, I fingered my hair a little to separate the curls and added moisturizer to a few areas of my body that could use some extra softening—the elbows, knees and ankles. Then, I noticed something move in the corner.

"Oh my God!" I grabbed my chest, still wrapped in a

P l a y e d

towel. James was in the room watching me. "Oh my God! You scared the hell out of me. How long you been standing there?"

He laughed. "You were just so sexy, and I didn't want to disturb you." He loosened his tie, removed it, and then threw it on the bed. "How was your day?" He kissed me.

"Good. Dinner is ready whenever you are."

"I know. It looks appetizing, too," he said, looking my body over. He loosened my towel, and as it fell onto the bed, I sat there, legs crossed and naked. He kissed my neck gently while he caressed my breasts. At that point, I knew it would be a while before we would go downstairs for dinner.

And it was. Dinner was cold after an hour of love-making. I turned on the oven and the stovetop to reheat the dishes. James poured two glasses of wine and sat at the bar, watching me prepare his dinner and grinning for some unknown reason.

"Wow." He laughed a little.

"What?" I turned around with a spatula full of sautéed potatoes.

"The only woman that has ever cooked for me was my mom. Oh, and maybe my oldest sister. You're something else. Beautiful and can cook—among one other thing."

I smiled at him, warm from his affection. I wanted to ask what the hell his ex-wife was good for, but I figured it wasn't a good time to mention her. In fact I couldn't think of any good time to mention her. He hadn't talked about her since our first date, and then he said just enough to let me know that their relationship existed but that he was completely over it. By the way he approached the subject, I couldn't tell that there was ever any love there for her at all. I pictured her as some dainty housewife who was only good for spending his money, and possibly that was the reason they didn't work out.

"Do you dance?" he asked, breaking my train of thought.

"Like a stripper, a clubber or an artist?"

"None of the above," he chuckled. "Just for fun—with a

partner, and not some random guy you meet and grind your ass on."

"I've never done it."

"Why don't we go out tonight? There's this spot with a live jazz band downtown—right on the riverfront. I know the owner. You interested?"

The invitation was shocking. James usually spent one night a week with the boys, Marcus and Tyson, if his schedule permitted. I learned a lot about them through conversations with James. Marcus attended college with James, and Tyson was a colleague at the hospital. Both of them were married.

"Yeah, it sounds nice."

"Well, get dressed after dinner, and I'll take you."

"Do I have to dress up? I don't have anything nice over here to wear. My things are back at the apartment."

"What apartment?" he asked sarcastically.

"*My* apartment."

"I saw the car moved, so where did you go today?"

"Nowhere—I mean, I went around the block. That's all."

"Around the block where?" He watched me, closely. "You didn't go and get your things?"

"I didn't know I was supposed to go to my apartment. You didn't say that in your note."

"No. I left you my credit card. I figured you would go to the mall or town center to pick up a few things."

"I didn't know that's what you meant." I put a dish in front of him and laid a napkin topped with silverware next to it.

"Well, we'll chill out tonight, but you know what's on your agenda for tomorrow. Tomorrow we dance." He picked up his steak knife and pointed toward me as he spoke. "And don't go back to that apartment. There's no point."

Before he could finish chewing his first bite, he was already cutting the tender, succulent meat for a second taste, an indication that I did well.

Although James opened his home to me faster than any-

P l a y e d

one had, I still found it difficult to open up completely to him. Comfort stood in for love. He found it necessary to take care of me, and I found myself in need of him. I became a home-body. Everything I wanted was within those walls. Besides the occasional trip to the town center to visit the spa or to do some shopping, nothing else would interest me unless it was done with him.

I prepared dinner on nights that he didn't plan to take me out. We had great sex all the time, all over the house. Between our wild escapades and fancy dinners, there was no room for arguments.

Triple Crown Publications *presents…*

15

Seasons came and went and James continued to take care of me. Nearly a year into our relationship, we were going strong. There were still things that I didn't know about him, but I didn't press him for information. I felt in due time we would learn everything about each other, but until then, I'd enjoy the ride as long as I was able.

James had made arrangements for us to have lunch at a bistro downtown near the river.

It was windier than it typically was in the city. The breeze from the river sent chills up my blue satin skirt straight to my white lace panties beneath it. Walking toward the bistro, I considered that the fragrance from my freshly washed hair hypnotized those walking behind me along the sidewalk.

We made it to the bistro and decided to have to a seat on the inside since it was so chilly out. We ordered a few appetizers and iced teas, and for a moment, we discussed the poor quality of water in the St. John's River.

"I forgot to ask you—how is the family?" I asked. He was talking to them a lot lately, but I never questioned him.

"My mom is great. She and my sisters are in Houston looking after my grandmother who isn't doing so well." He took a sip of iced tea. "They should be back in a few weeks though. They're bringing my grandmother here."

"Wow, I'm sorry to hear that." I rubbed his hand as it rested on the table.

The waitress interrupted to take our orders. James continued, "We're having a big cookout for my grandmother and my nephew, Tyler, when he returns from Iraq in a few weeks. Would you like to come?"

"Well, I don't know. I'll have to check my schedule," I joked. "Sure, I'll be there. I wouldn't miss it."

"Great. You'll get to meet the entire family then."

"Oh, really?"

The waitress returned with our appetizer and we continued talking.

"Yes, and oh, you're a beautiful woman, Taj. I just might have to watch you." James took my hand, stroking my knuckles as he grinned and lifted an eyebrow.

"What do you mean?"

"Oh, God. Where do I begin? My cousins are pretty flirtatious—nothing like vultures though." He chuckled then stuffed his mouth with spinach and artichoke dip.

"Really. So the men in your family are pretty aggressive, huh?"

"A little, but to tell the truth, it wouldn't be them I'd watch. It's my cousin Seymone who's the aggressive one—more so than the men. She's just really smooth with it."

"A woman? Smooth?" I asked. My pulse jumped in speed.

"Yes, Seymone is a beautiful girl, but we're still wondering why the hell she's so into women. I mean—are no men out there good enough? I've tried to introduce her to several of my associates and she turned them down quick."

"Wow, that's really something," I mumbled, then quickly

raised my glass to my mouth. I didn't know if I wanted to be having that conversation with James since we'd never discussed all of my history.

As we continued to chat, I thought of the secrets that I kept from James and how disappointed he would be if he found out about them. Although they occurred in the past, they could still affect the present and perhaps a future with him. It's one thing to have been with other men and another to have been with women. Some men laugh at the idea of two women being committed to each other. Others are disgusted by it. Secretly, it's because most men develop insecurities. They'll work their asses off to be the best man we've ever been with, but no matter how hard they try, a man could never be the same as a woman.

I was proud that James had asked me to join him for his family cookout. I never doubted his sincerity until three days later, when I overheard him talking on the phone from the other room—something he had never done before. I was in the middle of my dance aerobics video in the living room when I overheard bits and pieces of his conversation with someone. He didn't use complete sentences, and spoke in a serious, forbidding voice.

"... whenever I'm ready ... I'll do it on my time ... not tonight ... I understand."

I turned the television down a little so that I could hear him better.

"No, I don't want you to be with me when I tell her. You've done enough ... thanks for understanding ... soon ... I'm excited, too ... the two of us."

I stopped the video and ran to the shower to keep from overreacting and so James wouldn't see me crying. So many thoughts began to plague me at one time. For the first time since we had been together, I feared that I could possibly lose him, and lose him to someone else. Instead of discussing it with him, I directed all of my emotions inward.

16

A couple of days before the cookout, James asked me to get dressed for dinner. Since our dinner at the Bistro until now, things were pretty tense between us at home. I used all my reserve and deceit not to let on to him that I knew something was up, and his manner to me in turn seemed standoffish, too formal. Still, we were as civil as could be to each other.

The drive to the restaurant was quiet. Frankie Beverly's greatest hits played from the stereo system; every once in a while James would tap the steering wheel with his right index finger to the beat. I wondered if he could detect my feelings. Whenever he looked over to me in nervous, side-long glances, I pretended not to notice. I felt like a lost puppy at the local shelter who was in dire need to be adopted by this man, and to ensure that I stayed I was on my best behavior.

We arrived at a restaurant he had never taken me to before. **CYPRESS** was the name, lit across the front of the

Triple Crown Publications *presents...*

building in dignified block lettering. There was nothing fancy about it on the outside, no valet, no velvet rope or revolving doors. The inside was small, everything white. There were only about twelve tables in the entire space with a huge bar dividing the room into halves. Candles were lit on each table, and slow, melodic music could be heard coming from some place unknown. There was a hat and coat rack too close to the entry, which I couldn't entrust to hold the Burberry coat I just purchased. The hostess was a very petite white girl, probably no older than 19 or 20, and perhaps working to make some money while in college. She had emerald eyes and blonde hair that was swept neatly into a ponytail. Her smile was reminiscent of pictures I saw plastered on the walls of my dentist's office—beautiful. She didn't greet us or ask how many. She just smirked a little then walked us to a table in the corner of the restaurant.

"Do you know her or something?" I asked James, removing my coat and laying it across the unoccupied chair at the table.

"No, babe. I don't." He sat down and slightly loosened his tie, watching me take my seat.

We feasted on a seafood boil of shrimp, fish, clams, mussels and scallops. James also ordered a fancy shrimp and grits dish. He made small talk about the restaurant, the chef's techniques, and possible future business ventures as I half-listened and sipped my wine. When the waitress offered to bring us some dessert, James replied to bring us "something special." I imagined a nice chunk of chocolate cake or a velvety slice of New York style cheesecake. But on her serving tray was simply a box wrapped in red paper with a black ribbon tied around it.

"What's this?" I smiled as she handed the package over to me.

"Well, you have to open it to find out," James responded. "That will be all ma'am," he said, excusing the waitress.

"So, is this what you've been up to today?" My insides grew warm; perhaps I had misjudged him. "Awww. You

P l a y e d

111

thought of me. You're so sweet, baby."

Impatiently, he said, "Yes, I know. Open it!"

"OK. OK." I placed the box on the table and slowly tugged at the ribbon. I expected a blue Tiffany box carrying some new jewels or perhaps keys to a nice new Lexus or something. But as I lifted the lid from the box, I saw the color blue. Removing the lid further, I revealed metal and a rubber material. It was a stethoscope. I was puzzled, and I knew he could tell by the expression on my face.

"Surprised?" he asked, leaning in to reach for it.

"Well, I really don't know what to make of it."

"Well," he said, holding it up, "this is the stethoscope that was used when you came into the hospital. Can you believe it's been a year?"

"Wow!" was all I could say. I knew it had been that long, but the fact that he remembered is what shocked me the most.

"When you were in the hospital, I checked on you often. I monitored the rhythm of your heartbeat with this. I experienced what it was like for you to inhale and exhale — to feel your chest rise and sink so delicately with each breath. It became my mission to take care of you."

He pulled the tool from the box and placed them in my ears. "Now listen. Breathe slowly." He pressed the other end to my chest. "Can you hear that?"

"A little. Yes." I tried to ignore the fact that I was getting monitored in a restaurant, and embraced that he was illustrating my heartbeat.

He removed it from my chest then pressed it against his. "Can you hear this?"

I paused for a moment, waiting for silence. Once I found a break in the music and the waitstaff chatting with each other in the corner, I noticed that his heart was pounding.

"It's faster than mine. Is that normal?" I asked, concerned.

"It is when you're doing this." He pulled a small box from his coat pocket and kneeled on the floor next to my chair.

"Oh my God. Oh my God!" I suddenly wondered how fast the stethoscope would read on me now.

"Taj, I have been there for you since the very first day that we met. I have loved you and taken care of you in every way I know how. I live to know that you're safe and not in need of anything or anyone but me. I know it hasn't been long, but I want forever with you, baby. So, can I be all that you need for the rest of your life?"

"Yes, baby. Yes!" A tear began to stream from somewhere and my chest tightened. He embraced me like he never had before then placed the platinum, three-carat, round cut diamond ring on my finger. Ecstatic, I turned to look at the hostess, smiling. She smiled back at me then went back to her place at the front of the restaurant.

James later told me that he had his cousin, Seymone, help him pick out the ring and that she wanted to meet me and even wanted to be present at the proposal. At that moment, the phone call in the other room made total sense.

Played

17

*J*ames told his family of the engagement three days before the cookout. I didn't meet them when they arrived from Houston because James was on call, so the day of the cookout I was a nervous wreck.

At the cookout, everyone seemed preoccupied with cooking, serving food, and supervising the children. There were no formal introductions, so I just made myself comfortable in the living room area. I sat alone and observed while James talked to various relatives. My skirt began to rise as my legs shook rhythmically, a nervous gesture from childhood. Staring through the kitchen, beyond the group of men gathered around the table in line for a second helping, my eyes wandered for James.

I was momentarily distracted by all of James' childhood photos on the wall. There was even a picture of him and a man I assumed was his father. James appeared to be about 9 years old; both of them were shirtless, flexing their muscles for the camera. At that moment he walked up and hooked his arm under mine.

"What's on your mind?" he asked, smiling.

I smiled back. "You look just like your father," I told him.

I squeezed him tighter, unable to wrap my hand around his bicep. His body was something magical, maintained by his twice-a-day workouts—in the morning before work and in our bedroom at night. And his light, brown-sugar complexion seemed topped with the smoothness of honey. Even after a year, my chest would still sink into my stomach at his smile and touch.

He took my hand and led me to the most crowded space in the house: the den. The architecture of the room was a true masterpiece, however it was reduced by tasteless ceramic artifacts and artificial flower arrangements bought from the local flea market.

"OK, people, let's make a toast," James announced and poured both of us a glass of champagne. Many filled their glass to the brim. He handed a glass to me, winked an eye, and smiled as he focused his attention to the crowd. "I have to say we are blessed. Tyler is back home from war and in one piece." Heads turned with approving murmur toward the young man who stood in the middle of the room with his hands in his pockets and a sheepish grin. "And I thank you," he continued, looking straight at Tyler, "for your sacrifices and for your dedication to your family, and to your country. 'Cause believe me, no one else would have done it." The crowd broke into laughter. "So for that, and to welcome you back home, there's a little something for you outside cuz."

The family cheered, then rushed to the front door and scattered outside to get a look at Tyler's new ride—a brand new, fully loaded white Lexus. I gasped. It wasn't discussed with me first; I didn't even *know* about it. And now here James was as flashy as can be handing out cars like they were candy. But it was not the time to be confrontational with him. I hid my anger with a half-ass smile that helped me keep my cool.

P l a y e d

115

I took a sip of champagne and attempted to dismiss myself from the room. James grabbed me and placed an arm around my shoulder, knowing that I wouldn't make a scene by breaking away from him.

"Tyler, why don't you take your Aunt Taj here outside with you so that she can get a better look at the car? It was her idea, you know."

"Really? Aunt Taj? You have great taste." His five-foot-six figure stood in James' shadow as he reached out to take my hand.

"Oh, OK, yeah. Let's take a look. I didn't get to see what he actually picked out. I hope you like it though. You deserve it," I lied. There was nothing more special about this kid than any of the others who went over to serve our country, besides the fact that he had a successful doctor for an uncle who was willing to please others through his checkbook.

The party died down after everyone had a glimpse of the brand new, fully loaded white Lexus parked in the driveway. Several cousins piled in to take photos behind the wheel as if it was their car, which would probably show up on MySpace or some other site where fools can look like ballers and unattractive women claim photos of models or movie stars as their own.

A little bit later, I overheard one of James' cousins sharing some of the family business with a first-time visitor as I was standing on the front porch.

"Yeah, that's my cuz. He a rich man, you know."

"What he do?" A young girl, perhaps his date for the evening, inquired.

"Well, he's a doctor now, but man, if you would have known him ten years ago—"

"What was up with him then?" she asked. I was curious to know myself, so I listened.

"He was a screw up! His daddy died and left my aunt in the poorhouse. James didn't make it any better. He gave his mom a hard time. It wasn't until he met his ex-wife that someone was able to talk some common sense into him. That was all she was good for though." He laughed it off. "He always feels like he owes people something. Someday he'll learn that he can't help *everybody*."

I stood in the shadows, hoping that I could learn more, but the two of them walked farther into the front yard.

Keys rattled behind me as Seymone, the cousin James told me about over dinner, made her way to the front door. Immediately she reached out to give me a hug. "It sure is good meeting you, Taj."

I studied her for a moment. Seymone reminded me a lot of myself—young, soft-spoken, classy and even a bit mysterious. She had a pair of the longest legs I'd ever seen, a complexion that screamed milk chocolate perfection, and eyes like water. I was unable to discern their true color, they were so transparent. Her hair was short, which added a hint of sophistication to the package.

"It's nice finally meeting you, too," I told her. "James speaks of you often." I hugged her and got a whiff of her perfume, melting for a moment. "What are you wearing? You smell so good."

"It's a secret," she whispered. "I might tell you later though." She winked, gave a sexy grin and walked out of the room. My eyes followed her feet, admiring the three-inch BCBG pumps that I swear I'd seen in a magazine somewhere.

"Are you leaving, Seymone?" I called after her.

"No. I'm just stepping outside for a cigarette. I'll be back in a moment."

I returned to the living room and buried my face in my hands, thinking once more of the Lexus. The whole situation made me feel awkward and embarrassed. It wasn't the idea that he had spent so much money on a vehicle for someone else, but that he hadn't even talked to me about it. I was in the dark with so many of his decisions and interactions with other people. I was a separate entity from his life still, and I couldn't mesh with any of his other dealings. Where was our partnership? We *were* getting married, after all. And me, I just accepted my position beneath him on so many levels. At the very

Played

least, I wish he would have selected a better day and time to leave me out of the loop.

The front door slammed shut, then I heard two women giggling. I could immediately make out the clangor of Seymone's gold bangles and her deep sexy laughter, but there was something familiar about the other woman's voice as well. They spoke as they walked into the dining room area, but I briefly lost sight of them as they disappeared behind the three pillars that separated the large foyer from the living room.

Finally in my view, I noticed that the other woman was an inch or two shorter than me, a little lighter, and wore a blue strapless corset dress that hugged her body in all the right places. But I still couldn't see her face. I now wondered where James was—if he knew this person. Curious, I stood up slowly from my seat, grabbed my glass of champagne from the end table, and walked in the direction the two women had gone.

After a few steps, I came across them as they stood around the dining room table. Hovering in the doorway for a moment, I saw that their backs were faced toward me. I took this opportunity to examine the mystery woman's body and her interaction with Seymone. There was some familiarity in her movements and in the sound of her voice. In the purple butterfly tattoo on her shoulder.

"Taj. Hey, I want you to meet my friend," Seymone said, pulling at the woman's arm to turn and greet me. She hesitated, then turned around slowly.

"Hello, Taj. It's nice to meet you." She smiled.

It was her—the ghost from my past. It was San.

18

I stood and stared at her: it appeared she hadn't changed a bit. She was still as beautiful as I remembered her, but the thought of how beautiful she was became overshadowed by my memory of what occurred the last time I saw her. And she was smiling at me.

"Likewise," I responded, taking a sip of champagne while looking directly at her. I couldn't make a scene. No one was supposed to know about her. I wondered how much Seymone revealed about me to her— if San knew about my engagement. I wondered if she would jeopardize it—if she was there to hurt me again.

"Taj," said Seymone, "I wanted to invite you to a track meet for the kids that I coach at the high school tomorrow. San won't be able to make it, so I would like for *you* to come if you're not busy."

San's eyes wandered around the room, trying her best to

Played

remove herself from the conversation. It was apparent that she and Seymone were lovers—primarily by how close they stood to each other, how they touched, and how they smirked at each other. I was taken back for a moment, remembering what it was like to be with a woman, but the thought was short-lived. My insides were still jumping from the sight of San.

James walked into the room. "There you are, Taj." He stood behind me and wrapped his arms around my waist and kissed me on the neck. "I was wondering if you were ready to wrap it up here and go home."

He kissed me again, and I reciprocated. I could feel San's eyes on me.

"All right you two," Seymone said, then looked at San. "Oh, and San, this is my cousin, James." She smiled at him and nodded her head. "James, I was just inviting Taj to the track meet tomorrow. I know you'll be working, but it's the last meet of the year, and I would really like to see some of my people in the stands."

"Babe," James squeezed me, "you should go. Will you be going, San?"

"Oh, no, I have a meeting. We'll probably do lunch afterward or something," she responded quickly.

"Well, Taj, you should be able to make it, right?" Seymone asked again.

"Sure. I'll be there."

I was in a tight situation. I didn't want Seymone to think that I didn't want to be supportive; she was a very close relative to my fiancé. And although San said that she wouldn't be there, I didn't want her to get the impression that it mattered, even though it did.

I could barely sleep that night. I thought of San—ways to kill her and get away with it. Ways to hurt her the way she hurt me. I thought of my past life and all the secrets that I was afraid would be revealed to James. My life had to continue with him. I wasn't in love with him, but he was my

only answer to a life of normalcy: an escape from the edgy world of being a "showgirl," borderline prostitute, and drug addict.

Drugs. Damn, I missed getting high.

19

I owned only two pairs of tennis shoes. One was an all-white pair of Adidas, and the other was a European-style pair of Jordans for women. My short denim shorts and blue halter paired wonderfully with my Jordans, so I slid them on in preparation for the track meet. James was at work, as usual, so it was quiet in the house. His work schedule was becoming more frustrating by the day; I rarely ever saw him. Besides that, the only other thought in my head was that of San, and how she had appeared again.

Once I arrived at the school, I parked the Mercedes SL600 at the back of the desolate lot, away from reckless teenage drivers. Onlookers were already in the stadium cheering on the runners. I was late, but far from rushing.

"Hey! Excuse me!" I heard a male voice yell from across the lot. He closed the trunk of his all-terrain blue Hummer H2 that was parked near an office building on the opposite side of the lot and was hurriedly trying to catch up with me. I stopped in my tracks and shielded my eyes from the sun as I tried to look off in the distance.

"Yeah?" I asked and flashed him a little smile.

He was about six-foot-three, and had an even-toned dark chocolate complexion with a well-lined goatee and a freshly shaved head. I could see the outline of his pectoral muscles bulging through his T-shirt. His forearms alone were fascinating.

"How you doing today?" he asked, slowing his stroll.

"Do I know you from somewhere?"

"Maybe." I caught a whiff of his cologne. Damn, he smelled nice. He looked at me and smiled. I prayed he wasn't one of my old clients. That life was gone and I wanted no memories of it.

"Nah, cutie, we don't know each other."

"Then, what's your name? I'm Taj." I was relieved, so I reached out to shake his hand.

"Kelvin Ross," he announced, holding my hand for a long second before releasing it.

"Hmm—why does that name sound familiar?"

"Well, it should. I'll tell you why later. So, can I get your number?"

"Whoa, fast guy. I'm engaged." I flashed him a glimpse of the rock.

"Engaged isn't married. I'm sure your man wouldn't mind if you had friends. Let me take you out." He cocked his head and grinned at me, flashing those pearly whites.

"Well, I don't know if I—"

He lifted his arm to check the time on his diamond-studded Rolex, and I lost my train of thought. "Look, take my number. I'm running late for a meeting, but I want you to call me." He licked his lips.

I sighed. "Ok, what is it?"

I pulled my phone from my pocket and stored the number. We gave each other a quick hug goodbye, but instead of heading toward the office building he parked near, he ran back to

Played

his truck and drove away. Had he followed me?

I continued on to the track where there had to be at least two hundred spectators. Then, I bought a can of Coke and found a seat on the third row of the concrete bleachers between a heavy-set white woman and a group of Hispanic teenaged boys.

After a few minutes passed, I spotted Seymone on the far end of the field, talking to her athletes. A group of students were running the 400-meters while she assembled her group to run the relay. She was aggressive, not exactly what I expected from her. Her body language oozed confidence and authority.

Seymone looked in my direction and held the position as if she was trying to make sure it was me. I stood and waved to acknowledge my presence, but when she didn't respond to my signal, I sat down again.

"I don't think she saw you," someone said, tapping my shoulder. I turned my head slightly. It was San. She had come to the track meet after all. My chest sank into my stomach.

"What the hell?" I attempted to stand, and she pressed my right shoulder down to keep me from moving.

"Don't make a scene. Seymone could see you."

"I don't give a damn! Let me go!"

"I think you care more than you think you do. Come on, future Mrs. Doctor Carter." She giggled.

I turned to look at her. Now that I thought about it, there was indeed something different about her, but it wasn't phys-ical. Perhaps she had lost some of her innocence, some of her sweetness about life. There was a shrewdness in her pretty eyes that wasn't there before, and I could imagine it spreading through her whole body like a vine. At the same time. there was an air of pleasure surrounding her, an aura of infinite contentment. Whoever the person was in front of me, I never knew.

"So, how have you been?" she asked, bending over to tie her shoe.

"Making it. Come on, let's cut out all the small talk. Why do you even think you can talk to me? I should kill you right now." The lady next to me looked at the both of us then pretended to follow the activities on the track.

"I know, and I don't blame you. There is a lot that I could say, but I can't say it here."

"I don't want to hear anything you have to say, San."

"But you will. I know you will. I'll be at the coffee house we used to go to tomorrow around three. I'll see you then." She stood up and walked away, grabbing a bag of peanuts from the girl at the bottom of the bleachers before she disappeared.

I was being blackmailed. Initially, San's behavior seemed outlandish, but then I remembered Sarai, who I normally managed to block from my thoughts. San still might be making me pay for losing her daughter. And despite what she had done to me, could I blame her? Everything about San to me now represented pain and misery, where once it was love. Why did I ever let her, or anyone, in?

Seymone never looked my way after all. San already confronted me, so I had no fear of seeing her again when I went to greet Seymone after the meet. She smiled big and thanked me for coming. It felt good being supportive of someone else, but if I'd known that she wouldn't even notice I was there until the end, I would have stayed at home.

The next morning, I didn't awake until after 10. James and I were up all night watching various old-school videos on YouTube because we both had difficulty sleeping. I don't know what his excuse was, but I was plagued by thoughts of San.

By sunrise, James was gone. I could never get used to his long work hours: him being called away at all hours of the night, or not being there for holidays—even my birthday. If I had to analyze a side-by-side comparison of my life before James to my life with him, I would say they were extremely similar. Material things were easy to come by, but no one else was there.

I knew I had to meet up with San that day, primarily to keep her mouth shut, but a potential new friend had also been

Played

sparking my curiosity. My mind kept drifting to Kelvin, the man from the parking lot. He was mysterious, yet so familiar, and I was eager to learn more.

I sent him a text that said: *hey u. busy?*

who is this? he responded.

damn, u giv ur number out like that?

i think i kno who this is. r u 2 busy 4 me right now?

now?

yeah. i'm leavin in 2 days 4 business. meet me some-where.

I closed my phone, thought for a moment, then replied.

20

It was ten minutes to 4, and San hadn't showed. I didn't have a number to call her, so I waited in front of the coffee shop, hoping that she wouldn't come but desiring to know what it was she wanted.

By 4:15 San finally pulled up next to me in a brand new black Escalade with black rims and dark tinted windows. She rolled down the window slightly, only revealing her bug-eyed frames and freshly glossed lips.

"Hey. Follow me." She put her vehicle in reverse and proceeded to back away before I had the opportunity to respond.

We drove for at least six minutes through neighborhoods in the historic side of Jacksonville that most of us knew as Riverside or Avondale. All the "old money" citizens lived over here; I wondered where we were headed. We passed Memorial Park, where my mom took me as a kid, and the new Publix shopping center. Eventually we arrived at the newly

Played

built condos on the edge of the river.

We pulled up in the large parking garage, but I hesitated for a moment before exiting the car.

"What's this?" I asked, walking around to the back of the car to meet her.

"This is my place." She secured her Louis Vuitton bag on her shoulder.

"Why are we here, San? I thought you said to meet at the coffee shop."

She stopped walking and turned to me. "Yes, I said to *meet* there." Then, she continued walking.

I followed, wondering what surprises lay within the building. Although the sun was fairly high, the garage was extremely dark and quiet. The only other person there was a white brunette with a toddler in her arms struggling to unload groceries from her Lexus. I considered offering her my help, but San was almost to the elevator by the time I spotted her.

She swiped a key card, and we entered the building through a set of double glass doors. The lobby smelled of cinnamon and fresh baked chocolate chip cookies. San walked slowly toward the in-building elevator, and I followed, taking it all in.

"Good afternoon," the receptionist exclaimed, leaning forward in his seat to get a good look at us.

"Hey, Manuel. How's it going?" San replied.

"Just wishing I was off and able to join you ladies today." His hair was curly—most definitely of some Hispanic origin, and he had very rigid, sharp teeth.

She laughed. "Not today, babe."

The elevator ride to the eighth floor was silently tense. When we exited and arrived at her door, San announced, "You'll have to excuse my place. I've been pretty busy lately."

When she opened the door, it revealed a large picture window on the back wall with an amazing view of the St. John's River—no curtains, no blinds. Her place was smartly furnished with contemporary pieces that I recognized from the West Helm showroom. She had obviously done very well for herself, whatever she did.

Scattered around the space were twelve medium-size boxes. San walked over to one and opened it.

"This is why I brought you here," she said, removing the contents of the box.

"This is a very nice place, San," I said, staring down at the white, plush carpet. For some reason, I felt moved by her surroundings, by how her life turned out.

"Thanks. I've come a very long way." She laid the paper packaging on the granite countertop that separated the living room area from the kitchen, reached into the box again and withdrew a paperback book. "I owe this to you."

I read the cover. *Operation: Survival*. The back cover revealed that it was a nonfiction account of a woman who had been abused as a child, victimized by her lovers, who worked as a prostitute, and who had lost someone very close to her. Below the synopsis of the book was a picture of San, smiling.

So she wrote a book, had someone print it, and was now in the process of selling it. I wondered if I was in it — if she used my real name. I wondered how much of San's life it covered, and if it was the same piece she had been working on when we were still together. I wondered if any of it was true.

I flipped through the pages, trying to take in as much of the information as I could before turning to the next. The first chapter title read: ***An inch toward healing is better than none at all. Hand me my ruler, please***.

"No need to hurry," she said. "I'm giving that to you." I stopped flipping and looked at her. "Taj," she continued, "if it weren't for you, I wouldn't have had the courage to do this. And if it weren't for the experiences that you allowed me to share with you, I would have nothing extraordinary to talk about."

"So, this book is about me?" I could feel the alarm in my chest now; I held the book in my hand as if it were going to explode. Regardless of how she presented herself now, I was still on guard.

"No, me. You *are* in some chapters, but not throughout." I

lifted an eyebrow. "I didn't include your real name," she said quickly. "I call you T.J. in the book." She smiled, pleased with herself.

"How long did it take you to complete?" I was relieved, but still skeptical.

"A little over three months."

"And you're selling these?"

"Yeah. I published them myself, so I'm in the process of shipping them out to some local distributors and selling them on my website."

"Oh." I placed the book on the counter and took a seat on the barstool. San came behind me and gently touched my shoulder.

"Taj, I've wanted to talk to you for so long. I wanted to find you and make sure that you were OK." I looked away from her. "I know it may mean nothing now, but I was stupid. I was greedy. I was insecure. I—"

"Had me brutally raped and almost had me killed? Is that what you were going to say?" San's eyes began to water and her lips trembled. Now that I said it out in the open, the anger I felt toward her struck my brain like lightning. "What is there to cry for now San? I was traded. And for what? You betrayed me. You hated me so much that you wanted to watch me die in that hotel room."

My head began to throb and my face and limbs became warm to the touch. Before I knew it, I was bawling. The floodgates were opened but I didn't wail because of hurt. Forget the hurt. I was angry. I wanted to reach out and choke her, kick her in the stomach, slap her around until she lost consciousness, but I didn't. Instead, as San stood there abashed, I dried my eyes, regained my composure and stared at her seriously. "Are we done here?"

"Taj..." she spoke hesitantly. "I think we have a lot more to talk about. I'm not ready for you to leave yet."

"It wasn't my choice to come here."

"I didn't force you to come, Taj."

"Oh, really?" I responded, sarcastically.

Triple Crown Publications *presents...*

"What?" She thought for a moment. "Do you think I'm blackmailing you or something?" She half-giggled, looking incredulous.

"Well, things have been working out well for me. I don't want anything to jeopardize my current situation."

"He doesn't know, does he?"

"My relationship with him is none of your damn business, San."

"I'll take that as a 'no.' Well, I've changed, Taj. I'm not the same person anymore." She turned away from me and quickly removed her shirt, revealing the spaghetti strap top that laid underneath. "I want to see you happy—the same happiness that I have found for myself." She sat on the clean, white sofa and pressed both of her hands between her knees, staring at the wall in front of her. Suddenly I felt as though I were talking to Gandhi. "If you want to go, then go. We're done here."

I could tell that there was much more that she wanted to say, or at least, that I wanted her to say. I wanted to know where the hell she pulled all this happiness from. She had obviously been exploring the self-help book section at the bookstore.

I picked up my keys from the counter and walked toward the door, not desiring to speak another word to her.

"And I would appreciate it if you didn't mention anything to Seymone," she called as I opened the front door.

"I see I'm not the only one with secrets." I turned to leave and slammed the door behind me. I left her book on the counter.

21

Kelvin and I had been having an affair for four months. I was still comfortable with James, but I could no longer put up with the long hours and the loneliness. There was still no date set for our wedding. Our life at home had become routine, and neither of us made a move to change it. It made me nervous; I could feel the void growing with every day that I spent in his house alone. I couldn't go back to that feeling again, that feeling of being without. So I thirsted for more security and I found it in Kelvin.

One particular weekend, Kelvin and I planned to meet at the Sawgrass Marriott on Jacksonville Beach. James was working for the entire weekend—nothing out of the ordinary—so I made plans to spend time away from home, which at that point was also not out of the ordinary. Kelvin reserved the room and convinced the staff to issue me a key until he arrived. When I got there, I walked into the spacious two-bed-

room villa, dropped my bag of toiletries in the closest bedroom, and made myself comfortable. The balcony overlooked
the golf course, so I watched as white men teed off and
jumped in their little carts to chase the balls.

I heard a click and turned my attention toward the door.
Kelvin appeared, wearing a crisp blue polo shirt and jeans.

"I tried to call you," he told me. "What's up with your
phone?" He seemed flustered and looked as though he had
just run up eight flights of steps.

"I don't know. I didn't hear it ring. Maybe it's just poor
reception." I continued to watch the men on the golf course,
feigning indifference to his flawless body.

"Well, hello." He slowed his breathing, then walked over
and put his arms around my waist, kissing me slowly.

"Hey," I purred, "I missed you."

"Really? What'd you miss?"

"Everything." I smirked.

"Well, show me." He stared at me for a moment. Then, I
took his hand and led him to the master bedroom.

Our night ended with our sweating bodies lying next to
each other atop of white sheets. There was nothing else to be
said. We slept peacefully through the hours, and by morning
he was gone again.

"I hate the way you've been moping around here lately,"
James said the Sunday afternoon I returned home. He picked
up his reading glasses from the kitchen table and proceeded
to read the newspaper, still dressed in his dark red, Christmas-
colored morning robe.

It was true. I was happier when I wasn't sitting around at
home. "I'm fine, baby," I responded. "Just have a lot on my
mind." I was wrapped in a white blanket and lounging in the
chair next to him, staring at the pool from the window.

"I hate to pry, but it's hard to understand what could be so
wrong." He placed the newspaper down on the table. "Maybe
we both could use some time away. Let's drive to Miami for
the weekend." James' eyes lit up, and he clapped his hands

Played

together. "We can get a spot on South Beach and chill for a little while."

"That sounds great, but I'm really not in the mood for a vacation." I turned to look him. "I just need some time."

At that moment, I noticed the television in the background—or rather the image on it. And for the very first time, the two men with whom I was involved were in the exact same room. I couldn't hear, but there was no doubt that Kelvin was being interviewed, wearing a Denver Broncos jersey while standing on a field. The station was playing the highlights of the previous night's game and his name flashed across the bottom of the screen. The game he played right before he came to me. Eyes wide, heart thudding, I felt played. He told me he was into real estate when we met up after the track meet, not a professional athlete. Now I knew why his name was so familiar.

We sat in silence for a moment, me silently seething. After a while, it became apparent that both of us were thinking of what to say next.

"Get dressed," he whispered, looking above the frames of his glasses.

"For what?" I said, very distracted.

"Dress nice. Not too fancy though." He stood and walked out of the room.

My stomach was in knots, and I cringed a little more with each thought of Kelvin's lie, but I pulled myself up anyway.

I went to the closet, and I heard James messing around in one of the spare bedrooms. The black Chanel dress I chose fit too snug, so I went with the navy blue Calvin Klein pantsuit, slipped on a pair of Nine West pumps and topped it off with the diamond studded watch James bought me for Christmas.

I was on the bed, fastening my earrings when James appeared in the doorway, wearing an all-black suit and a beautifully patterned tie with crimson diamond shapes throughout. He drew the tie closer to his neck and looked at me for approval.

"I like it. You look nice, baby," I confirmed, looking him up

Triple Crown Publications *presents...*

and down. He did have a pretty great body.

"Thank you. And you're beautiful. But that's nothing new."

We were in the car for almost twenty minutes when James turned into a gravel lot off of the busy highway. The sign out front read: **United Church of Faith**. I became nauseated and feverish almost immediately, while James looked over to silently check my reaction.

It had been nearly fifteen years since I stepped foot into a church and I nearly vowed never to do so again. Atheism was never considered and I didn't hate God, but neither did I praise Him. After my mother was shot dead by three gang members during a Wednesday night service all those years ago, God and I had come to an understanding: I avoid Him, He avoids me.

"I used to come to this church when I was younger," James said, interrupting my thoughts. He unfastened his seatbelt, then leaned over to attain the Bible in the compartment behind the passenger seat. "This is the Bible my mom gave me when I was 18." He flipped through its pages with a smile in his eyes.

"You know, I'm not really feeling up to this today, James." He looked puzzled, staring me up and down as though I was the devil in disguise fearing the church house. "I mean, had I known we were coming here, I would have dressed different-ly. My hair makes me look like a slut, and—"

"You're fine, Taj." He pressed the release on my seatbelt, and without speaking any further, opened his car door and stepped out. I followed hesitantly, fidgeting with the straps of my handbag.

The church was small in size and in number of partici-pants. The entire congregation was gathered around the altar when we walked in. Dimly lit, the church was divided in two—four pews on each side, all unoccupied at that moment. It was warm. The ceiling fans did a poor job cooling off the room. We took a seat in the back of the church near a woman in a wheelchair who reeked of cigarettes and alcohol. James went down on his knees from his seat and began to utter words I

Played

135

couldn't discern.

The devotion leaders were in the front of the room humming harmoniously while men and women cried and shouted praises. The woman in the wheelchair, with her blank countenance, stared off into space, unmoved by any activity taking place within the church. I couldn't say the same. Maybe it was the atmosphere, but when my thoughts touched on Kelvin again I was overtaken with emotion. Teary-eyed and saddened, I looked down at James, still on his knees. There was a break in the praying, and I sniffled. It caught James' attention, and he looked up almost immediately, searching my face. I attempted to dry my eyes, but my condition worsened as I tried to wipe away how guilty I was feeling. James stood and pulled me up by the hand. We embraced. He cried, thinking he was sharing a moment with me. It was the first time I had ever seen him so overcome with emotion, and it was because of the wrong reasons.

Triple Crown Publications *presents*...

22

A week later, James attended a conference in Tennessee, and I was left alone in the house. Besides a few attempts to contact Kelvin with no success, I went through my typical routine: making breakfast, working out and then spending the the rest of the day in front of the television watching re-runs of several shows on BET. One particular morning, I must have pushed myself too hard during my workout because I became nauseated soon after. I jumped into a hot shower hoping it would relieve me, but it didn't work.

San called and asked if I could meet her for lunch so we could talk about an issue in which only I could assist her. I was reluctant at first, but considering that James was out of town and San had kept quiet about our ordeal, I figured I had nothing to lose. I agreed to meet her at a café downtown, a central location, in mid-afternoon.

As I dressed for the day, the nausea failed to subside. Then,

Played

this feeling as though someone punched and kicked me throughout my abdominal area began to overpower me, causing me to lie on the bedroom floor for a moment, unable to make it to the bed. After a while, the pain went away. I picked myself up and continued to dress—beginning with a layer of baby lotion and body spray, then a black Chanel cocktail dress and Ferragamo pumps. I pinned up my hair and added a hint of Dolce & Gabbana perfume behind my ears.

The pain came back to me enroute to the café. I pulled over to the side of the freeway and tears began to stream, an irrepressible reaction to the pain. My hands began to tremble while gripping the steering wheel. The need for fresh air was imperative so I drove to the closest exit, pulled over into a gas station, stepped out and circled the car. My legs buckled beneath me, and I could feel myself on the verge of fainting. I rested my back against the passenger side tire, not caring that I was sitting on the ground pressed against a filthy Michelin in an eight-hundred-dollar dress.

"Ma'am! Are you OK over here?" a male voice spoke, but I didn't see a face. "Can I call someone for you?"

"No ... I mean, yes. Please." I stared off into passing traffic, confused about what was ailing me. I wanted to lay my head on the pavement, knowing that I was unable to rise and get into the car. "Please hand me the phone from the front seat." For an instant, I considered that the keys were still in the Mercedes' ignition, and he could have easily driven away, but I didn't budge. "Thank you," I told him, as he handed over the phone and kneeled down to my level, looking at me. He was a white male, perhaps thirty-two or thirty-three, and fairly handsome. "Thank you again."

"I don't want to just leave you here. Can I ask what the problem is?"

"I don't know. I just don't feel too well. I'm gonna call someone to come and get me."

"Well, I'll wait around until someone gets here. You shouldn't be out here alone like this."

The only person I knew to call was San. She answered on

Triple Crown Publications *presents*...

the first ring.

"Don't tell me you're standing me up. I'm not taking no for an answer." She laughed.

"San, I don't feel well."

"Hell, me neither. I'm cramping, and I have a headache, but I'm not complaining." I could hear the sound of wind in the background as though she were already in her car.

"No, I was on my way, but I pulled over. I need you to come here and get me. Please."

"Where are you?" She sounded concerned.

At that moment, I began to see two of everything. My vision became blurred, and I could feel my temperature rising. I didn't have the strength to hold the cell phone to my ear, so I lowered it to my lap and the generous man picked it up and began to speak with her for me.

"Hello," he said, "she's going out. I'm calling an ambulance for her." He listened to the receiver for a moment. "Well, how far are you? ... OK ... We're off Exit 214. You're not far. Take the next exit and turn left. You'll see us out here." He placed the phone back into my lap.

"She's on the way," he told me. The man opened a bottle of water he purchased inside the convenience store and offered me a drink that I could barely swallow.

San pulled in moments later and rushed from her car.

"Girl, why are you on the ground? Come on, get up."

"I can't. I feel dizzy when I stand—like I'm gonna pass out or something," My own voice was faint in my ears.

"I got you. I'll help you into my car. Grab my hand." I could-n't lift my head high enough to see her, but her sweet fragrance occupied the air around me.

"Ma'am, I can pick her up and lay her in the back of your SUV—that's if you don't mind, ma'am," he said, turning his attention to me.

"No, I don't mind," I answered, offering my hand to him. "Thank you."

As he lifted me from the ground, San rushed over to the dri-ver's side and removed the keys from the ignition. I fit comfort-

P l a y e d

ably in the back of San's Escalade, which still had the new car scent. The alarm chirped, signaling that the doors had been locked.

"So, which hospital do you prefer?" she asked, fastening her seatbelt and looking over the seat at me.

"Whichever is the closest," I said in agony.

"You don't want that. I'm taking you to Baptist Medical Center. They're usually the best when it comes to ER situations." She paused for a moment. "Well, what's bothering you?"

"I don't know. I'm nauseated, dizzy, and there's a pain that's shooting through my entire abdomen. I don't know what the hell it is."

"Well, what did you eat? Any shellfish or red meat lately? Chicken?"

"No, nothing out of the usual."

"Hmm. Well, if you ask me, it sounds like your appendix. If that's the case, they'll want to operate on you today. That is a very dangerous organ to deal with. It can explode and possibly kill you."

She scared me with her appendix talk, but I wondered why I believed *her* of all people.

Once we arrived in the ER, they pumped me for a urine sample and took several vials of blood. Not long after, I was escorted into a room, even before others who were there before me. I thanked San for taking me to the hospital, but asked her if she could wait outside, in the lobby. We weren't friends, after all, and her nose was already too much into my business.

My assigned room was small; there was only enough space for two or three people to stand at any given time. The registration staff came in to inquire about insurance and financial matters, then the nurse peeped in to check my comfort and to inform me that they were waiting for my lab results before I would be seen by the doctor.

I lay on the bed staring at the ceiling, wondering what the hell was wrong with me and fearing surgery if San's assumptions were true.

After another half hour, there was a new face in the room.

"Ms. Jenson?" A short, gray-haired woman appeared in the doorway wearing a stethoscope and holding a chart.

"Yes."

"How are you feeling?"

"Like crap. Do you have any answers for me?" I stared at her.

She pressed her hand to my left thigh buried beneath the covers. "Well, your urine sample tells us that you're pregnant." My eyes widened.

"But I'm on my period. I can't be pregnant."

"You are also showing symptoms of someone who is miscarrying or may have an ectopic pregnancy. We won't know for sure until we can get an ultrasound on you."

"Wait. What? I don't understand!"

We're going to continue to watch your blood count and let you know for sure."

"So..." I raised my hand to my heart, alarmed. "I may have to have surgery, is that what you're saying?"

"It is likely, if it's a tubal pregnancy. I'll get you over to do the ultrasound as soon as possible."

"Wait a minute!" I tried to sit up but the pain knocked me back down. "Does that mean I won't be able to have children later?"

"No, not necessarily. You'll be fine. You should be able reproduce normally." She picked up the cTurner from the counter. "I'm going to get you in to see the ultrasound technician, OK?"

"Sure. Thanks."

In an instant, I thought of James and how he would react to the news of my illness. Then in another instance, I thought of the ordeal San put me through and how it could possibly be the cause of my situation. I wondered if the assault would prevent me from ever having children when I'm married. I even wondered if James would be willing to stay with someone incapable of reproducing. Having children was something else we had never discussed, not even after our engagement. I rolled back over onto my side and closed my eyes, forcing myself to sleep.

Played

23

When I awoke, San was sitting next to the bed wearing a loose-fitting black dress and a red scarf across her shoulders. Her face was hidden behind her hands and her legs trembled. Her three-inch, basic-black-pumps tapped the floor with each movement.

"What's wrong with you?" I asked.

"No. What's wrong with *you*? Have they told you anything yet?"

"No. I need to see a different doctor," I said, partially lying. The staff was in the process of contacting my OB/GYN to come in and assist me with my condition.

"How long do you think—" Just then, a female voice interrupted San from a speaker box above the bed.

"Yes? Did you need something?" she asked impatiently.

"Umm, no. I didn't call you," I responded. "I must have pressed the button by accident." She disconnected without saying anything.

San went on to question me about my comfort level and my health. To tell the truth, she was too concerned for my liking.

"James should be on the way here by now," I told her, "so you don't have to stay much longer."

"OK, that's fine. I just wanted to make sure you were OK." She looked toward the window, then hesitantly at me again. "There was still something I needed to discuss with you."

"YES?" a voice yelled from the speaker box above the bed.

"I didn't call you," I told the woman again. I looked at the button that I was sure I didn't touch. She disconnected again without saying a word.

"They should really get this damn thing fixed and stop giving me attitude." I positioned myself more comfortably on the bed. "What was it that you wanted to discuss?"

San took a deep breath, then said, "I forgive you."

I simply looked at her, blank-faced.

"No," she continued, "I mean really forgive you—for everything. I've been reading, meditating, praying even, and because I know that I have to forgive you in order to be the woman that I was before I ever met you, I have to confront you first."

What step in her self-help program is this? I thought.

"I knew about Sarai. I knew what happened the night Sarai died," she said. I raised and propped myself up on the pillow in an attempt to say something. "No, let me finish," she pressed on. "I was angry. You neglected something—someone—so important to me—for a couple of dollars. I heard the messages Tiki left on your cell phone about what happened that night." She shook her head. "I would have given you that money for the life of my little girl." San stood from her chair in the corner of the room and began to pace the floor on the right side of the bed near the window.

"You know, at first, I figured that you were jealous of me," she continued. "Jealous that I was able to get my daughter back. If you would have put in as much effort to get your son

P l a y e d

143

as you did into making money with those shows, you would have had him by now. You've probably forgotten you ever had one—so busy living the life." She stopped at the end of the bed and looked directly at me. I listened silently, wanting to scream and cry all at the same time.

"You've always been selfish, Taj, and I learned to hate you for it. I couldn't forgive you for what your selfish actions forced me to endure. And hating you took me to a lot of low places. A part of me wanted you to die that night. I was so angry." She pressed the back of her right hand against her mouth,. Tears now filled her eyes. "There's a lot I want to do with my life, but this can't keep hanging over my head. I realized that my healing wouldn't come from receiving your forgiveness for what I've done to *you*, but to forgive you for what you've done to *me*. This has to be the final chapter." She continued to stand at the foot of the bed silently.

I allowed what she said to process for a moment before I attempted to speak. I couldn't help but understand her frustration with me after what happened with Sarai, but her attempt to read me about my selfishness was a little over the top. I didn't know how to approach the argument. San was more upset than I ever saw, even more than the night Sarai died. Her behavior was reminiscent of a grieving mother saying her final words to her child's killer in open court, right before the prisoner is taken away for the last time. And this served as her way of healing.

As I made an attempt to speak, the door opened. I couldn't see immediately who was entering, but I could hear footsteps approaching quickly. Without saying a word, James rushed over to the side of the bed and pressed the Call End button on the railing. Then, Seymone appeared, but didn't fully enter the room. She crossed her arms and stared at San for a few moments before turning to leave. "Wait!" San called out to her. Then, she disappeared from the room.

Triple Crown Publications *presents…*

24

James walked over to the sink and washed his hands. Returning he asked, "How are you feeling?"

I was hesitant about responding, not completely aware of what had just taken place. I answered simply, "I've been better." He lifted my gown, and I touched where I told him it hurt as he questioned me about my symptoms, preparing to make his own diagnosis. There was no point in attempting to explain what other doctors told me. I figured he would better understand their findings, then inform me.

Within ten minutes, the grey-haired doctor re-entered the room. "Hi. You must be Mr. Jenson."

"No. I'm Dr. James Carter—Ms. Jenson's fiancé."

"Oh, I see," she said, possibly surprised by a handsome black man with such credentials. "Well, how are you feeling Ms. Taj?"

"I'm still in pain, but I really just want to know what needs to be done so that I can get out of here."

"Can you tell me what's going on with her, doctor?"

"Well, an ultrasound shows that she is pregnant, but it also shows quite a bit of internal bleeding as well. We're still running tests to determine whether she's suffering an ectopic pregnancy. We'll monitor her overnight, but we may have to perform surgery in the morning." The doctor looked at me, and I nodded my head in agreement.

James backed away from the bed, arms folded. He stared at my midsection, then the floor. He was silent for some time before he said, "So, you're saying she's pregnant?"

"Yes, her urine and blood tests prove it." She paused a moment. "I *am* sorry. Was this a planned pregnancy?"

"No, it wasn't," I said.

"So, there's no possibility of her keeping this baby?" James asked.

"Almost none. I'll give you two a moment. I will come back in to check on you in a few hours."

"Thank you," James and I said simultaneously.

He stood with his back pressed against the wall, arms folded and staring at the floor. Half of his face was hidden in the shadows of the wall. "James," I said softly, "it's gonna be all right."

"Umm." He cleared his throat. "I think I need some air."

"I want you to stay." I reached my hand out for him, but he ignored it and excused himself from the room.

I spent hours rummaging through all the thoughts in my mind—from San's comments to wondering whether we'd been heard, and then to the baby and James' reaction to the idea of losing it. Nurses came to take me to another room where I would be kept overnight. I called and paged James for hours, but received no response. I never expected him to be as upset about the situation as he was. Perhaps he secretly wanted to be a father or for me to mother his child, but it was nothing that we had ever discussed openly.

I laid in silence for hours, sorting through all of my thoughts until finally I fell asleep around 3:00 a.m.

Triple Crown Publications *presents...*

25

At 7:00 a.m. I was whisked away for another sonogram. My face wasn't washed, I still had morning breath, and my hair was a curly mess. But I couldn't be concerned with those things when I learned that the findings of the sonogram forced the doctor to rush me into surgery. The internal bleeding was worse.

James was nowhere to be found. Several nurses attempted to make contact with him, but there was never any response. I understood how devastating the situation might have been for him, but he hadn't considered how difficult and physically painful it was for me. I simply wanted him to be there.

The surgery itself passed in what seemed like minutes, although it had to have been hours. I awakened as I was being wheeled into the recovery area. As I became more conscious of my surroundings, the pain became more noticeable, but what I noticed the most was that no one else was there.

A nurse was adjusting my IV, and I called out to her. "Nurse. Have you heard from my fiancé?"

"No, ma'am. I couldn't get him."

I stayed in the hospital for two days to make sure infection didn't set in. The day I was released, the nurse offered to call James again, but I asked her to call a taxi instead. I dressed slowly, and was wheeled to the front of the hospital where the driver waited.

The taxi ride was dreadfully painful. My wounds were glued, not stitched, so I feared my incisions would be reopened with each bump and pothole.

Pulling up to the house, my mind moved far quicker than my body did exiting the taxi. Hunched over and slowly stepping one foot in front of the other, I made my way to the front door and let myself in. James was sitting in the family room—an open bottle of cognac on the table in front of him. He turned to look at me, hunched over.

"What the hell you doing? Why didn't you answer my calls, James?"

"You really need to calm down, Taj." He stood.

"What? I've been calling you all morning! I've been calling you for days!" I walked over to him. He seemed surprised by behavior.

"Have a seat, Taj." James sat down on the sofa and poured a drink.

"I don't want to sit. I want to know what the hell is wrong with you. What did I do so wrong to deserve this treatment?"

Agitated he said, "I know about you and Santina, Seymone's friend. I know now how you wound up in the hospital when I first saw you. Santina told me all of it yesterday. I know everything, Taj, and actually, I can let that go. That was in the past. But what I don't know now is you." He

Triple Crown Publications *presents* ...

took a sip of his drink. "Tell me, Taj, and your honesty is extremely important, what *man* are you cheating on me with?" He turned his head to look at me.

"What? I just got out of surgery, and I get the third-degree? This makes absolutely no sense to me, James."

"You better answer the damn question, and I mean truthfully," he said, staring directly at me, cold and frightening.

"I haven't cheated on you, James." Not an inch of me was willing to confess to him.

He placed his glass down on the table and walked into the kitchen. He reappeared holding a yellow legal pad and a pen. "Here." He shoved it near my face.

"What's this for?" I slowly removed it from his hand.

"I need you to write down a forwarding address." Standing, he reached down for his drink. "I will pack your things and send them there."

"This is ridiculous. Why don't you trust me?" I pleaded.

"Oh, and your son—I almost forgot about that part. Wow, Taj." He smiled, shook his head, and took a sip of his drink.

"OK, I know," I pleaded. "I had secrets but they're out now. I didn't want you to judge me. Is that what this is about? We can get past this because I'm still the same person. What can I do?" I heard the desperation in my own voice and it made my skin crawl.

"You can start by writing your *new* address on that sheet of paper. Then, you can get out my house."

"Wait . . . is this about the baby? I don't know what happened, James. It was beyond my control. I can't be the one to blame for what happened."

"Ding! Ding! Ding! Partially right! Where you're wrong is that you thought I gave a damn about that baby. It wasn't mine to begin with." He took another sip then took a seat.

"That's not fair, James. And don't you think you can sit there and treat me like I'm the only one with a past! You *never* mentioned why your ex-wife left. Maybe I didn't trust you with everything, but you could have opened up to me.

Played

Saying the baby wasn't yours is just really low."

"I had a vasectomy six years ago, Taj. I can't have children." He crunched on a piece of ice that he had taken from the glass, then stretched his arms across the length of the sofa. "Perhaps you also learned something *new* about me. As for the rest, you don't even deserve to ask."

He didn't say another word. Any other lie I would tell would be in vain, so I was quiet and did as I was told.

26

I packed a few items that I could carry in my condition—a toothbrush, a change of clothes, and some underwear. I called for a cab, and sure enough, the driver who'd dropped me off returned to pick me up again. My thoughts shifted from James, to Kelvin, and then to survival. I didn't know where I would sleep that night, where my next meal would come from, or how I would make another dollar. I figured I could maybe count on one person to be there for me, so that's where I went.

A bit of commotion came from inside San's apartment as my fist lightly pounded on the door. I held on to the door's frame, keeping my balance and realizing that I hadn't taken any medication for the pain that was becoming worse by the minute.

"Can I help you?" Seymone opened the door slightly, but I could see San sitting Indian-style on the sofa with her face buried in her hands.

Played

"Can I talk to San, please?" I pressed against my abdomen and grit my teeth.

"No, there's nothing that you need to say to either of us."

"San, I know you hear me. Please. I need your help," I attempted to yell. San continued to sit there. "I have nowhere else to go. I need this one favor, please."

"You heard me. Get away from our door." Seymone slammed the door, almost catching my fingers.

I felt myself go into a frenzy. "YOU OWE ME, SAN! YOU GOT THAT, BITCH? YOU OWE ME!"

"Go to hell!" Seymone retorted from behind the door.

I took the elevator and stumbled into the lobby. From the window I noticed a pharmacy across the street and managed to make it all the way there without collapsing. The twenty-minute wait for my prescriptions seemed more like a two hours. Elderly men and women stared as I was balled up in a fetal position and stretched over three chairs in the waiting area. I took the medication and sat there until the pain was manageable.

There wasn't a moment for me to stop and think about what had occurred—how reckless I'd been. What was in front of me was most important. I picked up my small sack of belongings and walked out to the pay phone in front of the store. It had been a while since I'd used one. I pondered who I could call. Clouds formed overhead, and the sun became lost behind them. I knew that soon it would be dark. My thoughts crossed Shai but she was out of the question. I shook my head at the thought of Kelvin. After I learned who he really was, and hadn't heard from him since we were together at the Sawgrass Marriott at Jacksonville Beach, it was evident that I was just something for him to do. There was only one person left to call and I knew that if I had a good proposition, she would come through. So, I picked up the receiver and dialed her last known number. Almost immediately she answered.

"Hello? Tiki? Is that you?"

27

Two months later, I looked at the water-stained mirror in the bathroom with disgust. After spending twenty minutes shimmying and jiggling for a fairly attractive 55-year-old white man who wanted to see my titties while he masturbated, I worked fast to rearrange my breasts inside my bra.

I looked down at the two twenty dollar bills and two five dollar bills clutched in my hands, then peeked outside the door to make sure no one was waiting on me to use the stall. I secured the lock on the door and quickly undressed as I turned the faucet on. The faucet slowly freed the water from the spickett before it flowed freely, like water escaping from a fire hydrant.

My life couldn't get any worse than this, I thought as I lathered the soap with the coarse wash cloth. Gently lathering my body, I made sure that I became fresh and clean—given the circumstances. This was the first bath I'd had in the past three days, and I was looking forward to doing the show with Tiki so I could get her money back, plus more. When I called Tiki two months ago, she took me in and nursed me back to health, but she made it very clear that I owed her for leaving her the way I did that night. And the only acceptable compensation for her was for me to get back into performing with her while she reminded me that she called all the shots. I didn't want to go back to that life, but I needed to survive.

Digging in my tattered fake Gucci purse, I pulled a clean bra and panties that I boosted from a discount store the day before, and squeezed the store brand cocoa butter lotion into my hand. "Damn, I spoke too soon," I mumbled, disappointed, to only get a small Skittle-sized drop into the palm of my hand.

I slowly turned the water back on and let two drops fall in my hand, then rubbed them together as I thanked God for having enough lotion to last for the job. I knew that with the money I was to make in the next few hours, lotion would be one of my first purchases.

I picked up the discount brand black dress from the floor, dusted off the dirt, and put it back over my body. I threw the bra and panties I'd worn for the past three days in the trash and vowed to get another set. Grabbing the key from the sink, I checked myself over once more, and walked out of the bathroom. After I looked to make sure an undercover cop hadn't spotted me as I fulfilled another one of my peepshows in the old gas station, I walked around to the entrance and returned the key to the attendant, who smiled. I gave the woman one of the five dollar bills and walked outside.

I walked around the building and folded the rest of the bills in half, dug into my bra, and placed the money over my left breast. That way, if someone jacked my purse like they did a few weeks before, they wouldn't have all of my cash. I lost two hundred dollars in that caper, causing my life to take yet another nose dive. Satisfied the money was secure, I arranged the bra for my comfort and walked back to the front of the building.

The prepaid phone buzzed in my purse, and I recognized

Tiki's number on the screen.

"Hello."

"I got the man to agree to let us rent the room for forty dollars. You got the money, right?"

"Yeah, I got it."

"OK, give the man that, and I'll give you the money back after we do our show. See you soon."

Before I could protest, she hung up. Shaking my head, I didn't know why *I* had to pay for the room when Tiki handled most of the money and the clients.

I shook my head as I reflected on my engagement to James—by far my greatest accomplishment—and all the luxurious perks that came along with being the future Mrs. Doctor Carter. With the same thought, I felt not a single ounce of remorse for what I'd done: how I'd managed to break the heart of the only man who ever loved me. No, my deepest regrets were that I was no longer taken care of and that I'd lost the multi-million dollar home, expensive cars, designer clothing, and a man to sleep beneath every night.

Tiki was the only person willing and able to come through for me. We had history, so begging wouldn't have been necessary—or so I believed. But the days of organized, classy shows in some of Jacksonville's premium hotels were now gone. Nowadays, we settled for anything affordable. I was stooping lower than I ever had before, but not so low that I couldn't grab hold to my game and eventually pull myself out of my own situation. It's just that I hadn't felt this despicable since before the birth of my son, when I was living in dope houses to avoid resorting to women's shelters—possibly where I would have been better off.

Even though I'd begged for help from San and Tiki, my pride refused to let me ask for help from those shelters, and my stubbornness refused to admit that I was in desperate need of it. Life after James was a temporary setback, but I would do whatever it took to ensure that I could spring back into the Taj I once was—bold, bossy, and beautiful.

I opted to walk barefooted to the peach-colored, no-named

P l a y e d   155

establishment a few blocks aways from the gas station which was my destination.

This is not the Hilton, the Marriott or even the Motel 6, I observed as I made my way inside the building. I missed the days when bright lights, palm trees and food from a nearby café or restaurant greeted me when I walked into the doors—when everyone looked like they were on business or trying to make it on someone's runway stage. Now, when I walked into hotels or motels, the buildings were usually dilapidated and the air was stale at best. If I was lucky, there was a snack and soda machine in the lobby and a way for me to get ice. The folks looked like they came off the streets, and the nicest thing the men wore were khakis or Dickies falling off their behinds.

As I stopped, I noticed that the man behind the counter was sporting the same bob-hairstyle that I was under his alligator print hat, except his relaxer appeared to be recent and fresh. I couldn't even afford shampoo and conditioner, let alone the relaxer my hair so desperately needed. I looked at his clean, white button-up shirt with the matching alligator print that he had for a bow-tie and a vest. His skin was smooth, and the oil he wore screamed money—at least it was more money than *I* had. I looked at his nails, and my brown-sugar eyes turned green with envy. They were manicured and freshly polished. His tips were sharp, and even his cuticles were on point. I didn't bother to look at mine because I knew I couldn't compete.

"Hey, baby, what can I do for you?" he spoke in a crisp, high-pitched, effeminate voice.

"I need a room. Smoking please."

The attendant, who I determined was named Freddie from his name tag, looked me up and down in pity. "Our rooms start at fifty-five dollars, and we take cash."

"Uh ... Tiki made an appointment. She said I could get a room for forty dollars."

"Oh, you're with *her*," Freddie responded with an attitude. He walked to the cash register and held his hand out. "Well, forty then."

I started to go for my breasts to pull out the two twenties, but decided I wouldn't give Freddie the satisfaction of degrading me any further than he did. I turned around for privacy, and, satisfied that no one else was coming into the building, I quickly reached into my bra, freeing my titty of the dollars it was protecting. I turned back around, walked to Freddie, and put the bills in his hand.

"Thank you, baby." Instead of putting the money into the cash register, he stuffed it into his pockets and pulled out a key labeled 112. "That's your room number on the tag. We just cleaned the room. You be safe now, and if you need me, call zero."

I looked at the effeminate man, but I didn't dare shake my head. Lord forbid if Tiki and I needed some real help. His skinny ass would break in half before mine would, that I was sure of.

I walked out of the building and followed the doors until I got to my room. As I stuck my key into the door, the smell of weed laced with cocaine hit my nostrils immediately, and suddenly, I had a craving for the drug that I'd kept hidden in my knock off purse.

"Um, who is you?" Some ghetto brown-skinned chick came to the door naked. I peeked in and saw a slightly older man, rock hard, on top of the covers, taking a few puffs of the drug. I looked at the door, and then at the keys: they both read "112."

"I must have the wrong room. I'm sorry."

Once I got back to the office, a fine thug-looking dude walked in in front of me. He looked like James. Knowing how I must have appeared, I became embarrassed. He didn't even acknowledge my presence.

"S'up, dude," Freddie greeted him with big eyes and a smile.

"I'm good, Freddie. What about you?"

I couldn't believe what I was seeing. He was all up in Freddie's face as if he were the best thing in the room. Compared to me, in my present condition, he might've been. I watched as Freddie licked his lips and leaned forward toward the man. Their eyes met, and Freddie seemed to taunt me, let-

P l a y e d

ting me know that *he* was going home with the prize for the night, not me. Freddie wrote something down on a piece of paper, then stuffed it in the man's hand. The man lifted his extra-long white T and put the folded paper in his back pocket. I admired how his red-and-white striped boxers followed the curve of his perfectly shaped behind. When the man turned around, I saw that he resembled a lighter version of Trey Songz more than he did James. He looked back at me and my heart broke.

Why do all the fine ones have to be gay? I wondered. I shook my head, trying to dispel the question.

Freddie turned his attention to me, breaking me from my thoughts. "What are you doing back so soon?"

"I need another room. Someone's in the other one."

"Oh, my bad." Freddie relieved me of the keys he gave me and handed me another set for room 115. He pulled out his walkie-talkie and paged the maid on duty. Upon getting confirmation that the room was available, he said, "Enjoy your night and get that money."

My eyes opened wide and my mouth dropped open. *No, he didn't call me out like that,* I thought, but I wasn't going to curse him out. I looked at the clock on the wall and knew that Tiki would be arriving in a few minutes. The men wouldn't be too far behind her. I'd have to deal with this he/she that called itself Freddie another day.

I walked to the room—my home for the night. At least this one had only a cigarette smell, and the bed was made. I wanted so badly to jump into the shower and give myself a real good cleaning, but I decided against it. I didn't want to use the washcloths or towels that hundreds of people probably used for hundreds of purposes. The wash up at the gas station had to do. I sat on the bed, and for a moment, stared at the reflection on the mirror. I dug into my purse and pulled out a bobby pin and pinned the left side of my hair.

There. That's better. I may not have looked much better, but it would have to do.

28

I sat on the edge of the bed and waited for Tiki, silently hoping that I hadn't been stood up after using my last forty dollars on a hotel room. I wanted to be reimbursed for at least half of what I'd spent.

There was no bond between Tiki and me. Everything was strictly business. I knew she pitied me, but most nights I would have to beg her for an opportunity to work, which she allowed at most only twice a week. Other nights, I was showing my breasts or trying to convince a bouncer at a strip joint to let me massage his loins for a couple of dollars and maybe something to eat.

My stomach growled, but I considered that my hunger pangs would subside once I hit a cocaine-laced blunt. I figured I would be able to sleep off the drugs and eat again in the middle of the following day.

Just as I considered using the loose change I found at the

Played

head of the bed to purchase a snack from the hotel's vending machine, there was a knock at the door. Tiki entered with another woman. She introduced herself as "Sunny" then went directly into the bathroom.

"What's up with her, Tiki?" I asked, combing through my hair with my fingers.

"Oh, that's my homegirl. Didn't she introduce herself?"

"I mean, what is she doing here?"

Tiki understood what I meant but was trying to avoid answering the question.

"She's working with me tonight," she finally said. "She had a couple of clients lined up, so I decided to bring her in."

I was pissed, but I knew that demonstrating my anger would cause me to miss out on future opportunities to work. "So, then—what about me?" My voice came out squeaky.

"You sound so helpless." She shook her head at me. "That's the problem. We don't get money—wait, no, *you* don't get money like you use to. So, tonight you'll just have to get in where you fit in."

Tiki dropped her bag and went into the bathroom with her new partner in crime. I walked toward the bathroom and knocked on the door frame, interrupting their conversation. "Well, what about the money I spent on the room? Can I get that back or what?"

"I'll give you twenty." She sighed and reached into her bra. "But I picked this up for you." She removed a small sandwich bag that was twisted tightly around a dollar-sized piece of cocaine and handed it to me. "Like I said, you get in where you fit in tonight, so you might make a couple of dollars."

I still waited on her twenty dollars, but she went on with what she was doing. Sunny walked out of the bathroom and set up the stereo she'd walked in with and played a few slow jams. She had a beautiful French vanilla complexion and extremely high cheekbones that seemed implanted. She was taller and thinner than I was, but not more attractive—even at her worst. She walked stiffly, and her voice was masculine. I noticed a bulge beneath her chin, which led me to believe

Sunny was a man—a very pretty man.

Great, I complained to myself, *not only is there a man who looks better than me, there's one that can pull more dudes than me, too. I wish I could die right now.*

"So, how long you been doing this?" Sunny asked, applying baby oil to her nearly naked body.

"About three years—off and on. And you?" I started to undress so that I could get into the shower, foregoing my earlier thought about using the washcloths. I wanted to demonstrate how confident and sexy I was. I'd be damned if another man showed me up.

"Umm, it's been about three months. Tiki put me onto it."

"And what did you do before this?"

"I used to dance at Kitty Kat's on the south side. Heard of it?"

"Yeah, that's the spot that was shot up a few weeks ago, right?"

"Yep. Glad I wasn't there. I know ol' boy who owns it. He'll put you in there if you ever want to dance or something." Sunny pulled down her thong to oil her butt thoroughly.

"OK, I'll keep that in mind," I lied.

I despised strip clubs. Judging from the ones that were in this city, I knew that if I ever tried to dance, by the end of each night, at least thirty men's filthy hands would have been shoved in my underwear, and I would have had to tip the DJ, the bartender, and the security staff from the tips I worked hard for. It was just too much work for too little pay. Perhaps there was a better market for stripping in other cities, but Jacksonville wasn't the place.

Tiki emerged from the bathroom wearing a boy's pair of Spider-Man underwear and a red sports bra. Her thick black hair was in a tight ball and her eyes, an indication of her Asian ancestry, were darkened with thick liner. She looked nothing like Amerie, though most men told her so.

Tiki's ensemble was beyond tacky, but possibly better than the hot pink bra and panty set I pulled out of my purse. I'd try to wear the sexy set when I performed, but often I found

P l a y e d

myself substituting the lingerie for underwear just so I could preserve the little bit of class I had left. I didn't realize now that the slightly irregular tag on this particular set was a warning that one bra cup was bigger than the other. I just hoped that our repeat visitors wouldn't mind.

"Anybody got some gum?" Tiki asked, spreading thick, pasty deodorant under her arm. I wished I had some deodorant I could use. That would've at least restored some of the dignity I lost when I watered down my lotion to apply to my body earlier.

"Nah, but I got some mouthwash," Sunny responded.

"You don't have no gum, do you, Taj?"

"No," I answered and picked up my lingerie set.

"I bet you don't," Tiki said, in addition to several other words she muttered beneath her breath. I was humiliated, and to add insult to injury, Sunny didn't chuckle, she roared loudly.

I wanted to say something to both of them, but I ignored them. I needed Tiki to make money. At this point, money definitely outweighed pride.

"I know one thing, neither one of y'all better mess with Anthony. He's mine," Sunny said with a stern countenance. She looked at me with contempt, as though the comment was more directed at me than at Tiki.

"Who's that?" I asked, curious to know who he was and why she was attempting to keep him to herself. If I was supposed to get in where I fit in, no man should've been off limits. After all, the three of us were there to perform and to provide whatever service we thought could get us the most tips.

"Someone for me to know and you to never meet." She smirked, but I knew her comment was serious.

"Girl, it's just her crush—something that she's too old to be having," Tiki added, trying to lighten the mood. The last thing I needed was for anyone to be fighting over a screw and messing up my money.

"Ooh, girl, I'm in love with him." Sunny smacked her lips. "Oh, I better not catch his baby mamma slippin', or I'm moving in on him with a quickness." She smacked her lips again.

Wasn't she the hypocrite? I thought to myself. *Got the audacity to be catching an attitude with me when she's the one who wants to hold on to someone else's man.*

"Chick, he done had you. That's the thing. Bye-bye, boo boo." Tiki was joking, but Sunny didn't respond.

I walked into the bathroom and was grateful to shower with the tiny bar of soap provided by the hotel, and I even used their lotion to moisturize. Though I smelled like a walking public restroom, I felt a little better about myself, as this was a big step up from the splish and splash I'd done in the gas station bathroom. Since I possessed no other toiletries, I decided to humble myself and wrap what was left in a small washcloth with the intent of using it when the show was over.

Before leaving the bathroom, I snorted some cocaine and immediately fell into a sneezing fit. My eyes began to water as I continued to sneeze. I could hear some of the men arriving and didn't want to go out in that state, so I waited for the sneezing to subside. Five minutes later, I emerged from the bathroom ready to perform.

One of the honored guests that evening was Taye John, a well known hustler who was due to turn himself in the following day to serve time in prison. Days before, his crew hosted a going away party for him in the most popular night club in the city, but I felt privileged knowing that he would spend his last hours as a free man watching us perform.

I snuck up behind him and grabbed his hand. "Hey, Taye, remember me?"

He turned and looked at me. His eyes were barely open and his breath reeked of alcohol and cigarettes. "How could I forget you, sexy?"

"Then, what's my name?" I flirted, clenching my teeth as my high elevated.

"Tanisha. See there, I know—"

"Nope. Wrong." I pointed my finger at his nose. "It's Taj. T-A-J." I drew invisible letters in the air and giggled.

"Yeah, yeah, that's what I said." He began to roll up his

Played

sleeves, revealing tattoos that covered both of his forearms.

Taye was not the person to argue with—notorious for his public brawls and weapon carrying—so I wisely dropped the subject and went back into the bathroom for another taste. My limbs tingled and my palms sweated, but I wanted to be sure my high would last through the night. The effect of cocaine couldn't be sustained like alcohol, and since Tiki nor I wanted to dish out the cash to buy liquor for our performances, there wasn't any. I noticed that Sunny hadn't offered up any funds to contribute to the upkeep of the business, even though she would reap more of the benefits. I thought that was foul, but I kept it to myself.

The show had already begun when I left the bathroom the second time. There was no major announcement. The men just lined the bed and watch as Tiki and Sunny slowly undressed each other in dim lighting. I was unable to view the show, so I stood near the back of the room with a shy attendee who was too much of a coward to actually step forward. There were at least eight men in the room and none of the attention was on me, so every ten minutes or so, I would escape to the bathroom to reboot.

My stash was dwindling down to the crevices of the sandwich bag, and I could barely keep my eyes open. I figured I would have one more trip to bathroom before it was all gone. I turned off the light and opened the bathroom door to leave.

"Hey, sexy. Where you going?" Taye's sleeves were rolled tightly at his elbow, and his dark complexion seemed to fade into the background. His voice sounded muffled.

"What? You gotta go?" I asked, assuming that he had to use the bathroom and I was in his way.

"Yeah. Don't *you*?" He stopped me from exiting by stretching his arm across the doorframe.

I caught on. "Yeah, but it's expensive."

"How much?" he asked impatiently.

"A hundred. Got it?"

"You know I got you, baby girl. What you gon' do for me?"

"Don't worry. I'ma treat you right."

Triple Crown Publications *presents...*

At one point, sex with clients was forbidden, but in Tiki's new game, any and everything went, and I didn't complain. Refusing men sex in the past caused Tiki to stop performing with me, and it hindered me from cashing in. I could no longer afford to miss out on the money.

He pulled five bills from his wallet, placed the stack in my hand, and gently pushed me further into the bathroom, closing the door behind him. He made every attempt to kiss me, but I turned my cheek to him.

"Wait a minute!" I commanded.

"What's up? I thought this was cool."

"Yeah, but I didn't say nothing about you putting your tongue down my throat." In the darkness, I reached under the dress I'd worn earlier and slid the money under it.

"OK. C'mere though." He opened his arms to pull me in.

I walked over to him and let him feel me up, starting with my breasts, and then downward. I could feel his excitement bulging through his pants before he took it out.

"Where's the condom?" I asked calmly.

"In my wallet. Hold on." He fiddled around in the dark for a little while before finally digging a condom out of what seemed to be his wallet's smallest compartment.

"You ready now?" I asked feigning a smile, anxious to get it over with.

"So, I'm paying for attitude...'cause I don't see nothing else I'm paying for. Come on, shawty."

He grabbed my arm and spun me around so that he was right behind me. I leaned onto the countertop and ran my hands along the cold surface. With one thrust he entered my walls, nearly tearing them down. There were moments when I felt everything and moments when I felt nothing. At a point, when I felt that I could take no more, I reached behind me and pushed his thigh with the palm of my hand.

"You like that, don't you?" he panted, and then placed my hand back on the counter top and held it down. "I'm right there."

He verbalized every moment of his climax and held me

Played

tightly. He stood there for a moment. Sweat from his forehead dripped onto my back.

"OK, you can get cleaned up now," he said.

He walked over to the light switch while I sat on the toilet to urinate. Looking up at him, I noticed he was not who I thought he was. I attempted to see more clearly by rubbing my eyes. It wasn't Taye. I looked for clues to his identity, but I couldn't find any. That was until he reached down to grab his jeans and flashed a tattoo on his forearm displaying his name written in cursive: *Anthony*. *Damn*.

"Where you from?" I slurred, still sitting on the stool.

"Around. Why?"

"No reason. Just asked." I wiped between my legs and attempted to stand but I was incredibly weak and high.

"You straight over there?" he asked, but didn't budge to help.

"Yeah. I'm just gonna sit here for a minute."

"All right." He turned to leave and closed the door behind himself.

I wanted to rest my head somewhere and not be bothered by other men. I knew that if I were to leave the bathroom, other men would line up for their turn, which would have been easy money, but the effects of the drug were too over-powering to go through another episode. I couldn't bear the idea, so I placed two fresh towels at the bottom of the bathtub and climbed in. Within moments, I was comatose.

By the time I awoke, Tiki and her new friend Sunny were gone, but someone left the faucet running full blast. The bitter taste of cocaine and mucus drained through my sinus passages and into my mouth, causing a numbing effect. My body lay naked, cramped in an awkward position. The heavy stale stench of marijuana filled the sticky air.

The room was silent. No one was there, except me. Everyone had gone, possibly to find another party elsewhere. I lay in the tub, feeling my chest rise and fall, sucking in the intoxicating, thick air, and playing back the details of that evening. Even more, I thought back to how I had come to this place again, and in an even worse situation than I was before.

Rising from the bathtub, I noticed that my dress and the one hundred dollars I'd earned from the sex I'd given Anthony were gone. Adrenaline kicked in, and I sprang from the bathroom in search of my clothing but found nothing. The room only contained items belonging to the hotel. I didn't have to guess who would steal my clothes and my money. Tiki only left one thing on the dresser—ten of the twenty dollars she actually owed me. But on the mirror, I noticed a message smeared in red lipstick from Sunny: *He's Mine*.

The words from the old Mokenstef song came and went through my head. I swore that the next time I saw Sunny, I was going to whoop her ass. However, this event didn't serve as the first time Tiki pulled a stunt of this caliber. Weeks before she'd left me at a bachelor party, only for the bachelor's fiancé to come and find me lying in bed with her soon-to-be-husband.

I admit to living recklessly, but Tiki and her agenda made it no better. I also felt that I needed Tiki as much as she needed me. If she didn't, she would've ignored me completely. Maybe I was delusional, but the truth was that Tiki would do anything to see me wallowing in the ugliness she created. Either way, I didn't have time to take Tiki's pettiness personal. I was too high most of the time to feel anything at all.

I no longer left performances at the end of the night in a hot, late-modeled vehicle. Instead, I slept in the hotel until morning, as I did that particular evening. I had no money and nowhere else to go. I had nothing.

P l a y e d

29

I awoke to a loud thumping noise against a wall as a house-keeper unloaded her cleaning materials into the hotel room. Even through drawn curtains, the sun's rays illuminated the space and heightened the temperature of the room. My mouth was dry. The stench of marijuana had faded, or perhaps I'd temporarily lost my sense of smell. My head pounded rhythmically, and my hearing was amplified.

"Check out at noon, ma'am!" a short Hispanic woman barked in an attempt to get my attention.

Stop yelling at me, I thought as I lay in my panties and bra, stretched across the bed.

"OK, I'll check out at 1 o'clock," I told her as I buried my face in the pillow.

"It's 2 o'clock now, ma'am."

I sat up, hair frizzled and eyeliner smeared. "Look, I know you're trying to do your job, but if you would just give me thirty minutes, I will leave," I said, staring at the woman like a crazy person.

She hesitated momentarily. "I'll go down the hall then come back. thirty minutes, OK?"

I planted my head into the pillow for another fifteen minutes before remembering that I didn't have pants to wear out of the hotel. Pacing the room for a moment thinking of what to do, I remembered the pool outside. I wrapped myself in a towel as if I were going to take a dip. I didn't know how far I'd get, but it beat walking out of the room in panties.

The housekeeping cart was at the farthest end of the hallway, and no one was in sight. I walked quickly toward the elevator in my lopsided bra and towel that was tied tightly around my waist. My intentions weren't to actually go to the pool, but when two semi-attractive men came toward me, I made a quick left and ended up at the pool entrance.

Two young ladies were doing cannonballs into the deep end of the pool when I walked onto the yellowing patio. Twigs, leaves and insects floated to the top of the pool each time one would dive in. They enjoyed themselves so much that they hadn't noticed me. I sat in a filthy lawn chair near the pool and took in my surroundings as I plotted my next move.

Three garments were laying poolside. I couldn't make out what they were, but they had to belong to the two in the pool. They skipped twenty feet from the pool in order to get a head start and yelled, "On your mark, get set, go!" On "go", I ran full speed for their clothing and managed to snatch up all three without anyone seeing me and ran inside before they reemerged from the water.

One piece was a small, yellow T-shirt, another was a black pair of shorts and the last was a blue summer dress with brown flowers printed throughout. Although extremely small, I pulled it over my head.

I returned to the lobby and noticed Freddie rocking a khaki-colored Dickie outfit with a nice rope chain and a peace sign emblem hanging in front of his chest. His bob hairstyle from the day before was replaced by zig-zagged braids that created

P l a y e d

intricate designs on his round head. The M&M-sized diamond in his right ear was so bright, it could probably light a room without the help of a flashlight.

When Freddie turned in my direction, my eyes shot up. I had to admit, when he put just a little bit of effort into looking more like a man instead of a fake, feminine broke-down pimp, he was fairly attractive.

"Marcus is coming by in a few minutes, you want to stay around and say hello?" Freddie asked. I was confused because I couldn't remember nobody by that name.. "Marcus," he repeated, noting my confusion, "the nigga that you was lookin' at yesterday and got jealous 'cause he took my number—him."

"Oh," I remembered. I wouldn't have minded seeing him if he weren't a switch hitter.

"Well, anyway, he said you was pretty and stuff and maybe you and him could get paid to do a show together."

"I don't do shows with dudes," I stated firmly.

"That's right. You play on the other team."

I looked at Freddie and shook my head. I had the right mind to slap him, but as I rolled my eyes, they landed on another sexy thug-looking dude who walked into the hotel. The guy smiled at me and licked his lips. I was about to forget all about Freddie and strike up a conversation with him until the same woman who opened the door to 112 butt-naked came in and grabbed the dude's hand. They walked to the counter, dropped two one hundred dollar bills on the table and walked right out. *Damn!*

The air was warm and dense as I left the motel. I didn't go far until the rain began to move in. I walked six blocks before I reached the Write On Bookstore. Although I couldn't buy anything, I figured I could get lost within the words of a book for awhile. The store was only large enough for fifty patrons to fit, though not comfortably, and was owned by an African woman who'd moved from Nigeria after her husband died four years ago. The store smelled of burning incense, and the air was extremely cold against my damp skin.

"Hi, there, again," she spoke in a rich accent.

"Oh, hey!" I pretended to be friendly. It wasn't that I didn't like the woman, I just had a lot on my mind.

"We have new titles in now," she told me with a smile.

"Where are they?"

"On that table there and over on the far wall. Some on sale," she remarked, accent thickening.

"Thanks," I replied shyly, then walked over to the far end of the bookstore that no one else occupied and browsed the titles along the wall, holding my chest tightly for warmth.

Since most of the work was produced by African-American authors, each cover revealed some part of me that I wanted back: the attractive woman stepping out of a limousine, a handsome man and a woman dressed in a skimpy bikini on the beach at sunset, and the urban model chick with glistening earrings and an erotic pose that accentuated her Coke-bottle frame. I looked down at the clothing I stole. The contrast was evident.

I studied the latest E. Lynn Harris and Eric Jerome Dickey book, then Kimberla Lawson Roby and J. California Cooper. I browsed the many titles on the new release rack until my eyes caught the attention of the third shelf and noticed a familiar work. It was San's book, *Operation: Survival.*

Perhaps her book was a sign; it seemed to laugh at me from the shelf, and dared me not to reach out and grab it. Nothing I tried could fill the inadequacies I faced, but I knew that San was somewhere enjoying her re-invented life with someone who actually cared about her. As for me, I was in a bookstore, tucked off into a dark corner, cold and alone and with no intentions of spending a single penny of the ten dollars I had tucked into my bra.

My life at that point was totally out of character for me. The worst part was admitting that I had nothing, but I knew that in order to dig myself from the hole, it would take a plan and a lot of action. I had no more time to waste.

The rain came down heavier than it did before I entered the store, but I began to feel claustrophobic, so I had to leave.

P l a y e d

There was a covered bus stop on the corner near the bookstore, so I figured I would be able to wait it out there. But where was I going to go? In order for me to rest my head somewhere, I needed more money. It was almost 5 o'clock, and it would soon be night. It was too hard trying to catch someone who would pay me for a peepshow. As much as I hated to admit it, my only avenue was Tiki.

I ran into the Korean-owned dry cleaners on the corner and asked to use the phone. I knew I would eventually have to replace the prepaid phone I got, but I needed way more than ten dollars in order to make that happen. Putting the phone up to my ear, Tiki answered on the first ring.

"Tiki?"

"Who is this?" she asked. I shook my head because I knew she was playing me. Tiki knew my voice, even if she didn't recognize the number that popped up on the screen. But I put aside my attitude. I knew that in order to get what I wanted, I had to play nice with her, but not too nice or it would come across as fake.

"I haven't talked to you all day," I began, "but was wondering what was up with tonight. Got something lined up?"

"Umm, I have a few people lined up, but—"

"But what?" I asked anxiously. I could feel the money and smell the double cheeseburger, fries and strawberry shake from McDonalds I was craving. *If I eat enough of them, I might be able to put some more curves back on my figure*, I thought.

"Sunny is in on this one."

I was irritated, stuck in an impossible situation. "Then, where the hell is my money?"

"Your money? What? What money?" Tiki spoke quickly.

"The hundred dollars Sunny stole from me—the money that was under the dress that she *also* stole from me."

"Come on, Taj, you knew screwing with her dude wasn't gonna make y'all friends, you know."

"I didn't know that was her man until after the deed was done. I thought Taye was screwing me. I didn't even know what Anthony looked like but that's beside the point. That ho was never my friend and I didn't know or give a damn about who *he* was. She can get over it and give me my money, or she can get her ass kicked!" I shifted from anxious to upset to irate in a matter of moments. I was ready to climb through the phone, strangle her and cry all at the same time. I just wanted a way out.

"Well, it is what it is, Taj," Tiki said calmly. I wondered if she had any remorse for allowing Sunny to take my stuff, but I knew better than to think about it for too long.

"I would never have done this to you."

"Yes, you have." Tiki hung up.

I stood there for a moment, not wanting to step out into the side-sweeping rain. Tiki was right. I left her hanging too many times to count—from when I was with San to when I was with James. In the same moment, I considered several people that I walked out on, including San and James. Karma served me well, and I got just what I deserved. But that thought only lasted a moment. Just as I found a break in the storm to walk outside, the phone rang.

"Tash? Tash?" the dry cleaner attendant called.

"Taj? That's me." I walked over and took the receiver from his hand. I was surprised that Tiki even bothered to call me back, let alone that quick.

"Meet me at the Greenbriar in about an hour."

"But that's all the way on the south side. How do you expect—"

"Look you gon' argue with me or you gon' try to get this money?"

"Yeah, I'll get there." We hung up.

I never understood what caused Tiki to change her mind, but I was grateful that she did. I called a taxi and hoped that the ten dollars would be sufficient enough to get me over the bridge. More importantly, I hoped that once I spent it, I would be able to earn it back—and then some.

Greenbriar was where local movers and shakers, promoters, business owners, and socialites would go for happy hour and live jazz. The spot was really upscale. I knew I wasn't dressed for the occasion, but I didn't have a choice. I looked down at the clothes I'd taken from the young ladies at the pool and knew I had to make it work.

I waited outside in the tiny summer dress and flip-flops while couples and singles hidden beneath umbrellas brushed past me in business attire—dresses, slacks, collared shirts and ties. I was looking in the opposite direction when someone grabbed my arm and rushed me to the corner, away from the view of others.

"What the hell are you doing?" Tiki was wearing a black cocktail dress that should have been classy, but her revealing breasts made her look like she was trying too hard.

"I was waitin' on you. What's up?" I responded.

"Girl, you look like a crackhead standing out here like this." Tiki held her umbrella over my head to shield her from the rain. "You messing me up."

I was ashamed, so I remained silent. It was written all over my face.

"How did you get here?" Tiki asked.

"Taxi dropped me off," I told her, pouting.

"OK, well," she looked out into the traffic, "I rode here with someone, but I got a spot at the Jax City Inn across the street. If you plan on pulling some people tonight for a show you'll need to go change." She pulled a hotel room key from her bag. "I have a bag in the closet. Find something in there. Room 105."

"OK." I grabbed the key from her hand, darted into traffic and crossed the street.

The hotel room was empty and nicer than the one we had the previous night. The air was freezing, so I turned off the air conditioner. Before going through Tiki's things to find something to wear, I rushed into the shower to wash away the day's filth. I blow-dried my hair and straightened it with Tiki's flat irons before putting on a short, pink-and-black halter dress that she had in her bag. I felt rejuvenated and even slightly sexy. I slid on her black pumps and left the room.

Please let this be it, I said to myself. *I need to get myself together.*

30

It had been so long since I'd gone looking for prospects that I thought I'd lost my touch. In the lounge there was standing room only; it was packed so tightly that it was nearly impossible to admire people's clothing. For once it seemed that men outnumbered women, but the women in attendance were still not pleased enough to flash a friendly smile toward me, another woman. They mean-mugged instead, even from a distance, obviously intimidated by what Tiki or I had to offer.

"Taj, this is Randy. Randy—Taj," Tiki introduced us and then sat on a stool between us.

"It's nice to meet you." I reached out to shake the man's hand, but he stepped around Tiki for something more.

"I'd rather hug you," he told me, reaching toward me. "You look so soft. It's nice to meet you, too." His light complexion made him appear biracial. The dimple on his right cheek was deep, and in my opinion it was his most attractive feature. His hair was curly, and although many women would have found him amazingly attractive, I thought he was too pretty.

"So, what you got going on tonight?" I asked.

"Taj, why don't you go and get us some drinks," Tiki interrupted.

I was puzzled, but I felt that she knew best in that instance. Besides, it was *her* party and I was just joining in.

"Sure." As I walked away, she leaned closer to him and spoke into his ear.

Space at the bar was limited. Women who'd been there since the lounge opened claimed their spot at the bar and knew that if they'd moved their seat would no longer be available. In this setting, for a desperate woman who was wearing someone else's attire, I felt confident and beautiful. The women at the bar must have gotten a whiff of it as well, because several of them moved in closer in order to close gaps and not allow room for me at the bar.

"Some women are so rude," a male voice said from behind me. "And they wonder why they're sitting alone." He was only an inch taller than me, but his height gave me a better view of his beautiful brown-sugar colored eyes.

I stared at him for a moment, not knowing what to say. "Why do you come here?" escaped my lips.

"Excuse me? Do I know you?" He tightened his expression.

"No. I'm sorry," I blushed. "I meant, how often do you come here?"

"Oh, not a lot." He was a little corny, but fairly attractive. "Do you?" he asked.

"Only with friends—just for a drink or two," I lied.

"I've never seen you here before."

One of the women left the bar, and I stepped forward in her place.

"What you drinking?" he asked.

"Umm, I'm thinking I'll get me and my girl some rum and

coke." I kept it simple in case he wasn't offering to buy me a drink.

"Bartender!" he yelled. "Let me have two rum and cokes, a Long Island, and two shots of tequila."

"It must be a special occasion." I smirked out of interest.

"Isn't every day?" He reached into his back pocket for his wallet.

"Well, what are you celebrating?" The bartender placed the shots in front of me and my new male companion then turned to make the other drinks.

"*We* are celebrating the beginning of a fun night together." He smiled as I tucked the One Free Drink tickets into the clutch I'd also borrowed from Tiki.

I was feeling his approach, but it had been a while since I engaged in conversation with a man who was not only appealing, but who wasn't just trying to pay me for sex. His actions reminded me of James and how the two of us were when we first met.

Tiki was still engaged in conversation, and I didn't want to throw a wrench into whatever plans she made with Randy by walking over with another dude, so I signaled for her to come to me.

"Is that your friend?" he asked when he noticed Tiki giving me the "one moment" signal.

"Yeah, here she comes."

As Tiki got closer, she looked uncomfortable. She openly fixed herself on the way over, and her facial expression made her look even more awkward.

"Hey, chick! What you got goin' on over here?" she asked as she reached across the bar for a napkin to wipe her glistening forehead.

I handed her a drink. "Tiki, this is—umm—I'm sorry. I didn't ask your name." I turned to look at him.

"Call me Dre."

"Well, Dre, it's nice to meet you." Tiki wiggled her way between the two of us. "Thanks for the drink." She clumsily lifted the glass into the air and splashed some of its contents

Played

onto the floor and over Dre's shoes. I didn't realize she was already lit or else I would've left her ass with Randy.

"Damn! Not my shoes, shawty." Dre was no longer the smooth talker he was moments earlier.

"Oh, my bad. Let me get that." Tiki reached over the bar again for another fistful of napkins, then kneeled down to clean his shoes.

I couldn't have thought of a tackier move. I knew that financially, and maybe even emotionally and spiritually, I was in a worse place than Tiki, but at least I still had a bit of class about myself in public. One thing I would never do was drop down to clean a man's shoes, even if I were responsible for spilling a drink on it. Putting my butt in the air and giving off the impression that I was easy was beneath me.

"That's alright, shawty. Get up."

When she did, her dress began to slip. Dre must have been as embarrassed for her as I was.

"Here, fix your dress," I offered, helping her to pull it back up.

Dre stared coldly at Tiki for a moment. "Do I know you from somewhere?"

"Who me?" She pointed at herself pathetically.

"I know you. I just don't know where from."

Most men who made that statement usually were at one of the performances Tiki or I put together. They would pretend to know us in an attempt to confirm *who* we were, then try their luck at getting some ass. Yet, I noticed there was something different about Dre. He seemed sincere—genuine—as though he was really curious about where he'd seen Tiki before.

"Well, let me know when you figure it out," Tiki said. She seemed defensive and began to pull me away. "You ready to go?"

I pulled her to the side. "How many do we have lined up for tonight?"

"About six. Why?" She started downing the rest of her drink.

"What do you think about inviting Dre?" I asked. Tiki looked over at him. "He seems harmless," I continued, "and I know he's good for the money." I wanted her to confirm or deny whether they had been intimate, because I really didn't want to mess around with a man Tiki had been with.

"Does he have friends with him?" she inquired.

"No, it's just him."

"OK. Tell him one hundred and fifty dollars. I'm tryna get paid tonight."

"I'll meet you across the street and I'll have him come with me." I handed her the room key and walked away. I rejoined Dre at the bar and was happy to see that he wasn't disappointed at seeing me again. "You'll have to excuse my friend."

"It's all good—some of my boys show out worse than that." He took a sip of his drink.

"Well, I'm gonna be leaving soon, and wanted to see what you were getting into tonight."

"This spot is going to close around midnight, so I'm probably gonna hit up another club or something. What? You tryna hang?" He eyed me.

"No. Are you tryna hang?"

"What's up?" He threw a couple dollars on the counter for the bartender.

"There's a little get-together tonight in the hotel across the street. The cost of admission is one hundred and fifty dollars." I smiled to soften the sound of the expense.

"Damn, it must be a great party." He smirked.

"You can say that."

"Is it going on right now?"

"It's waiting on you."

"Oooohhh—OK. Gotcha."

"Then, let's go. There's nothing better going on here."

I led him to the exit and waited as he walked toward the direction where his car was parked. He drove a black, late-model Chevy Corvette—not over the top, but impressive nonetheless. My self-esteem boosted for a minute as Dre

P l a y e d

acted like a gentleman and held the door open to let me have a seat. It had been a minute since I'd been on the passenger's side of someone else's ride, and I wanted to enjoy the moment. We were silent on the two and a half minute drive across the street. I had a thing for him, but didn't have expectations for what would come, aside from the fact that I'd get paid and possibly laid by someone I actually found attractive. At that point, I didn't care if his manhood was big or thick. I just wanted him to put it on me right.

"Here we go. We're in Room 105." I unfastened the seatbelt and stepped out of the car. I didn't want to get out, but I knew I had money to make and every minute counted. Dre remained inside for a moment, possibly preparing the cash required for entry.

"So, you gonna let me know what's up before I get in here," he asked, getting out, "or do you want me to be surprised?" A chirp indicated that the Corvette doors had been locked.

"Umm—a little of both." I stood in front of him and continued. "You're about to enter a room with a couple of other guys looking for a good time. All I ask is that you relax and try to enjoy yourself. Do you need anything before we go up?"

"I think I'm good, but I wouldn't mind another drink."

"I don't think there's any liquor in here, but we can run to the store, and you can pick up some there," I suggested. I wouldn't have minded stalling to get a few more minutes in the car. He shook his head, and we continued to walk toward the entrance. "One question: Are you a cop?"

He laughed. "I've never been asked that question before. Should I be?"

"Well—no. Are you?" I had to be sure. I may have been broke down and destitute, but I wasn't going to jail for anybody.

He scratched his head. "Then, no. I work for the Health Department. Been there ten years," he said proudly. He was obviously one of the few people I met who actually seemed to enjoy his job.

"Who would choose that as a career path? It couldn't be fun giving shots to whiny babies all day," I joked.

He laughed again. "That's not exactly what I do."

By the end of our brief conversation, Dre and I reached the hotel room. I knocked a few times, and Tiki opened it wearing only a pair of panties and high-heeled strappy sandals. She kissed me as I stood outside the door, which totally caught me off guard, but I figured she was putting on a show, so I went along with it.

"You missed me, huh?" I asked seductively.

"Yep. I sure did. Come in—your friend, too." Tiki walked slowly into the hotel room, and I followed behind her. Dre walked in last, eyebrows raised and obviously curious to see what would happen next. There were six other men in the room: two seated near the bed, one leaning on the dresser, and the remaining three on the balcony passing a joint. A neo-soul mixed CD was playing from the portable stereo Tiki used for most of our shows.

I turned to Dre and whispered closely to his ear, "Give me a moment. I want to get comfortable."

He stood in the shadows, near the door, away from Tiki and the other guests.

Beneath the vanity in the bathroom, I folded the tiny summer dress and underwear that I'd worn before. It was too late to handwash the garments to wear them again, so I had no idea what to put on. I wasn't wearing underwear because I refused to borrow a pair from Tiki. I paced the bathroom a bit, then undressed completely. I freshened up with soap and water, dampened my hair a bit in order to give it more of a kinky look, and tightened a towel around my body. I was more sober than I would've liked, but at least it would be beneficial.

There was a knock on the bathroom door. "Yes?" I called.

"Are you OK? It's taking you a minute," Dre said from the other side.

"Yeah, I'm coming out now." I opened the door, and he stood right in front of me.

Played

I smiled.

"Took you long enough, but I like what I see. What's next?" he asked.

"You'll see." I grabbed him by the hand.

Randy, to whom I was introduced at the nightclub, was sitting in a chair near the bed. Since he was the only other man I knew by name, I walked Dre over and introduced them, hoping to make him more comfortable. Dre wasn't like the other guys. It was obvious that he enjoyed being entertained, but even more apparent that he was a private person. In the company of the other men he stood away, and was mostly silent.

Since Tiki called all the shots, she insisted that she'd have fifteen minutes before each show for a solo act. That way she wouldn't have to split any tips that she earned. As she sat in the middle of the bed and removed every trace of clothing, the men gathered around her. She stroked herself seductively and moaned like a porn star.

I stood next to Dre as he watched, though his expression was not one of amusement. He stared at Tiki inquisitively. *Damn, maybe they have been together before,* I thought as I felt jealousy creep in. I moved to stand in front of him, pressed my butt against his crotch, tilted my head back, and asked, "You like it so far?"

"Yeah—yeah," he said, brushing me off without taking his eyes from the action in the room. I felt rejected, but was still motivated to move forward. I needed the money, and was focused on that.

I turned to face him, trying to tease him a little in hopes that we could hook up after the show. That way I would have an opportunity to rake in a little more cash. Maybe I could even make some extra tips during the show. But Dre had grown cold toward me as he continued to stare at Tiki. I was deeply envious, but I was also concerned that I wasn't going to make any money.

I kissed his neck. "What would you like me to do?" I whispered.

"Huh? Whhaaa—what?" he said, distracted.

I pressed my body firmly against his. "Would you like for me to join her? Would you like to see us together?"

"You mean—you're gonna have sex with her?" he asked.

"Mm-hmm." I nodded slowly in approval.

"So, is this what the two of you do?"

I slowly lifted one of my hands to loosen the towel tightly wrapped around me. As the towel began to drop, Dre grabbed my arm that held the towel in place so that it wouldn't fall.

"Wait!" he said, grabbing the towel and walking me into the bathroom.

"Oh, so you want some privacy, huh? You could've told me that crowds weren't your thing and I would've made plans for just you and me, baby," I said, continuing to flirt.

He didn't look at me, and I could almost swear that he wasn't listening. Instead, he stood in front of the door with his head down and his hand covering his mouth as if he wanted to speak, but was afraid to do so.

"Are you OK?" I asked.

"I could get into trouble for this."

"For what? Being here? You're safe with me, baby. I won't tell if you won't. These guys don't even know me, and I doubt any of them know you. They're friends of Tiki." I spoke quickly to help him feel comfortable, and to revive the mood. I was growing concerned by the second.

"That's not what I meant. I could get into trouble for what I am about to say." He paused for a moment. "But given the situation, and the risk that you run yourself, I have something to tell you."

The moment was suspenseful to say the least. *What could a total stranger really have to tell me?*

"OK, what is it?"

"Your friend in there—" he hesitated.

"Yeah, OK. What about her?" I attempted to rush him along.

"I know her," he said. I parted my lips to rush him along

P l a y e d

even further, but before I could speak, he quickly said, "Your friend in the other room is HIV positive."

There was silence. It seemed as if even the music in the other room stopped. When I became conscious of my surroundings again, everything came back into focus and I felt sick. I ran over to the toilet and dry heaved until I vomited. Dre stood still, watching me.

Tiki knows she's HIV positive. She's doing shows with me and putting me at risk? I couldn't believe the cards that were in my hand. All of a sudden, the spades I thought I had were turning into hearts, and they were breaking.

"She comes into the clinic regularly. That's why she looked so familiar. She knows she's sick, yet it's obvious that her lifestyle is extremely risky. I'm sorry to have to tell you."

"I'm sorry," I said as a long string of saliva ran from my mouth. "You can go." I pointed toward the door, head inches from the toilet.

"You want me to leave you here? Is there—"

"Just go. I can take care of myself." I vomited again. My anger was starting to rise, but I knew I had to play it cool, 'cause if I went ballistic on Tiki with all of those men in the room, they were likely to kill us both.

"Let me give you a ride somewhere," Dre pleaded. "I'll drop you off wherever you need to go. Just please, get dressed."

As devastating as the information I'd just learned was, I knew that if I left Tiki, any opportunity to work again would be out the window. In my state, I saw it as impossible to survive without money from the shows, but the thought of the numerous men and women I'd seen Tiki with, in addition to myself, I couldn't stomach being around her another moment.

"OK, let me get dressed." I walked over to the sink to rinse my mouth and stared into the mirror for a moment. There was nothing there—I couldn't see sickness or disease. Neither did I see any of it in Tiki. I quickly thought back. When I ended up in the hospital under James' care so long

Triple Crown Publications *presents...*

ago they must have tested me after I was raped. They never told me I had anything. Two months ago when I miscarried in the hospital they didn't tell me I had anything either. But maybe it hadn't shown up yet. Or maybe Tiki hadn't had it for very long. When did she have it? When was the last time we had sex?

I wanted to leave quickly to avoid confrontation from Tiki, so I didn't grab my bra or panties. I simply threw on the halter dress Tiki let me borrow, slid into my flip-flops, and was ready to go. Dre and I crept out of the bathroom. Tiki was still on the bed, but this time Randy was on top of her, putting his long thick member into her, unprotected, at the encouragement of the other guys. The way they moved gave off the vibe that they were familiar with one another. Dre and I walked out quietly so that we wouldn't distract anyone. That was the last time I planned to ever see Tiki.

P l a y e d

31

*N*umerous thoughts clouded my mind during the ride to nowhere with Dre. Fortunately, he didn't ask too many questions regarding me and Tiki, but he offered to take me into his place of business for HIV testing the following week. As much as I wanted to accept his offer, I felt better denying the fact that I was exposed to the disease in the first place.

"Where can I drop you off?" he asked.

We were headed toward downtown, so I figured I would come up with some location in that direction where he could drop me off to not inconvenience him.

"My cousin lives right over the bridge—downtown. You can drop me off there."

"Do you live there, too?" He was getting personal.

"I appreciate the ride and everything, but that's really none of your business."

I could tell that he was trying to comfort me and help me

feel less embarrassed about what occurred at the hotel, but it wasn't working. I was just ready to be rid of him.

"It's here on the right," I said, already tugging at the door latch before he could come to a complete stop. "Thanks again for the ride."

"Remember to come and see me to get yourself checked out. It's really important that you—"

"Thanks." I cut him off, jumped out of the car and slammed the door.

He drove off into the distance as I stood on the sidewalk. I folded my arms tightly, retaining as much warmth as I possibly could in a summer dress at a fifty-five degree temperature. It was after midnight, and most places of business were closed, but there was an after-hours restaurant on the corner that usually kept the doors open until 4:00 a.m. I headed that way, praying that no one would mind me sitting there until closing. Once I got to the restaurant, I told the waitress I was waiting for someone, and that worked.

For six nights after being dropped off by Dre, I camped out at a local shelter with battered and abused women or those with children and absolutely nowhere to go. In my condition, it wasn't difficult to convince them that I was abused in some way. After all, it wasn't a lie. It just didn't happen the day before as I told them. I held onto the two hundred dollars from the television I swiped and was doing all I could not to spend a single penny, but I knew there would come a time that I would have to get out of the shelter. Things were moving too slowly.

On the third night, the Duval County Health Department offered free health examinations, which included HIV testing. I decided to make use of the services and went to the lounge area to wait on my name to be called. I heard Dre's voice and when our eyes met, my heart skipped a beat.

I got up from my seat and walked into one of the offices that was being used for their portable lab.

"Nice to see you again, Taj," Dre said as he put my folder down and invited me to have a seat across from his desk. "I

Played

have your name finally."

I smiled. "And yours is Andreas. I take it that's what Dre is short for?"

"Yes, and you can still call me Dre."

As he beamed his pearly whites, my mid-region quivered. I looked to the door and thought, *He can still get me.* But then the memory of Tiki and Yayo, a guy whom we had a three-some with about a month ago, quickly crossed my mind. Fear struck my heart. *But if I got it, he probably wouldn't want me.*

"I wanted to let you know that we are going to be using the OraQuick Advance oral swab HIV test that is just as effective as the test you would get if we were to draw blood from you. After I perform the test, we will talk about your sexual history, and the risks of HIV, and within twenty minutes, we'll know your results."

I watched Dre open a fresh package, and then he encouraged me to open my mouth. He moved the top of the swab along the gums, and then placed it in a container.

Taking my paperwork and grabbing a pen that sat nearby, he asked, "How many sex partners have you had in the past year?"

I thought about James and Kelvin and Yayo. There were a bundle of other men that paid for random sex acts; then, there was Tiki.

"I'm not sure," I answered, hoping that Dre wouldn't judge me. "I think fifteen . . . or a number close to that. Mostly men—only one woman."

"Did you always have protected sex?"

"No."

Noting my answers, Dre asked me a few more questions involving the prostitution I was into and the types of sex acts I engaged in with men and women. It was strangely awkward since I had met him as a prospect, but I had no choice but to be honest with him. Afterward, he put a backpack on the desk and took out a few safe sex pamphlets, a plastic sandwich bag full of condoms, and other sex goodies. I looked at the bag and saw the logo of the health department and was shocked. I couldn't believe they had flavored lubricants and condoms. I just expected to get the free Lifestyle Condoms they'd given out for the past few years. By the end of our talk, twenty minutes had passed.

Checking the test, he noted more on the paper then looked at me. "Good news is that your test has come back HIV negative. However, because of your exposure to HIV, I recommend that you get two more additional tests within a year. Do another test about six months from today and another test a year from today. Limit your sex partners, and *always* use condoms. I would tell you to abstain from sex, but I am realistic about what you do and how you make your money. Encourage your partners to be tested as well."

I shook my head out of relief. One test down, and two more to go. At least the first test I passed with flying colors. I grabbed my bag of goodies and was on my way out of the door.

"I want you to be careful, Taj," Dre warned before I opened the door. "There are a lot of rumors out there about your girl purposely infecting others with the virus. Don't get caught up in that."

I acknowledged his warning and walked out of the door. I knew that from that moment on, I'd have to keep my distance from Tiki if I expected to survive.

Besides *taking* drugs, I never learned much about the drug game, so I never got into it to make money. But there was one exit strategy that I had yet to take: dancing. Although I was against stripping in nightclubs, it was my last resort, and I was at my low point. My greatest motivator was Tashawna, a young chick who was new to the area and living at the shelter. She had moved up from Orlando with nothing.

"So, where is it that you dance?" I asked her as we sat in the small cafeteria sipping on overly sweetened ice tea.

"Now, I'ma be real wit' you. I wanna see you getcho' money, but not where I'm makin' mines." Tashawna added another packet of sugar to her tea. I silently cringed to myself,

Played

as I desperately wanted to water mine down.

"I understand that." I couldn't be mad at her because I would've been the same way. Anyway, I already had a club in mind—one that I visited a few times over the years.

When I assured her that I'd be no competition for her, we discussed costumes and then took the 1 o'clock bus to the south side where most shops in Jacksonville were located. For the short amount of time that Tashawna was in Jacksonville, she seemed to know much about the city, from where the local Jaguars players resided to where the local drag queens would go to get injections for a plumper ass.

Tashawna was eclectic in all ways possible. She had skin as white as milk, but hair as kinky as Erykah Badu. She had tiny freckles that could only be seen at close range, and a brilliantly white smile that she exclaimed was afforded by one of her ex-boyfriends and a day-long visit to the dentist, all hidden behind the juiciest lips known to man. A part of me envied her—that was until she opened her mouth, and it became apparent how much of a hood chick she actually was. My motto was to do hood things, but not ever become a hood chick.

"It's dis spot right here." She pointed.

The bus let us off on the corner. We walked into a small lingerie shop that was disguised in what seemed like an industrial building.

"Good afternoon, ladies. Can I help you with something?" A petite woman stood behind a counter that looked more like a barricade. Behind her was a pile of costume material, some of them glitzy, neon-colored and bright. On the counter were baby wipes and body sprays.

"Umm, we jus' wanna check out whatchu got on sale." Tashawna shot past the counter and over to a rack toward the back of the store.

As I looked at prices, Wal-Mart's promise of guaranteed low prices kept calling my name. I shook my head as I picked up a box of a size 8 black, patent leather 5-inch stilettos and dropped them on the counter with my other items. The

woman at the counter rang them up and the total was nearly one hundred and twenty dollars. That left me with only eighty dollars to my name and no promise of being able to make more.

Tashawna was still browsing around the store when I left for the drugstore on the corner, where I purchased a pack of razors, baby oil, body spray, mineral makeup and lip gloss. This totaled fifteen dollars. By the time I left the store, Tashawna was waiting at the bus stop.

"What did you get?" I asked.

"Just some fishnets and dis bra thang that I can wear wit' somethin' else I got from here." Tashawna removed the items from the bag and raised them into the air in broad daylight at a busy intersection.

"OK, OK, that's cool," I mumbled, embarrassed.

We jumped on the next bus and headed back to the shelter. The shelter wouldn't allow the women to come in after 7 or leave in the middle of the night, so I showered, shaved, dressed and packed what little belongings I possessed into a plastic bag. I used the curlers belonging to another resident to spiral my bob, and then threw on the dress that I wore when I arrived. When I left for the evening, the plan was to make more than enough money to get a room for the night, so it would be unnecessary for me to return.

Played

32

The women inside the club sized me up as I walked in. My attire was that of a 12-year-old, but I had the face of a current-day model. My confidence had shown in spite of what I was wearing and the fact that I was carrying a now torn, raggedy plastic bag filled with my belongings.

"How you doing tonight?" a tall, bulky guy greeted at the entryway.

"Good. How you doing?" I attempted to flirt.

Just then a young white woman emerged from some other part of the club.

"You dancin' tonight?" She opened a notebook and picked up a pen.

"Yes." I became nervous. I was about to embark on a journey that I'd never be able to walk back from.

"What's your name?" She placed the pen on the pad.

"My name?" Just then I realized that I hadn't come up with

Triple Crown Publications *presents*...

one.

"Yes, your name. I don't have all night. We're busy."

I looked around quickly for a clue and noticed the shoes the bouncer was wearing. "Jordan!" I exclaimed.

The young woman wrote "Jordan" in the book. "OK, Jordan—that will be thirty dollars." I looked at her with anticipation.

"Thirty dollars? For what?"

"Your bar fee—twenty dollars before 7:00 p.m., thirty dollars before 10:00 and fifty dollars after that, and even more on busy nights. This your first time?"

"Yes." I swallowed my pride and reached into my top and pulled out the money. I was now down to thirty-five dollars.

The dressing room was empty. Twenty small lockers lined the room, most of them bearing locks. I didn't have one, but figured since I had nothing of value, it wouldn't hurt to leave my things unattended.

As I began to undress, another dancer walked into the room.

"What's your name?" she asked. She had an extremely high-pitched voice and skin so dark it was hard to discern where her dark hair began and ended.

"Jordan," I remembered, fastening my shoes.

"Well, I'm Mocha." She entered the combination on a lock 3 feet away from me.

"How long you been dancing here?" I inquired.

"Six months. It has its good nights. Like tonight—it's Jerome Rogers' birthday. They all wasted so they spendin' big money." Mocha wiped her black licorice-colored body with a towel and sprayed an enormous amount of fruity smelling body spray, then left.

I spent another fifteen minutes in the dressing room, guzzling a triple shot of cheap tequila that cost nearly twenty dollars—I was down to fifteen dollars.

There was never a moment that I felt I would have to resort to exotic dancing, so I was totally unprepared for the task. Walking out into the main area, I saw women winding

P l a y e d

193

their bodies around poles, some disappearing into the ceiling before crashing down into splits. I was a novice, so I knew I had to at least pretend to know what I was doing. Immediately going to the stage would've been a dead giveaway, so I made my way around the club, waiting for one of the guys to get my attention. It took almost a half hour before I was requested for a lap dance.

He said his name was Keith—a tall, dark-skinned guy with really bushy eyebrows, but there was no point in asking if that was his real name or not. I knew I couldn't make my ass jump like the other girls, so I kept a slow sensual pace regardless of what song played. Keith wasn't complaining. Four songs later, Keith was still unwilling to let me move on to the next patron. A quick trip to the VIP lounge sealed the deal and guaranteed that I would be taking home every penny he had in his pockets. I knew that women turned up the heat in private, so I allowed touching, some rubbing, and even flashed him some of my special treats. But I cut it short to prevent getting caught, fined or possibly escorted out.

It was almost 4 in the morning, and I managed to only dance for three guys. They paid pretty decent, primarily because they were a part of a group and probably didn't want to be the broke nigga in the crew.

The club was emptying rapidly, so I called a cab to make sure that I wouldn't be the last one standing after it closed. I walked into the dressing room, grabbed my things, thanked God that nobody went through my stuff or that nothing came up missing and went into a restroom near the exit.

In the stall next to mine, I heard someone struggling to get dressed. It was possibly an elbow or knee that kept hitting the stall's walls to which she would respond with an "Ouch!" or "Damn!"

We both exited the stalls counting our earnings. In all, I pulled in six hundred and forty-three dollars and was overly satisfied. It was the greatest amount of money I touched in months. I vowed that as soon as I got the chance, I was going to Wal-Mart.

"You ready to tip out?" she asked. It was the only white girl that danced in the club. Of course she stood out in the sea of black dancers with huge asses, but aside from the cheap red lipstick and her attempt to rock long cornrows, she was pretty. She could have passed for Christiana Aguilera's twin but she shook her ass like it belonged to Shakira.

"Tip out?" I chuckled. "Please. Ain't nobody taking this money home but me."

The girl looked serious. "They not letting you walk past them without a transaction."

"So what? You're bathroom enforcement or something?"

"No. I'm like you—don't wanna hand over the cash, but *just* like you, I have to hand over the dough."

"Then you ain't nothing like me," I said and tucked the money into my underwear.

"You'll see," she retorted.

I slipped out of the bathroom, heading toward the parking lot.

Before exiting, the club owner's wife spoke from behind, standing at the counter. "Hey, Jordan. You tip out?"

"Nah, not yet. I'm just checking on my ride."

"Make sure you tip out before you leave."

It was more of a demand than a request and the large bouncer standing near the exit doors made it more apparent.

Just then, I noticed the taxi pull up in front of the club. I walked back into the restroom, and the woman was still in there packing her belongings.

"How much are you tipping out tonight?" I asked her.

"A good one-fifty," she responded.

"Damn! I can't do it. I need this money."

"I feel you, girl. It's a lot of money to just hand over to people who've just been standing around or sitting on their asses all night. I work hard, but you know there's no way around it." She threw her bag over her shoulder and proceeded to leave.

"Wait!" I stopped her, speaking quickly. "I know a way we can make more money than this without all the work."

"I'm not with trickin'. That's for the other hos."

Played

"No—a show." I wanted to explain further, but I couldn't. "I can't tell you everything now, but I can guarantee that it will work."

"What you want from me? I don't know you like that," she said with an attitude.

What I wanted was a guarantee that if I wasn't allowed back in the club, I had another way to make money.

"You know—you're right. I don't even know your name. But what I do know is that we're both some money-makers. Have it your way."

I dropped the plastic bag of belongings that I was carrying, opened the heavy restroom door and peeked out in both directions. There were at least seven people standing in the main area, including two bouncers and the club owner's wife. I dashed for the door.

"Jordan! Jordan!" A woman called out, but I didn't turn to look.

I pushed the heavily tinted glass doors open, grabbed the handle of the taxi door and slid in. As I attempted to pull the door shut behind me, it didn't budge. The woman from the bathroom tugged on the other end.

She jumped in and slammed the door. "Drive!" I demanded.

We sped away, anxious and nervous at first, and then laughing once we were at least a mile away. The white girl said her name was Kristal and that she moved from a small city in Virginia three years earlier. She had been dancing ever since. Kristal explained that most of her money went back home to her mother who was fighting against cancer. She lived in a studio apartment and didn't own a vehicle. All of these things proved that she had a big heart and was a real down to earth chick. It didn't force me to trust her immediately, but I could give her some leeway.

Kristal and I discussed performances and she asked as many questions as she could think to ask. The plan was to meet at the Marriott, where I would be staying that evening and the following morning, so we could organize our first show. Before dropping Kristal off at her apartment, she wrote her phone number on a dollar bill with the taxi driver's pen and handed it to me.

"See you tomorrow," she said exiting the taxi.

After paying the fare, I checked into the hotel and happily showered with their cheap soap and slathered on their thin lotion, knowing that the following day I would be able to afford products of my liking. I slept peacefully in the dark and silent room. I didn't even bother to turn on the television. My thoughts were entertaining enough.

The following morning, Kristal met me in the lobby of the hotel. We spoke over free croissants and coffee.

"So, who do you know in the area?" I asked her, adding three packets of sugar to a cup of dark coffee.

"A few people ... all business men though. And—" she hesitated.

"And what?" I asked without patience.

"And they're all white. I don't know if they would be good candidates for our show. I mean—"

Thoughts raced quickly through my mind as Kristal continued to speak.

"Wait. That's a good thing!" I said, cutting her off. I had just realized that we'd stumbled upon a wonderful opportunity to make a lot of money.

"How?" Kristal asked, curious.

"One word—fantasy. A black and a white chick getting it on is a major fantasy for some men—it's something that's forbidden, especially in person."

I could see her wheels turning. Then, something finally clicked. "Yeah—like salt and pepper."

"O...K..." I said, balking at her corniness. "Maybe, umm, something like that. Anyway, do you have a way to get ahold of them? How many numbers do you have?"

"Well, I have two, but they're guaranteed to draw a larger crowd."

"It's almost 9 now. Let's make the phone call in an hour to allow them to gather a following. We'll take a count at that

Played

point before we move forward."

It felt like we were high school girls plotting something fun and forbidden.

I welcomed Kristal back to my hotel room where I briefed her on procedures for the performance. We basically reenacted scenes from one cheesy porno or another that we'd both seen in the past. She was fun to play with and our potential to make money together was vast. Since Kristal provided the contacts and I provided the hotel room, we arranged to split all of our earnings down the middle.

By noon, a phone call confirming at least a dozen attendees gave us the go-ahead to shop for costumes and alcohol for that evening's guests. We immediately took a taxi to the mall where we bought lingerie and fancy, strappy shoes. We also made a pit stop at the nearby Wal-Mart where we both bought the personal items that we desperately needed. We purchased two hundred dollars worth of alcohol, which we thought would appeal to our clients' tastes, and not before long it was showtime.

Kristal and I dressed and showered in the hotel room. I removed Kristal's cornrows and she washed her hair and straightened it. It made her more attractive, but more importantly it was suitable for the fantasy we were looking to bring to life.

The guest arrived, but the atmosphere was different than it had been in the past. The men were more standoffish and were reluctant to talk to me. However, when Kristal finally emerged from the bathroom, the tension in the air thinned. She walked in and kissed me on the lips. The onlookers' eyebrows raised, an indication that they were pleased by what they saw. The lights were lowered, and Kristal and I delivered a magnificent performance. Before the first segment ended, ten and twenty dollar bills littered the edge of the bed.

33

After returning to the hotel one day from hours filled with shopping, manicures and pedicures, Kristal and I felt that we deserved to go out and celebrate, so I called a taxi to take us downtown to a riverfront restaurant. We earned nearly two thousand five hundred dollars each in one evening, and were ecstatic to say the least. In spite of all the ways I considered to spend the money, what was most important was the fact that I was able to *make* money again. Kristal's thirst for quick, easy cash nearly guaranteed that I made a new, secure partner and that our time together wouldn't be limited.

"So, where we goin'?" Kristal bopped around the hotel room, giddier than anyone I'd ever seen.

"Someplace nice! A fine dining experience is long over-due."

"Oh, so we're going to Red Lobster?" she asked with a huge smile. At that moment, I was happy we didn't get paid for intelligence or good taste.

"No. Somewhere nicer," I said, fastening my earring.

"Oh, OK. Well, we have the money so it doesn't matter."

We arrived at Yiari's Steakhouse and dashed into the restaurant to escape the dropping temperatures outside. The hostess immediately escorted us to a table in the very center of the restaurant, and we both ordered a glass of wine. For the first time in months, I felt confident and sexy without having to rely on someone else—without having to borrow or steal.

Kristal and I split a shrimp appetizer and ordered fresh caught fish dishes for entrees. In spite of our laughter and good cheer, we discussed the previous nights' shows and future shows—things we would do differently. I offered her a few pointers, and Kristal happily accepted the constructive criticism.

"Wait. Don't look now," Kristal interrupted between another pointer I attempted to give her.

"What?" I placed my wine glass on the table.

"O-M-G. He is so hot, too." She smiled big and looked from the corner of her sparkling eye.

"Black or—"

"Black, girl. Come on now. You know the brothas is where it's at."

"Uh oh—looka here! Li'l vanilla girl likes chocolate men. That's cute," I said playfully, but inside I was annoyed. I didn't know how I felt about competing with Kristal for sexy, attractive black men. Dancing in front of them and doing shows was one thing, but dating them was something entirely different. In my subconscious, I hoped that a black man would never pick a white woman over me.

"Ah, man, he's walking over here! Uh oh—" Kristal smirked and lifted her glass to her lips.

Within seconds someone tapped me on the shoulder. "Excuse me, Taj?"

I turned slowly, fearing the worst. He was tall. Wearing a pair of dark-washed jeans and a navy blue collared shirt, Kelvin towered over me. Bittersweet memories of our affair popped into my mind as I felt my mouth prepare to drop open.

"Oh, wow!" I stood up quickly and regained my composure, then leaned in and gave him a hug. I didn't let my feelings be known for the moment. "How have you been?" I flashed a smile. He smelled as good as I remembered.

"I've been good—but not as good as you I see." He examined me from head to toe but focused hardest on the black, form-fitting dress I wore, which revealed every curve of my body. It was the best thing I'd worn since I was thrown out of James's house.

"It's been a while." I continued to smile. The last I heard from or saw Kelvin was in a fancy hotel room the morning after we made passionate love, which resulted in an ectopic pregnancy, surgery, and ultimately losing everything I worked for. And Kelvin didn't even know. I couldn't blame him though. His wrist and ears glistened, and I nearly melted. To be reminded of such luxury and comfort was most definitely appealing.

"You know," he said, "I tried to call you a few times, but I could never get through to you, so I figured that you changed your number." He stood there with his eyebrow cocked, waiting for me to respond.

"Yeah, exactly," I lied. I had tried calling *him* several times and not once did he answer. "How has the real estate business been treating you?" I waited for him to continue telling stories.

"Come on now. I know that you don't really believe that's all I do. It's been a while now."

"Well, *you* tell *me*." My tone became serious, but he laughed it off.

"You know I'm a ballplayer. I didn't have to tell you that, but for your sake, I'll play along." I pretended to look surprised. Then he said, "Here, take my number—and use it. Hopefully, I'll hear from you this evening."

He handed me a personal business card and kissed my cheek. When he walked away, Kristal grilled me about who he was and how long I'd known him. I explained that he was an old fling—someone I was over. But in my mind, I was thinking of a way to get him back and solidify my status as Jacksonville's baddest chick.

Kristal and I took a taxi back to the hotel, but not before I picked up a bottle of Riesling and a few wine glasses from a local liquor store. Kristal wasn't ready to end the night, and neither was I, so I called Kelvin.

"Hey you," I said when he answered.

"Hmm, let me guess who this may be. Kim? Tracey? Michelle?"

"What? OK, never mind." I went to hang up the receiver when I heard him yelling on the other end.

"Hold on! Wait! Wait! Taj, I know it's you."

"What?" I asked with an attitude.

"Wow—since when were you not able to take a joke?"

"I don't have time for silliness, Kelvin."

"OK, let's switch up the subject, because for some reason you're a *little* touchy." He paused briefly. "It's been a minute, Taj. Let's get up tonight."

"Tonight? Umm—I don't know about that."

"Well, what else you have to do? Where you at right now? I'll swing by and get you."

"I'm at the Marriott Southend."

"What you doing over there? Cheating on me?"

I had to think quickly. "Umm—no. I'm . . . uh, here visiting some friends. I relocated to Atlanta, so when I come into town this is usually my chill spot. You know, me and my homegirl."

"I see. I see. Well, let me come through and scoop you."

"No, not tonight. I'm chillin' with a friend, and we're both a little toasted, so I'm calling it a night. How about lunch or dinner tomorrow?"

"I don't have a problem with you having a buzz. You know that."

"Why? So you can take advantage of me? Please. Lunch or dinner?"

"Dinner—and hopefully some dessert," he said.

"We'll see about that." I disconnected the call and poured another glass of wine.

Triple Crown Publications *presents* . . .

Even though I was excited about seeing Kelvin, I just wanted to enjoy the evening without worries or cares, for I found peace for a change and believed everything would be uphill from that point forth.

The next morning I wanted to rent a car, but without a permanent residence or the driver's license that Sunny also had stolen, I had no choice but to call a taxi to take me to the hotel Freddie was working in to show off my upgrade.

My bob was fierce and freshly done and now had a nice bounce to it when I shook my head. My skin reeked of cucumbers and melons, and I was in my respectable Etruscan Red SONOMA life + style Floral Empire Dress with my brown SONOMA life + style Brinna peep toe heels that I got on sale at Kohl's. I felt pretty good walking into the hotel.

As I entered, I was amazed to see Freddie and Marcus standing at the counter hooting and hollering at something on the television screen. Instead of clacking my heels, I subtly took a step closer. Looking up at the screen, the naked woman and thugged out dude were recognizable even as their bodies clashed with the sounds of their lovemaking amplified on the security screen. It was the couple I'd seen when I was here last.

I shook my head and forced a cough. Strangely, I got a quick thrill watching Marcus move his hand quickly and Freddie trying to stuff himself back into his pants and turn around to face me.

"Well, damn," Marcus said, "I see you are better and looking lovely today."

"Thank you," I blushed at the compliment. I didn't have to think about which way Marcus swung; I'd definitely give him some.

"Bitch, you owe me fifty dollars," Freddie exclaimed.

I was shocked. "What you mean I owe you fifty dollars? You didn't give me no money for me to owe you fifty dollars. Boy, bye."

"You stole Tiffani's sundress, and her bra and panties, you

P l a y e d

203

nasty little girl you." Freddie moved from behind the counter and pointed his finger in my face. His mannerisms didn't match the Encye shirt and baggy pants he flossed. He turned his palm up and demanded, "So, just give me my money, and go on about your business."

I moved Freddie's hand out of my face. "I don't owe you no money. If anything, *you* owe *me* one hundred dollars, a new black sundress, and a fake Gucci purse 'cause that's what your girl Sunny stole from me." I rolled my eyes and crossed my arms to emphasize my point.

"I didn't have nothing to do with that," Freddie spoke fast as he put a hand on his hip. It was hard to believe that a moment ago, he was trying to get off watching a couple in the hotel trying to get their freak on.

"Whatever!" I threw my arms in the air.

"Yeah, whatever," he recanted. Freddie rolled his eyes and walked back around the counter to turn the television off. He then took out a book that caught my eye, temping me to take a closer look. "Maybe selling them old rags is how you got your hair did." Marcus chuckled as he tried to look over Freddie's shoulder.

"No, I got my money when I went to your mama's house and offered to donate these." I pulled my dress from the top and flashed my breasts in front of him, partly in an effort to see whether Freddie would jump into Marcus' arms. I could've used a good laugh.

"Well, if that's all you got then you don't got much," Freddie imparted, dismissing my D-cups verbally but looking at them like he wanted to cop a feel. "Whatever woman is fortunate enough to meet my mama, she's gonna have to be educated beyond high school and not working a corner and doing shows."

I scrunched my face and lowered my voice. "I didn't think you liked women."

"I didn't know you liked women either until Tiki sat on your face and was riding you like a cowgirl. Yee-haw." Freddie jumped up and pretended to throw a lasso in the air.

"Whatever."

"Yeah, whatever." Freddie picked up the book and handed it to me. It was *Operation: Survival*, and I briefly wondered what San and Seymone were doing.

"No, thanks," I said quickly.

I'd had enough: I turned around and sashayed out of the hotel.

I was almost to the cab when I felt a hand grab my arm. I was about to punch whoever it was when I looked up and saw that it was Marcus on the other end. Upon our faces meeting, he backed off and let go.

"I just wanted to give you my number, so we can chill sometimes or whatever." He passed a card from his hand to my fingers. When he flashed his smile, I almost fell for the line. I gave him the card back.

"Thanks, but I'm not interested."

I got in the cab and closed the door, instructing the driver to take me back to the Marriott.

The following evening, Kelvin pulled up in the same Hummer he was driving when we first met. He parked directly in front of the entryway, exited the car and opened the door for me to climb in.

"Good evening, gorgeous," he said as he took my hand.

"Oh, come on. It's a little too late for you to start spitting game."

"You know how to kill a mood now, don't you? Just smile for me. It's all you have to do."

He was right. I had become bitter, but I didn't want to ruin the evening because of my attitude. For once, I was with someone who was genuinely interested in me.

On the passenger seat was a bouquet of flowers: a combination of roses, lilies, and some others I didn't know the names of. I picked them up and smiled gaily. "These are beautiful."

"Not as much as you are," he responded.

Kelvin made reservations at a four-star restaurant near the

Played

beach. The atmosphere was exquisite. There were more freshly cut flowers, a wonderful aroma, and a warm dim lighting
that created a nice ambience and caused skin to glow.

We spent the evening discussing our history; the late-night
rendezvous and sexual escapades. He discussed a woman
that he dated for a short amount of time in Denver, but
explained that the relationship ended weeks earlier. He talked
about moving on to a woman that he could trust and be free
to be himself around.

"Dinner was great. Thank you." I wanted to be flattered,
but I was ready to change the subject.

"Thanks for joining me. It's been a while, and we really
needed this opportunity to catch up with each other." He
paused for a moment and took a sip of wine. "So, what's
next?"

"I don't know. I don't have anything to do until morning."

"Then, that means we have all evening then, right?"

"I guess so." I smiled.

"Then, let's get out of here." He took my hand.

Kelvin had purchased a condo that overlooked the St.
John's River. There were ceiling-to-floor windows throughout
the space without a single blind, curtain, or shutter. It was
possible for people to stand on the banks of the river and peer
directly into his condo and easily watch him in the living
room, kitchen, or the master bedroom. The walls were as
white as new linens and the wood floors shined throughout
his home.

"This is beautiful," I said, walking over to peer through the
window.

"Yeah, that's the reason I bought this place." He poured us
a glass of Pinot.

"You bring a lot of women here, huh?"

"What? Why would you ask that?" He grinned.

"Wine. That's not usually a man's choice of alcohol."

"I like it with my dinner," he replied.

"You've never cooked in that kitchen. There is not a single
thing out of place."

Triple Crown Publications *presents...*

"Well, that's my story, and I'm sticking to it." He laughed it off and joined me in the living room.

We sat on his plush, black couch and stared out into the night sky. We talked, then whispered a little, then our words turned into kissing. It was so familiar and all of the emotions came rushing back, but I wasn't as free as I was before. I had to act with some restraint, because my survival meant I couldn't get played again.

He leaned back on the sofa, then lifted my comparably small frame up to his chest where I rested my head. I listened as he inhaled and exhaled for a while and not before long, we both were asleep.

34

The following morning I had a serious case of déjà vu. From the floor to the ceiling, from the chill in the air to the sound of a dripping faucet, I saw the surroundings before, in some other space and time. It made me uneasy initially, given that I expected something negative to occur, but I brushed it off as silliness and went on about my day.

My evening with Kelvin was beyond amazing, but there was work to be done and money to be made. So, after promising to call him at the end of the day, I left him and met Kristal back at the hotel the following morning. We planned a fifteen-person party at the most exquisite resort in Jacksonville Beach, Cypress Suites, and prepared to charge each attendee two hundred and fifty dollars. Our earnings without tips would have been at least one thousand eight hundred and seventy-five dollars each at the end of the night.

After our plan was in place, Kristal and I rented a Charger

Triple Crown Publications *presents...*

for the week—the first car I rented in over a year—and went shopping for our wardrobes and the customary alcohol that would be required that evening.

The show was set to begin at nine o'clock that evening, so after arriving back at the hotel around 8:30, Kristal and I prepared as quickly as we could. I showered, loosely curled my bob, and put on the purple lace bra and panty set I'd purchased. I felt good knowing that, unlike the previous shows for the past couple of months, I was gonna start this one right.

"Damn! We forgot the ice," Kristal said, struggling to apply moisturizer in a hurry.

Initially, I figured that a request for room service would send a housekeeper or bellhop that could bring anything we needed to the room, but I knew that it would take twice the amount of time than if either one of us got it ourselves.

"Since I'm finished, I can run down and get it before anyone gets here," I offered, throwing on a robe and grabbing the ice bucket.

No one had arrived by the time I got back at the room, so I checked the prepaid phone I'd bought for messages. Kelvin called to tell me that he would be hanging out with his old manager and some friends that evening, and that he wanted to see me at the end of the night if I was free. It excited me to the point that I had butterflies almost instantly.

By the time the voicemail ended, there was a knock on the door. Three white men dressed in slacks and collared shirts entered the room. Kristal kept them company until three more men waltzed in, and another three, and another until there were twelve men. The last three were still missing, but it was already 9:15, and we had to begin.

Kristal laid down the rules while I approached the men near the door.

"We're expecting three other guys. I'll pay you fifty dollars if you let them in and collect their money."

"OK, no problem," a tall, bald guy responded.

I joined Kristal on the bed as I spoke. Within minutes we were naked, and Kristal began to massage my back. I lay at

Played

the end of the bed with my face toward the crowd, moaning and sensually maneuvering my body while Kristal massaged me. The hotel room door opened, and I wanted to be sure that the attendee near the door followed my instructions and collected the money. He did. The first two men that walked into the room handed over a stack of cash, but it was when the third man appeared that I realized how small the world actually was. It was Kelvin, the only black man in the room, standing near a guy wearing a suit and tie. And at that very moment, I wanted to be invisible.

I closed my eyes tightly, hoping that I could wake up. The day had turned into a nightmare. There was no way that I could talk my way out of this one; the show had to go on.

He watched as Kristal and I role-played. I tried my hardest to block him out, but I took note of everything he did, from how many times he refilled his drink to how close he actually came toward the bed. And although I was afraid to talk to him, I was relieved when the show was over. Immediately I jumped up from the bed, put on a robe, and went after him. I led him into the bathroom by the hand and closed the door.

"So, this is what's up." He laughed, staring at himself in the mirror.

I was relieved that he wasn't angered, although a little confused. "It's not funny! Don't laugh," I commanded as I tightened my robe.

"Don't try to hide your li'l goodies now. I've already seen 'em—well, hell, everybody *in* here seen 'em." He became serious, tightening his mouth and looking at me expectantly.

"I didn't mean to lie to you, Kelvin. I've just been in a tough spot lately and—"

"No need to explain," he cut me off. "You know, you could have told me about this."

"How was I supposed to know that?"

"You couldn't have."

"Well, can we meet up tonight? You know, get together?"

He laughed sarcastically. "Really? You need a shower—I need some time. I have a meeting first thing in the morning, and then I'm free in the afternoon. Hit me up then."

"OK," I replied. I felt ashamed, but not as bad as I before considering I had cash in my pockets.

After Kelvin left, I went into the room to count the cash with Kristal. We made more than the amount we expected, and for that, I was elated.

The next morning, I woke up and decided that I wanted to take a nice soothing bath with the Fresh Lavender 3-in-1 Bubble Bath, Shampoo & Body Wash that I purchased from Wal-Mart. Kristal was out on errands, so I had the place all to myself.

I set the water to the appropriate setting and poured the contents of the bottle in, as instructed. Watching the bubbles sprout to life brought back memories of my childhood, when I always took refuge in the ability to take a bubble bath as a treat to myself. I liked covering my chest with the bubbles and wrapping a towel around my head just like the white women did in the bath commercials. As the tub filled with water, I discarded my clothing and stepped my foot inside. I sat down, laid back, breathed deeply and closed my eyes.

Though I wasn't asleep, my body was so relaxed that I escaped this world and began to think about making love to James. I didn't want to remember how smooth, gentle and attentive James was with my body, but I couldn't help it. I blinked my eyes to get away from those thoughts, and next thing I knew I was thinking about Kelvin's lovemaking. He wasn't sensual like James. He was aggressive, but in a good way.

Thinking about their hard bodies and the way each of them felt caused me to subconsciously move my hand lower and slip a finger inside myself. But I didn't get a chance to move them; out of nowhere I felt my body jolt out of the water. I opened my eyes and a strong hand covered my mouth to prevent me from screaming. As my body was dragged out of the tub, I glanced at the mirror and saw Randy looking at me. My mind flashed to Tiki, and I knew I was in trouble.

P l a y e d

He dragged me out of the bathroom and threw my damp, naked body on top of the queen-sized bed. "Where is that bitch!" Randy shouted.

"I don't know!" I made a wise move to play dumb with him. I didn't need him going ballistic, hauling off and hitting me in the face. I still needed to make a few ends, and I had a long way to go before I got myself together.

"You know that bitch has AIDS?" Randy barrelled.

"She has what?" I screeched, pretending to be surprised and sickened. I wasn't going to tell him the difference between HIV and AIDS. Scared sick, I tried to get up and run to the bathroom because I had to vomit, but Randy caught me and threw me back on the bed where I let go of my insides. "That bitch has AIDS!"

I pulled my act together and hoped it would convince him that I was just as innocent as he was.

"Yeah, she has AIDS!" Randy roared as he paced frantically around the room. "And she gave that mess to me. I know it was her 'cause she was the only chick I hit raw, and I don't get down with that faggot-ass down-low shit!" I could see the tears forming in his eyes, and I could've sworn smoke was coming from his face. "I heard a few other niggas Tiki been doing shows with and some bitches got that shit, too. I heard about y'all nigga-killin' bitches doin' a show in this hotel room. Are you giving folks that shit, too?"

"No!" I trembled with fear. I knew in my heart I was telling the truth, that I didn't have it. But even if my results *did* come up positive down the line, I would never give someone a package intentionally. I had more class than that. "I promise you . . . I didn't know about Tiki having AIDS. And I just went for my test results last week. If you let me get up, I can even show you my paper."

"Naw, bitch. You just tell me where they are."

"In my bag." I pointed to my black Jansport backpack that had some of my dresses, bras and panties, and other belongings inside. I felt violated as this man opened my bag and threw everything inside it on the bed and on the floor. Finally he found the paper he was looking for, read it, got angry and crumpled it up. I didn't know whether I should've apologized to Randy or console him or just wait in fear, but I was saved from these thoughts when he suddenly when he jumped on the bed and started choking me. I struggled to breathe and found that I couldn't scream if I wanted to. My weakening body left me defenseless.

I could hear a zipper unzipping and felt his hardened manhood against me. *Oh no!* I cried in my mind as fresh tears fell from my face. *He's gonna try to give this damn thing to me.* I tried to move and get away, but what happened next surprised me. I heard something break and liquid was squirted all over the bed. I closed my eyes to avoid getting whatever it was on my face, but before I closed my mouth, I could taste what appeared to be wine. Randy's body fell on me. His penis, dripping with precum, was just centimeters from entering my walls.

"Girl, I got you," Kristal said as she pulled me from under Randy. "I came in when I saw him grab you from the tub, so I hid in the hall and called security. They're on their way up here now." She escorted my shaking frame, dizzy with shock and fear, to the bathroom to help me clean my face. Next, I heard footsteps as police commanded that everyone freeze. I just leaned into Kristal's shoulder and cried.

"Ma'am, are you OK?" I could hear the man ask. Kristal quickly grabbed a body towel and wrapped me in it. Nodding, I took a damp face cloth and cleaned the wine from my face.

We stood through the rest of the police's questioning and tried to comply as best we could. Eventually I opened my eyes, and even though I could see the attractive man whom I recognized from my first show with Kristal, I couldn't hear a word he was saying. I just wished I was in James's or Kelvin's arms, with all this mess behind me.

P l a y e d

213

35

It was almost 5 in the evening the day after my ordeal with Randy, and I was nervous. I decided not to press charges for the attempted rape, but the hotel chose to for the breaking and entering and trespassing. I briefed Kelvin on the situation, and he agreed to take me out in order to take my mind off of things.

Although I found no shame in performing shows in front of numerous men for money, I was embarrassed when Kelvin discovered my secret. With the exception of San, my personal relationships had been kept separate from my business as best as they could, and now in Kelvin those two sides of me had met. Doing shows was how I met Randy, after all, and if I hadn't been performing I would have never wound up in my current predicament. For the first time, I felt I had to come clean.

Kelvin answered the door shirtless, wearing only a pair of basketball shorts. Every inch of muscle was tight and bulging.

Triple Crown Publications presents...

Licking my lips, I entered and realized that the room smelled of household cleaning products blended with the scent of vanilla.

"I was just cleaning up the place." He pointed to the sofa, an indication that he wanted me to sit. He walked over to the bedroom and closed the door. "So, what have you been up to today, money maker?"

"Ah ha, that's not funny." I removed my bag from my shoulder; my bangles made a racket as I positioned myself comfortably on the sofa.

"No, seriously—tell me, how does it work? How long you been doing that?"

"Umm—" I thought. I wanted to be as honest as possible, and I wanted to feel safe. "On and off. Maybe since a few years before I met you."

"Do you make a lot of money doing it?" He slouched in the sofa and folded his arms.

The light from the blinding sun splashed rays throughout the living room and made it difficult to see him clearly. I placed my right hand near my forehead to block the sun. "Well, what's a lot of money to me may not be a lot of money to you. I mean—you make millions and I—"

"How do you know what I make?" He demanded.

"I mean—I don't know," I stammered.

He looked serious and unsmiling, as though the salary of most professional football players of his caliber were kept confidential. "So, how much is it? $10,000? $15,000? How much?"

"Well, no. Not that much," I hesitated.

"Then, I don't want to know the answer. You're worth more than the figures I just threw out there, so for anything less than that, you're definitely underpaid."

It was a moment meant for a father and daughter. Although it seemed to me that I was being scolded, it also seemed that it was done in love. A part of me was smiling, but I couldn't let it show outwardly and give Kelvin the impression that I wasn't proud of my actions.

Played

"You said you stopped, and then started again, right?" he questioned, leaning in.

"Yeah." I looked Kelvin in the face and answered him.

"If you stopped at one time, then why did you start again? What happened with your situation?" He stared at me, seemingly eager for an answer.

I could've lied and come up with some logical explanation as to why I found myself in such a difficult position; it would be simple to come up with a reason as to why I reverted back to my old ways. But I figured that I'd start whatever was blossoming with him in honesty, so I could continue in the same manner.

"I got pregnant."

"Whoa." He sat back in his seat. "Where's the baby?"

"I lost it." I looked directly at him. "It was yours."

"Wait a minute. Hold on." He made stopping motions with his hands and was quiet for a moment, thinking hard. "Baby? First, why are you just now telling me? And second, what does that have to do with you being in a hotel room surrounded by a bunch of dudes paying to see you feel up another woman?" He sounded confused first, then angry.

"Well, first, you stopped answering my calls. You totally ignored me, Kelvin, and that hurt. So why would I call you after losing my baby?" I made sure my tone was firm. I may have wanted or felt the need to have his protection, but that didn't mean I was going to let him intimidate me. "Second, I told you that I was in a relationship when I met you."

"Exactly, which brings me to my third question. How am I supposed to know that the dude you used to call 'fiancé' wasn't the daddy?"

"Let me explain a minute."

"Please do," he pressed coldly, eyes narrowing.

"When I became sick and he found out about the pregnancy, he knew that it couldn't be his."

"Y'all were screwin' weren't you? Or you were trying to do the proper thing?" he asked, making quotations in the air with his fingers.

"Wait a damn minute! Let me talk," I nearly shouted.

He folded his arms. "I'm waiting."

"My ex-fiancé can't have children. He had a vasectomy years ago. And *that* is why I am where I am today." I rubbed my fingers through my hair. "He put me out because you got me pregnant."

It seemed that Kelvin had stopped listening after I told him that the baby was his. "So, I mean, how am I supposed to know that there wasn't some other guy that you were with? I mean, you were with me while you were with him, so—" He shrugged his shoulders.

Outraged, I grabbed my bag and stood to leave. "Thank you so much for listening, Kelvin, but I'm gonna go before I let you get to me."

"Oh, and dramatic, too? What did you expect me to say, Taj? You want to run away because I have questions? I haven't seen you in months, and you want to spring this on me and expect for everything to be cool?"

"Exactly, Kelvin. It's been so damn long. I've already dealt with it and I'm over it. There *is* no baby, yet you're sitting here questioning me like I'm asking you for child support. You can go straight to hell."

There was no reason to re-open old wounds. I made a mistake trying to get back with Kelvin; I was done. He could see my actions as running away if he wanted to, but to me, I was moving on.

"I'm not finished yet. Sit down!" he snarled. His tone took me by surprise, but I didn't budge.

"Sit," he said again, lower but no less menacing.

I sat on the edge of the sofa with an attitude. "What? You want the number to the hospital that did the surgery? I know...how about you call my ex-fiance to see if he really had a vascectomy. Then maybe you'll believe what I'm telling you."

"No, no. I have to explain something." He paused for a moment to gather his thoughts.

"I'm waiting," I sang, mimicking what he told me.

Played

"I didn't mean to disappear on you like that. I just felt so many different emotions at one time that it was too much for me to deal with, so I had to leave it in the dust." He motioned for me to come and sit by him. Although I was still upset, he was not in the mood to be crossed right now. I shuffled over toward him.

"I loved you then, and I love you now," he went on. "You are a great woman—funny, attractive. I have to apologize for just burning out. I'm sorry." He kissed me briefly then continued, "I know I can't fix what you've gone through, but I can try and make it better if you let me."

I looked away, thinking that everything he said was garbage. I turned back and looked at him in the eye. "If you mean that, I'd rather you show than tell."

"You don't have to challenge me, babe. I'm a man of my word." He smiled.

The sun began to sink behind a building in the distance and shadows were cast across space. Kelvin walked over to the kitchen counter, retrieved his cell phone and sat close to me.

"What are you doing tomorrow?" he asked.

"Nothing planned."

"And the next day?"

"Umm—I don't know."

"Then that's a 'nothing.'" He began typing into his handheld, bunching his eyebrows as he read whatever was written on the screen, then made a call.

"Hey—Yo!" he said in a deep tone. "Get me out of here tonight. Same place—three days." He paused momentarily, then spoke again. "What time? Yeah … it's done."

He turned to me. "We're going to Freeport tonight. I have a nice chill spot there."

"What? Where is that?" I asked.

"About an hour away. It's a really quick flight honestly."

"Flight? Kelvin, how did you arrange something that fast? I mean, I need a passport and all don't I?"

He looked at me with his muscular arms outstretched, and

Triple Crown Publications *presents* …

smiled with a cocky smirk. "I'm Kelvin Ross baby."

I shook my head at his large ego. "Well, wait. If we're going out of town, I want to look nice, do my hair and everything. I don't want to look—"

"You're going to get your hair wet anyway. The Bahamas isn't the place to go and try to look like royalty. You'll want to have fun and let loose."

"I didn't know it was in the Bahamas. I've never been."

He looked happy to be the first to show me something. "Don't move. I'm gonna put on a shirt and some flip-flops, and then we'll leave."

"Wait! Are you not going to pack anything? I need to pack some things."

"For what? The fun isn't in the things you have, but in the things you do. Leave everything. I'd rather have you with nothing on at all."

The flight to the Bahamas was as Kelvin had described—quick, but by the time we got there it was night. It was at least 12 degrees warmer on the island and much more humid than in the states. Unfortunately, the darkness prevented me from admiring the beautiful, blue ocean water that I'd heard of so many times. We took a limousine—which was considered a taxi on the island—to a resort located directly on the beach.

While I expected slow jazz to play in the lobby, we were greeted by the upbeat sounds of drums and whistles. While I was completely excited and amazed by my surroundings, Kelvin played it cool, like he was accustomed to being in such an amazing environment.

A Bahamian woman with a really thick accent met us near the entryway and handed us the key to our room as if she were expecting us.

"I'll show you to your room, Mr. Ross," she offered.

"Umm—no thanks." Kelvin looked down at the key. "Same room, right?"

"Yes, Mr. Ross."

I looked at Kelvin, who ignored me. *I wonder what other*

Played

chick he has been bringing up here? Suddenly I felt self-con-
scious as he took me to the highest floor of the building, the
sixth floor. There were only six doors, and behind each of
them was a suite. When he opened the door to ours, I could-
n't help but gasp with wonder. The space was larger than the
size of an apartment and was equipped with every appliance
known to man. The living room was furnished with a choco-
late-colored sofa and chaise ensemble, two plasma televi-
sions mounted side-by-side, and a plush, luxurious cream carpet. Atop the granite countertops were two portable wine
racks, each filled with top shelf alcohol.

"Make yourself comfortable," Kelvin called as he walked
into the bedroom area. It appeared as though he certainly
stayed there often.

I sat down and took in my surroundings. For once in a very
long time, I had no worries. I didn't worry about Randy or
what he tried to do to me the day before. There was no way
that man got out of jail or especially out of the country, and
even if he did, with Kelvin at my side, I doubted he'd come for
my ass. Tiki and her AIDS status was a distant memory, too.
All the bad things that happened, I decided, stayed locked in
the past as I allowed the present to move me forward. I
refused to allow a single negative thought to cloud my mind
and my intent was to enjoy my time in my new surroundings,
which included enjoying Kelvin.

He emerged from the bedroom—wearing nothing. I hadn't
been intimate with Kelvin since our actual affair, but his
actions were definitely intending to lure me into doing the
deed.

"Shower?" I requested. "Please?"

"Sure, but only if I can join you."

"How could I part with what I'm looking at right now?"
Lust was clogging my vision. "Um ... don't do this to me."

"That's exactly what I want—to do it to you—all week
long."

As corny as that sounded, that's exactly what I wanted,
too.

36

When we returned from the Bahamas, Kelvin and I were both exhausted. We slept a lot and talked very little. On top of that, we were only back in Jacksonville for two days before he had to leave again for Denver for three whole weeks.

During the time that he was away, I continued what I did best and stacked some money. Kristal and I managed to pull in over eight thousand dollars since we'd started working together, four thousand of which was still in my possession. I opened a savings account at a local bank and stashed most of it there since I was trying to get my life back in order.

I decided that whenever Kelvin was in town for short periods of time, I would vow not work until he left. Like James before him, Kelvin was my closest thing to normalcy, so I figured I would do what I could to hold on to him, even if it led to nowhere.

When Kelvin returned from Denver, there was something different about him. He was cold, impatient, and even a bit harsh at times. My questions afforded sarcastic remarks. If I asked about his trip, he would reply, "Well, wouldn't you like to know?" Or, if I rephrased the question and asked, "How was Denver?" He would simply reply, "Cold."

One evening, after making love in his condo, he walked out onto the balcony in a pair of shorts and flip-flops. I rested for a while before I became curious about what was taking so long, so I threw on one of his button-down shirts and pretended to walk to the fridge for some water. I slowly drank it as I overheard fragments of his conversation.

"It's my money . . . you ain't going nowhere . . . like this for years . . . when will you learn . . . my kids . . . see what happens."

Overhearing that conversation gave me more than enough fuel to probe him. I walked back into the bedroom and sat on the edge of the bed, trying to put my thoughts in order. When he came in, he hit the light switch, and we were in total darkness.

"Can we talk?" I asked.

"No. I just wanna go to sleep."

"Well, what about what I want, Kelvin?" I sat there in the dark while he made himself comfortable under the sheets.

All of a sudden he threw the covers off and stood up in rage. "You know, I'm sick and tired of you women and whatever it is that *you* want! Between you and my wife, I don't know who's worse. Can I get some peace so I can rest, please?" He sat down on the bed, breathing hard.

"Wife?" My chest constricted. "You never said anything about being married." I knew I shouldn't have been surprised, I half-expected there were more girls than just me. Half the men who came to my shows were either married, taken, or in some other words claimed by some chick.

"Nor did you ever ask, Taj. We see what we want to see."

I was infuriated and hated to admit that he was right. I needed security and shelter after my ordeal with Randy, and after going from classy to bum, then bitch to riches, I wanted stability, and I thought I had finally found that in Kelvin. That didn't stop me from going off though. "How could I see anything beyond you spending days and weeks with me? Where is this wife? And you got kids too, huh?"

"Yeah, but none of that is your business, Taj."

"Forget this. I don't need this." I jumped up off of the bed and went into the living room where my clothes were. I began throwing them on madly with the intent to leave.

Kelvin followed me quickly. "And where do you think you're going, Taj? Back to the hotel with your li'l friend?"

I ignored him and continued to dress.

"Do you hear me, Taj? What's out there for you? Who's out there for you?" he yelled.

I ignored him and continued to dress.

"Fine! Leave! I've tried so hard." He paused for a minute. "Blame me! Blame me then! I can't help that I love you so much that I can't let you go even if it's the right thing to do! You didn't let me go when *you* were engaged, did you?"

I stopped moving. For a moment, I wanted to admit that he was right and that I was being a hypocrite, but this wasn't the time or place, it was a bad situation and I needed to be gone. But in my moment of hesitation, Kelvin gained ground.

"That's right," he pressed, "we're the same people, Taj, and everything is completely circumstantial."

"No Kelvin, I was honest about my relationship when I met you. You had a choice, but you've taken mine."

"So, if I'd told you I was married, when you were running back to sleep with your fiancé after spending long nights with me, would it have made a difference?" There was an awkward silence, and Kelvin folded his arms, standing tall. "You know I love you, Taj. I even loved you a year ago when we were kickin' it, but I've just been in a tough spot—trying to please everyone but myself."

"A tough spot doesn't mean that you hide the fact that you have a wife somewhere. What's that all about?"

"I married my wife when I was young—and stupid. She

P l a y e d

saw potential in me that I couldn't even see in myself. We're not together for love, but for what I could do for her and for what she would lose if she left me. I may have been young and dumb, but we signed a prenup, and for that reason, she's not walking out without a fight."

"Then, what is it that you want from me?" I asked, just as puzzled as I was upset.

"I want you to be my leading lady. I just feel so good when I'm with you. You take away my worries, baby—when other people just add to them."

"Leading lady? With what promise? What do I have to hold on to?"

"Me—everything. Have I ever not come through when I was supposed to?"

"The baby."

He sighed. He had no comeback for that. "Taj, say I don't make you happy, and you can leave right now. But you know you'd be lying if you said that. You feel exactly the way I do. I understand you, baby. We're both victims of circumstance." He kneeled on the floor near me and placed his head on my lap. "Don't leave me."

As dramatic as the scene became, not even an inch of me wanted to walk out the door. He took me by the hand and led me back to the bedroom where we held each other all night and slept peacefully.

I may have been wrong, but I fell asleep at night realizing that I was still safe.

I was doing shows at the Marriott so much that I almost felt like a hotel-certified employee. One Friday afternoon before a show, after I parked the car, I opted to walk outside to enjoy the breeze when my heart did a double take. I thought I saw Shai standing near the bus stop. As I attempted to get a closer look, I confirmed it was her as she spun around and we locked eyes. I was surprised to see the voluptuous woman in a tight mini-dress who, as usual, was showing off too much. Instantly, I flashed back to the day that Sarai died and how my world turned to utter hell. I thought about the beat down that was inflicted upon me because of my gross negligence and of Shai's useless, fried brain. I was about to turn away from her when she called out to me.

"Taj ... Taj!" She struggled clumsily to run in the heels she was wearing. I turned away and continued to walk, but she called out again, "Wait a minute, Taj! Can I speak with you for a minute?" Out of breath, she finally caught up to me.

"What do you want?" I asked with an attitude.

"Um ... I was wondering if I could get in on what you and Tiki was doing?"

I was shocked by her humility. Any other day she wouldn't give a damn about anybody other than herself, but here she was, asking me for help. Unfortunately it was in regards to Tiki. "Tiki and I aren't into doing anything," I said coldly.

"You know, the *shows*." Shai was all up on me in an eagerness to get down. "I really need this, and Tiki helped you out when no one else would. Why don't you do the same thing for me?"

I thought about how irresponsible she was. If Shai couldn't be trusted to keep a child safe for a couple hours, then why would she be able to handle anything else, like money? Besides, I liked the dough I was bringing in with Kristal, who had better upkeep than Shai, and I wasn't about to mess that up. Plus, I knew that Shai was just like Tiki, and who knows if she was HIV positive or worse by this time. Between her utterly negligent lifestyle and her failure to keep Sarai safe, was there even one small thing that Shai had done good for herself? For the world?

"I'm not interested," I said, turning my back on her before entering the hotel. "I'm on to bigger and better things, but I'm sure if you need money as bad as you say you do, Tiki would be more than available to help you out."

To prove himself to me, Kelvin gave me a key to his condo before he left for Denver again. He asked me to keep his apartment warm while he was away, so I tried my best to do as he

P l a y e d

asked. Although I knew I had to get out there and make some more money.

The week Kelvin was gone, Kristal and I performed three shows. At the end of each night, I returned to Kelvin's place to sleep and rejuvenate by preparing a healthy breakfast and working out on the equipment in the spare room.

For our fourth show, Kristal and I decided to do some role-playing—cops and robbers. I went out to purchase the cuffs and some other kinky tools at a local novelty shop to impress the crowd, but by six in the evening, I still hadn't heard from her. I made at least eight attempts to reach her but she never answered.

I checked into the hotel room and waited alone, listening for her call and watching the digital clock beside the bed. She never showed. Being a no show would mean bad business for more than just her—it was bad for me, too. Gathering my belongings, I rushed out to the car and drove over to her place.

Making my way to her apartment, I noticed that the door was cracked. I knocked on the door but no one answered.

"Kristal?" I called out.

Peeking in a little more, I saw that the apartment was blanketed in total darkness. I knocked three more times and called her name again.

No answer.

Just as I turned to leave, I could hear motion behind the door.

"Kristal? Is that you?"

Barely audible, she whispered, "Yes."

"Can I come in?"

She didn't answer, but because I knew she was there, I went inside anyway and closed the door behind me. "Girl, why is it so damn dark in here? Are your lights off?"

"No," she whispered again.

"Well, turn on a light or something." I walked over to the switch closest to the door and flipped it on. Nothing happened. "Come on now, Kristal."

I flipped the switch adjacent to the first one and light illu-

Triple Crown Publications *presents...*

minated the small apartment. But it also revealed something that I wasn't prepared for. Kristal stood behind the front door, holding herself tightly and shivering. Blood stained her white University of Miami sweatshirt. Her swollen lips and eyes made her difficult to recognize. Drying blood began to matte her hair and she cried silently. It took me a moment to take it all in.

"Oh my God, Kristal—what happened to you?" As I approached her, she went limp and fell to the floor, revealing droplets of blood on her jeans. I caught her and panicked.

"The guy—" she spoke from her swollen, bleeding lips.

"Huh? What guy?" I spoke quickly, half frantic.

"From the—the show," she spoke slowly.

"What? Was he here?"

She nodded slowly.

I looked around quickly for something on which to prop her head. Her bed was only ten feet away from us, so I slowly lowered her to the floor and went to retrieve a pillow. Kristal's place was a wreck. Broken dishes lay scattered on the floor and her tan sheets were saturated with her own blood. I rushed back over to her and Kristal's cries became audible. I felt guilty for not being there for my friend like she was for me when Randy almost raped me.

"Did he rape you?" I asked.

She cried, but didn't answer.

"I'm calling the police to get you some help, Kristal."

"No, no. Please," she pleaded.

"What? What do you mean? A man came in here and raped you. We have to get you some help."

"I don't want help." It looked painful for her to speak, but somehow she forced out her words.

"Then, what do you want me to do? I have to help you."

"Then, help me by leaving me alone." She lifted herself from the floor and propped her back against the wall. "I want you to get out of here. GO!" she cried.

Leaving her apartment, I felt deeply guilty for what happened to Kristal. Although I didn't know or understand the full

Played

scale of what happened, inside I knew it occurred because of our lifestyle. I realized that I forgot to warn her about not allowing our clients to know where we lived, and though that sounded like common sense, when trying to make fast money, sense is sometimes the furthest thing from our mind. Thinking back, I also never warned her about psychos, stalkers, and rapists. After all, no one warned me.

Immediately following the situation at Kristal's place, I called Kelvin, who told me to call and report it in spite of what Kristal wanted. Since he studied criminology in college, he'd studied the psyche of rape victims. He instructed me to go to his condo, lock the doors and not leave for a while, at least until things blew over.

"Go into my closet and look in the fourth Jordan shoe box on the left. Grab my gun in case you need it," he said. I followed his instructions, for he planted in me the fear of something unseen, something that Kristal obviously didn't see coming herself. I remained locked up for weeks.

37

I never heard from Kristal after the incident. I had tried calling her dozens of times, but eventually her phone number stopped working. I decided to lie low for a while, not wanting to splurge and spend the money that I'd saved. It wasn't in me to ask Kelvin for money since he had already been most generous in allowing me to stay at his place.

One evening, after a discounted facial and minimal shopping in the town center, I pulled into the garage and noticed Kelvin's truck parked in his reserved parking space. I became overly excited and proceeded quickly to the elevator and into the apartment.

Something smelled sweet, like perfume. A woman's cheap handbag sat on the countertop, but no one was in sight. The lights in the master bedroom were off, but there I could hear music playing from behind the door. Heart lurching, I pressed my ear firmly to the door to listen closely. Somebody was surely in there with him, some bitch, so instead of walking in to make a scene, I went into the kitchen and made a racket with some dishes in order to lure him out. It worked within moments.

He came out of the room and closed the door gently, "What the hell are you doing?"

"Excuse me?" I shrieked, appalled.

"Come on, Taj. I don't have time for your drama tonight." He walked over to the fridge and grabbed a bottle of water looking me up and down with something like disgust in his eyes.

I stood back and watched him. "You're just gonna walk past me like I'm not even standing here? Like I'm supposed to be OK with some bitch in your bed?!"

"I don't have time for your mess tonight."

"What?" I grabbed his arm. "Who the hell is in the room, Kelvin?"

"Keep your voice down before my neighbors start complaining about the loud, ghetto bitch next door." He looked down at my grip and ripped his arm away. "And take your damn hands off of me."

"What? Are you serious right now? Are you bipolar or have multiple personalities or something? What the hell is this!"

I hope you don't mind sleeping on the couch tonight," he said cooly, turning to enter the bedroom.

His actions left me speechless. I paced the living room for another twenty minutes, thinking of what I should do next. I heard Kelvin explain to his new lover that I was his roommate and deeply in love with him and to not pay any attention to the drama. *Oh hell no,* I thought. I wanted to break up everything in sight, but I didn't. I left my key on the counter and headed back to the hotel. I had no room in my life for mess.

Back at the Marriott, I drew a hot bath and tried to relax. There was no reason to shed tears. I couldn't expect anything more of Kelvin. He already had a wife and who knows who else. But, there was a fine line between settling for an unfaithful man and putting up with total disrespect, and Kelvin crossed it.

By morning, I had over twenty missed calls—all from Kelvin. He didn't leave any messages, so I ignored each of them. Instead, I spent the day shopping around for a car. Vehicles that were most tolerable were priced over $10,000, and I wasn't prepared to spend everything I saved, so I rented another car instead.

I drove to the beach, watched children play in the sand and adults jog against the friction. Birds swooped in for whatever crumbs were left behind by picnickers.

I knew that something had to give. I had to come up with a new plan and quick. Otherwise, all of my money would be gone, and I would be on the streets again.

Contemplating long and hard about my situation with Kelvin, I came to the conclusion that he was my only way out—for now. In spite of his doggish ways and dishonesty, he provided one thing that I found hard to afford without steady income—shelter. I couldn't run away from him, not at the moment, or I would be in an even worse situation without him than I was with him. Finally, after his fortieth phone call, I swallowed my pride and answered.

"Hello?"

"Don't answer all cool like there is nothing going on."

"What do you mean?"

"Come on, Taj. You're not sick of the games yet?"

The nerve of him! "Well, I don't know, Kelvin. Are you? Because it looks like you're full of them."

"I know. And I'm sorry. I can explain everything. Where are you? I'll come to you."

Kelvin and I had dinner on the beach—succulent shrimp and crab dishes that were pleasing to the appetite and my broken spirit. Kelvin laughed and joked as though everything were fine, and I decided to play along and not mention what had happened, not now. There was something tremendously wrong with his actions and his attitude. He had an addiction, covered by numerous excuses. He was incapable of being with

P l a y e d

one woman and couldn't possibly love any one of them. I tried to look at it objectively. In my situation with him, I had nothing to lose or anything to gain. To an outsider it would appear that I was using Kelvin, but he was certainly using me too.

Kelvin made another impromptu trip out of town and I decided that I wasn't going to sit around the house and wallow in pity. I needed to get back on my grind and needed to be proactive about getting my life together.

I paid for a room at the Mariott, then went back to the club in hopes of finding a new partner to do shows with for the night—perhaps for even longer. My situation may not have been ideal, but I knew that Kelvin was not and could never be the permanent alternative. I felt I deserved better than to have that man parade all of his whores in front of me while I was still living with him.

"Jordan," my alias at the club, owed them a few dollars for skipping on pay out, so going inside of the club was out of the question. I waited outside for the women to come out, wearing a respectable solid white Chaps linen jacket and matching Capri's that I got from Kohl's, making it appear that I went to work earlier in the day as a secretary or a bank teller. I didn't recognize any of the girls, so I wasn't sure quite what to say to them.

I approached a few suitable-looking prospects, but I was rejected by each. This was going to be harder than I thought.

After several rejections, I finally approached a woman who could give Lauren London a run for her money. Her hair bounced in such a way that I knew it wasn't weave. Her breasts and ass gave her a 36-24-36 vibe. I did a once over and then went to talk to her.

"Are you looking to make some extra money?"

"Sure, why not?"

I smiled, relieved. The money spent on the Marriott and the alcohol would not be in vain.

"I do performance shows for men—girl-on-girl action. Usually brings in anywhere from two thousand to five thousand dollars a night depending on the clientele, and that includes tips, and we split everything down the middle. All you need is something sexy, and you're good to go." I saw no need to lie to the girl; I needed her just as bad as she needed me. I had faith that I'd make the money back, because I already contacted some of the guys and at least eight dudes were down. All I needed was to call four more to confirm the location, get the one hundred and fifty-dollar admittance fees, and we were good to go.

"So, what's your name?"

"Prancer."

I looked at the girl again, not believing that she'd just given me a reindeer name. Then, I thought about what prancing meant and decided that I'd make it work.

"So, is what we're about to do going to make you uncomfortable?"

"No, I do a little tricking on the side, so I'm down for whatever."

I liked the sound of that. She made a phone call as I called up four more guys and made sure the man I hired to watch after the room and collect the money was in place. In no time, the two of us were at the Marriott, going up the elevator and heading toward our room, ready to perform. When I walked in, some of the men were already socializing and networking as if they were at a business reception. Prancer and I slipped into the bathroom where we removed our clothes. She revealed a pink and baby blue bra and panty set.

Damn, she looks good in pink, I thought as I watched her model the outfit. "I'll do most of the talking. You'll get in where you fit it."

Prancer nodded her head and followed my lead. I walked up to the man who took the attendance money and kissed him on the cheek.

"Guys, the show is about to begin. Now in order to stay, I need your ID. If you don't have a form of ID, I'm sorry, but you gotta go." I sounded just like Tiki did when we used to do shows together. Three of the guys held up empty hands and I

Played

informed my bouncer to give them back one hundred dollars of their one-fifty so they could leave. Of course they had to leave the rest for drinks because nothing in the room was free. Inwardly I was pissed, because that meant I had less than ten guys present, and I couldn't call anyone to replace that income.

"If you've been here before, you know the rules . . . no weapons, no touching, grabbing, fighting or jacking off."

"No touching us, right?" Prancer asked on cue, moreso because she didn't know the rules than to be caught up in the script.

"That's right, baby, no touching us." I smiled and looked at the bouncer. "Do we have fifteen hundred?"

I impressed the mixed crowd with my fast math skills. Normally, I'd collect the money, but since I hadn't done a show in a while, I got one of the customers I had grown to trust when I worked with Kristal to handle it instead. He was a regular and had helped out when a customer got rowdy with us before.

I collected the money, and then added, "One last thing. This is what I call your lifeline." I held my cell phone in the air and the light illuminated the darkest areas.

"At midnight, I will make a phone call. If for some reason that phone call is not received, the police will be here before you can think to run. Also, I only have to press one button to reach the authorities, so don't try anything slick."

Prancer took her place on the bed.

"Let the show begin," I said, meeting Prancer halfway. Feeling for each other, we kissed and then let nature take its course.

"What the hell is this?" I heard a complaint as Prancer started licking my areolas. I opened my eyes to see one of the black men sitting on the bed, caressing my legs.

"No touching," I said, tapping Prancer on the shoulder, giving her a hint that she needed to stop.

"Naw, these rules is bullshit, and I'm getting my monies worth," the man complained, taking his penis out. Pretty soon, another man had his penis out and walked to the other side of the bed, encouraging me to put it in my mouth.

"No, this is not that kind of show," I told them as three of the men left. Another man held the bouncer at gunpoint, and I knew that this was not going to end the way it was supposed to. I tried to remember if the four remaining men knew each other some kind of way. Looking at them, I remembered that three of them were at my "anything goes show" with Tiki. This was definitely the wrong clientele at the Marriott.

"It will be whatever kind of show we want it to be," one of the guys said as he grabbed me by the legs and pulled me all the way off the bed, forcing me to land with a thud. I could feel my bra coming off and the lace burns from the panties being ripped from me. I could see two of the other men climb on the bed with Prancer while I was pinned on the floor. I tried to close my legs, but the guy was too strong. "I want some of this good pussy, and you're gonna give it to me."

I cried because, not only did I mess up, but I got someone else involved and that would forever be on my conscious. "Look, don't hurt her," I sobbed. "I will do anything you want. Just let her go, please."

"Hell naw." One of the guys laughed. "I want to see how good Prancer can prance on my dick."

Out-numbered four to one, and with the bouncer abandoning us as well, I knew we were in trouble. I decided that it was just easier to comply and that maybe I'd be able to survive. I opened my legs, inviting my attacker in, hoping that all I would get out of it was a beat up pussy and a migraine.

"Let her go!" I heard someone yell, but then thought it was my imagination calling out for help.

I could feel the head of my attacker's member pushing into my walls, and I closed my eyes, so I could pretend that I was enjoying it. Just as the man nestled himself inside me completely and begin to thrust, I heard a soft pop and the man fell on the floor.

"Didn't I say to let her go, nigga?"

I opened my eyes and was surprised to see Freddie standing over me. He smacked my attacker again with his glock then stabbed one of the men on the bed with Prancer, causing him to howl. I scrambled away from the chaos and looked on.

"It's gonna be some raping tonight," he announced. I got a good look at him and couldn't believe that he was rocking some tight Shirley Temples, and that his fake Crip-look was completed with a blue and black-checkered shirt and black Timbs. "Strip butt-naked, faggots, since y'all into hurting females. Marcus, Katrina, get their clothes and their money!"

I looked at Katrina and realized that she was the naked lady at the hotel that Freddie and Marcus had videotaped. Then, it made sense. Freddie didn't run a hotel ... he was running a brothel *inside* of the hotel. He was the pimp and Prancer had to be one of his hos. How lucky was I to pick her out! As Marcus and Katrina did what they were told, I found my clothes and quickly got dressed.

"Line them fools up. I'm gonna show them how to rape somebody." The naked men who thought they were gonna take some pussy were now standing side by side. "Take my knife out of that fool," Freddie said, pointing to the wounded man. Katrina bent down and pulled the knife out of the guy's leg. "Meet me at Room 112."

One by one, Freddie smacked each dude in the face as they whimpered and wobbled out of the room just the way they came into this world.

In Katrina's room back in Freddie's hotel, we dumped everything we took on her bed, including the money that I collected for the show. The money totaled two thousand four hundred and seventy-eight dollars and was split into six equal piles. The jewelry and the clothes were put into a separate pile while the undergarments were put in the trash. Freddie gave everyone a stack of cash and kept two stacks for himself. I was disappointed to only end up with a little over four hundred dollars, but I was happy I got out of the Marriott with my life.

"Just think, if you hadn't picked one of my hos, you'd be in

the hospital or worse off— dead," Freddie said as he stuffed his money in his pocket.

"Thank you," I said, humbled and grateful.

"Well, you still got it, Taj. If you ever want to join my team—"

"I'm not really into tricking," I told him. "Shows are more of my thing."

"You can do that here. I'll make sure you're safe and don't nobody bother you. We split our cut like I do with all of my other ladies."

I looked up to see Prancer hanging on him and I couldn't believe how much Freddie reminded me of Snoop Dogg at the moment. Those Shirley Temple curls were still killing it. With his hat on, he did look like a pimp.

"Thanks for the offer, but I don't know if I'm going to keep doing them. How 'bout I make you a deal though ... I'll make sure I'll bring some business to you."

Freddie extended his hand. "Cool."

Played

38

Three months passed quickly. I couldn't line up a gig that would pay what I felt I deserved, so rather than become one of Freddie's whores, I decided that it was best to become accustomed to Kelvin's behavior. It was a roller coaster trying to determine which side of him would greet me at the door when he returned from his extended trips. Some days it was this warm, loving person who wanted to give me the world. And other times, it was a cold, callous man, who all but said that he couldn't care less about me. Eventually, his little game got old. Life existed beyond the walls of his condominium, and I wanted a taste.

It was a Saturday night and Kelvin was gone for a week, and popular R&B artists were coming into Jacksonville for the concert of the year. Several organizations promoted the main concert event as well as the after parties that would ensue. I picked up a flyer at a local beauty store advertising a more grown and sexy atmosphere for partygoers, so I made plans to join them.

I decided not to go against the all white party theme for the event, so I purchased a snug fitting dress from Bebe, a pair of four-inch heels, and simple accessories. After adding spirals to my now shoulder-length hair with a ceramic flat iron, I splashed on some sweet perfume—something by Juicy Couture—and dashed for the door.

The nightclub was warmer than I imagined, and the standing room was hard to come by. Every corner of the space was packed with some of Jacksonville's most attractive women and most eligible bachelors. The plethora of BMWs and Benzes parked outside was indeed a great indicator of the class and sophistication that the attendees had. Although I was alone, I knew I wouldn't have difficulty mingling with others and ultimately enjoy my night out.

Looking around at the place, I noticed it was darker in some places than others, but the use of earth tones in the establishment created a warm, inviting atmosphere. The music, though urban rap and hip hop, was not as loud as I expected. People were able to hold conversations without yelling at one another. There were no seats at the bar, so I shimmied up where I could and ordered a martini. I remained as close to the bar as possible in order to avoid having the contents of my drink spilled on my two-hundred-dollar dress.

After my first drink, I switched to a clear beverage, vodka and Sprite, and moved closer to the dance floor. My hips swayed to one of my favorite tracks, and I mouthed the lyrics to the song, only stopping to take a sip of alcohol.

"How are you doing?" A man stood on the other side of the banister, attempting to get my attention. I ignored him at first, playing hard to get. "How are you doing?" he yelled a little louder.

Looking at him, I saw that he was about three inches taller than I was and had a nice build. His pants were fitted better than most, but I found that look attractive—different.

"I'm OK. How are you?"

P l a y e d

"Better now that I have your attention. What's your name?"

"Taj," I replied and took a sip of my drink. "What's yours?"

"Ralf."

He seemed nervous, so I thought to take the lead.

"Where are you from, Ralf?"

"All over. I'm in the Navy, and I'm stationed at Mayport right now. I've been in for about eight years now. I've been in Jacksonville for almost a year." He flashed a charming half-grin and cocked his head.

I realized quickly that he wasn't shy at all. He told me that he was a full-blooded Puerto Rican, and with a name like Ralfael, I knew he was telling the truth. He discussed his children, a son and daughter, from previous relationships. His smile drew me in. The way he formed words with his mouth was simple, yet extremely seductive. In that moment, I yearned to know Spanish.

By 3:00 a.m., women and men scattered out into the dark parking lot to escape the bright lights that were turned on inside the club. Ralf walked me outside.

"Where are you going?" he asked.

"It's late. I'm going home of course."

"You don't have to. We can get into something." He stuffed his hands into his pockets.

"I don't know about that. You know what they say is the only thing that's open at these hours." I laughed a little. "And it's not that type of party."

"Actually, I was talking about breakfast. I would like to spend a little more time with you, if you don't mind."

I was hungry—or at least the alcohol caused me to feel that way—so I couldn't refuse his invitation. A friend of his followed us to the closest late-night breakfast spot in the area, where we were greeted by tired, overworked waitresses who seemed on the verge of quitting altogether. We all laughed and talked over hotcakes and eggs, but it seemed as though we were all curious about what we'd do after breakfast.

"Man, I would give anything not to ship out for duty," Ralf directed to his friend whose name I never caught.

 Triple Crown Publications *presents...*

"I'm not looking forward to mine either, man," he responded. "It's just two weeks. It'll be over quicker than you know."

"So, what—you leaving me already?" I teased him.

"I know right. There are no phones or anything. I thought I would be able to access my email, but I really doubt it now."

If Ralf's upcoming sea duty was his way to get me in bed, it wasn't working. As much as I was attracted to him, I couldn't see past the possibility of him throwing game. After breakfast, he dropped me back at the car. I kissed him good night and left alone.

For weeks, I didn't hear from him nor did I expect to. I figured that he saw me as a lost cause on the night that he actually wanted me. But I was wrong.

He called one afternoon, excited about being back on shore and explaining to me that he'd thought of me during the time that he was on the ship. I was charmed and quite delighted with him. Since Kelvin had been in Denver for weeks and only managed to call twice, I decided to make plans to spend the evening catching up with my new friend, Ralf.

We intended to go ice-skating on an artificial rink out in St. Augustine. I dressed warm in jeans and a fitted sweater and packed a pair of thick socks. But when we entered the city, there was an advertisement for comedy acts that would be performing that evening, so we ditched our initial plans and attended the show instead.

After a few drinks and lots of laugher, the crowd thinned, leaving us with a nice atmosphere to talk and become better acquainted. Ralf and I had a lot of fun. We had a way of making each other smile or laugh at the silliest things, and that was what I needed most.

"So, what do you have planned for tomorrow?" he asked, stirring his drink by whirling the glass.

"Nothing planned. I just thought I would relax a little. That's all."

"Um hmm." He continued to whirl his drink.

"What do you have going on?"

"I have to work first thing in the morning. I know it's gonna

P l a y e d

be cold, and I won't feel like doing it, but it's gotta get done."

"Well, what time do you leave in the morning?" I asked.

"From where? Your place or mine?" He smiled confidently.

I blushed, flattered by his comment. "I meant yours, silly."

"Around six."

I was curious. "And what time would you have to leave my place?"

"Around five. Not that I would mind at all though."

I considered that my activities with Ralf would only go as far as I wanted, and to have a warm body to cuddle close to that evening would have been beneficial, so I invited him over. Kelvin was still out of town and Ralf and I were just friends, so why not?

I turned Kelvin's old workout room into my getaway for those evenings that he would bring random women home with him. There was a chair, a full-sized bed, and a cableless plasma television mounted on the wall: all the makings of a comfortable bedroom. The apartment itself was bare. There were no photos on the walls, so Ralf had no grounds to ask questions.

We didn't have sex that night. We simply popped in a Denzel Washington movie and watched as much as we could before falling asleep, fully clothed. I found solace in his presence, and the fact that he required nothing of me in some way restored my power and control. He was masculine, yet gentle and kindhearted.

It seemed we were asleep for hours. After the DVD stopped, the blue light from the television shined brightly across the room. Ralf lay closely behind me with his arm wrapped tightly around my waist, breathing heavily and on the verge of snoring. I didn't want to totally break my sleep, so I blindly reached toward the floor for the fallen remote control. My hands patted around the carpet for the remote, and when I thought to quit my blind search and go back to sleep, I felt something brush against the back of my hand. Then, the cold, narrow device that I'd searched for was placed into my hand. I fully woke and sat up.

It was Kelvin. He stood over us wearing a gray sweat suit and hat. For a moment, I was speechless.

"Get up," he said quietly.

"Don't be upset, Kelvin. It's not what you think it—" I moved slowly.

"Bitch, get the hell up!" he yelled.

Ralf awoke. He rubbed his eyes for a moment in order to see clearly.

"Taj, who is this?" he asked sleepily.

"I'm her man—that's who, nigga. Get the hell out my house!" Kelvin removed the covers and Ralf sprang from the bed. He spent a moment searching the floor for his keys, found them, and left in an instant.

"It's not at all what you think, Kelvin. We're just friends. I just wanted some company over, and I figured you would be gone for a while—and I hadn't heard from you," I quickly attempted to explain.

"Shut the hell up," he demanded, sitting down on the bed and interlocking his fingers, obviously thinking of something to say.

I took a moment to think. "Wait, with all the women you screw up in here, why am I apologizing for having a *friend* over," I asked, then continued, "like I'm doing something wrong." He turned to look at me as I sat back on the bed and slid beneath the covers. "Good night."

"What did you just say to me?" He stood and walked to my side of the bed.

"You heard me. Turn the television off on your way out."

Quickly, he went for both of my shoulders and shook me as hard as he could. "What the hell did you say to me? Say it again! Say it again!"

He removed his hands from my shoulders, and in an instant drew a fist, cocked his arm back, and punched me in the center of my face. I heard a crunch. Screaming, I cuffed both my hands over my face, ran into the bathroom, and locked the door.

"Don't you ever in your life have another man in my damn

P l a y e d

243

house! You got that, bitch!" He bellowed and punched the door. "Trick ass bitch. You better stay yo ass in there!"

I didn't think to fear him; I was more terrified of how my face would look if I didn't seek immediate attention. The mirror revealed the obvious: my nose was busted, bleeding and broken. The sight of it made me nauseous. I ransacked the medicine cabinet for any pain reliever I could find and took four of them. I cuffed my nose again, sat on the floor near the bathtub and tilted my head as far back as I could to slow the bleeding. Within minutes, I became dizzy and then drowsy.

It felt as though someone poured glue down my throat. My face was stiff and there was dried blood on my skin. The pain was minimal compared to the pain of beatings I'd taken in the past, but I knew that I needed to see a doctor soon.

I rose from the floor, drenched a wash cloth in water, slowly washed away the dried blood and noticed dark circles forming beneath my eyes. I listened to the door for a while before emerging from the bathroom—silence. Kelvin was gone. The apartment was still. I grabbed my keys from the counter and went out to my car.

The emergency room was crowded with men, women and children—some of them coughing or shaking, others looking totally normal and patient. I hid my injuries behind a clean, white towel for fear that I would scare someone's child, or scare myself. I was always wary of the emergency room. Each time I walked past a free hand sanitizer station, I took full advantage of it.

For the sake of not running into my ex-fiancé, I drove to a hospital across town, nearly twenty minutes out of the way. My emergency room doctor was an older Asian male who acted as though he had one espresso too many.

"Well, hello, Ms. Jenson!" He announced cheerfully. "What can I do for you today?"

"My nose is broken," I told him. My voice was muffled behind the towel.

"What was that again?" he asked loudly.

"I said my nose is broken." I dropped the towel from in

front of my face.

"Oh my." He became serious. "Let's see here." He touched it slightly. "When did your injuries occur? Can you breathe a little?"

He asked me a series of questions, ruled out septal hematoma and other injuries, and told me that the swelling prevented me from breathing normally through my nose. He told me that my breathing would return to normal within a few weeks and that my nose would heal completely over the following months. He handed me a folder and sent me downstairs to check out after writing a prescription for some high quality pain relievers.

I went to hand the folder over to a woman behind the counter, but she sent me to Room 302 instead. It was a small office, cozy and clean. No one sat in the waiting area. A chime alerted a woman from the back room, and she came out to greet me.

"Good morning," she said gaily, although I knew she wanted to cringe at the sight of my face. She was a middle-aged white woman, about five-foot-six with a beautiful head of red hair and a pretty smile. Her presence spoke tranquility and peace.

"I just need to check out. Can I do that with you?" I went to hand her the folder.

"Ma'am, if you don't mind, I would like for you to have a seat," she said politely and signaled toward some chairs.

I sat down. "What's this about? Is it about my nose? The doctor said that it would be OK." I panicked.

"Yes, it is. And yes, you're right. We want to express a concern for your safety, and we want to prevent you from further suffering the injuries that brought you into this facility today." She looked directly at me. "Would you like to accept our help today, Ms. Jenson?"

She knows my name? I thought. I felt as though they were conspiring against me—as though the doctor couldn't wait to go and run his mouth about the busted black woman with the broken face.

Played

"What services?"

"If your injuries are the result of domestic abuse or violence in—"

"It's not," I cut her off. "I was playing basketball and my partner made a strong pass."

She looked down at my long, artificial nails and knew that I was lying. "Well, it's 9:00 a.m. When was this game? At six?"

It had to be irritating to be blatantly lied to when you're attempting to help someone, so I understood when the woman folded her arms and stared at me boldly.

"You're a nice person," I told her, "but if I wanted help from you or anyone else, I would have asked for it." I attempted to hand her the folder again and the papers fell out. I closed my eyes in disgust when I saw that the papers were blank. "The staff tricked me into coming here, which I don't believe is even legal."

"Feel free to leave, but take my card in case you ever need to talk."

I accepted the card, placed the folder on the seat, and left the room.

The pharmacy on the first floor of the building was my final stop. The pain had become less bearable, so simple walking around with the prescription seemed ridiculous.

"Drop off or wait?" the pharmacy tech asked from behind the counter.

"I'll wait."

I took a seat next to an older black woman, old enough to be my grandmother. Her dark hair color was outshined by her incoming gray hair. She wore glasses and was dressed in a long skirt-suit, like the ones my mother wore to church back in the day.

"Good morning," I said, and flashed a quick smile.

The table next to me was littered with various magazines, so I picked up a copy of *Essence* and flipped through its pages.

"The Lord has been so good to you," the woman next to me spoke, and I assumed she was talking to herself. "He's been knocking on your door. You can't keep telling the Lord 'no'."

"Are you talking to me, ma'am?" I was always taught to respect my elders, so I wanted to be polite.

"I'm not crazy. I know the Lord. His name is Jesus," she said with passion. "And you know him, too."

"Yes, ma'am." I simply agreed so that she could end the conversation.

"God says stop running. He sees that you've been going through some things. You don't see your way out of some situations you're in, but if you would just be still and wait on the Lord, I promise He'll bring you out."

"Ms. Thomas?" the pharmacy tech called.

"Believe what I tell you now. Pray, baby. You have a blessed day now."

Awkward, I thought. When someone gets an indication that another person was in trouble, they seem to have all the solutions. I believed that if my face hadn't been twisted into three shades of purple, then she wouldn't have said two words to me. Yet ... for some reason, her words resonated in my heart, and I spent the next ten minutes thinking of my mother—a beautiful, Christian woman who died before her time, but who loved me dearly.

P l a y e d

39

I drove around until I ended up in front of Freddie's hotel. I was going to run in there and tell him how Kelvin broke my nose and ask him for help to get away from him. In my mind, I decided Freddie was reliable, and I knew of anyone who was gonna bust a cap in Kelvin's ass it would be him.

I parked across the street in another rental car and wished I had something to cover my face with. I looked at the steering wheel and then at the hotel. All I had to do was get out of the car, walk across the street, and ask for help, and I would be free.

Instead of thinking about it, I was going to be about it. I grabbed my keys and prepaid phone, unlocked the door and stepped out of the car.

Only seconds later, Freddie walked out with Katrina on his arm and Marcus a few steps behind them.

Freddie stared at me. His mouth dropped, but he closed his

lips. A part of me wanted him to run to me and demand to know the name of the bastard that had the audacity to put his hands on me, but I knew that deep down inside, he wasn't going to do that. If I wanted help, I was going to have to go to him.

I turned, got back into my car and left. Fresh tears fell to my face as I realized I was in no better shape than when I met Freddie the first time.

I returned to the condo around noon with hopes that Kelvin was out of town again. He wasn't. His trucked was parked in his reserved space. I hesitated, contemplating what would occur when I encountered him again. After ten minutes of thinking, I mustered enough courage to get out of the car and go inside.

As I maneuvered the key into the lock, I detected the aroma of fresh garlic and basil. Jazz music played from beneath the door. *He got another chick over here*, I thought. My plan was to walk past them and go straight into my room.

I covered my face with the towel and held it with one hand while using the other to open the door.

"Baby, there you are." Kelvin was wearing a pair of boxers and a plain white T-shirt. "Where you been? I've been waiting on you for a while." He stirred a pot of boiling red sauce.

I stood, holding the towel over my face—speechless.

He danced around a little with the spoon, tasting here and stirring there. "Come on, baby, take the towel from your face. You look beautiful, and you know it."

He officially lost his mind: I was living with a mad man. Now, I was less afraid of him beating me and more afraid of his own state of mind. He was delusional.

"I just want to lie down, Kelvin. I don't feel well," I said.

"Lie down? I'm only here like once a month, and you don't want to spend time with me?" He put the spoon on the stove and placed his hands on the granite countertop. "What is it that you want from me? I bought you flowers, cooked your dinner. Damn that!" He grabbed my arms and forced me to sit on a

P l a y e d

barstool behind the counter. In front of me were two dozen of fresh cut, long-stem roses and a card that read: *I'm Sorry*.

"I can't breathe through my nose, Kelvin, so it's difficult for me to eat."

"Do I look like I give a damn about your nose? Here," he said as he threw a plate of spaghetti in front of me. "I want you to eat it all."

He stopped the music as he walked into the bedroom. It was silent for a moment, and then I heard a basketball game playing from the television in the distance, Kelvin cheering along.

I took a bite and was forced to chew with my mouth open. It was humiliating. But I wanted to eat as much as I could to prevent further confrontation, so I nearly licked the plate clean, grabbed some ice from the freezer and went into my room.

I wanted to pack up what few things I had, throw them into the back seat of the rental, and get out of there, but I didn't. I knew I didn't have a place to go at the moment, and I really didn't want to go to another hotel. I just wanted the storm to blow over—for him to leave again and allow me more time to get myself together. I couldn't be seen on the streets for a few days, because I looked like a freak.

After a long shower, I wrapped ice in a clean wash cloth and applied it to my face. The sun was high, but I wanted to sleep—to escape everything I felt. And again, for some reason, I thought of my mother.

My mother's spirit was so beautiful, and as a child, I yearned to be like her, to have everything in my heart and soul that she had. Although it seemed she had nothing, I never heard her cry or complain, even on the night she died.

"What you doing in there?" From behind the door, Kelvin's voice broke my train of thought. And just like that, the thought of my mother and her strength disappeared.

"I'm just lying down." There was a moment of silence, and then he walked in.

"What did I tell you? You won't sleep while I'm in town. Get up!" he screamed. I didn't move. "You know what? That's it. Lie

there," he said then dropped his underwear on the floor and climbed in bed on top of me. "Turn over. I can't stand to look at your face."

He forcefully buried my head in the pillow. "I can't breathe. Stop it! Please!"

"Shut up!" He thrust himself inside of me while I struggled and gasped for air. "What? You think you gon' leave me or something?" He continued to thrust himself inside of me without any regard to my pleas or cries. The ordeal lasted under five minutes, but he caused more damage than I could tolerate. He stood up from the bed and put on his boxers. "Try it."

Although I tried to regain my composure after he walked out and closed the door, the emotions built up inside me caved and I couldn't hold on any longer. The loudest wail that I'd ever heard escaped my lips. It was hard to breathe, and I began to pant. My heart rate increased as I realized that I ignored all of the warning signs to leave Kelvin because I wanted to live comfortably. And look how comfortable I was now! I dug my own grave. I had no one to turn to for help—no family or friends to call. And to Kelvin, I was already dead—worthless.

The kitchen was stocked with many types of liquor. I grabbed something clear, then walked back into my bedroom and locked the door. I retrieved the bottle of pain relievers prescribed by the doctor for my broken nose and took five of them, washing them down with the alcohol. Again, in a moment of weakness, I was running and found a solution to make a problem go away instead of dealing with it head-on.

After fifteen minutes, the drowsiness kicked in in full force. My body went limp across the bed. And although still lucid, my mind began to wander. As overwhelming as the emotional and physical pain I felt was, something inside of me yelled and demanded that I change my mind. I wasn't ready to go yet, it screamed. Not after all I'd already been through. My entire body was completely numb, yet tears began to well in my eyes and run past my ears.

Before closing my eyes completely, I whispered a cry that was long overdue, "Help me, Lord."

Played

40

The sun rose in the distance like it did every morning, casting shadows throughout my bedroom. The room was silent. The stench of vodka was heavy, and the liquid from the overturned bottle soaked my sheets. It felt as though someone wrapped rope around my head and pulled tightly.

I thought about how stupid I felt for driving to Freddie's hotel the day before and not even having the courage to ask for help. I could picture him and his people nursing me back to health, and Freddie and Marcus handling Kelvin like real men should. If I'd just gotten out of the car, Kelvin wouldn't have been able to rape me. If I'd just swallowed my pride and faced Freddie, I would probably be waking up in one of his hotel rooms instead of Kelvin's bed.

I coughed, trying to gather enough moisture to alleviate the dryness in my mouth. It didn't work. I showered and dressed before leaving the room to see if Kelvin was home. He

Triple Crown Publications *presents…*

wasn't. The plate that he'd piled with spaghetti the night before was still in the same place. His room door was wide open, bed completely made. Further examination revealed that his favorite overnight bag was gone. I knew I had to leave, and this served as an opportunity.

My bank statement revealed that I only had six hundred dollars, and the car rental was due back the following day. Everything about my situation pointed back to returning to the shelter, but I damn well refused to return there. I didn't want to go back to Freddie, either, because I felt I missed an opportunity for help when I had the chance.

The day came and went without a single word from Kelvin, and I was happy. The swelling inside and around my nose decreased a little, and my black eyes started to fade. I put on as much makeup as I could and hid what couldn't be concealed behind a large pair of sunglasses. I packed everything that belonged to me and placed it near the bedroom door. When I was done, I carried my belongings to the car, piece by piece, without a clue as to where I was going.

It seemed like one of the coldest days of the year. The air in the condo was warm and inviting after returning from each trip to the garage to load my things. Apart of the place was tugging at me, asking me to stay a little longer. I ignored the feeling. There was one more bag remaining in the condo, and I went to get it before saying my final goodbyes.

"Excuse me, ma'am," a man called out to me as I exited the elevator.

"Yes?"

"Do you live on this floor?" he asked, holding a large manila envelope.

"Yes, I do. May I help you with something?"

"I'm looking for ahh—" He looked down at the envelope. "A Miss Taj Jenson. Do you know where I can find her?"

"Who is the package from?" I asked out of curiosity.

"The Department of Children and Families." He stood there for a moment, awaiting a response. He was a short black man who probably could've passed for Johnta Austin's twin.

Played

Handsome, but from the way he spoke I assumed he was gay—there was too much of an emphasis on the "S" sound.

"That's me. I'm Taj Jenson." I reached for the package. I didn't know what to make of the situation.

"Actually, ma'am, may I come in to speak with you for a moment? I promise I will only take a moment of your time."

"May I see your identification please?"

He pulled an ID and a business card from his wallet and handed them both over to me. I invited him to follow me into the apartment, and he briefly looked around. "This is a really nice place."

"What is it that you're here for?" I asked impatiently.

"It's about a Micah Anthony Kingston. I believe he's your son. Right, ma'am?" He handed over the envelope.

I trembled at the thought that he was dead or hurt. It was a while since I last thought of Micah. I gave up trying to find him and get him back because to me, it seemed like a lost cause. "Yes, I'm his mother. Is he OK?" I opened the envelope anxiously.

"Well, he's safe, but he could be in a better situation."

"What's going on with him?"

"There was a fire. His foster parents lost everything, but they escaped injury, so everyone is OK—including Micah. For weeks now, we've been trying to locate relatives to see if Micah can be returned to the custody of his own family. The Henrys would like to piece their life back together again and—"

"I'm sorry. The who?" I asked, puzzled.

"Gregory and Destiny Henry were Micah's foster parents for the past eighteen months. They are in a bad place financially right now and can't handle the responsibility of properly caring for Micah."

I sat on the sofa, trying to take it all in. "And what is it that you want from me?"

He sat near me. "I've gone over your file several times and I know that you went through a rough time before and after giving birth to him. But that was over six years ago. I'm not an attorney, and believe me, I usually don't make house calls in situations like this, but one thing I do know is that people change."

"OK, you're right. So what?" I wanted him to get to the point.

"If you can prove that you have a stable environment in which to raise Micah, along with demonstrating your sobriety, then I'm sure that Micah can come home to you."

I was taken back and couldn't form a response. I found myself just sitting there quietly.

"I know it's a lot to take in, Ms. Jenson, and I don't expect an answer now. Take my card, and think about it. But understand that we'll have to place Micah with another foster parent if no one comes forth." He stood.

"Thank you," I said without looking up at him.

He stood up and began to walk to the door.

"Wait!" I called out, stopping him. "How did you find me?"

"I've been looking for you for awhile, but two days ago, I got a lead on this address. It seems that you updated your information at a hospital recently." He opened the door. "Enjoy the rest of your day."

His visit changed everything. My things were in the car, ready to be dropped off at a nearby shelter where I planned to take refuge until I was able to get on my feet. But now, along came an opportunity to regain custody of my son. Out of nowhere. I sat stunned, choosing between two decisions: Either I allow the opportunity to pass me by and let my son go back into the system, or I do everything I could to get him back. I opted for the latter.

In spite of the reasons that I showed up in the emergency room, something good came from it.

I sat in the living room in silence for at least an hour. Time passed quickly as I attempted to come up with a plan to gain custody of Micah and leave Kelvin altogether. There was no way that I would manage to get him back living in a shelter, so I couldn't leave. Asking Freddie for a room was out of the question because I needed a permanent address. I didn't know what would happen, or how far I would make it with my liv-

P l a y e d

ing arrangements, but I had faith that things had to work out somehow. If having Micah in my presence again was so impossible, how come this happened? How come this chance fell into my lap without any heads up? I looked at the card that I was given and knew that it was now or never.

The following morning, I dressed in a gray pant suit with gray and black pumps and headed downtown. Kelvin still hadn't returned, and I wasn't expecting him for at least another two weeks—his normal routine—so I was going to make the best use of my time alone.

Because of construction, traffic was backed up and the frustration added to my nervousness. Once I arrived at the brown bland building, I reached into my handbag for the social worker's card and approached the receptionist's desk.

"Franklin Turner's office please," I requested.

"Do you have an appointment with him ... um, Ms.—"

"Jenson. Taj Jenson. I don't have an appointment but he gave me his card and I'd lke to speak with him."

The receptionist made a phone call and within moments sent me down the hallway to Room 38A. The office was busy. Phones were ringing off the hook.

"Ms. Jenson." Franklin reached out to shake my hand. "It is really nice seeing you this morning. Step into my office."

Looking around, I saw the pictures he had scattered about, indicating he was married with children. Although the space was tight, he managed to have two book shelves, a file cabinet, and a full-size desk in the room.

"Have a seat." He reached for a file from his drawer. "I know why you're here today, so I'm going to get down to it."

I got comfortable. He explained that the process wouldn't be easy, but if I met certain criteria, it would be nearly impossible for the judge to rule against me. Amongst the criteria was a steady income, which I didn't have at the time. So anything he said following that went in ear and completely out the other.

"Do you want to see your son?" he asked, noticing my nonchalant attitude, and my thoughts shifted back to him.

"Whhaa—what? Is he here?"

"No, he's not here, but we can drive over for a visit."

I wanted to say yes but I was worried about how I would be perceived by not only Micah, but anyone who knew my history and would judge me for allowing my son to be born with drugs in his system. I was a teenager then, in pain and naïve, and although I wanted badly to prove that I was someone different, I really wasn't. In spite of all this, though, I accepted Franklin's offer, and we drove to see my son.

The building was in the very heart of downtown, brick, and smelled like a high school cafeteria. Everything was clean and sanitary. I could hear laughter and children playing from various areas of the building.

"Wait right here."

I sat in a waiting room with dolls and short, colorful plastic tables and child sized chairs. I wondered what Micah looked like, and the type of personality he had. Within moments, he was standing in front of me.

"Micah, this is Taj. Do you want to say hello?"

He had the biggest, most beautiful brown eyes that I'd ever seen. He had my nose and mouth, but his father's dark complexion. "Go ahead. Hug her."

He walked over to me and opened his arms wide without saying a word.

"Hey you," I said, hugging him as tight as I could, ignoring the involuntary tears in my eyes. For a while, he hugged back, then slowly loosened his grip and pushed away. I wondered if he gave up on me as I did him years ago.

"Say goodbye, Micah," Franklin said.

"Goodbye," he spoke and waved at me.

My heart broke.

"Wait a minute. Is that it?" I looked at Franklin, then back at Micah. "We just got here."

"Today is not a visitation day, and they try to keep the children on a strict schedule to maintain order."

"But, we can't just—"

"Listen. Someone let us visit out of a favor. I have to take

Played

him back now, but you'll see him soon."

Micah waved goodbye again.

"Goodbye." I tried to smile through my tears.

I returned to the condo late that afternoon and paced the living room floor, trying to come up with ways to get what I wanted—my son. I thought of robbing people or selling dope, selling sex or simply going downtown to kidnap him, but those were my old ways of doing things, and it was obvious that none of them yielded positive results in the past. I had to do something different. I had to find a legitimate job.

The following morning, I began my search downtown at various law firms. I figured that I would be able to hold a clerk position. And I knew I could have. But as it turned out, those positions were now being filled with high school graduates, and even some college graduates in the sluggish face of the economy. I tried the mailroom at several major companies; no one was hiring. Although I was intelligent and sophisticated, I'd never regretted dropping out of school until then.

Time was dwindling down, and I knew that if I couldn't prove myself able to care for Micah, then he would be swept back into the system. I swallowed my pride, and for the first time, really humbled myself in order to land a job. I stopped at various diners and restaurants and requested applications. Some of the managers were friendly and offered one to me, while others simply declared, "We're not taking applications. Try some other time."

By 2 o'clock, I was in need of an energy boost, so I stopped by a coffee shop on the corner near the condo, nestled between a smoothie shop and an upscale dry cleaner. The scent of fresh baked cinnamon rolls and blueberry muffins was intoxicating. The aroma alone gave me a sugar rush.

I rang the bell on the counter but no one appeared. I rang it again. "Hello?" I called.

"I'm sorry Miss," a man said quickly, emerging from the back of the shop. "Didn't want my muffins to burn." The stoutly looking man with kind, tired eyes gave me a grin and my heart melted. He had to be nearing 60. His white hair was combed neatly to one side and contrasted well with his dark skin. He hunched over when he walked. "What can I get you?"

I looked at the menu. "I'll have—hmm—a coffee and a cranberry muffin." I reached into my purse.

A buzzer went off in the back of the café. By then, three other patrons came in.

"Excuse me. If you would all bear with me for a moment, I have to check on something." He turned to walk away. I tried to look as far toward the back as I could to see if anyone was helping him, but there was no one. Two more patrons walked into the building.

"OK, ma'am, here is your order. That will be three dollars and sixty-five cents."

I handed him the money. "You're quite busy in here today," I told him.

"It's usually like this every day. I just can't manage as well as I did when Sarah was here."

"Who's Sarah?"

"My granddaughter. She left for college about a week ago. Now there's no one else to help me run the shop."

I thought for a moment. "If you don't mind me asking, how much did Sarah's position pay?"

"Well, eight dollars an hour. She had a lot of responsibilities." He returned my change.

I wanted to say more to him, but the other customers were becoming impatient. I thanked him, and then sat at a table near the window to enjoy my coffee and muffin and observed the old man.

When the last customer left the store, I approached the counter again. "If you don't mind, I would like to fill your granddaughter's position. I live just down the street, and I can be here every day and on time."

He hesitated. "I don't know. I didn't think of hiring someone so soon."

"Now is a better time than ever, mister—?"

"Kendall."

P l a y e d

"Mr. Kendall. With the rate you're going you'll tire yourself out before long. I can tell that your business means a lot to you, but you'll need help in order to keep it running."

"I can't agree with you more." He thought for a moment. "OK, first thing tomorrow morning, I want you to meet me here. I will go over all the responsibilities of the front store while I'm baking my first batches of muffins."

I shook his hand. I was proud to have talked myself into the first legitimate job I'd since I was a young teenager.

"You'll have to understand, I've never hired someone outside of my family to work in the shop for me, so, it'll take some getting used to," he warned.

"No problem. I'll see you tomorrow."

I returned to the condo and nursed my nose by massaging the aching spots. I wasn't excited about starting work the following day, but it was one day closer to getting my son. In any case, I tried calling around to other businesses looking for work, but no one was hiring. I slept hard that evening, knowing that the following morning I might endure backbreaking labor.

"So, are you really going to wear those shoes all day?" Mr. Kendall looked at me over the rim of his glasses.

"Yes, sir. This is my most comfortable pair. And cute, too." The way I admired my black Jimmy Choo stilettos by looking at them from every angle made Mr. Kendall smile.

He put me in charge of the dining area. I was to prepare orders, run the cash register, and make sure the counters and machinery were clean and tidy. Mr. Kendall observed me on and off but spent most of his time in the kitchen baking fresh goods.

By noon, my feet were aching beyond belief, but I never stopped to take a break. By closing, my feet hurt so bad that I walked back to the condo barefoot since I returned the rental the day before in order to save money. I was able to take a few leftover muffins and pastries that didn't sell, so I snacked on them that evening instead of purchasing a meal.

I soaked in a relaxing bath and rubbed my aching feet. This would have been the perfect opportunity to plot my next move, but I was sick of plotting. None of the plotting in my past ever took me anywhere. So, I thought to be as still as possible.

41

It could very well happen, I thought. The thought excited me—Micah coming to live with me. Now, I was finally put in a position to understand how San felt about the shows we performed—not to mention that my last show almost cost me my life. I knew that performing or even stripping had to be an absolute last resort, so there was no choice but to make it work with Mr. Kendall and the bakery. How else was I going to be able to provide for me and my son?

I thought back to the show I did with Tiki when I was supposed to be watching Sarai. I hoped I would be a better mother to Micah than I was an overseer to Sarai.

I decided to share the news about my pending reunification with my son with Freddie, so I took a bus and a cab to get to his hotel. When I walked into the lobby, I took notice of his thin twist braids. His back was to the hotel entrance.

"Hey, Freddie!" I chirped. He slowly and awkwardly turned

around. Bracing his hands on the counter, he looked at me through glazed eyes, but he appeared serene.

"What's up, Taj," he said, slowly and relaxed. Almost instantly, he closed his eyes, breathed in deeply and moved forward.

This nigga gotta be high, I thought, subtly inhaling the air around me. I walked to the counter with a huge smile on my face. Thinking I would smell weed as I got closer, I was surprisingly mistaken.

"I wanted to tell you that I was getting my son back."

"Oh, really?" He threw his head back, closed his eyes and jutted forward again. "That's nice. I wish I could get mine back," he choked out.

"You have a kid, Freddie?" In spite of myself, I couldn't mask my shock.

"Yes, but he's dead though." Freddie seems to struggle with his words, still slurring and slightly out of breath. "Oh yes!" he called out.

I looked around, then back at him. "I'm sorry." I felt guilty rubbing my accomplishment in his face.

"Oooh girl!" Freddie called out. "You didn't know." His body jerked, then he stood up straight.

"I apologize, Taj. I was just ... never mind." He laughed, smiled at me, then continued, "On the real, I'm happy you're getting your son back. I really am. I'd give my left nut if my son could return to me."

I nodded, sympathizing with him.

"I'll tell you this, too. Once you get your son back in your life, you gotta stop with the shows and stuff. I can't save you all the time. Oh yes!" he cried.

I nodded again, but this time I grew wary of how high he seemed.

"And," Freddie continued, "get you a good job ... something with benefits so you and your son will be alright. If you have to, go back to school so you can get a better job. Do something to better yourself because these kids are expensive."

P l a y e d

"Yes, sir."

"Ooh wee ..." he chirped, slamming his fist on the counter. "And if you can, find you a good man or a good woman to settle down with 'cause you are gonna need all the help you can get raising these children in these last and evil days."

"Man or a woman?" I asked.

Freddie twisted his lips at me. "Chile, I seen you when you and Tiki first got in here. We are just alike. I keep Marcus and Katrina around me 'cause most fags are selfish. They think that a man should be with a man only. Most women are selfish. They think that a man was only made for a woman, but I got news for you, my money goes like you and I do—both ways."

I chuckled. *Freddie is a damn nut,* I thought to myself.

"Damn, girl!" Freddie shouted as he wobbled back and forth.

"Huh?" I couldn't think of anything I said in the past few minutes to warrant that comment.

What the hell is he on? I thought as I watched him thrust his waist from front to back, as if he were tapping some ass doggy style. I stood on my toes and looked over the counter. I was shocked to discover Shai on her knees, licking Freddie's long, thick shaft slowly. I took a step back.

"I'm multi-talented. I can talk and screw at the same time." He looked down. "A'ight, Donner, get up." Freddie lifted Shai from her knees. She looked at me quickly then headed out to the pool, Freddie following.

I shook my head and attempted to wipe the grin off my face as I left the hotel, but I couldn't. Freddie was definitely hilarious.

I had a child over six years ago, but I didn't yet know how to be a mother. Six weeks passed since the last time I'd seen him. Kelvin had even come and gone twice, each time locked behind his bedroom door with a new acquaintance. The thought of failing Micah while he was in my custody plagued me more than the thought of someone else failing him.

Everything continued to line up properly in order to gain custody of Micah, and the day finally came for me to bring him home. I was excited, but so nervous I wanted to vomit.

Franklin opened the passenger door to let Micah out of the car. "He ate dinner before we left," he informed me, "so he shouldn't be hungry for the rest of the evening. If you need anything, Ms. Jenson, please don't hesitate to call."

"Thank you." I took Micah by the hand.

"Congratulations," Franklin said before kneeling to hug Micah goodbye.

Micah sat in the living room, quietly playing with action figure toys he was allowed to bring with him. He didn't say anything to me. I asked if he was thirsty, hungry, or bored. He denied each question. Finally he was mine again, but I had absolutely no idea what to do with him.

That evening, I drew a warm bath for him and made the water sudsy with some dish detergent. I threw a few of his waterproof toys in with him to keep him entertained. All the while he spoke little, if at all. Then, I dressed him in a pair of pajamas and clean underwear I'd bought from a discount store—the first thing I'd ever given him—and tucked him into my bed.

I sat in the chair pretending to read a book, but really I was watching him closely. For once, someone belonged to me—someone that I refused to have taken away again. I couldn't help but imagine everything he'd gone through. He wasn't as playful as most kids his age, and I was worried, but that was something that couldn't be fixed overnight.

His features, which resembled mine, were so angelic. As he fell deeper into his sleep, his nose expelled short puffs of air. I kneeled over him and kissed his cheek, and slept on the floor beside the bed that evening, on guard.

The following morning, I enrolled Micah into Peterson Elementary School along the bus route, where he began kindergarten. He was taller than most students in his class, but I knew that they were at least six to eight months older than he was, given that his birthday was in the latter half of

P l a y e d

265

the year. I hugged him goodbye, and again, he didn't say a word. I left him as he went over to play with a group of boys who were coloring handprints.

After standing all day—this time in better shoes—and taking the bus to pick up Micah from school, I was tired, and felt relieved once we reached the elevator. I leaned on the railing for support, just long enough to muster enough strength to get down the hallway and into the condo.

"Hold this for mama," slipped out from nowhere as I handed Micah a bag of baked goods from work. He looked puzzled and stared at me until I unlocked the apartment door.

I rushed into the bedroom and undressed quickly. The bed seemed to chant my name, so I threw myself into it and closed my eyes tightly. Within moments, there was a faint knock on the door. I sat up quickly.

"Yes?" I asked as Micah stood in the doorway.

"I'm hungry. I want to eat now, please."

I forgot to feed my son. I was so ashamed of my actions: and had he not come to me, it would have been morning before he ate anything.

I got out of bed. "Do you want a sandwich?" I asked. "I have turkey."

He shook his head, then climbed up into the barstool behind the counter.

"OK. Well, what about a hot dog? Do you like those?"

He said, "Yes," and smiled big. He reminded me of me in that moment.

I obviously took a step in the right direction. I stayed awake long enough to prepare him for bed and read a chapter in my novel as he fell asleep. I hadn't eaten all day, but my appetite completely faded.

The following morning went as the day before—up at 6 a.m., out by 7 a.m., and nearing home by 6 p.m.

"What did you learn in school today?" I asked Micah, who was busy tossing his action figure into the air and catching it.

"Dog is D-O-G. Cat is C-A-T. Blue is B-L—" He stopped, trying to think of the remaining letters.

"U," I offered.

"U-E," he added.

As we approached the door, I noticed that there was a light on inside the apartment. I thought I was sure to turn everything off in the morning before leaving for work. After considering that I possibly left it on by accident, I assumed the worst—that Kelvin was home.

I pulled the keys from my bag, unlocked the door, and moved Micah to the side while I took a peek into the apartment. I couldn't see or hear anything. Everything was in place. *I left the light on*, I thought. We went inside. Just as I closed the door a woman's voice startled me.

"Who the hell are you?" she asked, dressed in a long, colorful loose-fitting dress. Her complexion was that of a black woman, but her grade of hair indicated something different. Her eyes were exotic, and her makeup was applied flawlessly.

"What?" I said, confused about the situation. I assumed that she was one of Kelvin's whores. "Where is Kelvin?"

"No, I'm asking all the questions here," she barked.

"How did you get in here? Did Kelvin leave you here?"

"No. I'm Valerie ... Kelvin's wife." She put her hands on her hips, then dangled a set of keys in the air. "A wife has all the access to her husband's property. So, again, who are you?"

"I'm just a friend," I said hesitantly.

Micah was watching the entire time. "Go in the next room," I said to him.

"No, wait." She rushed over to Micah and roughly lifted his chin. "Is this—"

I grabbed her wrist as tight as I could. "If you don't get your damn hands off my son—"

"What?" She was at least three inches shorter than me.

I looked down to her. "I said get your damn hands off my son." I turned to Micah. "Go in the next room."

"Is that my husband's son?" she nearly cried.

"No, Micah is *my* son." I patted my chest.

"You wouldn't tell me the truth anyway." She turned away.

"I don't have anything to hide from you."

Played

She turned back and looked at me. Squinting her eyes, she pointed a finger toward me. "Really?"

I nodded.

"Well, what I want to know is why in the hell are you here, and where in the hell is my husband?"

I chuckled. "You know what? Your guess is better than mine." I dropped my keys on the counter. "I don't keep tabs on your husband."

"So, what ... he paying for you to stay here or something?" She walked into the living room and took a look around in disbelief.

"No, he lives—wait, this is a conversation you should be having with your husband, not me." I folded my arms.

"You know, I heard the same thing from the woman living in his house in Baltimore, the same thing from the woman in Cincinnati, again from the Hispanic chick in Miami, and once more from the woman in San Diego. I'm tired, and I want some answers." She plopped down on the sofa and covered her face with her hands.

"Have you called him?" I asked, moving in a little closer to her.

"Of course I've called him." She removed her hands. "He screens my calls." She focused her attention on me again. "So, tell me, are you screwing my husband, too?"

I hesitated and exhaled. I didn't want to add to her long laundry list, but I didn't want to lie to her either. "A long time ago I did. He spends more time with other women he brings in and out of here than he does with me to be honest."

"You mean, there are more?" She looked disgusted, but then chuckled silently to herself, unamused.

"More than are worth counting," I replied. I almost felt sorry for her. As I observed her, I noticed how beautiful she was. I couldn't understand if this is what he went home to, why was he cheating with me and every other chick?

"My God! He has an addiction."

"It's not an addiction," I told her truthfully. "Women are with him 'cause he has money."

She looked serious, and stood from her seat. "I'm sick and tired of you gold-digging hoochies trying to get something from my man. If it weren't for all of you, he would be at home with me and our four children."

She caught me off guard. "Four children? You and Kelvin have *four* children together?"

"Yes, we have *four* beautiful children," she spat. "And if it wasn't for sluts like you, then—"

"Hold on now. I've done a lot of things, but one thing I do know is that you can't blame me or any of the other women your husband has sprawled across the continent for his infidelity. At what point do you expect for him to take some responsibility for what he is doing?"

"Don't play Dr. Phil with me, bitch."

I shook my head at her in disbelief. "You know ... your husband's psycho, abusive ass can use some damn counseling. Does he beat you too or does he save that for his gold digging hoochie sluts as you call us? Or maybe it's just me he likes to put his hands on. I can't vouch for the other women."

Her eyebrows raised. "You liar!" she shrieked.

"You wish," I spat back.

"Why are you here if my man beats on you? Still in it for the money, huh?"

I couldn't find the words to say. For a moment, I imagined Micah overhearing our conversation and remembering it for the rest of his life.

"Please, keep your voice down. My son is—"

"I don't give a damn about your son. Actually, you can both gather your things and get the hell out!" She looked serious.

"What? You can't be serious."

"Oh, yes I am." She went to the bedroom door and knocked. "Excuse me, little boy," she called cloyingly and fake.

"Get away from my door." I pushed in front of her, daring her to knock again.

"Actually, this is Kelvin's door, my husband. And what is his, is also mine."

"Regardless of who the door belongs to, you can't evict us

Played

unless you give us thirty days. It's the law." I thought rapidly. "You may want to do your homework before you start trying to put people out."

She backed away and started bawling, obviously reaching the end of her rope.

"Why are you doing this to yourself?" I asked her.

"Kelvin owes me—everything. I birthed four babies for him, gave up all of my goals, all while he ran around the country on me, screwing everything in sight."

I offered a simple suggestion. "Then leave him."

"If I leave him, I'll have nothing."

"So, it's about the money with you, too, then," I recanted.

She looked up at me in shock. "You have no right to speak to me that way. I'm his wife, and I have his children."

"And he has no right to cheat on you ... his wife." I shot back. "Look, I don't know a lot about law, but I do know that infidelity is one of the easiest ways to get what you deserve."

"Oh, yeah? And by the time I'm able to really prove it, Kelvin would have made it go away. He's more powerful than you can imagine." He obviously threatened her as much as he'd threatened me. I could see a blink of fear in her eyes when she spoke of him. "I have to fly back to Atlanta to be with my children now. They can't be without their mother *and* their father."

"Atlanta?" I asked. "I thought you were in Denver. That's where Kelvin always claims he's at."

She shook her head, picked up her sweater from the back of the barstool and grabbed her expensive handbag from the seat. I followed her with my eyes.

"Enjoy him," she said, and walked out the door.

42

A week passed since Valerie's visit, and I hadn't heard a single word from Kelvin. He was like a ghost who showed up on occasion and made life a living hell. But for some reason he never kicked me out. I hoped that by the time he would come home again, I would have found a better place for Micah and me. With the eight dollars an hour I was being paid at the bakery, the cost of after-school care, and money used to feed us both, I only managed to save eight hundred dollars, which was enough for a deposit and one month's rent at a rundown apartment complex a few blocks from Micah's school. However, using the money would mean that we would go hungry until I made more. I needed more time.

"Tie your shoes," I said to Micah as I prepared to walk out the door.

"But I tied them," he responded.

"Do it again. The string has come loose."

Micah stood near the front door moving slowly as he attempted to retie his shoe. I wanted to hurry him along, so I knelt to help him. Suddenly, I heard a clicking noise behind me and keys rattling on the other side of the door. Before I was able to stand, Kelvin was standing over me.

He smiled and stooped near Micah. "Well, well. This is what my wife called blowing up at me about." He playfully grabbed Micah's nose. I didn't stop him.

"Come on, Micah. Let's go." The hairs on my neck began to rise.

"Go? Why is it that every time I come home you have somewhere to go? Are you not happy to see me?"

"Yes, but I have to get Micah to school, and I have to go to work and we're—" I spoke quickly.

"Micah? Work? Don't you think we need to talk about this?"

"Yeah, but not right now, Kelvin. I honestly have to go."

He grabbed me by the throat and squeezed tightly. I yelped, but didn't want to scream and startle Micah.

Kelvin whispered into my ear. "Do you want your little boy to watch me do this?"

"No," I responded, still in a chokehold. "Micah, go in the other room," I forced out.

"But I thought we were going to school," he talked back again.

"IN THE ROOM!" I yelled as loud as I could for someone being choked. He hurried into the room and closed the door.

Kelvin delivered a powerful blow to my stomach that forced me to the floor. Then, he pulled me by the hair into his bedroom. I didn't scream. He closed and locked the door behind us.

"Kelvin, I don't know what your wife said, but I didn't mean for—"

"Shut up! See that's the thing. You talk too damn much. I don't give a damn about what my wife thinks, or what she says, or whatever it is that you or the other bitches told her. This here is my world. But I'm guessing you forgot, and now

I have to remind you." He slapped me with the back of his hand.

"Do you think that if I don't go home to be with my own kids that I want to be around yours?" He slapped me again.

"I'm sorry, Kelvin," I offered, face burning and red.

"Sorry? You're sorry?" He dropped his pants to the floor. "Show me."

He was hard as a rock. Grabbing my head, he forced himself into my mouth, thrusting back and forth as if her were inside of me. I would have bitten the hell out him if I thought I would be able to grab Micah and make it out the front door before he could catch me, but if I couldn't we'd be dead. It was obvious that my efforts weren't good enough, so Kelvin lifted me from the floor to the bed and finished there. Afterward, he immediately jumped in the shower and didn't say another word.

I slowly got up from the bed, cradling my abdomen area. I didn't have time to nurse myself back or even cover any wounds before leaving the apartment. I opened my bedroom door and signaled for Micah to come out. The mirror on the ceiling of the elevator was my only shot at fixing myself up before missing another bus.

We stood at the bus stop for six minutes, waiting for the number eight bus. I leaned on the pole, hoping to regain my strength and not vomit. Micah continued to play with his action figures as though nothing happened.

"You were supposed to be here an hour ago, Ms. Jenson." Mr. Kendall stood near one of his industrial mixers with specks of flour on his nose.

"I know. I wasn't feeling well, so I missed the first bus to take my son to school."

"You have a son?" he asked, shockingly.

"Yes, he's in kindergarten."

Hunched over, I walked to retrieve my apron from behind the swinging door and tied it around my waist.

"Is everything alright?"

"I'll be fine."

P l a y e d

I wanted to ball up in a corner and cry my heart out. The pain was excruciating enough for a trip to the emergency room, but I knew that another visit could possibly result in me losing Micah again. When Mr. Kendall wasn't looking or when there were no customers, I caught hold of the pastry displays in order to keep from falling. Otherwise, I tried to stand as straight as possible and smiled to not indicate the pain I felt.

There was so much that I wanted to do, but couldn't. I wanted to scream and cry, but had to keep my composure. I wanted to go to the hospital, but was forced to endure the physical and mental hurt. I wanted to pack my things and leave Kelvin's place. Then in an instant, while counting back change from a twenty to a customer, I stumbled upon a way to do so.

It was near closing and the drawer contained at least eight hundred dollars. I thought to take only some of it and return to work the following day as though nothing had occurred. Then, I thought to take the entire stash, run like hell out the front door and never return. I nervously bit my bottom lip, thinking of what to do.

After the final customer, I locked the front door. Mr. Kendall was in the back, cleaning pans and the equipment while I swept the front of the café.

"Make sure you sweep the floor good tonight, Ms. Jenson. I saw a few crumbs this morning when I came in. We don't want roaches and bugs."

"Yes, sir," I responded.

My mind was far from crumbles on the floor. I had a decision to make. My heart pounded quickly as I ran to the cash drawer and emptied all its contents into my pockets. A twinge of guilt flashed through my mind, but I knew I must go through with it.

"Make sure you clean the outside of the glass display as well," he called. "Some of the children put their little handprints on the outside of the glass."

I stopped for a moment and thought of Micah. The money

would be useful in getting us out of our situation, but may ultimately result in me losing him again, which would create a major contradiction. I had come too far to lose him again.

"You worked really hard today, Ms. Jenson, and I could tell you weren't feeling well." The clangor of the pots and pans from the kitchen began to drown him out. "Go home and get some rest. Take a day off."

I felt so much remorse for attempting to steal from him. I emptied my pockets and replaced the money quickly. I couldn't stand to look at Mr. Kendall after what I'd done, especially when he had been so generous to me. I wanted to die. I left my apron on the counter, left the store and thanked God I hadn't got caught.

The bus let me off at Micah's school. For the first time, he ran to hug me when he noticed I was there to pick him up. His head pressed against my aching abdomen, and I reacted by grabbing his shoulders and pushing him away from me. He looked upset. I didn't want him to feel as though he couldn't embrace me, but the look on his face indicated that's what he perceived.

I squatted next to him. "I'm sorry, baby. My tummy hurts, and I just didn't want you to make it worse."

He nodded in understanding, and I took his hand and led him away.

We walked three blocks to a corner discount store. The sun was beginning to set, so the lights from inside the store were more luminous. Micah stopped down the toy aisle while I made my way to the hardware section. I needed to purchase a lock for the bedroom door. I knew that we wouldn't be totally safe until I moved, but I had to try something. I purchased an eight-dollar door knob and lock set, a Spider-Man figurine, and a pack of Skittles. With that, we sat on the corner until the next bus came.

Kelvin's truck was still parked in his space, and there was no way I could face him just then. Instead, I walked Micah to the indoor basketball court at the bottom floor of the building. There was a young man, possibly in high school, shoot-

Played

ing around by himself. When he saw Micah he offered him an opportunity to shoot. I sat on the bench near the court cheering him on as the young man lifted him into the air. After a half hour, I checked to see if Kelvin was still there. He was.

Next, we went into the building's library on the second floor of the building. Micah had no clue about what I was doing. He thought that we were simply playing and reading together. I found a couple of tattered Dr. Seuss books collecting dust in the corner of a bookcase and read them aloud to him. At the thought of green eggs and ham, Micah tightened his expression in disgust.

I could have read every book in that room in order to waste time and avoid confrontation with Kelvin, but the truth was that I couldn't avoid him forever.

"I'm hungry now," Micah said, rubbing his eyes.

"Oh, really? And what do you have taste for?" I asked trying to buy more time.

Micah shrugged his shoulders. "I don't know."

I walked to the basement door in time enough to watch Kelvin's truck pull away. My heart raced when I saw it, but I was relieved. I went back to the library and grabbed my son. We rode up in the elevator making silly faces in the mirror. He laughed harder at each one we made. I was glad he was coming around.

A can of chicken and vegetable soup warmed on the stove as I pried off the doorknob to my room and replaced it with the new one I purchased. I rushed Micah's dinner, and after cleaning the mess, brought him into the room and locked the door.

"I want you to stay in here tonight, OK?"

He nodded.

"Good, so, let's get ready for bed."

I ran his bath water and packed some of our things. I knew that we would be leaving soon, but I didn't know just how soon it would be.

After I tucked Micah in, I undressed and noticed a purple bruise the size of two grapefruits near my torso. I could barely touch it. I wanted to take something for the pain, but feared that I would lose alertness and ability to defend us if Kelvin were to return. As I showered, warm droplets of water blended with the tears that beaded down my body and ran off into the drain.

Getting in bed next to my son, he slept peacefully, though I couldn't sleep at all.

Played

43

The Winter Lake apartments required a three hundred-dollar deposit and four hundred and thirty-five dollars for the first month's rent. I submitted the application and timidly handed over a three hundred-dollar money order. The apartment wouldn't be ready to move into for another week and a half, so I attempted to stay put a little while longer.

After a month and a half of being in my custody, Micah opened up to me completely, sharing everything he learned in school including the drama that went on between him and his playground buddies. It was difficult being a parent, but to see him smile and sleep peacefully at night was rewarding.

Micah was due for routine shots, so I took a half day from work.

We sat in the waiting area of the clinic and Micah looked up at me as I looked around. There were women of all nationalities with their children. With their ongoing chatter, most of them barely spoke English. Micah tugged at my arm. "Will I have to get shots? I don't want shots," he pleaded, holding his arm tightly.

"Juliana Santiago," a nurse called, and a short Latina picked up the baby carrier near her ankles and left the waiting area.

"But shots hurt. Please don't make me get one," Micah continued, pleading his case.

"It'll be OK, Micah. Be a big boy for me." I handed him a piece of chocolate from my bag, attempting to pacify him.

In the same instance, a new woman walked into the front door. She was alone; there were no newborns or toddlers with her. There was something very familiar about her—tall, very pretty French vanilla complexion and high cheekbones.

"May I have your name, please?" the woman behind the glass asked.

"Sonya Robinson."

"OK, Ms. Robinson. Someone will call you back in a minute."

She sat across from me, avoiding eye contact. It was Sunny, Tiki's friend from the show. I shook my head. Now an opportunity came to get this chick, and it was bad timing on my end. I looked over at my son and knew I needed to play it cool. Micah just started warming up to me, and it would do me no good to go to jail now.

She lifted a magazine to her face in order to conceal her identity. Sunny was no friend of mine, so I didn't care to speak to her if she didn't speak first.

"Tashameka Billups." A nurse called for the next patient and a young, black mother picked up her toddler from the seat next to her and left the waiting room.

Sunny lowered the magazine in order to see the nurse and caught a glimpse of me.

"Taj?" She looked directly at me, pretending she didn't know me. "Is that your name?"

"Yes. You're Sunny, right?" I thought two could play that game.

P l a y e d

"Yeah." She paused. "Well, how have you been?"

"Making it. And you?"

"I'm good."

I saw that Micah was distracted, and so I moved to sit closer to her. I figured I'd try a different approach. "Look, that was messed up how you took my dress and my money—"

"Like it was messed up that you screwed my man," she cut me off.

"We were drunk, high and horny. You knew I didn't know who your man was nor did you make an effort to point him out to me."

Sunny rolled her eyes and turned her bald head away from me. "Bitch, you aren't getting your money."

I wanted to slap her right then and there but Micah ran up to me instead, preventing us from dueling. I gave him a few more pieces of chocolate and told him to stay close.

Sunny peeped at the scene and looked up when another patient's name was called. I was quiet for a moment. "When was the last time you heard from Tiki?" she asked seriously.

"It's been a long time. How is she? Still up to her old ways?" I didn't conceal the attitude in my voice.

Sunny placed her shades over her eyes. "No, not quite. Tiki passed away a week ago."

My heart stopped for a moment. "You mean, Tiki's dead?"

A tear streamed from beneath Sunny's shades. "Yeah. She was in the hospital for a few days. She was just sick, so we thought. We just didn't know how sick she was."

Everything came flooding back to me—the night I last saw Tiki and what Dre, one of the clients, warned me about. I've gone through a lot since then and suppressed the memory.

"What was it?" I asked.

"What was what?" She wiped her face with her hand.

"How did she die?" I stared blankly at her.

"Her parents won't say—and doctors couldn't tell us. Some people say that Tiki had AIDS. Everything points to it."

"Oh my God." My heart began to pound, but I didn't say anything else on the subject.

"Micah Kingston," the nurse called.

I looked over at the door, then back at Sunny. "I have to go." I stood and grabbed Micah's hand.

"Is this your son?" she asked before we walked away.

"Yes." I headed out the door.

The nurse set up a small tray of needles and several vials of medication to inject into Micah. He immediately began to cry. As full of thoughts as I was at that moment, I couldn't help but feel sorry for him.

"It will only take a minute, baby. I promise." He grabbed tightly and clung to me. It was as close as we had ever been.

"Ma'am, we'll need to calm him down, so that we can give him the shots."

"No! No shots! Please!" Snot oozed from his nose.

"Well, if you wouldn't have all the needles on display then maybe he wouldn't be so hysterical. There has to have been a better way to spring this on a kid," I yelled over Micah's cries.

"Please!" he pleaded and looked at me.

"Mama can't stop her from giving you the shots now. I'll give you something if you're a big boy though." I reached into my purse and pulled out the Spider-Man figurine I bought him.

"But I don't want it. You can have my Spider-Man. I don't want it," he cried.

I sighed, then came up with a good idea to calm him.

"Nurse, may I speak with you outside for a moment?"

She nodded.

Moments later, when I re-entered the room, Micah swung his legs from the edge of the exam table. His eyes were puffy, and he rubbed his nose.

"See, I have to get a shot, too," I told him as two nurses followed me in.

He looked surprised. "You have to get one, too?"

"Yep, but I'm going to be a big girl. Can you be a big boy for me?"

He looked as though he wanted to cry again, but he didn't.

"OK. Sit in my lap. I'll hold you, and we can do it at the same time."

P l a y e d

281

One nurse moved in on my left carrying a tray with a tourniquet, three empty vials, and a needle. The other nurse slowly approached Micah, cleaned his arm gently with an alcohol pad, then filled the first needle. He nestled his head against my chest.

"You don't have to look, baby," I told him.

The nurse found a good vein, and I pumped my fist a little before she inserted the needle. While Micah was getting his shots, I took the initiative to take another HIV test.

"Ooouuucchh!" Micah yelled after his first injection, face still pressed against me.

"See, it's over. Now that wasn't so bad!"

The nurse attached a new vial and continued to draw blood from me.

"Ooouuucchh!" Micah screamed again when the other nurse gave him his second shot. By his third shot, he didn't say a word. He merely jumped a little. After his third shot, I was all done.

With the two of us bandaged and achy, I treated Micah to a cheeseburger and milkshake in a diner across the street from the clinic. I was proud of him—proud to have him, but I feared the worst. In spite of the reckless life that I lived, even taking beatings from Kelvin, I never considered dying. I always thought that I would end up in jail before I wound up dead. Perhaps I was wrong.

I watched Micah play with his milkshake for an hour before we headed back to the apartment. Again, no one was at home. Football season started, so I knew that Kelvin's visits would be few. Besides, I only needed another week or so before my apartment was available.

I removed Micah's bandages and ran a hot bath for him.

"You know I can make my own water now."

"Oh, you can?" I was impressed by his comment. "Well, let's see you do it." I sat down on the toilet beside the tub.

He took the bubble bath from beneath the sink and poured it into the water.

"That's enough! That's enough!" I called to him.

He swished the water around a bit with his hand, undressed, and climbed in.

"Wow. Who taught you to run your own bath?" I asked.

"Ms. Henry," he replied.

I took it as an opportunity to really talk to him—maybe probe a little. "So, who was Ms. Henry?"

"I lived with her. Then, her house burned down," he said as he dipped Spider-Man into the water.

"Were you in the house?"

He nodded.

"Well, were you scared?"

He nodded again.

"You're such a brave boy." I paused for a minute, thinking that my son could have died in a house fire, but no, he was alive and with me now. "Do you miss Ms. Henry?"

"She was nice, but I like you better."

He smiled big, and all my worries melted away.

Played

44

"There is so much to be done, Ms. Jenson." Mr. Kendall was driving himself crazy preparing pastries for his niece's wedding.

"Calm down, Mr. Kendall." I softly patted him on the back. "We have time. I'm here to help you."

"The wedding is tomorrow, and I have to bake goods for the shop today on top of everything for her wedding tomorrow. And I couldn't start earlier, they wouldn't be as fresh." He tightly tied his apron around his waist.

"You've shown me how to bake muffins. How about when the store is clear, I come back here and help you bake as much as I can."

"I don't want to put too much on you."

"Believe me," I chuckled, "you can't do that."

"Well, let's get to it!"

A couple of days passed since I got tested and on the

third day, I received another negative result. I felt better, but I still had to do what I needed to become free. Every day, I worked to show Mr. Kendall that it wasn't a mistake to hire me and that I could be trusted. I busied myself sweeping, wiping countertops, taking orders, and baking when I had a free moment. The shop was as busy as any other day, but this day, we were busier than normal. Mr. Kendall never left the kitchen, so I would only see him when I stepped in the back to lend a hand.

The bell on the counter chimed, and I went to the front, dusting traces of flour from my apron. Out of the corner of my eye I saw the customer approach.

"May I help you, sir?" I asked.

"I'll have—hmm." The man stared at the menu for a moment, and then looked at me. "A muffin."

His skin color said that he was black, but his eyes were green and almond-shaped. He looked like the black version of David Beckham, and he walked like him, too. I felt guilty for looking at him in that fashion because I usually preferred my men taller and darker, but like Boris Kodjoe, he was starting to put a dent into that preference.

"What kind, sir?"

"Wow, you're so polite."

"Well, I would think I have to be, given that I'm supposed to provide good customer service," I told him.

"So, you're telling me that you're not always this polite?"

I ignored him. I wasn't in the mood for flirting. I had a job to do. "What kind of muffin would you like?"

"No 'sir' that time? Wow. How quickly we lose politeness." He smiled.

"Do you want the muffin, or don't you?"

Just then, Mr. Kendall sprang from the back for the first time all day.

"Quentin! Are you out here giving Ms. Jenson are hard time?" He cheerfully walked toward the man and hugged him.

"You know me, pop."

P l a y e d

285

"Taj, this is my youngest boy, Quentin."

"It's nice to meet you." I extended my hand to shake his, but he folded his arms across his chest.

"Is that right?"

"Never mind him, Ms. Jenson. He's a spoiled, rotten child."

"I'm kidding." He reached out to shake my hand. "It's a pleasure."

Just then, in that awkward moment, the phone rang. I hurried over and answered.

The phone call was from Micah's school. The nurse on the other end explained that Micah had come down with some kind of stomach flu and needed to leave school immediately.

"But I'm working right now ma'am, and I can't—"

"He can't stay here in this condition, Ms. Jenson. We don't want to be held accountable for his condition worsening or for him passing it along to other students."

"OK. Thank you."

I hung up the phone and loosened my apron.

"Is everything OK, Taj?" Quentin asked.

"It's my son. He's sick, and I have to go and get him." I threw the apron on the counter. "Of all days, he picked the busiest one to get sick."

"I'll bet you anything that right now he'd rather not be sick," Quentin remarked, eyeing me closely. "He's a child. They never choose when or how to get sick." He picked up the apron from the counter. "Go ahead. I'll cover for you for a few hours, but I can't stay all day."

"Thank you. Thank you." I grabbed my bag and headed out the door, too quickly to express my gratitude to him.

By the time I took the bus and arrived at Micah's school, he lay weak on the cot in the nurse's office.

"He won't have an appetite for a little while, Ms. Jenson, but you need to make sure that he gets plenty fluids," the nurse said.

"Like what? Water?"

"No, something a little better. Gatorade usually works with keeping them hydrated. Otherwise, you'll be in the ER with a dehydrated little boy."

I most definitely wanted to steer clear of any hospitals, so I carried Micah to the bus stop and waited. We stopped in the convenience store on the corner near our building, and I stocked up on four of the largest bottles of Gatorade that I could find and a few cans of soup. Micah walked faintly to the front door and nearly passed out in the bed once he was inside. I forced him to drink nearly a half bottle of the sports drink and asked him a series of questions that would indicate his level of pain or discomfort. He only wanted to sleep.

He dozed off for a half hour, then I woke him and had him take in more fluids. He drifted back to sleep immediately afterward.

It was almost three in the afternoon. I was away from the shop for nearly three hours and knew that I had to return.

"Micah, baby?"

He mumbled.

"I'm going to leave your juice right here, OK? When you wake up, I want you to drink a whole cup of it, OK?"

"OK," he said sleepily.

I locked the room door and left the apartment. I knew that I would return in two hours, even if I had to run home. Even so, the memory of Sarai flooded my mind and I felt guilty for leaving him there by himself, especially in the house of a madman. But what choice did I have? I couldn't bring him to the job sick, and I still needed to work to make that money so we could finally be independent of Kelvin. As I walked to the shop, I looked at the sky, thought of my mother and said a quick prayer that my son would be OK when I returned home. And that I wouldn't turn into a bad parent.

The line was nearly out the door when I returned to work. We were out of fresh coffee, and Quentin was slow on restocking the racks with products. I jumped right in and helped where I could until the line dwindled down significantly and only Quentin and I remained.

Played

"It's great that my dad hired you. Usually he's really a stubborn man. Has a lot of trust issues, too."

"I can't see all that. He's been really nice to me," I said, wiping crumbs from the counter. I thought about the time I was going to steal from him, and was glad instead that I earned his trust.

"Well, I can see why."

"So, are you getting ready to leave, son?" Mr. Kendall came into the front store.

"Yeah, pop. I got a lot to do before the sun sets. Gotta get to it."

"Alright then, be safe out there." They hugged.

"It was really nice meeting you again," he said to me. We shook hands, and he was gone.

I spent the next hour wrapping individual muffins into colored plastic wrap and discussing Mr. Kendall's family. He explained that his wife had birthed three children and died of cancer, leaving him to take care of the kids, which he claims to have done the best he could given the circumstances. He said that he started the bakery with his children after she died in order to keep them busy and bring in a steady income. Each of his children and his older grandchildren had worked in the café, but now that most of them were older and had their own lives, he was left to run it alone.

"I'll retire soon. I just know it. I'm getting to be an old man."

"What do you mean? You're already an old man." We both laughed.

The last muffin was wrapped, the floor swept, and the counters cleaned. Mr. Kendall decided to close the shop to attend his niece's wedding, so he offered me a paid day off from work. I quickly accepted, thinking I would have time to nurse my son back to health before sending him to school.

Mr. Kendall and I left the shop and I rushed home to be with Micah, praying along the way that he was OK. Each step I took, my heart beat faster, hoping nothing happened to him. The elevator couldn't reach my floor fast enough.

When the doors opened, I rushed inside. Everything was still as I left it. I unlocked the door to my room and could hear water running in the bathroom. Seeing that he drank the rest of the Gatorade, but he wasn't in bed, I walked to the bathroom door.

"Micah?"

The water was still running.

"Micah?" I turned the nob but the door was locked. Sarai and the lake crossed my mind again. "Micah!" I pounded on the door and shook the doorknob furiously.

"Shut up, bitch!" yelled a deep, masculine voice from inside. It was Kelvin.

I pounded on the door as fast and as hard as I could. I tried ramming it with my shoulder, hoping to knock it off the hinges. "What are you doing? Get out of there! Leave my son alone! Micah!"

Just then, the door swung open. "What the hell is your problem?" Kelvin was standing in front of me in his underwear. His erect penis fought to peek through the fabric. Micah stood naked near the tub, holding himself.

I found it hard to stand or breathe. My first instinct was to attack Kelvin and literally rip out his eyes. Instead, I ran as fast as I could to his bedroom, into his closet and flipped over as many Jordan boxes as I could before he could come in and stop me. By the eighth box, his pistol fell onto the floor. I picked it up and ran back into my bedroom. I didn't care whether the gun was loaded or not, I was going to find a way to use it.

"You son of a bitch!" I didn't think to aim, I just lifted the gun up in Kelvin's direction and fired one shot, shattering the mirror above the vanity.

Micah screamed, but I ignored him.

"What the hell is your problem? Put the gun down!" Kelvin stretched out his hand to take the weapon.

"Get out!" I screamed.

"This here is my house! Now give me my gun!"

"Get out!" I screamed again as I brought the gun up and

Played

tried to line it with Kelvin's face. I fired the gun, this time taking a chunk of Kelvin's ear.

He touched the side of his head and examined the blood on his hands. Immediately, he lunged toward me.

"Get out of here or I'll kill you! I swear, I'll kill you!" I aimed directly for his chest.

Kelvin grabbed his ear as he walked past me. "You think you'll get away with this?" he roared, furious.

"I'm going to get away with it! But don't you think, not even for a minute, that *you've* gotten away with this. What would all your fans and your teammates think when they find out that you like playing with little boys, you sick bastard!"

Kelvin looked serious and lowered his hand from his ear. "I'm leaving. See." He grabbed his keys from the counter and walked backward toward the front door leaving in his underwear.

I fell to the floor in disbelief for a moment and cried. It would be the last time that I shed tears over Kelvin or any situation that he'd take me through. I was fed up. There was no more time to lie dormant. I waited long enough.

We had to make a move before Kelvin returned or before one of the neighbors called to report gunfire in the building. I stood quickly and turned the water off.

Micah looked scared and I grabbed him and held him. "I'm sorry, baby. Did he hurt you?" Although he shook his head no, I inspected his body for any types of signs of violation. *Thank God,* I thought to myself. I wanted to question him more, but we had to go. I wrapped him in an oversized towel as tears continued to burn a path down each of my cheeks.

"Is he gone, Mama?" It was the first time that Micah had ever referred to me as his mother. Although I was still furious at what transpired, on the inside, I was smiling.

"Yes, he's gone. We won't see him again."

I turned off the running water and rushed Micah into the bedroom to get dressed. I threw all of our possessions on the

bed and packed them in every empty box or bag that I could find. Micah sat in the chair near the bed, subtly watching me yet pretending to be interested in his figurines. I called a taxi and fifteen minutes later, it was waiting for us outside.

"Carry this for Mama." I handed Micah a large overnight bag that was nearly larger than he was.

"But it's heavy."

"We're not going far, baby. I promise."

He stuffed his toy into the side of the bag and began to drag it down the hallway toward the elevator. My hands were stacked with boxes of our belongings, so I didn't lock the door. There was no need to. I knew that we would never return.

45

That evening, we made it to Freddie's hotel. I never felt as safe as I did at that moment in time. I was slightly disappointed that Freddie wasn't there to check me in, but Katrina helped me carry my things and Micah to the room.

"I'm glad you finally left him," Katrina told me as she brought the last box to my room. My mouth dropped, not realizing she knew about the abuse. "I've seen enough women get up enough courage to leave to know what I'm walking into," she continued, reading my expression.

I smiled. "I won't be going back."

"I know you won't."

I couldn't believe that I once performed in this hotel. It seemed as though it was decades ago, but in actuality, it was months. We piled our belongings near the door, and I double checked the locks.

"Mama, I'm hungry." I looked at Micah.

I was glad he asked for food. That meant his stomach flu was short lived.

I picked up the phone on the desk and ordered Chinese food. It arrived within forty-five minutes and we inhaled it like we were starving. Then we watched throwback episodes of "The Fresh Prince of Bel Air" and giggled at funny actions from Carlton's dance to Will's sly remarks. We both slept peacefully that evening, knowing that Kelvin couldn't find us.

The following morning, I awoke early, and packed our belongings as tight as I possibly could into one box and the one overnight bag. I had to get rid of several items of clothing and some shoes in order to make room, but I knew that I wouldn't be able to lug those things around by myself. Once Micah got up, I got him ready and warmed up some of the left over Chinese food for breakfast. After we were done eating, we headed out of the room.

"Leaving so soon?" Freddie asked. I didn't even recognize him as his hair was pulled back into a ponytail. He wore a slightly oversized black Phat Farm jogging suit with matching shoes—a far cry from the shirts and slacks or Dickie outfits that he usually wore.

"Yeah, it's time for me to get my own place," I insisted. I started pushing Micah toward the door, but Freddie walked around and grabbed one of the bags I carried.

"And who is the little one?"

"That's my son, Micah. Micah, say hello to Mr. Freddie."

"Hey, Mr. Freddie." Micah stuck his hand out and Freddie shook it.

"Good morning, Mr. Micah. Nice to meet you."

Micah smiled, and then looked up at me. I knew we were going to have to have a conversation about Freddie's hair and limp handshake later. Freddie looked at me.

"If you need a place to come back to, you always have a room here."

I smiled. "Thanks."

I walked to the bus stop and waited for eight minutes until it arrived. We took it to the apartment complex where we

Played

would be living. No one was there initially, so we waited one hour, then another, before the complex manager showed up to work. She was a black woman that was most likely in her early 50's given the amount of noticeable wrinkles throughout her face.

Micah and I sat on the overnight bag outside the leasing office. "Excuse me, ma'am," I called out to her as she went to unlock the office doors.

"May I help you?" She looked at me in disgust, like a beggar asking for change. Instead of addressing the unprofessional attitude, I decided to take the higher road. At that point, I needed her, not the other way around.

"Yes, please. I paid my deposit over a month ago, and was told last week that my apartment is supposed to be ready in a week and a half. That would be the middle of next week, but I was wondering if it was ready before then. I need a place for me and my son."

"What apartment?" she asked, looking at Micah then at me.

"Umm—6—625," I offered.

"There is no 625. Our apartment numbers only go up to unit 540. Are you sure you set up a leasing arrangement out here?"

"Yes, I even paid the three hundred dollars."

"We'll see," she said with an attitude. "Come in." Micah and I followed her in and watched as she went through mounds of paperwork. "See, it's not here. What's your name again?"

"You didn't ask for it a first time. It's Taj Jenson," I said with the hint of an attitude.

She paused, obviously affected by my quick tongue. "See, I told you. It's not here."

The door chimed and another property agent walked in.

"Good morning," he said.

"See, he knows me. I signed my lease with him." I stood and pointed, then walked to the counter in an effort to meet him halfway.

"Whoa. Yes, Ms. Jenson, right?"

"Yes, yes, that's me," I responded.

"What are you doing back so soon?

"You see, that's the thing. I need to move in sooner. Can we make that happen?"

"I couldn't find any paperwork on her," the manager butted in.

"It's right here." He went into his drawer and pulled out a folder. "The apartment hasn't been cleaned for you, Ms. Jenson, so we have no choice but to ask you to wait."

"I'm sorry, but I can't wait. Is there anything that I could do? Please."

"No, the carpet needs to be replaced, which it looks like will occur in two days and tomorrow the walls need to be painted."

"I can paint the walls. I don't care."

"We can't allow you to do that, ma'am. It's our policy."

"Listen, my son and I don't have anywhere to go. If I continue to spend money on hotel rooms, eventually, we'll run out of money to eat. Please. Is there anything you can do?" I heard the desperation in my voice I'd heard all my adult life.

For some reason, the property manager seemed pleased with my circumstances. She stared at me for a moment, then walked into her office and closed the door.

The man looked around toward the supervisor's office then back at me and began to whisper. "I understand your situation—I do—but there is really nothing that I can do."

"Thank you." I sighed, then turned to Micah. "Let's go."

We were near the end of the walkway when the gentleman called out to us.

"Ms. Jenson, maybe I can help you."

I turned around and looked at him.

"Give me your things." He walked us near the leasing office and opened a utility closet door. "I'll leave your things in here." He placed the bag on the floor. "Here. This is the key to your apartment—Number 525. After 5:00 p.m., when the office is closed, I want you to come back and grab your belongings

P l a y e d

and sleep in the apartment. Please make sure that you leave by morning when the office reopens." He handed me a key.

"I'll put a rush on the apartment, so I'll try to have everything complete in three days, but I can't promise any sooner," he said.

"Thank you. Thank you so much." I grabbed his hand, near tears.

Micah and I jumped on the next bus and wound up at a diner. I reflected on my life and how much I'd done to other folks in order for it to return to me tenfold. If there was any way I could right the wrongs I'd done, I would do it in an instant.

I took Micah to the park so he could burn off some energy, and then found a comfortable spot in a local bookstore to cuddle up to a book that I couldn't afford to buy at the time.

"I like books," Micah said as I noticed that he had picked up one of the *Encyclopedia Brown* books. I remembered reading the Donald Sobol tales as a little girl, and then moving on to Nancy Drew and the Hardy Boys. "These and *Goosebumps* were my favorites."

"Mine, too." I reminisced.

Micah and I stayed in the store for another hour reading and sharing books until it got dark.

Retrieving our things from the utility closet, we entered our apartment. Both of our noses turned up at the smell. The carpet inside smelled sour, as though a pipe had burst, and the carpet was left to dry on its own. The walls were dingy and marked by nails and handprints, but I was happy because it was ours. Trying the utilities, I saw that they were already turned on. In order to not make too much noise and alert anyone that we were here, we only used the bare minimum. We didn't have any blankets, so we threw our dirty clothes from the night before unto the floor and used the bag as a pillow. Neither of us slept comfortably, but we slept safely.

Micah bathed early the following morning and dressed himself in wrinkled jeans and a T-shirt. I packed our things and dropped them off to the utility closet before leaving for the day.

Micah complained a little about his stomach, so I kept him with me for the day. I was glad that Mr. Kendall gave me a day off. Micah and I did the same routine—the park, bookstore, and the diner before returning to our apartment.

The next morning, I headed to work after taking Micah to school. When I arrived, there wasn't a fresh aroma of baked cinnamon rolls or muffins coming around the corner. When I went inside, it was dark and instantly, I knew something was wrong.

"Hello? Mr. Kendall?" I called as I walked toward the rear of the shop, but no one responded.

"He's not here," a man's voice spoke from behind me and I jumped.

"Man, you scared me, Quentin. Where's your dad?" I reached for my apron behind the door and went to tie it.

"My dad collapsed at the wedding. They say he has a heart condition. He's been in the hospital since yesterday." He looked upset.

"Well, how is he?" We both stood in the dark.

"Alive. He has to take it easy for a while. This shop has gotten to be too much for him."

"We just spoke about that. I just didn't see it coming so soon."

"You don't have to work today. Feel free to go home. I can close up until he's better."

I thought for a moment. "Did your dad not teach you to run this place?"

He laughed. "Yeah, a long time ago."

"I doubt you've forgotten," I said and threw him an apron.

I turned on the light, and we got to work kneading dough, baking, and grounding coffee beans. Within an hour, customers began to pour in. Quentin maintained his position in the front store while I continued to kick out some of Mr. Kendall's favorite recipes, and by the end of the day, both the equipment and I were extremely exhausted.

"You work really hard around here. How much is he pay-

Played

ing you?"

"That's for me to know and your father to pay," I said, cleaning the last dirty baking sheet in the sink.

I turned toward the counter and nearly bumped into him. "Excuse me."

"No need to excuse yourself. I guess I'm in *your* way."

"Well, the kitchen's clean, and I hope you swept the floor out front. Your dad would have a fit if there were crumbs," I replied, remembering one of the first things Mr. Kendall told me as I hung my apron behind the door. "I'm guessing I'll be seeing you again tomorrow." I grabbed my bag. "Good night!"

After Micah and I spent some time at a local park, watching people and reading some books that he got from the school library, he snacked on one of the left over muffins that Mr. Kendall always told me I could take. For dinner, we both had cheese breadsticks and water.

After a while, we returned to the apartment. This time the wall had a fresh coat of paint, which was nice, but the fumes were unbearable. We opened every window and camped out near the biggest one. Micah didn't complain. He drifted off to sleep unfazed by our situation and I realized how content I was by just having him.

The following morning went as the day before, only we returned home to fresh, new carpet and fumes from the paint had totally dissipated. Micah flipped and rolled around the floor until he tired himself. I cleaned the apartment thoroughly with cleaning products I'd purchased and stocked the bathroom with toilet paper, soap, toothpaste and a few other things we'd need. Placing a sheet on the floor and topping it with two pillows, it had officially become our first night in our new place—together.

46

Piece by piece, I loaded furniture into our apartment, beginning with a twin-size mattress for Micah's room that I scored from a mattress shop that was going out of business. The pots and pans were next. We didn't own a television, so we resorted to reading instead. Micah nestled up close to me as I read aloud to him. My life was getting back to normal. Before I knew it, two weeks passed.

Mr. Kendall's condition was worsening. He never returned to work after collapsing, and Quentin had low hopes that he ever would. Each morning, I picked up a copy of the classified section of our local newspaper in order to find a new position. Again, very few people were hiring, and those who were sought highly qualified individuals—like those with experience or diplomas. I felt like all hope was lost and it was only a matter of time before the bakery would close for good.

"So, what you looking for?" Quentin walked up behind me

as I was reading the classified section during my break.

I sat on an overturned bucket. "A job. What else?" I responded.

"So, what is it that you do besides bake a damn good cinnamon roll?" He laughed.

"I don't really know what I'm good at," I said seriously. "What do you think?" I asked out of curiosity.

He pulled up his own bucket and stared at me through his green eyes. "Well, first, you're really organized. Second, you're a really hard worker. Third, you're about as loyal as we come. This shop would have been closed down by now had it not been for you."

"I guess you're right, but none of that stuff amounts to anything on paper. I have to actually land a job and work for a while before an employer can see those qualities."

"I don't foresee you ever having a problem finding a job." With that, he stood from his bucket.

"I never graduated from high school. This is really the first legitimate job I've ever had." He looked down to me. "See me any differently yet?" I asked.

"No, but I must admit I'm curious. What are you doing about your education?"

"I can't focus on that right now." I folded the newspaper and placed it on my lap. "I recently gained custody of my son, and I just want to stay on the right track. A diploma won't pay the bills right now."

"You're such a brave woman," he whispered.

"What? What was that?" I pretended not to hear him.

"Well, I'm a professor during the fall and spring at the community college here. I'm sure there are programs you can take advantage of in order to gain your diploma...and maybe even a degree."

"But I can't pay for that. I can barely take care of the costs I've already incurred."

"Well, all of the costs don't have to come from your pocket," Quentin informed me. "There are scholarships and grants available for single mothers and low income families. Your son

does receive assistance for his meals at school, doesn't he?"

I quickly nodded and remembered the headache to get him on reduced breakfast and lunch. Those were two meals out of the day that I didn't have to worry about, at least. The rest of the time I made note to pay attention to what he liked and didn't like so I could make him pleasing dinners at home. Getting him on the meal plan at the school was probably one of the smartest things I'd ever done.

"Also available to you are low cost and affordable loans that you don't have to pay back until six months after you complete the program," he continued. "But if you go on to earn an associates degree or to a four-year institution where you can get your bachelors, you have more time to pay back those loans because as long as you are in school, the federal government and some private lenders will not make you pay the loans back."

"OK, that sounds nice...but what happens if I get out, and I get all these degrees and still can't get a job? There are people with master's degrees and doctorates who don't have jobs now."

Quentin chuckled, because he knew it was true. "They give you up to three years for hardships, in which you can put off paying the loans, but I will tell you what I tell my students who run up thousands of dollars and get bad credit and wonder why they are stuck. If you don't call the people and talk to them and let them know what's going on, folks won't know you need help."

"Well, I need all the help I can get. If I decide to go further than getting a GED, who's gonna watch Micah while I'm at school?"

"Do you believe in the Bible?"

I nodded, even though I couldn't remember when the last time was that I opened a Bible or went to church.

"The Word says, *Ask and ye shall receive, seek and ye shall find, knock and the door shall be opened unto you.* You have to take that first step or else you won't get anywhere."

"Well, what is that first step?"

Played

"Get the application, fill it out, and turn it in. Get started, and just take it one day at a time. I promise, it will come," he said, then walked away.

The following morning, Quentin greeted me with a stack of GED applications and various other program materials. I never took the opportunity to go back to school seriously, but I knew that in order to be successful, I had to have a diploma. Between serving patrons and removing hot pans from the oven, Quentin helped me complete each form. He even called and scheduled an appointment with an advisor.

No other man, not even James or Freddie, expressed as much concern for me as Quentin did. Amazingly, I had informed Quentin of the raw, unadulterated truth about my life, and he did everything he could to help without throwing stacks of cash my way, or putting me up in elegant homes, or allowing me to drive his expensive cars. He just genuinely cared.

I left Micah in the apartment with some books and some crossword puzzles I was able to get at the discount store. I hoped that the puzzles would keep him engaged and out of mischief while I went to Freddie's for a little while. At times like this, I wish I had family or even a good girlfriend I could depend on to keep an eye out for my son and make use of what I had.

As I stepped into the hotel, I noticed Marcus and how tight his pants were. I was surprised to see he was able to move around. My observation served to strengthen my argument for why men should never wear skinny jeans.

"Where's Freddie?" I asked.

"Room 112. Where else would he be?" Marcus answered.

I turned with nothing more to say and headed toward Room 112. When I got there, I saw Katrina and another man coming out of the room.

"Is Freddie inside?" I already knew the answer. I just needed to know whether the man was decent.

"Yeah, he's fine. I'll let you in," Katrina said as she put her key back in and opened the door. The pungent smell of marijuana freed itself from the room. "Freddie, you got a visitor."

302

As I walked in, I saw Freddie lying in the bed with the sheets covering his body. His hair was in disarray and desperately needed to be combed. I was going to offer, but I changed my mind when I saw Freddie sit up and bring the sheets up to his waist.

"What's up?" Freddie quickly reached to the right side of the bed and picked up a thin pair of black and red pajama pants, turning them over to pull the pants over his naked body. He reached down and grabbed the black robe on the floor and quickly stepped into his leather house shoes.

"Look, I came here to talk to you about one of your girls."

"OK, what about them?"

"I was wondering if one of them had any free time in the mornings and wouldn't mind being a babysitter."

Freddie's neck rotated like the exorcist. "Are you serious?"

"I don't have no family or home girls I would trust with my son, and if I got to pay somebody, I at least want to pay someone who can pack a pistol and protect my son."

"Did you read the book *Whoreson?*"

"Donald Goines, right?" I flexed, showing that I was up on my street lit.

"You want a pimp and some whores to help raise your son—think about that for a minute."

"Y'all won't be raising my son," I defended. "Just helping me out while I'm in school—keeping him out of trouble. I'm still going to work to keep a roof over our heads while I go to school and work."

Freddie looked at me. "You really are trying to turn your life around."

"Of course. I got a job, and I applied to get my GED. Now I just have to go. And I just need a little help."

"OK," Freddie answered, a few octaves higher. "We'll help you. But if that boy ends up to be a cold-blooded pimp, I don't want you coming to me with no problems."

I hugged Freddie, and then followed him to the lobby.

P l a y e d

47

As promised, Freddie kept true to his word, and the girl who I knew as Prancer gladly watched Micah as I worked and studied for my GED. Even Freddie watched him from time to time, keeping him entertained. The people who I thought I could count on played me, but the people who I thought were against me turned out to be those I could really trust.

They were there, Freddie, Marcus, Katrina, Prancer and Quentin, when I passed my GED. Quentin helped me enroll in the local community college and my plan was to study law. My life was changing, and for the better.

Another six months had passed, and so did Mr. Kendall, but with the help of Quentin, we both kept the bakery running and became friends.

I sat inside of the clinic, flanked by Freddie and Quentin, awaiting the results of the last of my HIV tests. Although 2-0, I was still nervous. Reality was, Kelvin did rape me, and he

Triple Crown Publications *presents...*

had women all over the globe, so between him and Tiki, there was still the possibility of my being positive. I nervously tapped my toes rhythmically on the tile floor, and sighed deeply every other minute, but I knew God wouldn't give me more than I could handle. A young mother, no older than seventeen, sat to my right holding her toddler. Freddie and Quentin engaged in conversation while I waited for my name to be called.

"Jessica Smith," the nurse called, and the young girl stood and walked away.

Just as she disappeared behind the doors, another nurse appeared and called out, "Taj Jenson."

"That's me." I stood and walked into the nurse's office. The original plight of the situation that brought me to the clinic returned in my mind. I thought about the men I engaged in risky sexual acts with when I was doing shows with Tiki, and how low I stooped to earn a few dollars just to buy personal items.

"Have a seat." The nurse motioned to an empty chair and closed the door. She already succeeded in breaking my concentration. The moment of judgment was here. Although I wasn't ready, I had to face what the cards held for me and I would accept whatever consequences there were for my actions. "Let's see here," she hummed and pulled a card from a folder with the letters J-E-N written across the tab. Time seemed to slow down as I could see all the good things I did with my life and all the bad things I wished I could take back.

"Yes? What is it?" She moved too slowly.

"Well, your HIV test is negative, which is a great thing. We are concerned and want to make sure that you refrain from activities that would put you back in this position. Do you use condoms or are you—"

I was relieved. Anything that she said after the word "negative" was definitely a waste of breath. I rejoiced that my life would be spared and promised myself that from then on, I wouldn't give myself to another man or woman until I was in a committed relationship, preferably where someone put a

P l a y e d

ring on it.

"I understand that. I will be more careful." I hurried out of the office. When I saw Freddie, I rushed to him and gave him a big hug. "I'm negative," I whispered. I turned to Quentin and hugged him, too.

I felt like the weight of the world was lifted off my shoulders. I looked at the time and realized that I would need to pick Micah up from school soon. Quentin dropped Freddie off at the hotel and drove me to pick up Micah.

Hours later, Quentin dropped Micah and me off, and I began dinner—chicken and rice. As it cooked, I went to my closet to find something comfortable to put on and saw the bag that I packed when I was at Kelvin's. It was *his* bag, and my first thought was to throw it away as it was a reminder of him. Yanking it out of the closet, it fell to the floor, but something rattled inside. I reached in and felt around. I pulled out a faded address tag, but at the very bottom of the bag, tucked tightly into the corner, was something plastic. I pulled it out and it was a translucent blue jewel case. Inside was a DVD labeled "Taj in the Caribbean." I didn't remember where the video came from or how it wound up in my possession. I remembered foolishly taking part in Kelvin's exploits, but the intent was for the moment to remain private and never be transferred to a DVD or worse yet, put into a medium where it could end up on the Internet.

I didn't want to watch it. For as good of a time as I'd had in the Caribbean, the later memories of the abusive Kelvin and finding out he was married outweighed it. I didn't want it in my possession any longer. As I thought back and reflected, I came up with an idea.

When dinner was ready, Micah came out of his room to join me for a bowl of well seasoned chicken and rice. We ate together and laughed about his school day. He practiced spelling three new words he learned that day in his new first grade class, and I stuffed some muffins in the oven to heat and enjoy for dessert. Afterward, we sat on the living room floor going over math homework while I studied legal terminology.

The following morning, after dropping Micah off at school, I made a brief stop at the post office. I was thankful for Mr. Kendall's old Sentra that Quentin gave to me. It wasn't what I was accustomed to, but it got me where I needed to be. I placed the DVD I found into an envelope and sealed it tightly. In my neatest handwriting, I made it out to Valerie Ross and used the Atlanta address that was written on the tag I found and mailed it off express. If anyone deserved more closure than I did, it was Valerie. I later learned she used the DVD to win a multi-million dollar suit against Kelvin for infidelity, neglect and abuse—the last offense one that she never admitted to me. Valerie then rewarded me with $50,000 of her $3.5 million settlement.

As for me, I found a small church just outside of Jacksonville. I discovered it when I gave my life back to the Lord. At this point, I knew I was making my mother proud. After all, in my life, I had done it all. Although I was once a deceitful, conniving, prostituting thief, all of my transgressions have been cleared, and I started anew. In short, never mind the stunning mansion, exotic cars, and jewels. I dare anyone to get like me: FREE.

P l a y e d

♛Triple Crown Publications

Order Form
P.O. Box 247378 Columbus, OH 43224

Name	
Address	
City	
State	Zipcode

QTY	TITLES	PRICE
	A Down Chick	$15.00
	A Hood Legend	$15.00
	A Hustler's Son	$15.00
	A Hustler's Wife	$15.00
	A Project Chick	$15.00
	Always a Queen	$15.00
	Amongst Thieves	$15.00
	Baby Girl	$15.00
	Baby Girl Pt. 2	$15.00
	Baller Girls	$15.00
	Betrayed	$15.00
	Betrayed Again	$15.00
	Black	$15.00
	Black & Ugly	$15.00
	Blinded	$15.00
	Cash Money	$15.00

Shipping & Handling
1-3 Books $5.00
4-9 Books $9.00
$1.95 for each add'l book

Total $_____

Forms of accepted payment: Postage Stamps, Personal or Institutional
Checks & Money Orders. All mail-in orders take 5-7 business days to be
delivered.

♜Triple Crown Publications

Order Form
P.O. Box 247378 Columbus, OH 43224

Name	
Address	
City	
State	Zipcode

QTY	TITLES	PRICE
	Chances	$15.00
	China Doll	$15.00
	Chyna Black	$15.00
	Contagious	$15.00
	Crack Head	$15.00
	Crack Head II	$15.00
	Cream	$15.00
	Cut Throat	$15.00
	Dangerous	$15.00
	Dime Piece	$15.00
	Dirtier Than Ever (hardback)	$20.00
	Dirtier Than Ever (paperback)	$15.00
	Dirty Red	$15.00
	Dirty South	$15.00
	Diva	$15.00
	Dollar Bill	$15.00

Shipping & Handling
1-3 Books $5.00
4-9 Books $9.00
$1.95 for each add'l book

Total $_____

♚Triple Crown Publications

Order Form

P.O. Box 247378 Columbus, OH 43224

Name	
Address	
City	
State	Zipcode

QTY	TITLES	PRICE
	Ecstasy	$15.00
	Flipside of the Game	$15.00
	For the Strength of You	$15.00
	Game Over	$15.00
	Gangsta	$15.00
	Goonette	$15.00
	Grimey	$15.00
	Hold U Down	$15.00
	Hood Richest	$15.00
	Hoodwinked	$15.00
	How to Succeed in the Publishing Game	$15.00
	Ice	$15.00
	Imagine This	$15.00
	In Cahootz	$15.00
	Innocent	$15.00
	Karma	$15.00

Shipping & Handling
1-3 Books $5.00
4-9 Books $9.00
$1.95 for each add'l book

Total $_____

Forms of accepted payment: Postage Stamps, Personal or Institutional
Checks & Money Orders. All mail-in orders take 5-7 business days to be
delivered.

♕Triple Crown Publications

Order Form

P.O. Box 247378 Columbus, OH 43224

Name	
Address	
City	
State	Zipcode

QTY	TITLES	PRICE
	Karma II	$15.00
	Karma III	$15.00
	Keisha	$15.00
	Larceny	$15.00
	Let That Be the Reason	$15.00
	Life	$15.00
	Love & Loyalty	$15.00
	Me & My Boyfriend	$15.00
	Menage's Way	$15.00
	Mina's Joint	$15.00
	Mistress of the Game	$15.00
	Played	$15.00
	Queen	$15.00
	Queen of Thieves	$15.00
	Queen of Thieves II	$15.00
	Rage Times Fury	$15.00

Shipping & Handling
1-3 Books $5.00
4-9 Books $9.00
$1.95 for each add'l book   Total $_____

Forms of accepted payment: Postage Stamps, Personal or Institutional
Checks & Money Orders. All mail-in orders take 5-7 business days to be
delivered.

♛Triple Crown Publications

Order Form
P.O. Box 247378 Columbus, OH 43224

Name	
Address	
City	
State	Zipcode

QTY	TITLES	PRICE
	Road Dawgz	$15.00
	Sheisty	$15.00
	Stacy	$15.00
	Stained Cotton	$15.00
	Still Dirty	$15.00
	Still Sheisty	$15.00
	Street Love	$15.00
	Sunshine & Rain	$15.00
	The Cartel's Daughter	$15.00
	The Game	$15.00
	The Hood Rats	$15.00
	The Pink Palace	$15.00
	The Pink Palace II	$15.00
	The Reason Why	$15.00
	The Set Up	$15.00
	Torn	$15.00

Shipping & Handling
1-3 Books $5.00
4-9 Books $9.00
$1.95 for each add'l book

Total $_____

Forms of accepted payment: Postage Stamps, Personal or Institutional
Checks & Money Orders. All mail-in orders take 5-7 business days to be
delivered.

♜Triple Crown Publications

Order Form
P.O. Box 247378 Columbus, OH 43224

Name	
Address	
City	
State	Zipcode

QTY	TITLES	PRICE
	Vixen Icon	$15.00
	Whore	$15.00
	Wife	$15.00
	You Knew Betta	$15.00

Shipping & Handling
1-3 Books $5.00
4-9 Books $9.00
$1.95 for each add'l book

Total $_____

Forms of accepted payment: Postage Stamps, Personal or Institutional
Checks & Money Orders. All mail-in orders take 5-7 business days to be
delivered.